SCEPTER OF FIRE

THE MIRROR OF IMMORTALITY BOOK 2

VICTORIA GILBERT

License Notes

Print ISBN: 978-1-948661-40-9
eBook ISBN: 978-1-948661-39-3

Published by Snowy Wings Publishing
https://www.snowywingspublishing.com/

Cover Design by Deranged Doctor Design
Formatting by Deranged Doctor Design

Dedicated to my Mother
Barbara King Lemp

Who loves books and reading as much as I do.

CHAPTER ONE:
ANOTHER PATH

A POTION CAN CURE OR KILL. This is the first thing a healer must learn. Life or death lurks, silent as snow, within the same bottle. I steady a small metal funnel with one finger as I ladle liquid into a brown glass bottle. It is a tincture of horehound blended with coltsfoot—an excellent remedy for the cough.

"Is this all you desire, Varna?"

My mentor, Albrecht Olsen, stands so close his breath stirs the hairs on the back of my neck. If he was younger, or I fairer, I'd suspect seduction. No, that is ridiculous. Master Albrecht only wishes to train me as a healer.

"Many villagers suffer during the long winter months." I spoon medicine into another bottle. "And our soldiers are often plagued by hacking coughs."

"I could teach you so much more." Master Albrecht's reedy voice twists its way through my mind.

For a moment my thoughts take wing, like the finches fluttering amid the trees outside. I crave more, but such promises are a trap, stirring desires that can never be fulfilled. I must bottle my passions as securely as these potions I create.

I pluck a cork from a wicker basket and hold it up to the light to search for defects. "And I hope you will, in time. But with the war raging around us, for now I must concentrate on learning all I can about curative potions and salves."

So I can at least take over as village healer when you die. I cork the bottle before turning to face Master Albrecht. *Which might be soon.*

It's his appearance, not my cruelty, which makes me anticipate his death. I don't know his exact age, but his face is crisscrossed with as many grooves as a walnut shell.

He scuttles backward, clutching at a stain on his worn tunic. "There is much more to our calling than that."

"So you say. However, I want to learn useful skills."

Albrecht's eyes, dimmed with an overlay like pearl, appraise me. "Yet you refuse to create love potions. Surely love is useful, in the grand scheme of things."

"Is it?" I study my mentor. Once, he might have been handsome. A fine bone structure still lurks beneath the wreck of his face. "I've always thought love should take its own course. Interference seems so … "

"Intrusive?" A cackle of laughter escapes Master Albrecht's thin lips. "Of course. Yet when did love follow logic?"

This is true, as I well know. My sister, Gerda, has refused several suitors, despite their looks, charm, and wealth. She claims she will only marry for love, although she cannot describe what that means. "I've felt it before, so I will know it when I feel it again," she says. "It will come, in time."

I am sure it will, for her. She is lovely and sweet and everything a young man could desire. As for me, I will be a healer, and God willing, live out my days here.

I survey the cottage. It is only one room, with a deep niche providing sleeping quarters. A row of windows frames a colorful assortment of glass bottles and ceramic jugs, while multicolor rag rugs enliven the plank floors. All the surfaces gleam with recent scrubbing, and the whitewashed plaster walls shine in vivid contrast to the smoke-blackened wooden rafters. A stone fireplace fills one end of the room, with a tarnished copper pot swinging from an iron bracket above ash-whitened logs. Bunches of dried herbs and other botanicals dangle from hooks screwed into the rafters, their mingled scents lending the cottage an exotic air.

Master Albrecht shuffles to the rough-hewn shelves lining one wall of the cottage. As he rifles through a jumble of ceramic jars and dark glass bottles, I question his connection to my previous mentor. My apprenticeship began when I was fourteen, and never once in the four years I studied with Dame Margaret did she mention this man as her heir. Yet he appeared at her funeral six months ago, brandishing letters declaring him owner of Margaret's cottage and land.

I move a bottle from one end of the row to the other. *It should have been mine.*

Master Albrecht teaches me many skills Dame Margaret lacked. He shows me bags filled with strange herbs and roots, and promises to tell me where to procure such rare items. He's an excellent mentor, but …

It should have been mine.

"Love is a great force, Varna," says my master, keeping his back to me. "I hope you will learn that someday."

I stare at his hunched shoulders, fighting the bitterness that taints my tone. "Love? Love is all very well, for those it favors."

"Why not you?" Clad in a simple woolen tunic and baggy breeches, Albrecht resembles a vagrant more than a learned purveyor of charms and cures. Since he always appears indifferent to the bustle of everyday life, his interest in my love life—or lack thereof—baffles me.

"Because I am not a fool, Master."

Albrecht turns, his ancient face somber. "No, that you are not, my girl. But I think perhaps you underestimate your own special qualities."

I snort. "Special qualities? What do you mean? If you're talking about something more than looks, it's Gerda who has the good nature in my family. She's even forgiven that girl who stole her first love away. Now, *that* is a special quality."

"Ah yes, Thyra Winther. The village orphan who became a Snow Queen."

I narrow my eyes and instinctively grab the metal ladle. "You've heard that story?"

"Of course. It is not every day a young girl returns to her village after a sojourn in the wilderness—accompanied by a mysterious reindeer and telling tales of a Snow Queen, sorcerers, and an enchanted mirror."

"It isn't tales, it's the truth. My sister would never lie about such things." I slap the ladle against my left palm.

"I never said she would." Master Albrecht looks me over, his eyes oddly bright. "It is a strange story, you must admit. The thing that confuses me"—he scratches his crooked nose—"is why your sister would ever befriend the Snow Queen who stole Kai Thorsen's heart."

"It's because she has a forgiving nature. She even claims to be friends with Thyra. I don't know if that's true, but Gerda has received a few letters from abroad. She says Thyra writes to her, as well as to Kai."

"Most peculiar. Still, Gerda is an exceptionally sweet girl. Not like your younger sisters." Albrecht clicks his tongue. "Quite lovely, Franka and Nanette. But not particularly kind, I fear."

I narrow my eyes. What does this old man, a stranger until six months ago, know of my family? "The twins? They're simply young and headstrong."

Albrecht snorts. "Spoiled and self-obsessed. Still, they *are* gorgeous. Like Gerda, they take after your mother. I suspect you resemble your father."

"Yes." I set the ladle back on the table with too much force, and it clangs against the wood. Unfortunately, I do take after my late father. His sharp jaw, small hazel eyes, and beak of a nose did not look unattractive on a man. On a woman it is another story.

I may call Gerda's spurned suitors "unfortunate," but I know it's me the townsfolk pity. I can read it in their eyes—poor Varna, the ugly duckling who will never transform into a swan.

My fingers clench, digging the nails into my palms. "As for Franka and Nanette, they're only fourteen and already besieged by suitors. Since, as you note, they are gorgeous. But surely you're not interested in silly village gossip."

"On the contrary, I find it enlightening." Albrecht shuffles over to me. "Knowing such things helps determine how many bottles of love potions I should prepare and stock. Now, don't make that disapproving face. Despite the value of our healing work, you must admit it is not a lucrative profession. Love elixirs, there's where the real money lies, my girl. People will pay any amount to achieve success in love." He tilts his head, looking like some grizzled vulture. "Wouldn't you enjoy wealth? It might make young men take more notice of you. Riches can prove a mighty aphrodisiac…"

A swear word flies from my mouth. I flush and turn my head, but not before catching my mentor's sly smile.

I must compose myself. Master Albrecht holds the keys to my future. I cannot allow anger and resentment to destroy my dream.

A loud series of knocks rescues me. I wipe my hands on my apron and hurry to open the front door.

Nels Leth fills the doorway. He's a tall, bulky, young man, whose small eyes and shaggy brown hair match his nickname perfectly. "The Bear," they call him. Well, many of the villagers do. I don't, having sympathy for anyone whose appearance gives rise to jokes.

"Oh hello, Varna." He whips off his cap and twists it between his hands. "I was looking for Master Albrecht. Is he at home?"

"Yes indeed, young man. Come in, come in." Albrecht slides next to me, so close I must step aside.

As I turn, Albrecht's boney fingers grab my wrist. "Stay. You might learn something useful."

I yank my arm free, surprised at the force of my master's grip. Although I have seen him lift patients much larger than himself, I always assumed that skill came from long practice, not strength. Rubbing my wrist, I back away. "I thought we should allow Master Leth to enter. No need to keep him loitering in the doorway."

"Ah yes, how rude of me." Albrecht waves Nels inside. "Now, young man, I assume you're here to collect that potion you requested the other day?"

Nels shoots a sheepish look my way. "Must Varna stay? It's rather … personal."

"Don't fret, Master Leth. Varna is the model of discretion. Let me collect the bottle." Albrecht toddles toward the back of the cottage.

Nels's gaze wanders. He looks at the back wall, the table, the sleeping niche—anywhere but my face. From his obvious discomfort, I suspect the elixir he is purchasing is somehow connected to his futile pursuit of my older sister. He's loved her for years, but Gerda has never shown any interest in him, not even after she abandoned her childhood infatuation with Kai Thorsen.

"Ah, here we are." Albrecht grabs a clear glass bottle filled with a pale blue liquid and shuffles back to stand before Nels. "All I need is our agreed payment …"

Nels fumbles with his money pouch before pulling out a gold coin.

"So much?" I shoot Albrecht a sharp glance. "We don't charge that much for healing draughts."

"It's fine, it's fine." Nels thrusts the coin into Albrecht's open palm, grabbing the elixir with his other hand. He stuffs the small bottle into his jacket pocket and crams his hat over his bushy hair. "I must go. Still need to harvest some peas before dark."

He tips his hat to both of us and backs away, making for the open cottage door.

"It's important work you do, Nels," I call after him, as he turns in the doorway and flees. "Well, it is," I tell Master Albrecht, who's eyeing me with far too much amusement.

"I never said it wasn't."

"People call Nels a coward, you know, because he hasn't gone to war like most of our other young men. But someone has to stay and raise the crops needed to feed our soldiers and their horses and ..."

"My, my, such a fierce defense. Perhaps you have feelings for this Nels fellow? Which would be quite a shame, since he bought that love potion to use on your sister."

All the humor has fled Albrecht's face. I wonder why. *He probably fears you might marry and leave him without an assistant, Varna.*

But of course that's not going to happen. I lift my chin and meet Albrecht's gaze squarely. "No, what a ridiculous notion. I just don't like to see someone like Nels treated unfairly. It's not his fault he was forced to stay and manage the farm, and he can't help looking the way he does, or being the son of a dreadful mother."

"Yes, I imagine Inga Leth would prove a stumbling block to any young man's marital prospects." The strange flash of anger that shadowed Albrecht's face a moment before has given way to his typical sly smile.

"I'm not comfortable with you charging him such a price for whatever it was you gave him.

"A love potion, of course."

"Which is useless, whatever you say. Really, Master, I sincerely doubt some potion will make my sister fall in love with any of her current suitors. Anyway, Gerda's marital status seems beneath your notice."

Fire flashes in those veiled eyes. "I have many interests."

I look away, surveying the place I hope to call home one day. If I do well, if I prove myself, I believe Master Albrecht will leave this cottage to me, just as it was bequeathed to him by Dame Margaret.

"You covet my home."

I grab the edge of the table. It's as if he can read my mind, but that's nonsense. Through my knowledge of Gerda's adventures, I believe magic exists, but I scarcely think an ordinary healer possesses such powers.

"I simply admire."

"Varna, Varna." Master Albrecht's voice is oddly seductive. "You are a terrible liar. I'm afraid you suffer from the curse of a truthful tongue."

I stiffen my spine. "I am not ashamed to speak honestly."

Albrecht laughs. "No, indeed you are not." He rubs at his rheumy eyes. "My dear, sometimes a healer must tell a few lies. We may be required to convince someone to take a necessary draught of medicine, or give hope to the hopeless … "

I tug loose the ties to my apron. "Better to cure them. I don't think lies aid anyone, in the end."

"Even if they provide comfort?"

I pull off my apron, fold it, and place it on the table. "I've found that type of comfort of little value. My mother told such lies when I was young. She insisted I would grow into my looks, that one day I would wake and find myself as lovely as my sisters. This magical moment never occurred, as you can see. I am the starling amid the goldfinches, the thistle in the rose patch. This is the truth, and no pleasant lie will change it."

Albrecht clasps his knobby hands. "So you seek to embrace this truth and… what, Varna Lund?"

"Make a useful life."

"Useful? What about matters of the heart? You possess quite a fiery heart, I believe."

It is true. Despite my plain appearance, my wandering mind ensnares me in ridiculous fantasies of passion. I'm too often haunted by foolish daydreams of romance that leave me flushed and breathless.

I meet Albrecht's amused gaze. "Love is not for me."

"You are young to resign yourself to a life without love."

"Master, although I am only eighteen, I'm not foolish. Under your tutelage I will become a fine healer. I will embrace this calling and be content."

"My dear girl, I do not believe such a life will satisfy you, but we won't quibble about that now. And you can indeed become a great healer. You have skill, and a determination few can match. You possess passion, too, although you seek to hide it. Yes, I spy your true nature, despite your attempts to bank your fires."

I bow my head to hide my astonishment. He's read me like a book fallen open, no matter how hard I've tried to mask my feelings. "Thank you for your encouraging words, Master Albrecht. Now, I must go. It's almost time for supper and my mother will be displeased if I'm not there to help."

"Very well, but I shall expect you back here tomorrow, as soon as your morning chores are done. I still have much to teach you."

"For which I thank you." As I leave, I lower my head to avoid his gaze.

I pause outside for a moment, leaning against the heavy wooden door of the cottage, and tuck stray strands of my brown hair under my white linen cap. *Bank my fires* ... Yes, that's what I must do. Albrecht may believe I should chase love, but I know better. It doesn't matter how I feel, life is what it is. If I wish to achieve some measure of happiness, I must embrace reality. So many of my young countrymen have already died in the fight to protect our lands from the invading emperor, there will be few left around my age. Certainly not enough to make me, with my face and figure, sought after as a sweetheart or wife.

As I hike the path that leads from the healer's cottage to my small village, my thoughts swirl like the leaves kicked up by my boots. Master Albrecht's insightful assessment of my character makes me gnaw the inside of my cheek. I've never shared personal feelings with him. He should not be able to discern my deepest desires. It's unnerving. Even my family hasn't seen the truth so clearly.

A low growl startles me into stillness. I look up. A wolf stands on the path before me—a bulky creature with silver-tipped brown fur and golden eyes. I hold my breath.

The wolf tips his head to one side.

I've seen wolves before, but always at night, and from a distance. I know they have no particular desire to harm humans, and can often be scared away by loud noises. *They are not mindless killers.* Kai Thorsen told me that once, when we encountered a pack while sledding with our families.

I know this, yet my heart clatters against my ribcage, and my fingers clutch the folds of my woolen skirt.

The wolf yips, then turns and trots down the path, glancing over its shaggy shoulder once, as if it wishes me to follow.

I must be insane. I rub at my eyes, but the wolf is still there. I know I shouldn't run. That's the worst thing I could do.

Placing one foot in front of the other, I follow the wolf's lead, turning from the main path at one point to take a narrow track barely distinguishable from the surrounding woods.

Definitely mad. Yet something draws me on. I trail the wolf to the door of an abandoned cottage, its stone walls fallen in on one side like a shoe run down at the heel.

The wolf yips once more, then bolts. The tip of its tail waves like a pennant as it disappears amid the green sea of the woods.

A loud groan rends the quiet. I spring toward the cottage, pushing one hand against the door that hangs drunkenly from a single hinge.

A male figure fills the opening, blocking my view inside. He yanks a flintlock pistol from his deep jacket pocket and brandishes it in my face.

"Stay out! I will shoot if you take another step." He levels the pistol at my forehead.

CHAPTER TWO:
ANGUISH AND ANGELS

I STARE INTO HIS SHADOWED FACE as I smooth down the laced bodice of my gown. "I mean no harm. I heard someone in pain and thought … "

"What?"

As my eyes adjust to the dim light, I realize the voice belongs to a young man in uniform.

He's a soldier. Although his colors are veiled by a film of dust and splotches of mud, I determine he is one of ours. "I am a healer. I might be able to offer some aid."

Before I can say more, the soldier grabs me by the forearm and drags me into the cottage.

"My friend." He points to a corner where old sacks and a horse blanket cover what might be a human form. "He's badly injured, and overcome by fever. You must help him."

I examine my captor. His face would be handsome if it were more than pale skin drawn over sharp bones. He's tall, and, despite his broad shoulders, thin. No doubt life in the camps has reduced him to this lanky scarecrow. A finger of light poking through the shattered roof reveals the fiery tint of his hair.

"You must help him," the soldier repeats, shaking my arm. His face is gray with fatigue, but his green eyes gleam with a ferocity that makes me curl my shoulders inward.

I jerk free of his grip. "Excuse me—I don't have to do anything. I am willing to help, if you'll give me your name."

He straightens, clicking his heels together. "Erik Stahl, soldier in His Majesty's army, fighting the Usurper."

"And your friend?" I motion toward the covered figure, who stirs and groans again.

"His name is not necessary."

I lift my chin and stare up into Erik Stahl's angular face. "It is if you wish me to help him."

The emerald eyes narrow to slits. "Anders. Anders Nygaard."

"How long has Anders been feverish?" I push past Erik and cross to the far side of the room.

"A day. Maybe two? I don't know. I've lost all track of time."

I kneel beside the bundled form. Throwing back the blanket and bags, I uncover a slender young man wearing only the tattered pants of his uniform. His skin is clammy, and his light brown hair is plastered to his skull.

I press the back of my hand against his forehead. "God in heaven, he's burning up."

Erik crouches beside me. "Can you help him?"

"I'll try. Where is his injury?"

"Leg." Erik pulls a flap of fabric back from Anders's left leg, and I shove my fist against my teeth to stifle a gasp.

The wound itself isn't ghastly—a deep puncture caused by shot or some type of shrapnel—but contagion has set in, turning the skin about the wound black and streaking red rays up and down his leg.

"Why are you here? He should be at the field hospital." I press my fingers against Anders's calf. He twitches and moans.

Erik slumps onto the damp planks of the floor. "Not your business."

"I think it is. This man needs expert care, in clean conditions. Why did you drag him to this moldy, makeshift shelter?"

Erik's gaze slides quickly from my face to my hands. He's not impressed by my appearance. This is nothing new. *And neither is your anger.*

I grip his shoulder. "Why are you in hiding, Erik Stahl? I know a battle took place, not far from here, several days ago. Surely your company would not abandon you, so why aren't you with them? Do not lie. I will help your friend, but only if you're honest with me."

He shakes off my hand and averts his head. "We were involved in that battle. It did not go well, as I'm sure you know. Anders was hit right before we were forced to retreat. My company wanted to leave him, to let the enemy troops take him prisoner. I've heard about their prison camps. It would have meant his death." He rubs his hand over his face. "Who are you, anyway? You're young to be a healer."

"I have been training for years," I reply, which is close enough to the truth. "My name is Varna Lund. I live in the nearby village."

"Lund?" Erik studies me. "Like the Lunds who own the mill?"

"Yes, with the Thorsen family."

"It was one of the buildings we fought to protect."

"I know."

Yes, I know this only too well. We supply the local troops with grain and flour—assistance the invading emperor called "The Usurper" seeks to curtail. So far the mill has escaped the enemy's wrath, but it's only a matter of time before it is targeted.

"So, Varna Lund, what will you do for my friend?"

"Whatever I can. However, I need answers first. You still haven't told me why you're in hiding."

Erik rises to his feet. "I deserted. There. Happy with that information?"

I stroke Anders's hot brow. "To save him."

"Yes. I carried him from the battlefield in the confusion of our retreat. I refused to allow him to be gathered up like kindling for a fire."

"Why not simply follow the company back to camp?"

Erik shifts from foot to foot. "It was not that simple."

Anders groans and rolls to one side. My stomach clenches.

"Can you help? Honestly?" Erik kneels back down.

I study his drawn face. "Perhaps, but I must ask my master for assistance. He is a great healer," I add, when Erik shakes his head.

"No one else can be told. The enemy is likely to occupy these lands soon, if they have not done so already. They offer a reward for any of our soldiers handed over to them. I cannot risk Anders's life to the whims of some villager's greed."

"Do you care for him so much?"

Erik grips my right hand. "Anders is my best friend. We joined the army as a team, and swore we would stay together until the end. That's not a promise I will break."

"Very well, but I must go and collect some things from my mentor's cottage." I squeeze Erik's fingers. "I will return."

"Alone." He uses our clasped hands to pull me toward him.

I stare into those green eyes—as bright as if they too burned with fever. "Yes, alone. If you know of any source of clean water nearby, go there." I yank my fingers from his grasp and stand, glancing about the deserted cottage. "Locate some vessel, and collect as much water as you can."

He jumps to his feet. "What else?"

"Do you have a knife? If not, find one, and hone it as sharp as humanly possible."

A drift of freckles stands out in sharp relief against Erik's pale cheeks. "You mean to cut into him?"

Although my lips quiver, I refuse to drop my gaze. "The contagion must be sliced away."

He grimaces, but nods. "I will do as you ask. Only, return quickly. I fear there is little time to waste."

I fear this as well. "I swear I will come back as soon as possible."

"Thank you, Varna Lund."

"Collect water and sharpen the knife," I say, as I back away. "If you have any spirits, I will need those as well."

I push my way through the half-open cottage door, my hands clenched at my sides. I've never cut into flesh before. I may do more harm than good, but Anders Nygaard will die if I do nothing, and I cannot allow that to happen. Not on my watch.

Luck or something like it is with me—I return to the cottage to find Master Albrecht gone, allowing me to collect supplies without fear of betraying the soldiers' location. I throw some potions, ointments, and other items into a canvas satchel.

Despite the bulky bag banging my hip, I quicken my pace as I head back to the abandoned cottage.

Clomping hooves disturb the leaves blanketing the main path. Rounding a corner, I encounter the age-whitened muzzle of a reindeer.

"Varna, why aren't you at home?"

I look up into the face of my older sister, Gerda. Perched on the reindeer's broad back, her legs barely reach around to grip his flanks. Her plump fingers are buried in the thick fur of the reindeer's neck.

Something must be wrong. One of Gerda's wheat-gold braids has sprung free of her plaited crown, lending her round face a lopsided appearance, and she's wearing her heavy work boots. Even her cloak is pinned wrong—one side of the collar pokes up higher than the other.

"I've been working with Master Albrecht."

"So late?" Gerda's eyes, blue as a spring sky, are puffy and red-rimmed.

I study the worn tips of my boots. "If you must know, I left something at Albrecht's cottage and had to retrace my steps."

The reindeer butts my shoulder with his nose. "The little miss is simply concerned, Miss Varna."

When I first heard Bae speak I sank to my knees on the straw-strewn floor of our livestock shed, overwhelmed with fear. I was skeptical when Gerda told me of the transformation the mage Mael Voss had wrought on the reindeer who had accompanied her home from her journey to rescue Kai Thorsen. A few words from Bae, and I believed her—the entire story she told, not just her tale of the enchanted reindeer. But on Bae's urging, Gerda and I are the only ones who know of his magical abilities. He doesn't speak in front of anyone but us, and does not fly at all, although that is within his power.

I grab his rope halter and force the reindeer's head up, so I can stare directly into his liquid brown eyes. "Concerned about what?"

"Soldiers."

I glance up at Gerda. "Ours?"

She shakes her head.

"In the village?"

"Yes, they marched in a few hours ago. I was heading home from the mill when I spied them coming over the hill beyond the lake. I took the forest path and managed to get home before they stormed the town. After I warned Mother and the twins, I hid with Bae until I could slip away. I wanted to find you and alert you, before you wandered home and stumbled into danger."

"Thanks, but why do you think I'd be in more danger than anyone else?"

"Well, you do have a habit of speaking your mind." Gerda's smile takes some of the sting out of her words.

Some. I tug down my rumpled bodice. "I think I know better than to deliberately offend a troop of enemy soldiers."

Bae snorts.

"Are we sure what might offend them?" Gerda pulls one hand free of Bae's fur and fiddles with the end of her loose braid. "We don't know these people, Varna. Not their language, or their beliefs. All we have are stories."

Not pretty ones, either. I dig my boot into an anthill on the side of the path. The ants dash off in formation, like good soldiers. "Did they take the mill?"

"Yes, but I heard their commander—who does speak our language—promise Mother he won't burn it. He plans to keep the mill running, using our workers. To supply their troops, I suppose." Gerda frowns. "We shouldn't dawdle. They may impose a curfew. Hop up—Bae can carry us both."

"I cannot."

"You must. Surely you don't plan to run away? That would be foolish. There's more danger on the road than in our village. These soldiers, they aren't monsters, as far as I can tell. Well disciplined, and their commander ordered no looting or … or other actions. On pain of death."

"I'm sorry, but I can't come home yet. I have a chore to complete first."

Gerda eyes my canvas bag. "Someone needs help? That's what you carry when you're doing healing work."

I sigh, knowing I must break my promise to Erik Stahl. Still, there's nothing for it—Gerda never gives up, not when she has set her mind on something.

"There are two of our soldiers hiding near here. Just young men— boys, really. One of them is injured and overcome with fever. I said I'd do whatever I could to help him." I tighten my lips and press my boots into the ground. No matter what my sister says, I will not be moved.

Gerda slides off Bae's back. "Where are they? I will help too."

I relax my posture. What was I thinking? Of course Gerda, being Gerda, is willing to risk anything, even her life, to aid someone else. "Down this track." I motion toward the woods.

Bae swings his heavy head around to face Gerda. "It could be dangerous, little miss. Perhaps we should go to the village and ask for assistance … "

"No!" Gerda and I shout in unison.

Gerda pats Bae's nose. "Don't fret, my friend. We'll be quite safe. I know Varna will not lead me into danger."

"I cannot promise that, but it's a chance we must take. They are our countrymen, and the one boy is very ill. If it were Kai, lying there … "

"Come on then." Gerda sets off down the track.

"Hold up, wait for me," I call out, before turning to Bae. "Stay here, within these trees, and keep watch over the path. Alert us if anyone comes this way."

He bobs his head, his dark eyes solemn. "Very well, Miss Varna. But you must take care of my mistress."

"Of course." I turn on my heel to follow Gerda.

But who will take care of me? I shake my head and hoist the canvas satchel higher on my shoulder.

When we reach the abandoned cottage, I motion for Gerda to stay behind me before I knock on the door.

Erik peers out. His eyes widen at the sight of Gerda.

"I warned you to tell no one." He fumbles for his pistol, but he has shed that, along with his uniform jacket.

"This is my sister. She was looking for me, and when she discovered my plan, would not allow me to come alone." I glare at Erik's flushed face. "Her name is Gerda. You will treat her with courtesy or I'll walk away and leave your friend to die."

Erik is obviously too incensed to recognize my lie. "Come in."

He steps away from the door to allow us to enter. Barely sparing a glance for me, his gaze lights on Gerda and lingers with appreciation. "Erik Stahl." He clicks his heels as he bows.

Gerda smiles and bobs a curtsey in return. "Gerda Lund. Pleased to meet you, Master Stahl." She holds out her hand.

"Erik." He clasps her fingers and presses a light kiss on the back of her hand, then gestures toward the other side of the room. "My friend, Anders Nygaard. I'm afraid he is in no condition to be courteous."

Gerda smiles gently before walking toward Anders's bundled form. "We'll make him better, right, Varna?"

I drop my bag on a rickety table shoved against one wall. *Well, what did you expect, Varna? Men always overlook you and are all smiles for your sisters. This is nothing new.* I rummage through the bag, banging two metal flasks together. Their clang rings through the cottage.

Erik jumps and grabs a knife from the table.

"Steady." I touch the back of his hand. "This is not the battlefield."

He blinks and lowers his arm.

I motion toward his hand. "Is that the knife?"

Erik takes a deep breath before handing the weapon to me. "Yes. Will it work?"

I have no idea, but that is probably not the best response.

"I think so." I twist my wrist, turning the knife to examine the blade. "It's sharp, I'll say that."

Anders groans and thrashes beneath his makeshift covers. Gerda sinks to the filthy floor beside him.

"Poor dear boy." She rearranges the horse blanket over Anders's prone form. "Don't worry, we are here now. We'll stay with you, and Varna will make you better, I promise."

Anders stirs as Gerda's fingers brush his forehead. His eyelids flutter open, and his right arm shoots up. He clutches Gerda's hand so tight she is pulled down onto his chest. "My God, Erik," he says, his voice hoarse as the caw of a crow. "It's another angel."

CHAPTER THREE: WELL OF TEARS

I GRAB MY BAG AND HURRY to the two linked figures, Erik close on my heels.

Anders stares into Gerda's face for a second, then slumps back, his eyes closed. His grip relaxes and his hand falls to his side.

Gerda rises to her feet, cradling the hand Anders clutched. "You must help him, Varna."

"I will, if possible." I kneel by Anders. "Do you have the water, Erik?"

His boots vibrate loose floorboards as he dashes to another corner of the room. He returns, carrying a wooden bucket.

"I cleaned it out as best as I could. There's an old well outside, and the water seems fresh." Erik sets the bucket beside me. "What else?"

"The spirits. I suspect you carry some."

Erik produces a small metal flask and hands it to me. I open it and sniff.

"Brandy? Well, it will have to do." I glance from Gerda to Erik. "Both of you must help. It won't be pleasant."

Erik's freckles glow against his blanched skin. "You mean to cut away the contagion?"

"Yes, I must. At least the worst of it. Hopefully he'll remain unconscious, but if not …" I take a deep breath. "You must pin him down."

Gerda's round face is pale as the moon. "I will hold his legs."

"And I his arms." Erik looks me over. "You're certain this is necessary?"

"Yes." I am certain of nothing, but I can't imagine Anders improving with that contagion breeding in his leg.

"First, we need to tie off his leg above the wound. Strap it as tight as you can, using this." I toss Erik a roll of soft rope.

"A tourniquet? I've seen that used in the field."

I nod. "It will prevent him from bleeding out."

Erik wraps the rope around his friend's thigh and ties it tight. This unfortunately wakes Anders, who groans loudly.

"Tear the fabric away, would you, Erik?" I take a clean cloth I've draped over my arm and soak it in the water bucket.

Erik leans in, grips the loose flap, and rips the tattered trouser fabric away. Anders's leg is exposed all the way to his hip.

Gerda wobbles slightly.

"Grab some of those bandage rolls from my bag, Gerda. We'll need them to staunch the blood."

Wringing the excess water from the cloth, I wipe blood and mud from Anders's leg, then toss the cloth across the room. "Now, sit down and hold his ankles, Gerda, and you grab his shoulders, Erik."

You have never done this. You don't know what you are doing. The words swirl through my mind. I wipe my brow with the back of my hand, banishing all distraction, all doubt.

I pour some of Erik's brandy over the blade and lift the knife.

There is no second-guessing, there is only this—a blade before my eyes, my fingers gripping the handle. My slight tremor calms and ceases. My hand is perfectly still.

There is no fear, no hesitation.

There is only the patient and me.

The first cut is the most difficult. Anders cries out, still feeling the blade despite his delirium. I bite my lower lip and continue slicing away dead skin, closing my ears to his anguish. *Steady your hand, Varna. Focus on herbs for a poultice—barberry, garlic, goldenseal … Do not think of the knife, think of potions that can lower a fever—meadowsweet mixed with parsley and white willow.*

When I sit back Gerda's cheeks are streaked with tears, although she made no sound during the grisly procedure. Erik's face is as stony as a statue.

"Done." I drop the knife into my lap, ignoring the blood. "Now, Gerda, use some of the bandages to staunch the bleeding. You must apply steady pressure. I will create a poultice to pack the wound before I bandage it."

Anders is silent as one dead, yet the slight rise and fall of his narrow chest reassures me. I stand, the knife clattering to the floor.

Swaying, I fight an urge to retch. The taste of bile coats my tongue. Erik leaps to his feet and grabs me by the arm. "Steady."

"Get my bag," I say, between chattering teeth. "I need some herbs and potions for the poultice."

Erik leads me back to the table, my canvas satchel slung over his shoulder. He sets down the bag. "Should I bring the water bucket?"

"No, you still need it. Go and help Gerda slow the bleeding." I meet his anxious gaze. "You must remove the tourniquet, wash the wound with water, then apply pressure. Steady pressure, understand?"

He nods. "I have an extra shirt in my pack, if we need more bandage material."

"Good. Grab that, then go to Anders." I touch Erik's arm. "You did well."

"As did Gerda," he replies, with a glance in my sister's direction.

"Yes, she was very brave. Now let me work." I wave my hand to shoo him away.

It is true, Gerda was brave. This doesn't surprise me. I've heard tales of her unwavering courage before, from Kai Thorsen. The surprise is how much it seems to impress Erik Stahl.

Never mind that, you have work to do.

I concentrate on mixing the correct herbs in a willow bark paste for a concoction to heal Anders's leg and soothe his pain. Behind me, Gerda's voice lifts in a lullaby.

Smearing the herbal paste thickly on some bandages, I fold the soft material so the poultice is contained inside.

"Wash the wound again," I call out as I tuck some additional rolls of bandages under my arm. I cross the room in a few strides. "Then sit back and give me space to work."

I pour a little of the remaining brandy on the wound and wipe the excess, then apply the poultice and securely bandage Anders's leg. Exhausted, I brace myself with one hand to keep from collapsing onto the dank floor.

"Now what?" asks Erik, lifting hands stained with blood.

"Clean up and prepare for a long night. We'll need to sit with him, feeding him sips of this." I pull a small brown bottle from my skirt pocket. "It will ease the pain, and hopefully reduce his fever. Don't worry about using it up as I have two more bottles in my bag."

Gerda rouses from her focus on Anders's bone-pale face. "What is it?"

"To be honest, I'm not entirely certain. But Master Albrecht swears by it." I meet Erik's questioning gaze. "It's no poison, I can assure you."

"I did not think it was, only ... " Erik wipes his hands on his extra shirt. "I don't know this Master Albrecht."

"You did not know me either."

The faintest hint of a smile curves Erik's thin lips. "True, but I felt you could be trusted. I haven't looked into the eyes of this Albrecht person, as I have yours."

"I will take the first watch." Gerda settles on the floor near Anders's head. "Hand me the bottle, Varna, I'll make sure he gets some of that potion."

I pass her the medicine, relaying instructions on how much Anders should receive, and how often. "I think I'll step outside for some fresh air."

"I will join you." Erik stands, casting a glance at my sister. "That is, if you feel comfortable watching Anders by yourself, Gerda."

Gerda's eyes focus on our patient. "I'm fine. Anyway, you'll be within shouting distance." She lifts her head and smiles at Erik. "Thank you for asking."

Well, that should do it. If Erik was not already enchanted, surely he is now. I press my trembling hands together as I stride to the door. "You said there's a well outside? Can you show me?"

Erik crosses in front of me and kicks open the cottage door with his foot. "Around the back, beyond the blackberry bushes."

I slide past him without allowing our bodies to touch. *Don't show me then, Master Stahl. Let me wander, alone. I imagine you would be more solicitous if I were Gerda.*

Wiping dampness from my cheeks with the edge of my sleeve, I stumble to the well. I wind up the old bucket, still attached to its winch by a frayed length of rope, and tip it until water rinses most of the blood from my skirt, then winch up another bucketful to wash my hands.

It's no surprise a young man prefers my sister to me. I am used to that. No, Erik Stahl's disinterest only stings me to tears because my emotions are as raw as the hands I've scrubbed far too long. *The blood, the whimpers and howls of pain, the sight of the damage to muscle and bone ...* I long for arms to wrap about me, to keep me from flying apart, but there's no one to offer such comfort.

I sniffle once, then swear. The cursing makes me feel a little better. I wipe my wet hands on a dry portion of my skirt and experiment with a few more words I've heard from the workmen at the mill.

"Colorful, although rather limited."

As I spin about to face Erik my damp skirt and petticoat cling to my legs in an unseemly fashion. I pull the fabric away from my body. "I thought you decided to stay inside."

A spark of amusement lights Erik's tired eyes. "No, forgot this." He lifts his arm, revealing the bucket. "I thought we might need more clean water."

"Good idea." I shove my lank hair away from my eyes. "Listen, you do need to watch Anders, and make sure he takes that medicine. Because I cannot guarantee … "

"I know. Please don't fret. I am not expecting miracles. You've done more than most would have attempted."

"I still wish you would allow me bring Master Albrecht to attend Anders. He's a much more experienced healer than I am."

Erik shakes his head. "No. I am willing to trust Gerda, and you, but no one else. Besides, you seem more skilled than most so-called doctors I have seen operate on our soldiers."

I make a disparaging noise. "Most of them are hacks. More likely to butcher than heal."

"That they are." Erik looks me up and down. "You were perfectly calm. You must have great confidence in your abilities."

I wring the damp fabric of my skirt between my hands. "No." I lower my voice. "I'm afraid I have failed— that Anders will die, that I have tortured him to no purpose." When I glance up, I realize Erik is not listening.

"Odd. It looks like a trained falcon. Over there, on that branch." He points with his free hand. "See—it has something attached to its leg, like fetters."

The bird flies off before I can see anything other than a sweep of wings, and I question Erik's observation. It would be strange to find a trained falcon around here. That's a gentleman's sport, and none of my neighbors are rich.

Still, it seems to be a day for peculiar events involving animals. "A wolf led me to you," I say, recalling the creature's unusual behavior.

The empty bucket clatters to the ground. "What?" Erik grabs me.

I take a step back, jerking my arm from his grasp. "A wolf. I saw it on the path. It led me to this cottage, then disappeared."

"That's impossible."

"Are you calling me a liar?"

"No, but there was a wolf"—Erik's eyes glisten—"on the battlefield. It's how I found Anders."

"What do you mean?" I lean back and use both hands to grip the edge of the stone wall encasing the well.

Erik rests one booted foot on the overturned bucket. "We were separated during the battle. There was so much confusion." He rakes his hand through his red hair. "I could hardly glimpse my boots, much less the men around me. All I could see were rolling clouds of smoke from the muskets and cannons, then a bayonet slicing through, stabbing before you knew what was happening … Sorry, forgive me, that's not important to the story. Anyway, Anders was on my right—I glimpsed his face as another wave of smoke engulfed us. There was cannon fire, and I hit the ground. When I rose again, I couldn't find Anders. I had to keep fighting—I couldn't take time to look for him." He sweeps his hand across his eyes, as if to wipe away the memory. "When it was over, and we were told to retreat, I tried to find him, but my company forced me to march away. I checked each face as I stumbled over bodies, but none was his." Erik drops his head into his hands. "Every face."

The silence of the woods is broken by the cheerful chirps of crickets.

"War is a terrible thing," I say, and curse my inability to say more.

Erik lifts his head. "We reached the road before I looked back. I saw it through the veil of smoke—a wolf, staring at me with its great golden eyes. It looked like it could speak."

"The same." My voice is barely audible. "I saw the same."

Erik, lost in his memory, doesn't acknowledge my words. "The wolf turned and headed for the battlefield. I knew I had to follow. I left my company. I walked away and deserted them without a second thought. I followed the wolf to the edge of that terrible meadow, its grass trampled to mud and blanketed with bodies. The wolf veered into the woods encircling the field, and led me to the spot where Anders lay, then disappeared."

"Anders crawled from the battlefield?" I shiver as I picture this action, given his shattered leg.

Erik shakes his head. "No. He was still speaking, then—the fever had not overcome him yet. He told me … " Erik shoots me a challenging look, as if daring me to disbelieve his tale. "He said an angel pulled him from the field, dragged him into the woods, and made sure he was hidden from the enemy troops. An angel pale as early morning light, with clear eyes, bright as the blade of a sword."

I loosen my grip on the well. "He was in great pain and probably delirious."

"Perhaps." Erik jumps to his feet, grabbing the bucket. "Let me get that water. We shouldn't leave Gerda alone too long. If Anders wakes he may thrash about, and though he is slight, I doubt she could hold him."

"You might be surprised what Gerda can do." I move aside as Eric reaches for the handle of the winch.

"No, actually I wouldn't." He glances over at me as he fills the bucket. "She has an air about her. Something special."

"Yes," I say, because it is true. Because I can feel jealousy, yet don't have to show it.

We walk back to the cottage, Eric toting the bucket of water as if it were filled with feathers. When we enter the dilapidated building, I stop for a moment to allow my eyes to adjust to the dim light. The sun is setting and shadows stain the vacant window panes.

Gerda looks up at our approach, her finger against her lips.

"How is he?" Erik sets down the bucket and sinks to his knees beside his friend's prone form. He clutches Anders's limp fingers. "He feels less feverish."

That is impossible. It must be the well water, cooling Erik's hand.

Gerda strokes Anders's shoulder. "He's sleeping more peacefully. I was able to give him some of the medicine, and it did seem to help."

"Good." I kneel beside Erik. "You can take a break now, Gerda. Stand and stretch your legs."

Giving Anders's arm a final pat, Gerda sits back and places the brown medicine bottle out of reach of flailing limbs. She then struggles to stand, her legs obviously asleep. Erik leaps to his feet and lends her his arm. He escorts her to the center of the room, where she delicately shakes out one foot and then the other. I watch this pantomime over my shoulder, half-expecting Erik to kiss her fingers again.

"Thank you." Gerda slides away from his steadying hands.

"Not at all." Erik's voice is infused with charm.

A gallantry he does not waste on me.

I look away. *Varna, you silly goose, you have more important things to think about.*

Pressing my fingers against Anders's forehead, I am shocked to find he does feel slightly cooler. I stare at the bottle I stole from Master Albrecht's shelves. What is in that potion, to affect such a change so quickly? It was something Albrecht brought with him when he arrived in our village—not anything he taught me to make, or distilled in my presence.

A rustle—Gerda must be shaking the dust from her skirt. "Erik, who is Christiane?"

Erik makes a noise that sounds suspiciously like a swallowed curse. "Why?"

"Anders called out the name a few times. It was the only word I could understand."

"A girl," Erik tosses off as he crosses the room. "Christiane Bech."

"His sweetheart?"

"Well"—Erik stares down at his friend—"Anders loves her. How she feels about him, I'm not entirely certain. She's a ballerina at the Opera House in our city."

Gerda claps her hands. "Is that the city with the university? My friend Kai studies there. Perhaps he knows her." She crosses to stand near me. "Or maybe he's met Anders."

"I doubt it. If this Kai is a student—well, students at the University don't typically mingle with workers." Erik crouches next to me. "Anders and I, we grew up together, as neighbors in the tradesmen's quarter. My family runs a dry goods shop and Anders used to help out, at least until he was apprenticed to a cobbler." Erik gently brushes his fingers over Anders's upper arm. "He's talented, a first-rate shoemaker. He learned so quickly, his master soon had him making ballet slippers for the dancers of the Opera. That's how Anders met Christiane. She is young, barely sixteen, but he's only eighteen so it was not surprising they were drawn to one another." A smile lights Erik's face. "He likes to dance too. Not ballet, of course, but he often escorts Christiane to the public dance halls. I must admit they are beautiful waltz partners. I love watching them."

I sit back on my heels, staring at Anders's leg. "Erik, you should know … "

Erik's smile twitches into a grimace. "He will never dance again? Yes, I realize that."

Gerda gasps. "Surely his leg will heal."

I shake my head. "I believe he will live and even be able to walk, assisted by a cane. But will he ever dance again?" I glance at Gerda's stricken face. "No."

"Oh, the poor boy." Tears fill Gerda's eyes.

"There are worse things." Erik rises to his feet. "Now, you two must hurry home. Yes, I know you planned to stay the night, but I don't think it wise. Your family will be frantic, and I doubt you wish to draw too much attention, what with the enemy camped in your town."

"They are camped outside of it, actually." Gerda's gaze is focused on Anders. She shakes of her head, as if to clear her thoughts. "Can you take care of him, Erik? Surely we should stay?"

"No. Go home. I hope you have some plausible story to tell?"

"I've already thought of that." Gerda helps me to my feet. "I will say my reindeer, Bae, escaped his pen and when I searched for him I met Varna, and asked her to help me. Bae's waiting for us by the path," she adds, obviously sensing Erik's confusion. "We can go home with him in tow, so it will be perfectly believable."

I blink as I examine my sister. I didn't expect Gerda to produce so glib a lie. Still, it *is* believable. I turn to Erik. "Unfortunately, you must stay up all night. Give Anders more medicine whenever he wakes. Get him to at least take a sip or two, and some water as well. Can you do that?"

"Yes, Madame Doctor, I think I can manage."

"It is important." I brush past him and stride to the table to collect my bag. "I'll come back tomorrow, although I must wait until I can get away without alerting anyone."

"So will I." Gerda scurries to my side. "We'll return to watch over Anders so you can rest. We will also bring you food and drink, right, Varna?"

Erik's amused expression makes my fingers twitch. "We'll bring what we can. Come, Gerda, we'd better go if we hope to sell your story. Mother might believe it now, but not if we're out after dark."

As we head out the door, Erik grabs my arm. "Remember, not a word to anyone."

I shake his fingers loose. "You claim to trust us."

His intense gaze sweeps over my face. "I do. I'm just worried about Anders."

"The best thing you can do is watch over him tonight and continue to trust us."

As Erik holds the door open, the light filtering through the tree leaves tints his face green. Coupled with his sardonic grin it lends him the appearance of some elven creature. "Very well, Doctor Lund." He bows from the waist. When he straightens, a more genuine smile graces his face. "Goodbye, Miss Gerda, and thank you. Try not to let your sister get you into any more trouble."

The door closes before I can reply.

CHAPTER FOUR:
AN EYE FOR BEAUTY

MASTER ALBRECHT STANDS AT THE entrance to a tent, his scuffed boots sinking into a puddle of late spring mud. The papery skin on his neck jiggles as he lifts his chin and stares at two enemy soldiers and their interpreter.

"If you wish more of your troops to die, please do keep me out." He adjusts the heavy canvas bag draped over his sloping shoulder. "I am offering my aid, and that of my assistant, to treat your injured soldiers. Not for money, or concessions, but to prevent more needless deaths."

One of the soldiers jabbers with the other. The interpreter looks pained and shuffles his feet. "They say—we already have a doctor."

Obviously, they said more than that. I assume the interpreter is unwilling to translate insults.

Albrecht's expression signals he may know a few of the words. "Doctor?" His laugh emerges as a bark. "More like a butcher. But have it your way. Come, Varna, we shall return to our work at the cottage." He turns and trudges toward the dirt path that leads away from the enemy camp.

As I follow two soldiers point at me and laugh. The village boys often do the same, although they tend to wait until they think I cannot see or hear.

But I do. I hear their snide laughter, and catch them staring at my flat chest and questioning whether I'm actually a boy. Once, the pastor's son said no one would ever make love to me, unless it was very dark and the man was very drunk. Yes, I hear such taunts and sometimes, even worse.

I quicken my pace to catch up to Master Albrecht. "Talk about ungrateful. I can't imagine why you even bother. Here, do you need me to carry that bag?"

Albrecht raises his bushy brows. "You have your own burden. I can manage." He stares at the horizon, where hills rise like stair steps to meet the mountain range. "Still, thank you."

I frown. "To be honest, I don't understand why you offer aid to the enemy."

Albrecht scans one ridge as if seeking some hidden object. "Those soldiers are simply men. Or boys, many of them. They did not ask to be transported to this country to be shot to pieces on a battlefield near a village whose name they cannot pronounce. A healer heals, regardless of the patient's allegiance or nationality."

"Yes, but ... " I shift my bag from one shoulder to the other. It *is* heavy. Master Albrecht filled it with bottles of his mysterious potions as well as the typical ointments, herbs, and rolls of bandages. "Many in the village will label you a traitor for offering assistance to our invaders."

"I am not concerned about the opinions of the townsfolk. It's best to ignore such things." Albrecht shifts his gaze back to the path. "You should do the same."

I sneak a glance at him. Had he heard and understood those mocking soldiers?

Or read my thoughts?

No, that is ridiculous. I roll my shoulders to relieve the numbing pressure of the heavy bag. "I should, I suppose. We heard enough talk when Gerda returned four years ago. She didn't even tell the whole story and people were ready to label her mad. Not to mention those who thought she'd compromised her honor, travelling alone with Kai, although they relented on that point when she told them of the presence of Thyra Winther and others during her travels."

Master Albrecht stops short and grips my wrist. "Did she tell *you* the whole story, Varna?"

For a moment the fingers encircling my wrist appear young and strong, but when I blink and look again it's Albrecht's gnarled digits, splotched with liver spots and engraved with wrinkles.

Perhaps I *am* going mad.

I raise my eyes. "Most of it, I think. There were some details she would not discuss. Too painful, I suppose."

Albrecht drops my wrist and steps back. "She told you of the mirror?"

"Yes, she mentioned a shattered enchanted mirror. She said the mage Mael Voss thought it would grant him immortality if he could reconstruct it. Unfortunately for him, he died before that happened."

"At the hands of Thyra Winther."

"True, but Gerda claims Thyra only killed Voss to save her and Kai." I gnaw the inside of my cheek for a second, discomfited by his piercing gaze. "I'm not sure why this matters to you, Master Albrecht. Did you know Voss?"

Albrecht wheezes out a laugh. "No, I never had that pleasure. What would an ordinary healer have to do with a mighty mage? I've heard tales of him, of course, and his mirror." Albrecht resumes his typical shuffling gait. "Whatever happened to it, the mirror? Did Gerda tell you?"

Did she? I search my memories. "She said it was taken somewhere safe, to be kept hidden. She didn't say where, although I suppose it might be in the mountains, in Voss's old kingdom."

Albrecht glances at me over his shoulder. "It is a powerful object, that mirror. Or so I have been told. Perhaps your sister knows its location and keeps it a secret?"

"I suppose that is possible." I clear my throat. "Master, I would like to beg off working with you this afternoon. Traveling to the enemy camp has taken up the entire morning, and I do have chores."

Albrecht grunts. "You seem to be burdened with more chores than usual these days. What is it this time?"

"Mother needs me to help put up some preserves."

"Really, Varna, you must learn to lie better than that. What sort of preserves would these be? No fruit is ripe this time of year."

Once, I could've claimed we had bartered our flour for some pears from Inga Leth. When I was younger her garden produced fruits and vegetables impossibly early in the spring, as well as long past frost. Strangely, that changed after Gerda returned from her journey to find Kai. Now Inga's garden is as limited by the seasons as any other plot of land.

"You have found me out, I do have another reason, but I must beg you not to question me further. I've made a promise."

"Do you hold promises in such high regard?"

"Yes, I do." I lift my head and gaze up at the tree limbs that canopy the path. Their pale green leaves flutter like moth wings. "I also value the truth."

Albrecht stops short, causing me to step on his heel. "So if I were to ask how three bottles of my special potion disappeared, would you give me an honest answer?"

I drop my head to hide the flush in my cheeks.

"I took them. It was necessary." Images of Erik and Anders flood my mind. I must concoct an acceptable lie. "Gerda asked me. She said there was a workman at the mill whose child was ill. I saw you use that medicine on the cobbler's wife and she regained her health. I should've asked, but you were off somewhere … "

Albrecht snorts. "Three bottles? I doubt your sister truly requires that much, not to help one person, especially not a child."

"She said she needed more. After I gave her the first one, I mean." I study the tips of my well-worn boots. "I did not question her. What else would she want it for?" I look up, meeting Master Albrecht's eyes.

"Perhaps Gerda is keeping secrets? Is she always absolutely truthful?"

I steel myself not to look away, even though Albrecht's gaze is boring a hole in my forehead. "She is. Absolutely."

To be honest, I've been astonished at Gerda's ability to lie. Every morning Gerda tells Mother she's headed to the mill to oversee our workmen and ensure they are treated fairly by the enemy soldiers. She offers this lie with a smile. Oh, it is true she goes to the mill, but she leaves at midday, claiming she must hurry home to help with chores. Of course, she's actually sneaking off to supply Erik and Anders with food and drink. She's even provided them with some of Kai's old clothes, pilfered from his mother's house while Olivia Thorsen was at the market.

"Kai wouldn't mind," she said, when I questioned this behavior, and I know she is right. That's not the problem. No, I worry someone at the mill will inform Mother about Gerda's true schedule. Mother is so fearful lately, concerned the enemy will retaliate and burn down the mill on the slightest provocation. If she suspects Gerda of any rebellion …

"I wonder." Master Albrecht's words slice through my thoughts. "Sometimes we cannot see our family or friends clearly." Inexplicably, he leans in and strokes the side of my face. "Love blinds us all. Now, I must leave you, my dear. It seems I am required to distill medicine to replace my missing stock."

Before I can form a proper response, he trundles down another path, leaving me alone. I turn my gaze from the hunched figure and step onto the main road.

As I draw closer to the village, I glance up at a tall hill overlooking the town. I stop in my tracks.

There is a horse and rider atop the ridge, paused near a stand of firs.

I shade my eyes with one hand. It is a cloaked figure, which makes it impossible to tell if it is one of their soldiers, one of ours, or simply a lone traveler. I squint, hoping to capture more details.

Something stands beside the horse, a creature of some kind. My satchel slides off my shoulder and hits the ground with a thud.

It looks like the wolf who led me to Erik and Anders.

It cannot be. Although, the wolf *was* unafraid, almost tame. I lift my bag and run my fingers over the rough material, ensuring no bottles have broken.

Steady, Varna. Decide if you will speak of this rider—if you will inform the enemy soldiers posted in town, or our own men.

Or, perhaps, no one at all.

Gerda speaks of a young woman always accompanied by a wolf— Kai Thorsen's love, who travels the world. She supposedly left Kai to learn on her own terms, while he studies at the University. But if the former Snow Queen planned to return to our village, surely Gerda and Kai would know.

The rider leans forward, lifting a pale hand to shade hidden eyes.

I drop my own hand and raise my skirts so I can move as quickly as possible. The heavy satchel swings from my shoulder, banging against my hip. I ignore this and run, only pausing when I reach the narrow trail that intersects with the path to Master Albrecht's home.

Learning against the rough bark of a pine tree, I take deep breaths. I must calm my racing heart before I enter the abandoned cottage. I can't appear anxious, not when Anders is improving day by day. Erik might decide to move him too soon and destroy all my good work.

I tuck the loose strands of my hair up under my cap and smooth the wrinkles from my bodice and skirt. Slowing my steps to a walk, I reach the half-open door of the derelict cottage.

"It is Varna," I call out as I push my way inside, aware Erik keeps a musket handy, in addition to his pistol.

He meets me right inside the door, silently taking the bag from my shoulder and placing it on the table.

"How is he today?" I ask, keeping my voice low.

Erik nods his head in the direction of the makeshift bed. Anders sits up, propped by the folded horse blanket and a pillow Gerda stole from our house.

Gerda's seated next to the young soldier. They study a book open in Anders's lap. I recognize a collection of stories and illustrations I read as a child—humorous tales of talking animals and a young man who gets into dangerous scrapes.

The golden head bent close to the light brown one, the hands touching as they turn the pages, the peals of laughter ... This is not good.

I cough, loudly.

Gerda looks up, her blue eyes merry. "Varna! Come and see. I'd forgotten how funny these stories are."

"I remember," I say, without moving.

I also remember Gerda's pain, as she struggled to overcome her feelings for Kai Thorsen. I recall how she put on a brave face, expressing her happiness over Kai's love for Thyra Winther. I remember she claimed she only wanted the best for both her friends.

I can't forget how she wept, when she thought no one could hear.

It took some time, but Gerda finally moved beyond the pain, or at least far enough to cease shedding tears for her thwarted love. Now when she speaks of Kai it's like someone talking about a beloved brother.

"Anders is feeling so much better." Gerda's smile would warm the coldest heart.

I remember another fact Gerda seems to have forgotten—Anders already has a sweetheart. He loves that ballerina in the city, Christiane Bech.

"I know," Erik says, under his breath. "I see it too."

"It would be better if it were you."

He shrugs. "She does not see me."

I study his profile. Erik is the handsomer of the two young men, despite deprivation sharpening his features. He is tall, and big-boned, and—with food and rest—would cut a splendid, masculine figure.

A flush rises up the back of my neck. I need to banish these thoughts. I must stop imaging every good-looking young man in my arms.

Or your bed.

I slap my upper arm. "Going to sleep," I say, when Erik shoots me a questioning look. "That heavy bag."

Erik apparently finds this explanation acceptable. "Anders is much improved. His fever has receded."

"That's good, but I need to check him over." I cross to Anders and Gerda. "Let me examine you then, Master Nygaard."

"Sorry, I still cannot stand." Anders's voice is delicate, much like his body. Considerably shorter and slighter than Erik, his light brown hair spills over his forehead, brushing his eyebrows. His hazel eyes are wide and fringed with soft lashes, and there's a delicacy about his mouth that reminds me of pictures of cherubim I once saw in a book of Bible stories.

"No need," I say, kneeling before him. I push up his loose trouser leg and unwind the bandages. "Erik says your fever is gone."

"Quite gone." Gerda stares at my hands.

I know what she wants to see. The truth. What damage remains.

It is not pretty. Although the flesh is growing back, it's puckered and red, and there's a deep indentation where a chunk of leg muscle is missing.

I force a smile. "Healing nicely."

"It looks horrible." Anders's eyes cloud with tears. "Yet it is healing, and I will live, and for that I thank you again, Varna."

Gerda places her arm around Anders's narrow shoulders. "It is a war wound, honorably received. Many soldiers have them. It's nothing to be ashamed of."

A shadow crosses Anders's face. I know he must be thinking of Christiane, of how she will view such a wound. Now, if she wishes to go dancing, it must be with other men.

"You should be able to walk soon, although perhaps with help."

Anders's lips curve into a sad smile. "Erik's already carving me a cane."

I glance up at Erik, who has crossed the room to stand beside me. "Good for Erik. You must build up your strength, though. Do not expect too much too soon."

"It is beautiful," Gerda says.

I shoot her a sharp glance, then realize she's staring at the object Erik clutches in his left hand.

It is a cane unlike any I have ever seen. Formed from a single oak branch, it's carved with a skill that makes me catch my breath.

I stare at the gorgeous wolf head topping the cane. "You are an artist."

Erik's face reddens. "No, a craftsman. My grandfather taught me. It's something I can do, you see, minding the counter in the shop, or at night, by the fire. It keeps my hands busy."

"Do not believe it." Anders casts an indulgent smile at his friend. "Erik is a connoisseur of beauty. He protests when I drag him to the ballet, then is transfixed by the dancers. If you visit a cathedral or art gallery with him, you should expect to spend hours. If he sees anything beautiful, he stops and stares and stares."

I drop my hands in my lap and fiddle with the light fabric of my apron. This explains his total disinterest in me, outside of my healing skills. *That is fine, Master Erik Stahl. I know I would not attract a man like you. You will never look at me with the gaze you use to admire beautiful things.*

Like the look Anders has turned on Gerda.

Oh no, I won't have my sister's heart shattered again. "Come, Gerda, we should get home."

"Really?" Gerda's lips roll into an adorable pout.

"Yes." I rise to my feet, barely acknowledging Erik's hand under my elbow. "You know how Mother is these days. She's interrogated me a couple of times about your whereabouts. We don't want to give her more reasons to question us."

Gerda sighs, but pulls away from Anders and stands. "You keep the book," she tells him.

"Thank you, Gerda."

There's that smile again. I bite the inside of my cheek. "We must hurry. If we are home early, it will look less suspicious." Erik, who has followed us to the door, hands me my bag as we pass the table. "We don't want to betray Anders and Erik to the enemy," I whisper in Gerda's ear as I push her out the door.

We walk home in silence. I shift the heavy satchel from shoulder to shoulder to lessen the burden. It's a measure of Gerda's preoccupation that she does not offer to help carry the bag.

Entering town, I lower my head as we pass the enemy soldiers posted in the square. No need to draw any attention. Thankfully, we reach our house without incident.

Stepping into our bright parlor, its white-washed walls displaying splotches of bare plaster from Mother's constant scrubbing, I notice my twin sisters, Franka and Nanette perched on the oak settle. Their golden hair falls below their shoulders in soft waves and their eyes sparkle like sapphires in their perfect, porcelain doll faces.

Mother stands in the center of room, clutching a wrought iron poker. She slaps the poker against one callused palm.

"Gerda and Varna Lund." Her tone is icier than a mountain lake in winter. "Get in here."

I grab Gerda's hand and grip it tightly as we cross the room.

Mother's face is pale and drawn. She straightens and stares at us with hard eyes.

"I know what you have been up to, and I am going to put a stop to it."

CHAPTER FIVE:
CAGE OF BRANCHES

G ERDA STEPS FORWARD TO STAND between me and Mother. "What do you mean?"
I glare at Nanette and Franka, who meet my furious gaze with identical self-satisfied smirks. Maybe, just maybe, Master Albrecht is right about the twins.

"Do not play the innocent with me, Gerda Lund." Mother taps the wooden floor with the end of the poker. "It's bad enough you ran off before, in that totally irresponsible fashion, now you endanger all of us with this foolishness. Hiding and aiding soldiers … "

"*Our* soldiers." Gerda's implacable face mirrors Mother's.

"That may be, but you heard the proclamation. The orders are to turn over any of our troops hiding in the area. Not nurse them and take them food. On penalty of death, or worse."

"Not sure what you mean." I curl my fingers until my nails cut into my palms.

"Prison camps." Mother shudders. "Do you know what happens to girls in a place like that?"

I unclench my fists. It's clear Mother is more terrified than angry. She is afraid something dreadful will befall her daughters. Something she will be powerless to prevent.

When I was a child, my mother was a cheerful woman, always ready with a hug or laugh. Now responsibility weighs down her shoulders, heavier than any sack of grain, and her blue eyes, once as clear as Gerda's, are shadowed. Losing my father years ago was difficult, but at least she had Nicholas Thorsen to lean on. After my father died, Kai's father stepped in, managing our family affairs as well as the mill. Sadly, when Nicholas died in a freak blizzard four years ago, Mother was forced to take responsibility for both families. Olivia Thorsen is no use, preferring to sit and embroider rather than have anything to do with the business, and as for Kai ...

"If only Kai were here, where he should be," says my mother, with a heavy sigh. "But no, he must pursue his studies. For all the good that will do."

"We are not having this discussion again." Gerda's tone is firm. "I know you think Kai should abandon his studies to return to the village. Even though he is the most brilliant mathematician the University has ever seen. Even though our productivity is up, along with sales, since I have taken over management of the mill."

"You have done your best." Mother leans the poker against the stones flanking the fireplace. "Still, you should be thinking of marriage, Gerda, not running a business. Or dashing off to spend time with young soldiers. Have you no sense of propriety?"

"Varna was with me the entire time."

This is another lie, but I'm not about to contradict her. I move to stand by Gerda. "These are just young men, Mother. Boys like Nels or Kai. One of them is seriously injured. We could not leave them to die."

"So you decided to sneak around, right under the noses of the enemy? You know I've struck a bargain with the occupiers. They have agreed to keep the mill running, and even give us a cut of the profits, if we cooperate." Mother's gaze rakes over my face. "How do you think we would eat if they took the mill from us or, God forbid, burnt it to the ground? That is the least they might do, if they find out what you've been up to."

"It was my idea." I take hold of Gerda's hand.

"No doubt."

"I am a healer. I'm not going to let someone die, especially not one of our own, if I can help it."

Mother shakes her head. "I have no quibble with your healing work, Varna, but this is different."

I notice Mother does not speak of me giving up a vocation for marriage. No, she's pleased I've found work that can provide me with a home and a livelihood. Because, of course, she does not believe I will ever marry. Especially not now, when so many of our young men have died in the war.

I turn to Franka and Nanette. "I know it was you two, sneaking around and following us. Little snitches."

Mother bustles over to the settle. "The twins were doing their duty." She lays one hand on Nanette's shoulder.

Franka tosses back her lustrous mane of hair. "We didn't plan to spy on you. We just overheard you and Gerda talking one day, after Gerda snuck into Olivia Thorsen's house and dashed out carrying some of Kai's old clothes. We thought it was odd."

"So you eavesdropped?" I stare at Franka, who has the grace to blush.

"No, we just happened to be there, behind the grape arbor, hanging up the laundry. We heard you ask Gerda what she was doing and then talk about the men you are helping. Nanette and I didn't say anything for a week, but there was that proclamation about aiding soldiers ... "

Gerda pulls her hand from my grasp and points a finger at the twins. "The words of our enemy. Do not forget that. They take over our town and then expect us to betray our own."

Mother pushes back her linen cap with her free hand, revealing hair as bright as corn silk. "Still, we must follow their orders, or be tossed into a prison camp. Did you think of that, Gerda? Not only you, but your sisters as well." Her fingers tighten on Nanette's shoulder until my younger sister squeaks in protest.

I level a frosty stare at the twins. "So, doing your duty, huh?"

"If the enemy finds out, who knows what they would do." Nanette's words end in a whine.

The fact the twins are speaking the truth about the danger doesn't mollify me. I long to slap those pretty faces, but crumple a wad of skirt fabric in my hand instead.

"I hope you haven't said anything to them."

Franka jumps to her feet. "It would serve you right if we did. You didn't think about us when you decided to take the risk, did you?"

"Hush, Franka." Mother releases her hold on Nanette and steps forward, until she is standing face-to-face with Gerda and me. "So far there is no harm done. But I insist you break contact with these soldiers. You have helped them all you can. Now you must protect yourselves, and your family."

Gerda holds out her hands in supplication. "Mother, how can we abandon them? They are as likely to die in a prison camp as we are. We cannot allow that to happen."

My mother's eyes narrow. She examines Gerda while the grandfather clock my father hauled back from one of his rare city trips ticks off the minutes.

"Gerda Lund, do you have feelings for one of these soldiers?"

Gerda lifts her chin to meet Mother's glare. "Yes. I do. I feel they are heroes, and don't deserve to be betrayed by the people they fought to protect. I believe we owe them our loyalty."

I tug on the tie dangling from my linen cap, pulling the hat from my head.

Mother takes a deep breath and straightens like a ramrod. "You will go to your room. You will stay there until I tell you to come out. Varna as well. As for you two," she shoots a sharp glance at the twins, "you will stay in the house until I decide whether, or what, we tell anyone concerning this matter."

There's nothing more to say. I share a glance with Gerda, then silently follow her to the stairs that lead to our bedroom.

Behind us, Nanette whines about the unfairness of her life. I concentrate on the ticking of the clock to still my desire to run back and give her a good thrashing.

Gerda paces the floor of our small room while I slump on the bed. "We must warn them. They need to leave the area as soon as possible. I think Anders can be moved now, although he's likely to need Erik to lean on."

"And how, exactly, will they get away?" I pull a pin feather through the exposed ticking of one of our pillows. "Even if we sneak out of the house and reach the cottage, how do we smuggle them beyond the village? There must be enemy guards watching the roads."

Gerda stops and leans against the carved wooden wardrobe. "I have an idea. I'm just not sure if I should pursue it."

"What?" I tickle the back of my hand with the pin feather. It is gentle, but can draw a line like a brush. *Could be useful to paint a tincture onto damaged skin.*

"The Upper Branch flows through the woods, not far from the cottage where Anders and Erik are hiding. It eventually feeds into the river, and Bae told me our troops have a camp along its banks, not far downstream."

I sit up, dropping the feather onto the pieced counterpane. "That sounds good, but what do you expect them to do, swim?"

My sister's eyes are shadowed beneath her golden lashes. "Nels has a boat."

"Nels Leth? You want to involve him?"

"No, I do not, but I will if I must. His boat is moored on the Upper Branch. We could easily get the boys to the boat, under cover of darkness, and they could make their way to safety. A short trip down the river and they could join up with their company."

Gerda's face is alight with passion. I take a deep breath before I trust myself to speak. "Erik abandoned his company to save Anders. I'm not sure he would be any safer with them than with the enemy. He would probably be shot as a deserter."

"Then another company, where no one knows them. In the confusion of war, who will ever find out? Or perhaps they can escape and head back home, to the city."

"Still a problem." I rise to my feet and cross the room. "But they do need to leave. I'm afraid Mother or one of the twins might let the truth slip, trying to protect us."

Gerda's eyes flash. "Protect? They are playing both sides."

"In order to save our family business and keep us out of a prison camp." I look Gerda over, reminding myself this is the same girl who braved blizzards and a Snow Queen's wrath to save someone she loved. "Gerda, you've not fallen in love with Anders, have you? You know he already has a sweetheart."

"I know." Gerda stares out the window. "Which is why, if I involve Nels, I must promise to marry him once the enemy soldiers leave town. Which they will, you know, sooner or later, no matter who wins the war."

"What?" I reach out and take hold of Gerda's chin, turning her head to face me.

Her blue eyes brim with tears.

"Oh, Gerda, I am sorry. Still, you cannot throw everything away to help Anders Nygaard. You can't swear to marry Nels, even if it does convince him to lend his boat."

"Nels will do as well as any other man. He is not so bad, and he's a patriot. He would be fighting too, if he did not have to manage old man Hendersen's farm. Someone has to supply food to the troops, you know."

"I understand that. But you don't love Nels, and there is his horrible mother ... "

Gerda sniffs back a sob. "It seems I am destined to love people who cannot return my feelings. Well, if that's my destiny, I might as well accept it, and do whatever I can to help those I care about."

I touch the tears on Gerda's cheeks with the tips of my fingers. "Wipe your eyes. I will help you, and our new friends, any way I can. First, we must get out of the house."

Gerda uses the edge of her apron to dry her tears. "That is not a problem. Unless you are afraid to climb down a tree."

"Afraid?" I make a pffing sound. "I've done it before. It might be more difficult in the dark, though."

"Nonsense." My sister wrinkles her pert nose. "I have crossed mountains on foot before."

"Then you go first."

We wait for the night to cloak our actions, using the time to dress in our darkest clothes and walking boots. After Gerda determines everyone in the house has gone to bed, she opens our window.

The misshapen limbs of the tree testify to its survival through many hard winters. Gerda crawls out the window and climbs down a few branches, perching on a lower limb to wait for me.

"Come along," she whispers, as I pause with both feet resting on a branch and my hands gripping the sides of the window frame. She slips down the tree, clambering from limb to limb until she is close enough to drop to the ground.

The tangle of dark branches looks like so many arms, reaching out to pull me down. I close my eyes for a moment. *If Gerda can do this, you can do this. If you can cut into a man's leg with a knife, you can do this. Concentrate, Varna.*

I open my eyes and reach for the closest limb. Digging my fingers into the rough bark, I cling to the branch and pull myself to a standing position. I carefully navigate the lattice of branches, finally reaching the lowest branch, where I sit for a moment before launching myself forward and tumbling onto the grass.

"Are you all right?" Gerda leans over me, holding out her hand.

"Yes." I allow her to help me to my feet. "What next?"

"I'm going to locate Nels. I know we could simply take his boat, but he keeps his oars at the house, and it won't be much use without them. You go to the cottage and instruct Anders and Erik to prepare for their escape. I will meet you there."

"Wait." I grab Gerda's arm as she turns to go. "Why not ask Bae to fly them away from here? He could do that, right?"

"Yes, but … " Gerda bites her lower lip. "I made a promise to keep Bae's magical abilities secret. Think of what could happen if word got out. There would be circuses, and hunters, and wealthy men trying to capture him as a curiosity. You found out by accident, and now he trusts you, but I cannot risk anyone else knowing."

"All right, we will leave Bae out of it." I pull the hood of Gerda's dark cape over her bright hair. "Be careful."

"You as well." Gerda flashes me a smile before heading off into the night.

I move swiftly toward the path to the woods, careful to remain hidden by foliage and the shadows of buildings. The guards clustered about an open fire do not notice me as I pass by, silent as a cat. Once on the wooded track, with the trees arching above me, and a bend in the path cutting off the view into town, I relax my hunched shoulders. The full moon is bright enough to light my way. I increase my strides, determined to reach Erik and Anders and share Gerda's plan.

A figure appears from the mass of trees lining the path. I gasp and instinctively throw up my arm, as if fending off an attack.

The figure steps onto the path. It is hunched over and dressed in a tattered dark cloak. I squint and release a gusty sigh.

"Oh, Master Albrecht, it's you." I hurry forward, concocting a story to cover my late night wanderings. *Coming to you for medicine, Master. Someone in the village is ill. Could not wait until morning.*

Before I can open my mouth the figure shifts and changes.

The cloak falls back and whips away, disintegrating like burnt paper blown by the wind. The figure straightens and broadens, until it's no longer a ragged old man. It is a gentleman, tall and imposing.

I rub my eyes with the back of my hand. The man strides toward me, his black greatcoat billowing.

He stops a few feet from me and looks me up and down. Dark eyes flash in a face that could turn heads anywhere, even at court. His ebony hair falls back from his forehead in waves, tumbling to the high collar of his coat. High cheekbones and a narrow nose speak of nobility and restraint, but the sensuous curve of his full lips suggests something else.

He is stunningly handsome, and not at all the man I thought I knew.

"Hello, Varna." His silky voice caresses every word. "Do you not recognize your old master?"

CHAPTER SIX:
SWEPT AWAY

I CLUTCH MY UPPER ARMS WITH both hands. "I don't know you."
"You do." As the man's fingers encircle one of my wrists, his other hand brushes against my breast. It feels as deliberate as a lover's touch.

Collect yourself, Varna. This is a dangerous individual. Someone who has lied to you for months.

Because it is the same touch, the same strong fingers I thought I saw once before, when he gripped my wrist outside the enemy camp. Foolish me, I dismissed that as a hallucination. I now see the real illusion was always the old man who worked beside me.

I twist my wrist, yanking it from the stranger's grip. "Who are you?"

He bows from the waist, elegant as a courtier. "Sten Rask."

"I thought you were a healer."

"That is one of my skills."

"In addition to transforming into other people?"

His lips twitch. "Yes. Now, shall we dispense with these pleasantries? Like me, I believe you are in something of a hurry."

I square my shoulders and stare up into Rask's hooded eyes. "I do have an important mission, but I must know—why tell me now?"

"Because I am running out of time. As you will be, if you do not rush to your young soldiers. Yes, I know about them."

A mage. A wizard. A sorcerer. Rask must be one or all of these things. I recall Gerda's tales of the mage Mael Voss and shiver.

"Why the deception? Why pretend to be a doddering old man?"

Heat flushes my face. *Why stand close, why guide my hands, why breathe upon the back of my neck? You who look like that, who exude sensuality like a scent?*

Sten Rask's dark eyes are cool and unreadable as stones. "So I could get close to you and your family without drawing the notice of certain … individuals."

"My family?" I clench my fists at my sides. "Why my family?"

"Your sister Gerda in particular. You see, I think she knows more about the location of a particular enchanted object than she lets on. I'd hoped to convince her to speak with me—a harmless, doddering old man. But matters did not go exactly as I planned. For one thing, Nels Leth could not bring himself to give her that potion, poor fool."

As I take two steps back my cloak slips off my shoulders. I ignore it. "You search for the enchanted mirror Thyra Winther hid from the world. Why? For what purpose?"

"Yes, I seek the mirror. Now that it is been made whole, its considerable powers may be wielded once again."

"By you?"

"Hopefully. That is to say, I believe I can do so. Though in the service of someone else—the emperor you call the Usurper."

The light wind rustling the new leaves roars in my ears like the ocean. "You serve our enemy? You would betray your own country?"

"It is not my country, but that is neither here nor there. This is simply politics, and it's obvious you know nothing of such matters, my dear. As it happens, the emperor's plans coincide with my own desires."

I stare into Sten Rask's handsome face and spit.

Rask whips a silk handkerchief from his inside coat pocket and calmly wipes his face. "Really, Varna? Frankly, I have always admired your pragmatism. Drama does not suit you."

I refuse to look away from his amused gaze. "I don't care what you do to me, I will protect Gerda. Or at least warn her."

"I thought you might, which would be unfortunate, since she could inform others who may have the power to thwart my quest. No, I do not think such a plan will suit my purposes. I will tell you what we shall do instead." He circles me, pausing long enough to pull my cloak over my quivering shoulders. "I will allow you to help your soldier friends escape, as I have no quarrel with them, but when they are safely away, you will return with Gerda and allow me to question her."

"I will not."

"You will, unless you want me to raise an alarm that will bring every enemy soldier to the door of your friends' hiding place. Consider as well—you and Gerda out so late, in the company of strange young men—what will the town think? Not to mention the enemy? On the other hand, in my scenario everyone is protected. Erik Stahl and Anders Nygaard can escape to safety, and I—in my Albrecht form, of course—can swear you and Gerda were working with me all night. You walked out to view the full moon and stumbled over an injured traveler. You brought him to me and helped bind his wounds before we sent him on his way." Rask languidly lifts one olive-skinned hand and brushes a lock of black hair from his eyes. "So you see, my dear, my plan is the best option. The soldiers still escape, yet no one can accuse you of aiding them, or any other impropriety."

"What will you do with Gerda?"

"Simply question her. Help her to remember. Then return her home, no harm done."

The moon slips behind a bank of clouds. I cannot read Rask's expression, yet his plan does sound sensible, and might be the only way to save Erik and Anders.

"I will agree to those terms. Where should we meet you?" I turn from him and step onto the trail that leads to the young soldiers' hiding place.

"At my cottage, of course. Ah yes, I did steal it from you. I apologize."

I spin on my heel and glare at Rask. "You used magic to fake the will and those letters?"

His grin displays perfect, white teeth. "No. I simply had them forged. I do not believe in using magic when human trickery will do. It's much more efficient."

"You never met Dame Margaret, did you?"

"I did not, but hear she was an estimable woman. Now, don't pout, my dear. I will provide documents to transfer the cottage and its grounds to you before I leave town."

Pout? I dig my boots into the dirt to avoid flying at him. After viewing him as old Albrecht for so long, I must rethink every action. It's likely Rask has the power to reduce me to cinders where I stand.

"I will bring Gerda to you when the young men are safe," I call out, not looking at the sorcerer before I stride down the narrow track.

When I do glance back, there is no one on the path.

Pressing my hand against the rough bark of a pine, I pause to catch my breath. I cannot risk Erik and Anders learning of my encounter with Sten Rask. They will refuse to go if they think Gerda is in any danger.

Gerda in danger ... A thought buzzes in my mind like a horsefly. What was it Rask said? Something about Gerda contacting others who could destroy his plans. Which I know she *will* do if Rask sends her home after questioning her. She will inform Kai, or Thyra, or both, and they will contact the enchantress Sephia, who protected Gerda and aided in the destruction of Mael Voss's mad plans.

Varna, you idiot. Rask will never release Gerda unharmed. You sensed that—the threat beneath his honeyed words. He will transform her into a duckling first.

Or kill her.

I straighten and run toward the door of the abandoned cottage.

I must convince Erik and Anders to leave. To take Nels's boat and head to the river. To flee this place.

And take Gerda with them.

Anders insists he stay behind.

"I will only slow you down," he tells Erik. "I can barely stand, much less walk any distance, even with a cane."

Erik doesn't look up as he shoves items into a large rucksack. "Stop being an idiot. I will carry you if I must. You know I can."

"Varna, tell him how foolish it is to take me." Anders, already dressed in traveling clothes and boots—after much tugging and swearing by Erik—sits on his makeshift bed. He looks to me with pleading eyes.

"I will do no such thing. You both must escape. Otherwise, one might betray the other. They won't be looking for you on the river, but if they hear of a boat ... "

Erik casts me an approving glance. "You won't need your legs, Anders. Your arms can still work an oar. Speaking of which, I think I spy Gerda. There, through the window."

I go to the door to let her in. She clutches the heavy wooden oars with both arms, balancing the paddles against her shoulder.

"Finally." She lowers the oars to the floor before collapsing beside them.

"Where's this Nels fellow?" asks Erik. "He should've helped you carry those."

"I told him to stay home. I didn't want to involve him any more than necessary." Gerda pulls the pins from her hair. "This way he can claim someone stole the oars along with the boat."

She looks like a child, sitting there on the floor with her skirts spread about her and her braids falling below her shoulders. Her round face is flushed pink from exertion.

I won't allow her to be harmed. No matter what. "I bet you had to do some talking to keep him from coming with you. Did you promise to marry him or something?"

"I said I would think about it." Gerda gathers up her skirts and rises to her feet.

Anders examines his fingernails. The color brightening his face moments ago has bled away.

Erik grabs a sheepskin flask from the table. "I need to head out back to fill this. The river is all right in a pinch, but I prefer well water." He strides out the door.

I follow, leaving Gerda and Anders staring at one another.

"Wait up, I must ask you something." I grab Erik's coat sleeve.

He pauses, one hand on the winch, and gazes down at me. "What is it? Look, there's nothing I can do about the situation with Anders and Gerda. Fortunately, we're leaving, so there's an end to it."

I release my grip. "That's what I want to talk to you about. I want you to take Gerda with you."

Erik mutters some obscenity under his breath. "Impossible. It is a dangerous trip, worse if we're caught by the enemy, which is quite likely. You must also think of Gerda's reputation."

"Oh, reputation." I snap my fingers under his nose. "It is her life I am worried about."

"Now look," Erik avoids my gaze as he fills the flask with water. "I know Gerda has a big heart, but no one has ever died of love. She will get over Anders in time."

"That is not what I mean." I pinch Erik's lower arm. "Look at me. I'm talking about her life, not some silly love-sickness. She's in real danger if she stays here. You must take her with you."

Erik studies me for a moment. "You are serious, I can see it in your face. Still, what are Anders and I to do with her? We can't drag her into some military camp."

In my panic to get Gerda out of the clutches of Sten Rask, I have not given thought to this. I close my eyes for a second, recalling the stories Gerda told of her previous travels.

"The Strykers!" I register Erik's astonishment and lower my voice. "You know them, certainly."

"I know *of* them. I'm not exactly on close terms with lumber barons."

"Gerda is. Yes, that is perfect—she said they had a townhouse in the city. Get Gerda there, and someone will surely look out for her. Even if it's only the servants, if you drop Clara Stryker's name, that should work. And Kai—you know, the friend she mentioned at the University? He will help too, if needed."

Erik lays the filled water flask on the edge of the well and takes hold of my upper arms. "Varna, you are blathering like a madwoman. Yes, I might be able to get Gerda to the city. Honestly, it would be easier for me to disappear there than in the woods. I know the city well enough for Anders and I to hide, at least until we sort out the deserter issue. I even have friends who would help." He shakes me gently. "That doesn't answer my question, though. Gerda's life is in danger? Why?"

"I cannot tell you."

"Does she know?"

"No."

Erik stares into my eyes for a moment before releasing me and stepping back. "Why not?"

I shake my head. "If she knew, she would likely do the very thing guaranteed to endanger her further. I'm sorry to be so cryptic, but you must trust me."

"It seems I am always forced to do so." Erik picks up the sheepskin flask and tucks it into the inner pocket of his long coat. "Very well, we will take her along if we can. But what about clothes and such? She'll have nothing."

"The Strykers can provide everything she needs. It will only be a few days before you can leave her in their care."

"I hope." Erik turns to head back to the cottage. "I cannot give you any absolute guarantees."

I follow him. "I know. But getting her away from here will … "

Erik spins around and clamps his hand over my mouth. "Someone is coming. Did you tell anyone we were leaving tonight?"

I grab his little finger and jerk it back, forcing him to remove his hand. "No, of course not."

This is not precisely true. Sten Rask knows. Still, he said he would allow Erik and Anders to escape.

And you can trust Rask? The man who has lied to you for months?

"How do you know someone is coming? I hear nothing," I whisper, matching Erik's stealthy movements as we make our way back to the cottage.

"Lights, in the distance, bobbing through those trees." Erik grabs my hand and pulls me along. "Come, we must get out of here right now. I can carry Anders, but it will slow me down. How far to this Upper Branch you mentioned?"

"Not far. A few minutes."

"We might make it then."

Erik says nothing more until we are back inside the cottage. Slinging the rucksack over one shoulder, he directs Gerda and me to each take up an oar. He shoves the cane into his bag before hoisting Anders to his feet.

"Is there some rush?" Anders leans heavily against Erik's arm. "Truly, if I'm going to slow you down enough to get captured, you should leave me."

"Shut up and stay still." Erik swings the smaller man up and over his shoulder, toting Anders like a sack of grain. "Gerda, can you lead the way? As quietly as possible, please."

Gerda nods and heads outside. I hang back to hold open the door. As Erik walks past I pat Anders's shoulder. "Hang in there."

"I must, it seems," replies Anders, pushing his hands against Erik's broad back in order to lift his head.

"Hush," Erik says.

We follow Gerda through the woods. For a few minutes, all seems well, until a rumble of voices breaks the silence.

"There they are!" shouts someone.

A shadowy mass of bodies is at our heels. They carry torches that bob like candles set adrift on the sea.

"Pick up the pace!" I yell at Erik.

He increases his stride, pulling ahead of Gerda, who points before her with her free hand.

"The river is just around the bend." She holds out the oar.

Erik adjusts his grip on Anders and grabs the wooden paddle with his right hand.

I shove my skirts into my waistband, lifting them almost to my knees. The hell with modesty, I must reach Erik and hand him the other oar.

I also must get Gerda into that boat.

The roar of mingled voices grows louder, along with the crunch of boots breaking through underbrush. I reach the stream bank as Erik crab-walks to the water, his boots sliding on the damp ground. Somehow, he keeps his balance and stays upright, but Anders's white face betrays the pain inflicted by this maneuver.

Thank God, Nels Leth's small wooden boat is there, its back half bobbing in the water and its prow perched on the bank. Erik deposits Anders in the boat, lowering him gently onto one of the plank benches. He lays the oar beside Anders and glances up at me.

"I need the other one. Quickly, we must push off." Erik throws the rucksack into the boat.

I stand at the top of the bank and extend the oar. "Gerda, take it to him. You are more agile."

Gerda shoots me a dubious look, but grabs the paddle and makes her way down the bank. She reaches the boat and hands Erik the oar as a group of villagers, flanked by enemy soldiers, bursts though the cluster of trees behind me.

"There!" screeches Inga Leth. Of course *she* would be leading the mob.

I turn and dig my boots into the damp ground. Placing my hands on my hips, I confront the crowd.

Lit by the torches, their faces look like macabre masks. I scan the group as one of the enemy soldiers barks out an order. Two of his compatriots raise their muskets.

"Wait!" screams a familiar voice.

Mother shoves her way to the front. Her cap is askew and her hair has sprung free from its pins, allowing her braids to flop onto her shoulders.

For a moment, with her cheeks rosy from exertion, she looks like Gerda.

"Please stop, these are my daughters." Mother lays her hand on the commander's arm.

"They aid our enemy," he replies, speaking our language with a thick accent. "They are traitors."

"No, misguided. Just foolish girls." Mother grips the commander's arm and gazes up into his face, her blue eyes brimming with tears. "When I told you about the soldiers, I did not think my daughters would be with them."

"You told them?" I can barely form the words. I thought someone else had seen Erik in the woods, or overheard the twins chattering, or something. I never expected my own mother to betray us.

The commander motions for his men to lower their weapons. "No shooting the women. We only want the soldiers."

Inga Leth spits on the ground. "Take them all. Thieves—stealing my son's boat."

"No." The commander uses his free hand to shove Inga behind him.

I realize Nels is not part of the crowd and wonder how he managed to avoid joining the mob.

Mother turns her pleading gaze on me. "I didn't know you were with them. You were supposed to be in bed."

"How did you know we were here, near this place? Did the twins follow us, the little snitches?" There's a splash as Erik shoves the boat into the water. If I can stall the mob long enough …

Mother shakes her head. "No, I guessed you would be in the woods. You had to pass this way to get to Master Albrecht's cottage, and no one saw you elsewhere, so I thought … I simply guessed."

The shuffle of boots on the leaf-strewn ground grows louder, along with the murmuring of the crowd. Someone shouts something about traitors and whores.

"No, no, what are you doing?" Gerda's voice cuts through the rumble.

I glance over my shoulder.

Erik hauls Gerda into the boat. "Sit or we will tip."

"See," my mother points toward the water. "They are kidnapping my Gerda!"

The commander barks another order. His soldiers advance on me.

When I take a step back my boots slip on the slick leaves and I fall. As I tumble down the bank, my skirt and petticoat rumple up to my waist, exposing my pantaloons.

This does not matter. Broken bones matter. Clutch your knees to your chest and roll.

I land at the pointed end of the boat, which still touches the shore. I cannot tell if the screams I hear are coming from Gerda or my mother, or both. I uncurl and sit up, my muddy garments clinging to my body.

A shot rings out and an object whizzes over my head.

"Get down!" Erik's voice roars over the noise of the mob.

I scramble to my knees. Erik shoves Gerda to the bottom of the boat, where he has already deposited Anders.

More gunshots pierce through my mother's shrieking and the shouting of the crowd.

"In the boat!" Erik's green eyes flash as he turns his gaze on me. "In the boat now!"

I'm not going with them. I cannot—I must stay and deal with Sten Rask. It's up to me to stall him until Gerda is far from his grasp.

Erik thrusts out his hand as I scramble to my feet. "Gerda won't let me push off without you. Get in if you want to save her. But keep your head down, for God's sake."

I grab his hand and climb over the side of the boat. Safely inside, I slump onto the damp floorboards.

Erik sits and grabs up the oars. I crawl onto the seat next to him.

"No, stay down."

"Faster with two, and I can handle an oar." I grab one of the paddles and slide it from his grip.

"Head down!" Erik thrusts his oar in the water.

I bend forward as I follow his lead. A shot hits the stream, splashing water into the boat.

Ignore it. Just row.

"Pull, pull, pull!" Erik sets up a rhythm for our strokes.

Once we glide into the center of the tributary, the swift current catches and carries us. Erik and I keep paddling, even as the voices fade behind us.

"They will follow us downstream!" Anders shouts over the rush of the water. He struggles to sit up.

Gerda lends him her arm and they both crawl onto the front seat of the boat.

"They can't move fast enough on land." Erik plies his oar with grace. "I hope."

My strokes are less polished. Still, I am able to match his movements well enough to keep us from sliding toward the shore.

"What is going on?" Gerda turns her head to look at me. "What's this all about, Varna?"

"It is about saving your life," I reply, "and helping Erik and Anders escape. I will explain later."

"Once we hit the river you can help." Erik meets Anders's confused gaze. "For now, take care of Gerda."

Anders nods and faces forward. He places one arm about Gerda's shoulders.

"I can take over." Erik leans across me to grab the oar from my hand.

"You cannot maneuver the oar with me here." I am acutely aware of Erik's body pressed against mine.

"Slide back, then climb over the bench and sit on the seat behind us. That will balance us better anyway." Erik applies himself to rowing, paying no attention to my awkward scramble to the rear of the boat.

Huddled in the back, my damp clothes cold against my skin, I lift my head and stare at the sky. The moon sails out from behind a dark mountain of clouds and casts a ribbon of light across the water. It is a silver path, leading us onward.

I lower my eyes. Erik's strong arms pull the oars through the water. "What if they're waiting for us?" I ask, keeping my voice low so Gerda and Anders cannot hear. "The villagers know where this branch spills into the river."

Erik does not turn around. "If we get there before them, we will be fine."

"And if we don't?"

There is silence before Erik speaks again, a span of time in which I am acutely aware of the violin screeching of tree frogs and the unearthly hoots of owls.

Erik rows faster. "We will get there first."

CHAPTER SEVEN: MAELSTROM

W E TRAVEL IN SILENCE FOR some time. Erik ceases rowing when the tributary spills us into the river, but keeps his fingers curled about the oars. "The current will carry us for a while. I'll watch so we don't drift too close to shore." He rolls his shoulders.

He must be in pain, but does not complain. I make a note to recommend some of the muscle ointment I stuffed into his rucksack.

Anders lifts one hand and points to Gerda's head resting against his shoulder. *Don't wake her,* he mouths, before turning to face the front of the boat.

I lean forward and tap Erik's shoulder. "This Christiane, is he truly engaged to her?"

"Not officially, but he believes he is. Which, to him, means the same thing."

"Shame." I sit back, pondering this information. It's clear Gerda is smitten with the young soldier.

We are the lone boat on the river, which is just as well. I watch the banks, but only the occasional otter or beaver prowl the shoreline. When I spy something that looks like a solitary reindeer I dismiss it as the sighting of an ordinary deer.

As the sun rises higher in the sky, I shake out my mud-caked skirt, but can only release a few of the stiff folds. I lean over and unlace my boots. Pulling them off proves more difficult than I expected, and my final tug sends one boot flying forward. It slides under the middle bench seat and strikes Erik's calf.

He jumps. "Don't startle me like that."

"My stockings are soaked, and won't dry stuck in those boots."

I catch Erik's glower before he looks forward again. "Warn me next time. I don't appreciate objects flying at me out of nowhere."

My lips form a sharp retort, but I swallow it, recalling his description of the battlefield. "I will try to remember."

"Pull off those stockings as well," he says, not looking at me. "You don't want to get trench foot."

I can't help myself. "By your command, *Doctor* Stahl."

Erik's only reply is a grunt.

We float in silence for some time, until Gerda wakes and peppers me with questions. I am finally forced to speak of Sten Rask.

"He must be stopped." Anders has scooted back to sit beside Erik. His fingers grip one of the wooden paddles, ready to man the oar if necessary. "If the Usurper gains control of this mirror … "

"Do we know what it can do?" Erik directs his words toward my sister. "Did you see a demonstration of its powers?"

Gerda pauses in her deft braiding of her golden locks. She glances over her shoulder. "No. I only saw it prevent the Snow Queen—Thyra Winther, I mean—from being transformed into a wraith. It also freed the former Snow Queens from their ghostly forms, allowing their souls to depart in peace. That is all I saw." She dips her head over her hands so I cannot examine her face.

There was something else. I always knew it, from the first moment Gerda told me this story. Something she would not say. I am curious, but now is not the time to press the point.

"Rask seems to think he can use it as a weapon," observes Anders.

"If he's involved, it certainly can't be anything good." Erik looks up. "Like that sky."

"Did we pack any food?" asks Gerda, reminding me breakfast and lunch have passed us by.

"Just some hardtack left over from company rations." Erik reaches for the rucksack. "You're welcome to it. I think I would rather starve."

Gerda shakes her head. "You would not. I've gone without food for days at a time, and I would have eaten a boot if I could have spared one."

It's easy to forget that part of my older sister's life, when she was only fifteen. She departed our village carrying nothing but her courage—traveling to find Kai Thorsen and bring him home. She braved many dangers on her journey, including traversing the frozen lands of the Snow Queen. Without magic or weapons, she was alone much of that time, except for one enchanted reindeer.

If only we'd brought Bae with us. Well, maybe not on the boat. I chuckle.

Erik shoots me a sharp look. "Something funny?"

"No. Thinking of Gerda's reindeer. It might have been useful to bring him along, but then there is the boat … "

"He's tracking us," Gerda says calmly.

I almost jump from my seat but—*boat, Varna, boat.* "You told him to follow us?"

"From a distance." Gerda swings her legs over the bench and faces us. "I thought we might need him, after Erik and Anders got away. I didn't envision us escaping on the river." She adjusts her skirts and meets my astonished gaze with a smile. "I learned to take precautions, some time ago."

Anders's profile is clearly visible, as is the admiration on his face. "Clever, yet … " His expression shifts to one of confusion. "How do you tell a reindeer such a thing? I know they can be trained, but that seems rather complicated instructions for such a creature."

Gerda takes a deep breath. "Well, you see, Bae is not just any reindeer … "

Her words are cut off by Erik's string of expletives. "Storm," he says, as Anders elbows him.

The clouds are dark and rolling in fast. I grip the side of the boat. "Should we put to shore?"

Erik shakes his head. "Not yet. I've seen no evidence that we are beyond enemy-held territory. There's a bend in the river where one of our encampments is located, but we haven't reached it yet."

"We can't keep going if this weather brews into a storm." Anders's expression remains calm as his knuckles blanch. "This boat is not built to withstand heavy winds."

"I know. If we can get a little farther … " A flash of lightening punctuates Erik's words.

Gerda's face betrays her fear, but her voice is perfectly steady. "Perhaps the opposite bank?"

A crack of thunder splits the air.

Anders and Erik deploy the oars, pulling as hard as they can, while the wind rises, scattering a spattering of rain. The sky darkens to a sickly gray-green.

"Gerda, get down!" I yell over the roar of the wind. Sliding off the bench seat, I slump to the bottom of the boat, gripping one side with both hands.

Oars swing through the air and slice the water, but the men's efforts are thwarted by gusts blowing the boat from side to side. We tip precariously, forcing Erik to drop his oar and grab the rucksack. Anders pulls his oar into the boat and slips off his seat, landing next to Gerda. He pulls her into his arms.

"Hang on!" Erik follows Anders's lead, ending up by my side. The boat spins like a leaf caught in a drain.

Erik wraps his arms about me and presses my head against his chest. His heart beats under my ear, a rhythm at odds with the swirling motion of the boat.

I can't believe this is the way we will die, sucked down into the river like minnows swallowed by a trout. I hold onto Erik as if he's the only rock wedged between me and the abyss.

I have never experienced a kiss. Such a foolish thought, but the only one flitting through my mind.

The prow of the boat lifts, slamming Anders and Gerda into the middle bench. Water floods the back end of the boat, sweeping away my boots and stockings. Only Erik's iron grip on the rucksack, and me, keeps us secure.

Erik says something under his breath. I realize it is a prayer, and repeat "amen" until my lips can no longer form words.

The wind roars as rain falls in a barrage of needles against my skin. It's impossible to know if the dampness on my face is rain or tears.

All at once there is silence, as if the boat has been enveloped in a bubble.

I free myself from Erik's embrace and stare at the sky. Rain falls in sheets that curve away so not a drop hits us.

"What's this?" Erik scoots to one side of the boat.

The bubble glides over the choppy surface of the water, toward the far shore. Inside the protective globe, there is only a slight bounce, like a stone skipping over waves.

Gerda looks at me, her eyes bright. "It is some sort of magic."

"Good or bad?" I climb up onto the seat.

She shakes her head. "Hard to say. It's definitely better than being battered by the storm."

"Nothing natural." Erik swings his body up onto the seat next to me.

"Maybe not, but I'll take it over the alternative." Anders crawls onto the front bench and offers his hand to Gerda, pulling her up beside him.

As the storm rages around us, we glide in our bubble until it rolls onto the river bank. When the boat slides up over the grass and comes to rest, the clear globe disintegrates. Rain pelts us, soaking us to the skin.

Erik clutches the rucksack to his chest and rises to his feet. "Out! We must seek shelter."

He jumps over the side, drops the rucksack to the ground, and holds out his arms to assist Gerda. The boat slides backwards as her feet hit the ground.

"Grab Anders!" I scramble toward the front, ignoring the wood scraping my bare feet.

Erik leans in and flings his arms about his friend. He pulls Anders out of the boat and both men tumble to the ground.

The boat groans and slides back into the water as I throw one leg over the prow. Straddling the edge of the boat, I attempt to pull my other leg over, but my wet petticoats bind my limbs like rope.

The boat falls back into the rushing river. I register Gerda's screams as I fight to free myself from the leaden weight of my garments.

So this is it—I'll be swallowed by the river, food for fishes. I drop back onto the front seat of the boat and close my eyes. Rain washes over me until I can barely breathe, even before being dragged to the depths.

The boat halts as if steadied by unseen hands, then glides forward. My eyes fly open on a tall, slender figure standing on the shore, stretching out her arms. It is an auburn-haired woman wearing a flowing gown the color of lilacs. The rain has plastered her dress against her body, outlining every inch of her lovely figure. Her fingers reach and pull, as if drawing an invisible cord. Obviously controlled by her magic, the boat moves toward her, until the prow slides up onto the land. Erik leaps in to drag me onto the shore. As soon as my feet touch the grass, the rain ceases.

I lift my head as Erik helps me stand, and come face-to-face with the strange woman who saved me.

"Thank you." My voice is as hoarse as a frog's croak.

"No thanks necessary," the woman replies. "I have not brought you this far to lose you now."

I stare into clear green eyes, bright as new leaves. Only then do I notice Gerda standing beside the stranger. The woman smiles and drapes one arm around Gerda's shoulders, pulling my sister close to her side.

Of course, there is only one person this could be.

"Are you Sephia?"

She inclines her head. "Yes. Welcome to my home, Varna Lund."

CHAPTER EIGHT:
A CUP OF TEA

"COME," SEPHIA SAYS, "MY HOUSE is just a short walk." She leads us to a path that twists through a forest of slender pines. Pausing at the head of the trail, her gaze focuses on Anders, who drags his bad leg and leans heavily on Erik.

"Forgive me. I forgot your injury." Sephia moves swiftly to Anders's other side and offers her arm. "Take hold. Your friend and I will help you."

After a few turns we step into a clearing where a cottage sits, squat and gray as a mushroom. The rough stone building is crowned with a thatched roof, and a curl of smoke rises from the chimney. I'm glad to see evidence of a fire. Although the late spring day is not particularly cold, my soaked garments weigh on me, heavy as wet mortar.

Sephia releases her hold on Anders long enough to push open her bright green front door. "Come in and rest."

The cottage feels familiar—one room, like the home I hope to inherit, and a mirror of its rustic charm. It's warm inside, even though the stone fireplace is filled with pots of bright red geraniums instead of flames.

Magic crackles in the air like static before a storm. I cross to the fireplace and soak in the warmth emanating from the flowers.

Erik and Sephia guide Anders to a small settee with cushions covered in an intricate floral pattern. Gerda hurries to sit by him. She puts her arm around his shoulder, and he slumps against her, blindly reaching for her other hand and clutching it against his good leg. His face is pale as the moonflowers twining through the settee's colorful embroidery.

"I can make you a draught of something to ease that pain," Sephia says. "But let me find you some dry clothes first."

I narrow my eyes and examine the tall, slender woman. I imagine she might have something for me, or even Gerda, but what would this solitary creature own that Erik or Anders could wear?

I glance away and realize I'm not the only one studying Sephia. Erik stares at her with blatant admiration.

Sephia crosses to a wooden wardrobe and motions for me to join her. "Here, take this." She presses a soft bundle of material into my arms. "You and Gerda can change over there, behind the curtains of the little alcove. The young men can change in the main room, so Anders does not have to move too much." She pulls out another pile of fabric and glances at Erik's bemused face. "Fear not. I shall step outside."

He flushes as red as the geraniums. "Thank you." He takes the garments from her hands.

Gerda joins me as I push back the sea green curtain and step into the sleeping alcove. We undress and toss our wet garments on the floor. When I unfold the bundle, I discover two gowns—both woven of some wool as soft as silk. I reach for the one the color of sunflowers and hold it up against my body. It is the right length, which is odd, since Sephia is a few inches taller than me.

"There are no petticoats," whispers Gerda, donning the other gown, which is blue as a hyacinth. Strangely, this gown fits Gerda perfectly, its beautiful cut enhancing her figure in a way I fear may further confuse Anders.

I slip the yellow gown over my head. It is true, there are no petticoats—only a pair of silken pantaloons for each of us. But these gowns do not require any other undergarments. They fall in perfect folds, graceful as flowers swaying in a light wind. I run my fingers across my body, marveling at the lightness of a fabric that provides perfect coverage. Modest as a nun's habit, and yet … My gown doesn't grant me Gerda's voluptuous figure, yet makes me feel more attractive than anything else I've ever worn.

Gerda loosens her hair, allowing it fall in golden waves about her shoulders. She looks radiant. She calls out to Erik and Anders. "Are you dressed?"

"Yes, come on out."

There is a tinge of embarrassment coloring Erik's voice. I understand why as soon as Gerda and I step into the main room.

Both Erik and Anders wear silken robes like those I've seen depicted in old paintings of royalty. Long sleeves fall open at the wrist like a bell, and high collars are decorated with more of Sephia's floral embroidery. Erik's robe is the soft green of a spring meadow, while Anders's is the tawny brown of a young deer.

Men's robes, cut in an old style, in sizes that fit both large-boned Erik and slight Anders? I cast a look at Sephia as she comes through the front door, carrying an armful of wood. Her lilac gown is perfectly dry.

Sephia's smile lights the room. "You look splendid. I chose wisely."

Unsure if she means us or the clothes, I decide to swallow my questions for now. "We left our wet clothing on the floor, but if you want me to hang it outside … "

Sephia crosses to her black stove and stuffs the kindling into the firebox. "No, you sit and rest."

I choose a wooden rocker, while Gerda sits beside Anders on the settee. Erik slumps into a deep armchair. Although he faces me, his eyes are on our hostess.

Sephia strikes no match, but the kindling bursts into flame. She reaches for a copper kettle dangling from a hook sunk into one of the ceiling beams. "I imagine some tea would be welcome, but I must cut a few herbs from my garden—would you assist me, Varna?"

I spring to my feet and cross the room, noticing as I pass how Anders stares at Gerda. Her head's down, but I spy a rosy blush rising in her cheeks. "Trouble, trouble," I mutter, as I follow Sephia out the back door.

Sephia smiles. "It will be all right. Come into my garden, Varna."

I gasp and clutch the doorframe. The enclosed garden is a brilliant tapestry woven of vegetables, fruit trees, and flowers. Roses from purest white to deepest crimson drape the stone walls, their green vines buzzing with honeybees. The scent of all these growing things is overpowering. I press the back of my hand against my forehead.

I stumble after Sephia as she gracefully navigates paths that wind like emerald streams through the garden. Miniature chamomile covers the paths, soft as feathers under my bare feet, the sharp scent rising with each step. Sephia pauses at one corner of the garden.

It's a bed of lush and vibrant herbs. What I wouldn't give for such a garden! It could supply me with everything needed to concoct healing potions and ointments. I recognize most of the plants, although not all, and make a mental note to query Sephia later.

We gather mint and beebalm and a few sprigs of lemon verbena, along with a cutting of the taller form of chamomile. I raise my fistful of herbs to my nose, breathing in the luscious scents. It seems to clear my head.

"You cannot grow all this without some sort of magic." I cast one longing look at the garden before following Sephia back into her cottage.

"That is true." Sephia drops her herbs on the wooden counter near her stove. "I am, as you know, an enchantress. But I prefer to use my powers only when necessary, unlike many others of my kind."

"Are there many others?" I strip the flowers and leaves from the stems of the herbs, tossing the foliage into a small copper bowl.

"Not so many. Not anymore." Sephia presses the leaves and flowers into a pewter tea ball shaped like a large acorn. She dunks the ball into the hot water in the kettle before turning to me. "You have heard Gerda speak of Mael Voss."

"Yes. He stole young girls from villages like mine and transformed them into Snow Queens, hoping they could repair some shattered mirror." I meet Sephia's steady gaze. "But only Thyra Winther could reconstruct the mirror, with the help of Kai Thorsen. Gerda was present when the mirror was made whole."

"Yes, Gerda was there." Sephia's eyes glitter like emeralds. "Didn't she tell you about her part in the mirror's restoration?"

"No." My sister has fallen asleep, her golden head resting on Anders's shoulder. A little smile tugs at the corners of her mouth. Anders is also asleep, as is Erik. They look so peaceful …

I whip my head around. "Have you enchanted them?"

"Only for a moment." Sephia lays one slender hand on my shoulder. "Varna, you should ask Gerda what transpired that day. Ask her about her tears. It is important you understand what happened—why there are those who believe Gerda holds a key to the mirror's location."

I step back. "What do you know?"

"I know someone seeks the mirror. I can feel it. Someone who wishes to use its power for evil." Sephia sighs. "Such ancient power, neither good nor evil, is sadly always a danger to our world."

I study Sephia's lovely face for a moment. The honesty in her eyes spurs me to speak freely. "There is someone. He impersonated an old healer and took over my former mentor's home and practice. I even studied with him for a time." I shake my head. "I did not know who he was, I swear."

"Of course not." Sephia's voice is as gentle as the brush of her hand against my cheek. "Do not blame yourself. You were tricked by a sorcerer who wields great power. Maintaining such a transformation is extremely difficult."

"He revealed himself to me right before we escaped with Erik and Anders. It's why I forced Gerda to go with them, and why I joined them when she would not leave without me." To my embarrassment, I realize tears are sliding down my cheeks. "He threatened Gerda. He thinks she knows where the mirror is hidden, and is determined to use her to find it. I think"—I wipe away the tears with the back of my hand—"I am afraid he will kill her."

"He will not." Sephia hugs me to her breast. "Do not worry. I will not allow harm to come to Gerda, not if I have any power to prevent it. Now"—she pulls away while still holding onto my arms—"did he give you his name, this sorcerer?"

"Sten Rask."

Sephia's eyes betray an emotion that clenches my hands at my sides. *Fear. She is afraid. Oh, dear Lord, if this enchantress is afraid of Rask, what are we to do?*

"Do you know him?" I fight to keep my voice calm.

"No. I've heard of him, but we have never met." Sephia tosses her auburn hair as if shaking something from her mind. When she looks back at me, her face is perfectly composed. "I met his mentor once, the sorceress who took him in and taught him the ways of magic. She calls herself the Lady Dulcia. If Sten Rask is anywhere near as skilled as she, he is a serious threat."

"She is powerful?"

"Very. And dangerous, although she appears as delicate and lovely as a flower. You would think her as innocent as Gerda, were you to meet her. Which I hope you never do."

The whistle of the tea kettle pierces the silence following Sephia's words. Erik leaps to his feet. "What is that?"

"Just the kettle," calls out Sephia in a bright voice. She busies herself pouring tea into four ceramic mugs.

Gerda sits up and rubs at her eyes. "Was I asleep?"

"We all were, I think." Anders lifts his arm from Gerda's shoulder.

Erik eyes me with suspicion. "Except for Varna."

I grab two of the mugs and head back to the rocking chair, handing Erik his tea before I sit down. "I was gathering herbs."

"Now, drink up." Sephia crosses the room with the other two mugs and hands them to Anders and Gerda.

"You're not having any?" Anders stares into the pale green liquid.

"No, but I was not dunked in the river." Sephia sits on the raised stone hearth. "Go on, it is not some magical potion. It is tea. Varna watched me make it, if you are concerned."

I take a sip. "Just tea."

Erik sits up straighter in his chair. "One thing I don't understand," he says, after a long swallow. "How did you guess we were in trouble, Sephia? No one knew we were on the river. At least, no one who could tell you."

"Ah, there you are wrong." Sephia's face glows, as if lit from within. "Someone did know, and he warned me." She crosses her hands in her lap. "He waits outside, on the edge of the clearing. Go and take a look, Gerda."

Gerda sets down her mug and jumps to her feet. "Bae?"

"Yes," replies Sephia, as Gerda runs to look out the front window.

"The reindeer?" Anders furrows his brow. "How could he tell you anything? I mean, reindeer do not speak."

"Is that so?" Sephia's voice is laced with amusement.

Erik stands and hands me his mug before striding across the room. He flings open the front door. Gerda is instantly at his side.

Bae pokes his muzzle inside until he is eye-to-eye with both of them. "Hello, Master Erik," says the reindeer.

Erik stumbles, tripping on the hem of his robe and landing, flat on his backside, on the floor.

Gerda giggles. Erik shoots her a sharp look, then stares at the reindeer. "It talks."

Gerda fights back more laughter. "Yes."

"It talks?" Anders slides to edge of the settee, his hazel eyes round as coins.

"Yes. Bae was enchanted by the mage Mael Voss. He can speak and"—I look to Gerda, who nods her head—"he can also fly."

Erik makes some unintelligible comment.

Anders stares at Gerda with a question in his eyes. "Voss is dead. I thought his enchantments died with him."

So he knows? And you thought she only shared the details with you, did you, Varna? Seems she told Anders all about her journey to find Kai. I finish off my tea in one swallow.

Bae dips his shaggy head. "I was able to decide, in the moment of the mage's passing, whether to break his enchantment or remain as he made me. I choose to stay as I am, in case Miss Gerda ever needed my help."

"And a good thing you did, my friend." Sephia rises to her feet and crosses to the door to rub Bae's velvety nose. "Now, go rest under the trees. I have provided water and hay for you."

"Thank you, Mistress Sephia." After a gentle bump of his muzzle against Gerda's shoulder, Bae backs away from the door and lumbers toward the woods.

Erik rises to his feet. "This is astonishing." He offers his arm to Sephia. "May I escort you back to your chair, my lady? I think I will pace for a bit to clear my head. I'm not used to such enchantments." The smile he turns on her clearly indicates he includes her in the things he finds entrancing.

Sephia's laughter cascades like a string of sleigh bells. "You have recovered quickly, Erik Stahl."

Erik leads her to the armchair where she sits down and arranges her lilac gown until it falls in perfect folds to her feet. "I think you should stay here for the night. Rest, then set off for the city. It is probably best if you travel to a place where you can mingle with a large crowd of people, and I believe Erik and Anders may have friends there."

"And Kai is there." Gerda perches back on the settee. "He'll help us if we ask, I'm sure."

Sephia nods. "Kai Thorsen could prove a useful ally."

Erik pauses in his pacing. "Some University scholar? How can he help?"

"Do not underestimate Kai, or his friends," replies Sephia with a smile. "Finish your tea, Anders. I put something special in your cup."

"So that's why I feel less pain." Anders stretches out his injured leg. "Can you do anything about this?"

"Sorry, no. At this point I can do more than Varna has done." Sephia leans back into the cushions of the armchair. "Tell me about yourselves, Erik and Anders. I would like to know more."

As the men take turns talking, I stand and walk to the alcove. "Excuse me, I believe I will hang our wet clothes." I pull back the curtain and gather up our cast-off garment, then pause beside the settee to collect the men's clothing. "No, Sephia, please sit and talk. I will only be a minute."

I push my way through the front door, half-expecting Gerda to follow. She does not, and I realize why—Anders is talking about making shoes for the Opera dancers, and she's hanging on his every word.

Oh, Gerda, you are skating too fast on a thin-iced pond.

I sigh and cross the clearing to reach a low branch I spied earlier, nodding to Bae who stands behind the front line of trees, his head down in a water bucket. I drape our damp clothing over the tree limb, cursing the fact I have lost my stockings and boots. Hopefully, Sephia can loan me something before we depart for the city.

A rustling in the underbrush makes me look up, as Bae lifts his head and stares into the woods.

A cloaked and hooded figure, holding the halter of a dark horse, is visible between the layered rows of trees. I press my lips together to keep from crying out.

Bae seems to have no fear of this stranger. He simply shakes his heavy head and resumes eating hay.

A creature appears at the stranger's side and stares at me with golden eyes. It is the wolf.

I back away, concentrating on each step. When I reach the front door of the cottage, the stranger lifts one pale hand and presses a forefinger to her lips.

I shove the door open and stumble into the cottage as Erik finishes recounting some story that elicits laughter from the others.

"All done?" Sephia's bright smile fades as she studies me. "Come and sit down. You need rest too."

Her green eyes remain fixed on my face, even as Anders urges Gerda to tell some humorous anecdotes about our family.

I know who is out there. Sephia's unspoken words ring in my head. *It is all right, Varna. No harm will come to you, or Gerda, from that quarter.*

Nodding to indicate my understanding, I sit in the wooden chair and rock back and forth, until I can speak without betraying Sephia, or the mysterious stranger.

CHAPTER NINE:
ROSE AND FLAME

S EPHIA WAKES US AS SOON as the sun peeps over the mountains. Having insisted Anders take the bed, Gerda and I crawl out of the pile of downy comforters Sephia produced from the wardrobe—an object I suspect possesses magical properties. Erik, who fell asleep in the armchair, stretches before jumping to his feet. As for Sephia—I'm not sure where she slept, or if she slept at all. Based on the opening and closing of the front door, I know she left the cottage at some point in the night. She claims it was to retrieve our clothes, but I suspect it was to meet with the cloaked stranger lurking in the woods.

Still, what do I know of the habits of an enchantress? Perhaps she no longer requires sleep, just as she seems to survive without food. She provides an ample breakfast of fried potatoes along with fruit harvested from her trees, yet does not sit down to eat.

"I do not have time right now. I need to pack some food for your trip," she says, when Erik questions her.

He raises his eyebrows and digs into his potatoes without another word.

We change back into our old clothes as soon as we finish breakfast. I hate giving up the sunflower gown, although I know it's impractical for travel.

Sephia sticks her head around the curtain as I finish lacing Gerda's bodice.

"I have boots and stockings for you, Varna. And please, keep the gowns. I will give you each a rucksack to carry them, along with some other clothes. More practical than the gowns, of course."

"Thank you, Sephia." Gerda shoves back the curtain and hugs the enchantress. "You've always been my guardian angel."

"Angel? No, far from that. Still, thank you." Sephia kisses Gerda on the forehead.

Gerda smiles and heads into the main room to assist Anders with his boots and cloak.

"Thank *you*." I bob an awkward curtsey. "You've been more than gracious. Truthfully"— I look up into the enchantress's eyes—"I wish I could stay with you. Learn about your garden, study all the herbs, and discover what you know of healing. Might I do that, someday? Come back, when we are sure Anders and Erik are out of danger and Gerda is safe?"

Sephia's expression grows unexpectedly solemn. "I believe you must walk another path, Varna Lund. If I am wrong, yes—please return. If you find yourself alone, and all those you care about safe, come back to me."

I nod. I *will* be alone someday, and soon. Gerda will find a husband, as will my other sisters. Erik and Anders will return to their old lives, and my mother will find joy in the children Gerda and the twins will surely have. Sephia may think I possess some other destiny, but I doubt this. I will return to this cottage, and learn all I can, and—if Sephia refuses to take me as her apprentice—at least carry this knowledge back to my village, where I will take possession of Dame Margaret's cottage and the position of healer.

If Sten Rask did not lie and gives me back what should be mine.

I frown and flop down on the bed to pull on my new stockings and boots.

When we leave the cottage, Sephia walks outside and points toward a wooded path that apparently intersects with a back road. "It will lead you to the city, although in a roundabout fashion. Still, I do not think it wise for you to use the highway."

"No, we need to stay away from roads heavily traveled by the enemy." Erik hoists his rucksack over his shoulder. "Are you sure you can walk?" he asks Anders, who stands beside Gerda, leaning heavily on his wolf-head cane.

"Yes. It's still difficult, but my pain has lessened." Anders glances at Sephia. "I suspect the medicine you gave me includes more than a touch of magic."

"It could be." Sephia taps him on the arm. "There is more, in bottles I have stowed in Erik's rucksack. Make sure you add a bit to your tea or coffee from time to time."

Anders's smile lights up his face. "Thank you."

Gerda whistles for Bae, who steps forward, shaking his head. "You need not walk, Anders. Allow Bae to carry you." She grabs the reindeer's leather halter and pulls his face close to hers. "Is that all right with you, old friend?"

"Yes, little miss. It is the wisest thing, all in all."

Erik helps Anders up onto Bae's broad back and we depart, Gerda waving farewell to Sephia and promising to visit soon.

Our travel is blessedly uneventful. We walk throughout the day, reaching the road Sephia mentioned—a packed-dirt track riddled with ruts—and following it west.

As the sun slides behind the mountains, Erik suggests we make camp for the night. Abandoning the road, we settle in a small clearing surrounded by a hedge of blackberry vines, and search our rucksacks for food. I realize Sephia has provided us with blankets and other supplies along with a change of clothes.

Erik holds up a box of matches. "Do you think she simply materializes these?"

"It's possible." Gerda drapes one of the blankets across the ground and helps Anders sit down, with his bad leg stretched out before him.

"Sephia is an enchantress of great power," Bae says, as he rubs his flank against the rough bark of a pine tree. "Sorry, little miss, I have an itch."

"I'm not offended, Bae." Gerda walks over to him and scratches the side of his neck. "We don't have food for you, or enough water. Can you find your own?"

"Of course." He tosses his head until the metal on his halter jingles. "I lived many years in the wild." He places his nose against Gerda's cupped hands. "I shall return with the morning light."

"Go on with you then." Gerda gives him a final pat.

While Anders rests on the blanket, his head bobbing in exhaustion, Erik gathers fallen branches from the surrounding woods.

"I'm not sure he will stay awake long enough to eat." He motions toward Anders. "Although, truthfully, he probably needs sleep more."

Gerda settles next to Anders and allows him to rest his head on her shoulder. "We should give him some more of that medicine, though."

I fill a cup with water and pour in a few drops of Sephia's tincture before handing it to Gerda. Turning back to Erik, I help him pile the branches and brush in the center of a cluster of rocks. As he lights the pile with one of Sephia's matches, I sit on a large stone close to the fire.

Erik settles near me, on another stone. "Hand me my pack, would you?"

I grab up the rucksack and toss it to him. "Do you think you can disappear in the city? I'm worried you might be arrested as deserters."

Erik pulls a wrapped object from his pack. "Bread," he says, unwinding the fabric. "Want some?"

"Sure." I take the chunk of bread, which is soft and smells of rosemary. "Seriously, Erik, do you believe you and Anders will be safe?"

"I'm not sure, but we have a better chance in the city than anywhere else. I do have friends there." Erik chews on the bread for a moment. "What about you and Gerda? Still planning to leave her with the Stryker family?"

"If I can." I hand over a flask of water. "There is Kai Thorsen too. He will help."

Erik's eyebrows rise to meet the russet hair spilling over his forehead. "What can he do? I suspect he's no fighter."

"No, but he's smart. Very smart," I add, to counter Erik's dubious expression.

I offer some bread to the others. When I cross back to Erik, I notice he's whittling.

I sit and watch his flying fingers. He has a gift, no question. A shape blooms under his hands. It is a rose.

"Is this a gift for Sephia?"

Erik glances at me. "Yes, a brooch. I may never get a chance to give it to her, but I wanted to create something to commemorate our meeting."

The knife carves layers from the wood, revealing the beauty hidden within. "She is a stunning woman."

"True, although not exactly a woman an ordinary man could hope to love." Erik looks over at me. "I may admire beauty, but I'm also pragmatic."

"So what is it you want?" I know I am posing a question he may not be able to answer. Still, lulled by the warmth of fire, I must ask.

Erik's fingers maneuver the knife, cutting and shaping wood. "It's hard to say, although Anders is right—I am obsessed with beauty. It's not as simple as a pretty face, though. I always feel there must be something more, something beyond the surface. I've seen many lovely women over the years, but somehow, none have been exactly what I want. I mean, what I am searching for. Damn." He glances up from his hands. "I sound like such an idiot, seeking some ultimate beauty."

"No, I understand." Erik's words cut me like the knife he handles so deftly, but I refuse to betray my pain. "You have a dream, and will not be satisfied until you achieve it."

"Yes, that's true." He shoots me a grateful smile. "I keep thinking I will find it, but I never do. Gerda comes close."

"Beautiful inside as well as outside?" I stare up into the tree canopy. A single star winks through the collage of leaves, bright as a diamond.

"Yes." Erik slips the knife back in its sheathe and tucks the rose brooch into the pocket of his jacket. "No, even that is not quite it. I mean, Gerda is lovely and sweet and all, yet somehow it is not enough. It should be, but it isn't." He slumps and stares into the fire. "Go ahead— call me a foolish dreamer."

"I will not. I believe in dreams, and hope one day yours will come true." I look away, unwilling to witness his longing expression.

Never for you, Varna. All these young men, with all their dreams, but never of you.

The fire sputters. As Erik leans forward to feed more kindling into the blaze, I glance over my shoulder, and notice Anders slumped over, his head resting on the ground. Gerda is not beside him. Perhaps she has gone to fetch water. It would be like her to head off without saying anything, especially if she thought she might interrupt my conversation with Erik.

I rise to my feet. "I need to check on Gerda."

Erik, lost in his own thoughts, just grunts in response.

I walk deeper into the woods, looking for any sign of my sister. It's possible she simply slipped away to relieve herself, but I must be certain. As I search, the orchestra of crickets, tree frogs, and owls continues its eternal tuning, never to break into song.

I step into another clearing. Sten Rask stands before me, holding Gerda against his body like a shield.

I run at him. "Let her go!"

A blast of wind blows me back. I fall to the ground, my face pressed into a pile of decaying leaves.

"My dear Varna." Rask's voice pours over me like honey—sticky, clogging all my thoughts. "Shall we start over? Rise, my girl, and let us discuss this matter in an amiable fashion."

I struggle to my feet, spitting out bits of dead leaves. "Release Gerda first."

Rask tsks. "I am afraid that is not part of the bargain. We can talk about a reasonable trade."

"What sort of trade?" I examine Gerda's face. It's clear Rask has muzzled her. Her mouth opens and closes, yet no sounds emerge.

"I will exchange information for your sister's freedom." Rask steps closer, hauling Gerda like a sack of grain. "Frankly, I'd be delighted to release her, if only she would tell me—or you—where Thyra Winther hid the mirror."

"Gerda does not know." I move closer, my eyes locked on my sister's face. "You cannot make her tell you what she does not know."

"Ah, you see, I don't believe that." Rask shrugs and tosses Gerda aside. She slides across the leaf-strewn ground, coming to rest at the base of a pine tree. From her stillness and pleading eyes, it's obvious Rask's magic still holds sway.

He advances on me. I cross my arms over my breasts and stand my ground.

"Now, shall we discuss a deal?" Rask gestures in Gerda's direction. "I will free her from my spell, if you promise to obtain the information I need."

"I'm not sure I can promise that."

"You underestimate your abilities, my dear." Sten Rask stands directly before me, the tips of his boots touching mine. "I believe if you were to speak with your sister and convey the gravity of the situation, she would tell you anything."

I press my boots into the dirt. "She does not know."

"Varna." Rask strokes my jawline with one finger. "I do admire your courage and tenacity, as well as your intelligence. It's a shame your exterior does not reflect your true nature. Of course, if you wish, I can change that."

I stare into his dark eyes. "What do you mean?"

A slow smile curves Rask's sensual lips. "I can grant what I know you desire. Outward beauty to match the passion of your soul. Power to enflame the coldest heart."

Remembering Erik's earlier words, my own heart contracts. "I want you to let my sister go."

"What a pity you have been cursed with that face and figure. You deserve so much more." Rask leans into me. "You *are* so much more. Trust me, my dear, I see the real Varna Lund. And if you allow me, I can reveal her to a world blinded by superficial beauty."

His breath is warm upon my cheek. I turn aside.

This is not important, Varna. Gerda lying on the ground is important. Freedom is important.

Strong fingers grip my chin and twist until I am forced to look at into Rask's handsome face. We are nose to nose as his fingers slide down to caress the soft skin of my throat.

"Varna." His voice rolls over me like the purr of a great cat. "You crave what only I can provide, while you in turn can give me what I desire. A fair trade, I believe."

I close my eyes. "Even if Gerda knew where the mirror is hidden, even if she would tell me, I would not offer you such information." I open my eyes on Rask's burning gaze. "At any rate, it's all nonsense, because she does not know."

"Someone must." Rask's voice cracks like pottery smashed against a wall. Strong fingers slide to my shoulder blades and tighten. "I will find it, whatever it takes. I will have it, and everything else I seek. Everything I need."

I claw at his hands, but he simply shifts his hold and clutches me to his chest with one arm.

"Give over, my dear. Stop fighting your own desires." Rask tips my chin back with his other hand and presses his lips against mine.

I feel as if I am drowning, as if the river did take me. Stunned, I sink to the murky bottom and am lost. I am the river and its current roars through my body, vibrating every inch until I feel I must explode.

"Release her!" The words ring through the clearing, rattling the leaves on the trees.

Freed, I slump to the ground, burying my face in my hands.

"Varna!" Gerda crawls toward me, released from enchantment as well. Thank God, and whoever spoke those words Rask had to obey.

Gerda reaches me and falls into my arms. "It's Sephia," She shakes my arm. "Look, Varna. See her arrayed in all her power."

I raise my head and stare across the clearing, where a blaze of light illuminates the shadows. Within the glow, I can barely discern the shape of a tall, slender woman.

Rask shakes off the lethargy cloaking his limbs and spins about to face her. "Do you truly think your power can rival mine? You may be able to take me by surprise once, but I know your limits, Lady of the Roses."

"As we know yours." The cloaked figure I spied at Sephia's cottage materializes from the woods, a wolf padding by her side. I fixate on her cloak, which is the pure green of new leaves and decorated with embroidered vines and flowers.

The stranger shoves back her hood, revealing a wild mane of white-blond curls. Her eyes are pale as crystal in her strangely beautiful face.

It is the face of some fey northern creature, born in caverns of ice.

The face of a Snow Queen.

"You may be a sorcerer, but you are still flesh and blood." The young woman drops her hand, resting it on the powerful shoulders of the wolf. "One word and my companion will rip you to pieces. Sephia can hold you motionless long enough to make you suffer the agony of such a fate. Choose, Sten Rask. Depart now or be torn limb from limb."

Rask's voice fills the clearing. "You've caught me unaware, unprepared, for the last time. I will go, but keep watch. I shall obtain what I desire. The mirror and more." Freed from the last shreds of Sephia's enchantment, he casts one last glance in my direction before he strides off, disappearing into the shadows of the forest.

As the light surrounding Sephia fades, she crumples. The blond woman rushes to her side and holds her upright until the enchantress regains her bearing.

Gerda stares at the white-haired young woman, her eyes wide with amazement. "Why are you ... ? What are you doing here?"

A smile curls the thin lips of the other girl. "Watching over you, of course."

The wolf trots forward. I shrink back as Gerda throws open her arms. "Luki!" She snuggles against the wolf's broad chest.

I look up and over the creature's shaggy back. "Thyra Winther, I assume."

Thyra inclines her head. "The very same. Now come, Varna Lund, and let us rejoin your companions."

CHAPTER TEN:
TRUE STORIES

ERIK AND ANDERS ARE BOTH asleep when we return to our camp. Sephia snaps her fingers and they sit up, startled as deer facing a hunter.

"I did not mean to … Sephia, what are you doing here?" Erik leaps to his feet, his searching gaze sliding from my face to Gerda's and Sephia's before focusing on Thyra. "And who are you?"

"You were under an enchantment." Sephia brushes back her hair with one hand. "No, not mine. It was Sten Rask, who captured Gerda and Varna. He has gone now," she adds, as Erik reaches for his musket.

Anders looks stricken. "Gerda, are you all right?"

"Yes, I'm fine." She sits beside him.

"This is Thyra Winther." Sephia gestures toward the other woman. "She is a friend."

The smile that brightens Thyra's sharp-featured face holds more than a trace of irony. "Hello, you must be Erik Stahl and Anders Nygaard. I just met Varna, and of course I know Gerda." She glances into the woods. "Luki, you may come out now. I think these men will act sensibly." She eyes Erik until he lays down his musket.

The wolf trots out from the trees to stand at Thyra's side. Erik gasps and Anders grips Gerda's hand while staring at Thyra and Luki. He opens his mouth as if to speak, then shakes his head and remains silent.

"Is Freya with you too?" Gerda pats Anders's shoulder. "Her horse."

"Oh." He blinks rapidly.

"Yes, in the woods. Bae's watching over her." Thyra whistles and a compact bay mare appears, trailed by the reindeer.

Erik gazes at Thyra with blatant admiration. "Have you been following us?"

Thyra grabs the horse's bridle and strokes the animal's satiny neck. "Yes. I've been shadowing you, to keep watch over Gerda in particular."

"Because of the mirror?" I ask.

Thyra shoots me a look cold as an ice spear. "What do you know of that?"

I meet Thyra's piercing stare and hold it. "It's what Rask wants—for Gerda to tell him the location of the mirror."

"She does not know where it is," says the former Snow Queen.

"Yes, but for some reason Rask will not believe us."

"Because of the tear." Gerda rises to her feet. "He must have obtained that information, although I don't know how."

"Tear?" Erik glances from Sephia to Thyra. "What is this? Varna and Gerda told us about Rask, and the whole mirror thing, but no one has mentioned a tear."

"You must get Gerda to explain." Thyra's expression softens. "It was her magic, after all."

"Magic? Gerda isn't a sorceress or mage or anything like that." It's clear from Anders's expression that he desperately hopes this is true.

"No, and neither am I," Thyra says. "Not anymore. Still, not all magic is wielded by sorcerers."

"You stood up to Rask without possessing any magic?" I examine the pale young woman, who meets my gaze with a lift of her pointed chin.

"I had Sephia at my back and Luki at my side. Besides"—she shrugs—"I have faced worse."

Erik kicks a smoldering branch back onto the fire. "I'm still confused. I understand how Thyra was able to be here, since she was following us, but how did you arrive so quickly, Sephia? We left your home this morning, and have traveled far."

The enchantress smiles. "I have my ways, although I prefer to use them infrequently." Her eyes cloud over. "Magic, despite what many may think, is neither simple nor painless. There is thought and preparation involved in wielding great power. It is how I was able to overcome Sten

Rask, at least for the moment. Sometimes a sorcerer can be defeated, if they do not expect the attack." She casts a significant glance at Thyra, who turns away and toys with the girth of Freya's saddle.

"You're only a day's journey from the city." Thyra places her booted foot in her stirrup and gracefully swings up onto Freya's back, exposing a pair of breeches beneath her rumpled skirt. "I will continue to shadow you. First, though, I must deliver some messages. Bae, will you carry Sephia back to her home before you rejoin Gerda and the others?"

"Yes, my queen." Bae lowers his head.

Thyra frowns. "I am no one's queen."

"You will always be mine." The reindeer's glistening dark eyes focus on the former Snow Queen.

Gerda steps up and grabs Freya's bridle. She stares up at Thyra. "How is Kai? I've received letters, but he has not been home in some time."

Thyra's face freezes into an icy mask. "I don't know. I have not seen him."

Gerda's blue eyes widen. "Why not?"

"Do you remember the letter I sent you, Gerda? The one where I confessed what I had done?" Thyra glances over at me. "I could have rescued Kai's father from the blizzard that froze him into insensibility, and eventually killed him. But I did not. Oh, I did not mean for anyone to die," she adds, obviously reading the horror on my face. "Still, I choose to protect myself and abandon Nicholas Thorsen to his fate." She fiddles with her reins. "At the time I thought I had good reason to do so. I now know better."

"The letter? That was months ago and I told you ... " Gerda shakes her head. "I wrote you back and said it was fine to inform me in a letter but you should tell Kai in person. I warned you to wait until you came home."

Thyra's clear eyes narrow. "Yes, but I had already written you both. I sent those letters on the same day."

Gerda takes two steps back. "How did he respond?"

"He didn't." Thyra lays one rein against Freya's neck and turns her away from us. "I never heard from him again." She gives the mare a gentle kick and heads off without looking back. Luki follows the horse, his tail swinging from side to side.

I watch until they disappear amid the trees. "That's a sad turn of events."

"It is tragic," says my sister, her eyes brimming with tears. "I will not allow that to stand. I will talk to Kai and sort this out."

She has a mulish look on her face—the expression she wears when determined to follow some course of action, no matter where it leads.

Kai Thorsen, you do not stand a chance.

Erik runs his hands through his hair, obviously uncomfortable with our conversation. "Since we must travel at first light, we need to get some rest." He sketches an awkward bow in Sephia's direction. "Thank you again, my lady."

"No thanks needed, Erik Stahl, but your courtesy is appreciated." Sephia tears her gaze from the spot where Thyra disappeared. She turns to Gerda and embraces her. "Do not fret, little one. We shall set this right, in time."

"Of course we will." Gerda huffs back a sob and returns the hug. "Bae, come and carry Sephia home."

The reindeer ambles forward and stands quietly as Erik helps Sephia climb up onto his broad back. She flashes us a dazzling smile before Bae trots toward the road.

Gerda pulls another blanket from her rucksack. "Grab yours as well, Varna. I'm sure Sephia provided us each with one." She spreads the blanket near Anders. "We can curl up together."

"Bring me your pistol, I'll keep watch." Anders waves away Erik's protests. "I've had more sleep than any of us. You grab some rest and relieve me later."

Erik grumbles, but hands Anders his flintlock before slumping onto the blanket beside him.

I lay my blanket over Gerda's and sit down. It does feel wonderful to be off my feet, and to have a chance to think. Rubbing a spot on my shoulder where Rask clutched me, I sigh deeply.

"Are you all right?" Erik glances at me as if he has just realized I exist. "Sephia said you were held captive as well."

I lower my head. "I am fine."

"He did not hurt you, did he? You or Gerda?" Erik's voice trails off as his head droops to his chest.

"No. At least, nothing serious." I press two fingers to my lips, which feel odd. They're tingling, as if some numbness is wearing off.

Gerda snores lightly. I glance at Erik, who has drifted into sleep. Giving Anders an encouraging smile, I sink down onto the blankets beside my sister.

Behind my closed eyelids, all I can see is Sten Rask's face.

Desire. He said he could give you what you desire, Varna. Beauty, power...

I break into a sweat, but wrap one section of the blanket tighter about me. It clasps me like hands, clutching me close, holding me. I fling one arm over my face and press my mouth against my damp skin.

I can still feel those lips on mine. They were so fierce, and yet, there was a frisson of pleasure amid the pain.

It is a great relief when the darkness takes me.

After an uneventful day of travel, we reach the gates of the city. It's simple enough to blend in with the crowd filling the main square. Erik has us stow our rucksacks in a lean-to shed behind a dilapidated tavern.

"I've used this before," he says, when I shoot him a questioning look. "For the occasional bottle of brandy and such."

"That we were not supposed to have," Anders says.

"Right." Erik wipes the grin from his face. "Now, let's go. We don't want to linger."

I spy a large fountain and make my way to the stone wall enclosing its basin.

"Heavenly." I splash my face with the cool water.

"We should move along," Erik says, as the clock in the tower overlooking the square chimes the hour.

The figures in the clock chase one another around their mechanical track. Anders, who has walked the entire day, slumps next to me on the stone rim of the fountain.

"One moment of rest, please," he begs.

Erik's gaze darts about. "Very well. Just remember, we cannot stay in the open for long."

I dip my hands in the fountain, enjoying the cooling touch of the water. For some reason, ever since Rask laid hands on me, I feel as hot as if I've been overcome by fever. "Erik, give Anders some of that medicine Sephia packed. It should help."

Erik grumbles but pulls the bottle from his rucksack and hands it to Anders.

"There's the University." Gerda points toward the towers rising above a mosaic of tiled and thatched roofs. "Kai said there were towers."

Erik stuffs the medicine bottle into the pocket of his long coat. "I think finding the townhouse owned by the Strykers is probably more useful than tracking down this Kai fellow."

Anders wipes his mouth with the back of his hand. "It would be in the better part of town, close to the Opera House."

Erik's sour expression conveys his opinion of this information.

"We could take Anders by the Opera House," Gerda suggests, "then Varna and I could investigate the location of the Stryker's' home. If you would rather check on some of your friends, Erik, and see if they will help you and Anders, I believe that might prove a good division of labor."

I study my sister's deceptively innocent expression. I must remember she's managed a mill and its rough workers for a few years. Despite her gentle appearance, there is a core of iron inside my sister's soft body, and a fine mind beneath her crown of golden hair.

"Very well." Erik adjusts the collar of his loose white shirt. "That does sound like a reasonable plan."

Gerda smiles sweetly. "Where can we meet you? We should rendezvous somewhere, just to make sure we are all safe."

"Why not the Opera House? The stage door. Anders knows where it is." Erik narrows his eyes at Anders. "Just don't expect too much. You haven't seen Christiane in some time."

"You mean, since I became a cripple." Anders's expression matches his resigned tone. "Yes, I know she may reject me, but I must let her know the truth. It's only fair."

Erik's eyes cloud with doubt. "I'm not sure fairness comes into it. Still, I suppose it is best to approach such challenges head on." He lays one hand on Anders's fine-boned shoulder. "Just be prepared, my friend." Giving Anders's shoulder a final pat, he disappears into the crowd.

Anders pushes himself to his feet with the aid of his cane. "I think I can walk now, although I may need to lean on you from time to time."

Gerda's expression is uncharacteristically solemn. "We will help anyway we can, right, Varna?"

"Of course." I place my hand under Anders's elbow. "Anyway we can."

Even if it breaks my sister's heart. I peek around behind Anders's back and catch Gerda's eye. *No need for this,* I mouth at her.

She shakes her head and stares straight ahead, matching her stride to Anders's halting gait.

I know she won't come between Anders and his sweetheart, no matter how much she loves him. Because she is Gerda Lund, and she'll always do what is best for others, regardless of what it costs her.

I set my mouth in a tight line. I am not so nice, or kind. We shall see what can be done about this Christiane Bech.

CHAPTER ELEVEN:
BEHIND THE FACADE

I T'S NOT EASY MANEUVERING ANDERS through the crowded streets of the city, especially with cobblestones catching his cane. "Steady." Gerda grabs his arm.

Anders's face is ashen. "Can we stop for a moment?"

"Of course. Here we go, the perfect spot." Gerda guides Anders to a small alcove, where a wall fountain spits water into a shallow basin.

As Gerda fusses over Anders, I watch people passing by. A cluster of young men, clad in wide-collared white shirts tucked into dark pants—University students I suspect, from the books they carry—pause long enough to look us over.

One of them says something about Gerda giving up the cripple for a real man.

She spins on her heel and faces them, hands on her hips. "I will have you know this man was wounded in the war. He was protecting the likes of you, who have nothing better to do than insult a true hero."

Anders flushes pink as a sunrise. He leans over and splashes water from the fountain onto his face.

The young men simply laugh, admiration for Gerda gleaming in their eyes. They barely spare me a glance, but as they move away I hear something like "plain as a post."

Anders, bent over the fountain basin, casts an apologetic look my way.

"They're obviously crude louts, despite their pretense of scholarship."

I smile while something twists like a serpent in my stomach.

Yes, Anders, you are a kind and gentle young man. Yet even you look at me without seeing me at all.

Unbidden, the vision of a savagely handsome face floods my mind. Sten Rask said he saw me, the real me. *No, Varna, those are the lies of a deceiver.*

Yet, as I hand Anders his cane I imagine how I would treat those students if I were as gorgeous as Sephia. I picture how they would all kneel before me. They would grovel, begging for my love. I would make sure of that.

"Here we are." Gerda's sweet voice breaks through my bitter dream.

I stare at a poster plastered on a signboard before an elegant brick structure. It's an advertisement for some new entertainment. I realize we have reached the Opera House.

"How do we find your friend?" I ask Anders, as I study the flight of marble stairs leading to a pair of double-height, gilt-encrusted doors. To the right and left of the doors the upper landing spreads out into a balcony. It's the perfect spot for the wealthy and beautiful to pause and pose. "I doubt we can just march into the lobby and call for her."

"No, as Erik said, there is a stage door. Just around the corner." Anders lifts his cane and points toward a narrow alley. He sways slightly, and Gerda's immediately at his side, steadying him with one hand pressed into the small of his back.

"Are you sure she will be here?"

"Oh yes." Anders peers up at the sky. "This time of day they are between rehearsals, but cannot leave the theater."

We walk down the alley until we reach a plain wooden door sunk into the side of the Opera House. This part of the building is constructed of plaster and lathe, rather than the brick and marble of its grand entrance.

I smile grimly. It is always the façade that matters.

Anders knocks on the door, which is opened by an older man who ushers us inside.

"Heard you enlisted. Injured, were you?" The doorkeeper examines Anders with sympathy. "It is a blessing your hands were spared. At least you can still make shoes, even with a bum leg."

A slow smile spreads across Anders's face as he stares at the man. "You are right." He claps the doorkeeper on the back. "Thanks for reminding me. I hadn't thought of that, strangely enough."

"Eh, you young men never consider the important details." The doorkeeper shuffles off, disappearing into the wings of the stage.

Anders points down a narrow hallway. "Dressing rooms are that way. The girls usually rest there between rehearsals." He slumps into a chair near several hanging panels of black velvet. "Could one of you go and ask for Christiane Bech? I cannot walk into the dressing room unannounced."

"Of course." I examine Anders with a critical eye, noting how tightly his fingers grip his cane. He's nervous, which is only sensible. The girl he loves is about to find out something that might change the way she feels about him.

"We will both go." Gerda takes me by the hand and leads the way.

At the end of the hall we step into small room filled with a variety of chairs, their upholstery a jumble of fabrics and colors. "I imagine they use these in productions," I say, as a petite girl enters through one of the room's unmarked doors.

Her dark hair is pulled into a tight bun and she's wearing pink tights, as well as a ragged gray sweater over a fitted black garment resembling a chemise with an attached tulle skirt. She is obviously one of the ballerinas.

A muscular young man bursts through the door behind her. He's dressed in black tights and a white tunic belted at his slender waist. "Christiane!" The young man grabs the girl by the arm and swings her around to face him.

I am ready to intervene, until I hear her peal of laughter.

"Stop it, Nicolai." She playfully slaps his arm. "You know I can't walk out with you tonight. We have a performance."

"Then after." The young man shoves back his blond hair, pressing his palm against his forehead as if his head aches. Lines drawn by frustration mar his otherwise perfect features.

"No. *After* is when I have a dinner date, with a wealthy patron, not some poor dancer." Christiane's flirtatious smile seems designed to give the other dancer hope, despite her words. "It is so difficult these days, with all the best young men off to war. I've had to make friends with some older gentlemen."

All the color drains from Gerda's face. "Are you Christiane Bech?"

"Yes, but who are you? I don't believe we know one another, Miss … ?"

"I am Gerda Lund. This is my sister, Varna. We are friends of your fiancé."

Christiane flutters the black lashes fringing her luminous dark eyes. "Whatever do you mean? I have no fiancé." She turns to the other dancer, who backs away and places one hand on the doorknob. "Truly, Nicolai, they must be confusing me with someone else."

"Anders Nygaard." Gerda steps closer to Christiane. Although they are the same height, the ballerina's slight body makes her look like a child, especially in contrast with my sister's womanly figure. "I believe you know him."

"Anders?" Christiane's voice betrays her. Her blond companion swears and stomps from the room.

"Yes, he's come to visit you." Gerda throws out an arm to prevent Christiane from darting down the hall. "You should know, before you see him, he is much changed."

Christiane's rosebud lips quiver. "What do you mean?"

"She means he has suffered a serious injury to his leg. He now must walk with a cane, and will do no more dancing." I keep my unflinching stare focused on Christiane's heart-shaped face. "The good news is that he's alive. It was questionable for a while."

The young dancer blinks rapidly and sways on her turned-out feet. "No, that cannot be. Poor Anders."

"He is brave and strong and there is nothing poor about him." The vehemence of Gerda's tone causes Christiane to still all her movements.

"Of course." The dancer straightens and throws back her shoulders, as if striking a pose for the stage. "Is he here now? Can you take me to him?"

"Yes, this way." Gerda sets off down the hall.

The dancer licks her lips and pinches her cheeks to bring up their color, then follows Gerda with her head held high. As I walk behind her, only her odd, duck-waddle gait breaks the illusion of dignity.

When she spies Anders, she runs to him with exclamations of surprise and joy. Gerda, who has just helped Anders to his feet, steps away. Christiane's bird-like twittering over Anders soon has him blushing and kissing her hands.

"We should leave them." Gerda's smile, no doubt plastered on to reassure Anders, pulls her mouth higher on one side than the other.

I squeeze her shoulder. "Yes." I fight to keep my voice cheery. "Anders, we will meet you back here in a bit. Just stay put until Erik arrives."

I don't know if he has heard me, or cares, but I have done my duty.

As Gerda and I shove open the stage door I hear Christiane complaining about "that Erik person."

"God in heaven," Gerda says, as we make our way to the street, "but that is one annoying little bundle."

I stop and stare at her. A chuckle wells up in my throat. "Indeed."

Gerda's grin is worth looking like a fool as I stand in the street and laugh like a loon.

After a moment, Gerda offers me a handkerchief to wipe my eyes. "Come on, we need to waste some time before we meet up with Anders and Erik again. I know you want to locate the Strykers' townhouse, but I would like to wait on that." Her eyes light up. "Perhaps we can find a chocolate shop. A cup of cocoa would be heavenly right now."

"We don't have any money." I sigh. It *would* be nice to sit and drink some cocoa, or even tea. I would love to pretend for an hour that we are not on the run, harboring fugitives and fleeing a dangerous sorcerer.

Whose kiss you can't forget ...

I shake off this thought as we turn a corner onto street featuring several bookstores, a coffee house, and a tavern. As we peer in the shop windows, my stomach rumbles and I realize we haven't eaten a real meal since our breakfast at Sephia's cottage.

The scent wafting from the coffee house draws me to its open door. "I wonder if they would trade a cup for this." I touch the simple pewter pin fastening my cloak.

"I doubt it." Gerda pulls me away and drags me through a maze formed by the shelves of a bookstall. We navigate the narrow aisles, almost reaching a clear stretch of sidewalk, when a young man with his nose buried in a book plows into us, knocking me to the ground.

"Oh, forgive me!" He pockets his book.

I look up into a pair of familiar brown eyes just as Gerda squeals "Kai!" and throws her arms around his neck.

After a few chaste kisses, Kai apparently recalls my unfortunate tumble and sets Gerda aside. He pulls me to my feet.

"What are you two doing here?" His intelligent dark eyes search my face. "Are you in the city alone?"

"Not exactly." Before I can say anything else, Gerda grabs Kai's arm and shakes it.

"We can't talk in the street. Is there somewhere else we can go?"

Kai runs his fingers through his thick dark hair, which is quite a bit longer than I remember. I suspect this is due to forgetfulness rather than the adoption of a more poetic style. "There is my room. We are not supposed to have female guests, but I know from my fellow lodgers that my landlady tends to look the other way." A little smile twitches his lips. "Especially if one presses a few coins in her palm."

"Let's go then." Gerda links her arm with his. "We have so much to tell you, right, Varna?"

"A bit, yes." I glance across the street and stifle an exclamation. In an alcove, hidden by the shadow of the doorframe, stands a slender cloaked figure. A finger of sunlight reveals the glint of white-blond hair. "Yes, we should get inside. Lead the way, Kai."

He nods and offers me his other arm. "My landlady will think me quite the man-about-town, bringing home not one but two young ladies." He bends his head closer to Gerda and winks. "Especially since she has never seen me out and about with any woman before. No doubt she suspects I contemplate converting and joining the priesthood."

"Hah!" Gerda bumps her head against his shoulder. "Little does she know."

Kai's expression sobers. "Well, perhaps that fate is not so far off, these days."

I glance at the green-cloaked figure following us from across the street. "Oh, you never know." I tighten my grip on Kai's arm. "Love can be just around the corner, or so I am told."

He sighs. "I'm not sure I believe in such things anymore." Rolling his shoulders as if to cast off some burden, he bombards us with questions about Mother, the twins, and his own mother, until we reach a sliver of a building wedged between a pub and an apothecary shop.

"Home." Kai pulls a large metal key from his jacket pocket and opens the scarred wooden door.

I stare at the steep, switchback set of stairs. "We have to climb all the way up?"

"You've guessed correctly." Kai motions for us to walk in front of him. "Go on, it's the only room on the top floor. The attic, really, but it suits my purposes. Let me go and inform my landlady of your presence. If she gets the news from someone else—and trust me, she will—I won't ever hear the end of it."

I wait until he disappears into the only room off the front hall before I turn back and wedge Gerda's folded handkerchief between the door and its frame.

SCEPTER OF FIRE

Gerda pauses on the second floor landing, her hand resting on the worn wooden balustrade. "What are you doing?"

"You will see, and I think, approve." I bound up the stairs to join her. I tap her shoulder. "Trust me and keep climbing."

CHAPTER TWELVE: REUNION

G ERDA AND I WAIT ON the top landing until Kai, taking the final set of steps two at a time, joins us and unlocks his door.

It opens onto a large space under the eaves, filled with a minimum of furniture and a surplus of books. A narrow bed with an iron rail headboard faces the dusty skylights stretching from the roof halfway down the wood slat walls. Sheets of paper are pinned to the opposite wall, and blanket the large desk that dominates the center of the room. The papers are covered in equations written in black ink and pencil. In one corner of the room, calculations scribbled in white chalk decorate the dark surface of a large slate board.

"Sorry for the mess." Kai scoops piles of paper from the room's two chairs. "I've been working on a few equations … "

Gerda smiles indulgently as she settles into one of the chairs. "I know you, Kai. I would have been surprised to see anything else."

He offers an answering grin. "Well, I've been trying to write a paper. I want it to be published. It's difficult to make your name when you are still a student, but I hope I can manage it. It would help my future prospects."

"Speaking of the future." Gerda primly arranges her hands in her lap. "Not long ago I heard something peculiar."

Here it comes. I sit in the other hard-backed chair as Kai perches on the edge of the wooden desk.

"Oh, what was that?" Kai lowers his eyelids, shadowing his eyes.

"Well, you know Thyra and I have been exchanging letters."

"Hmmmm." Kai picks up the nub of a pencil and rolls it between his fingers.

"She told me something recently, about the blizzard that hurt your father."

Kai stares at his hands. "That killed him."

"Yes, eventually. Anyway, she confessed she could have saved him, and did not. She didn't want him to come to harm, of course, although that did happen." Gerda tips her head to the side, studying Kai's busy fingers. "She's sorry about it now."

"She left him there."

When Kai looks up, I stifle a gasp at the pain reflected in his eyes.

Gerda scoots forward until she's sitting on the edge of her chair. "Yes, and she had her reasons at the time, but now deeply regrets her actions."

Kai meets Gerda's implacable gaze without blinking. "She also lied to me."

"It was a lie of omission."

"Still, it was a lie, and not the first one she told me." Kai sweeps a pile of papers from the desktop with one hand. They flutter to the plank floor like snowflakes drifting to hard ground.

"So she confessed all this to you as well?" Gerda's eyes are innocent as bluebells.

I lean against the hard rails of my ladder-back chair, knowing I should remain silent. This is Gerda's battle. Only she has the weapons to fight it.

"Yes, in a letter. It was probably similar to the one you received."

"How did you reply?"

Kai leaps off the desk and circles our chairs. "I didn't."

"That seems unnecessarily cruel."

"Why do you care?" Kai stops in front of Gerda and grips the arms of her chair with both hands. "I thought this might please you. My break with Thyra gives you a chance again, right?"

"I only want what's best for my friends. Besides, you know I don't feel that way about you anymore." Gerda reaches up and taps his lips with two fingers. "You *do* know that, I hope?"

I bite the inside of my cheek to check a smile. *Well played, Gerda. Well played.*

Kai releases his grip on the chair and jumps back. "Of course."

"It seems you could make some allowances. You know why Thyra was so focused on her survival, and how she has changed. I understand your anger at this revelation, but now, after you've had time to consider everything … "

Kai stalks to the windows and stares at the rooftops of the city. "Honestly, I don't know if I can move forward, even if I forgive her. It seems she is only capable of thinking of herself. I'm not sure I can live with someone like that."

"Kai." Gerda's voice is sharp as a well-honed blade. She rises to her feet and crosses to him. "Perhaps you should look to your own house before you burn down another."

He turns, his face a study in confusion. "What do you mean?"

Gerda sweeps her hand through the air, taking in the slate board and the sheets of equations papering the walls. "This is your obsession, Kai. It's the thing you chose above all else. It may be a noble endeavor, and I do not begrudge your pursuit of your dreams. Still, you must admit your own selfish streak."

When Kai protests, Gerda takes hold of his hands and shushes him into silence. "You left us, my friend—your mother, my mother, my sisters, and me. You abandoned us to follow your own dreams. You forced us to manage the mill—the very thing that keeps you, as well as us, fed and clothed. Oh, I don't think you are wrong. This is what you were born to do. I simply believe you should think carefully before you claim someone else is focused only on themselves."

Kai studies her face for a moment before drawing her into a tight embrace. "Thank you." He brushes her hair with his lips. "I needed to hear that."

Gerda pulls back and swats him on the arm. "Yes, you did." She steps away and gazes toward the door. Her eyes widen. "You do still love Thyra?"

I follow her gaze and throw my hand over my mouth.

Kai presses his palms against his temples as he stares out the window. "Of course. That's what makes this such torture. Even though my mind says I am traitor to my family, my heart will not listen. I still love Thyra. I always will."

"Well, that is something, I suppose," says a cool voice.

Kai spins on his heel to face the open doorway.

Thyra steps into the room, closing the door behind her. She pushes back the hood of her green cloak, allowing her pale hair to spring free and halo her face. Her crystalline gaze sweeps over the room, finally coming to rest on the slate board.

"Interesting." She crosses the room without looking at Kai and studies the board for a moment before wiping away a small section of the equation with her fingers. She picks up the chalk and scribbles a new set of numbers. "This might work better, though. What do you think?" She turns to Kai, still holding the bit of chalk aloft.

He stares at her with a look that makes me suck in a swift breath. "What are you doing here, Thyra?"

"I am sorry, Kai. I would've stayed away if I could." Thyra drops the piece of chalk into the gutter of the slate board. "You see, I've been living with a woman, a fine mathematician, who is quite wealthy. I would have explained how she took me in and mentored me, but since I've not received any recent letters from you I thought it best to respect your silence. Anyway, this lady entertains a wide variety of people, including those who support the Emperor invading our lands." Thyra twists a loose curl of her white hair about one finger. "I attended her parties and heard talk. It wasn't difficult. These people took no notice of me—simply dismissed me as some unfortunate waif my mentor had taken in out of charity." Thyra casts me a look conveying her opinion of such behavior. "At any rate, at one of these parties I overhead discussion of a mighty weapon the enemy hopes to us against us, and the sorcerer who swears he can find and deploy it. The weapon is the mirror. The sorcerer is … "

"Sten Rask." Gerda moves close to my chair and clutches my hand.

"Yes. A man known for his ambition and power. Also the student of a respected and feared sorceress." Thyra turns her gaze on Kai. "That's why I returned—to ensure Gerda's safety, and warn you about the mirror."

Kai clenches and unclenches his fingers as she crosses the room to stand before him. His entire body appears to vibrate, despite its unnatural stillness.

"I will go away again, once I know you are both safe." Thyra strokes his rigid face with her fingers. "My feelings for you have not changed, Kai Thorsen. I will leave if that is what you truly desire, but I too, will always honor our love."

Kai's hands shoot out, gripping her wrists. He pulls her to him and kisses her.

When their lips meet, she yanks her wrists from his grasp and throws her arms around his neck.

That kiss—like a drowning man breaking the waves and finding air. Like a soldier, returning from battle, sighting home.

Heat rises in my own face and I look away, while Gerda studies a page of calculations as if she actually understands such things.

"No, I cannot do this." Kai's anguished voice breaks the silence.

I turn to the couple silhouetted at the window. Kai has pushed Thyra aside and stands facing Gerda and me. Even across the room, I spy the rapid rise and fall of his chest.

Thyra smooths down the bodice of her plain dove-gray gown and lifts her chin. She turns from Kai, her face an unreadable mask.

Behind them, the sky darkens, as if thunderclouds have rolled in over the span of a few minutes.

I leap to my feet. "It's a fire."

Thyra looks out, pressing her palms against the dirty window panes. "Yes, something is going up in flames. What is that?"

Kai peers through the streaked glass. "My God, the Opera House!"

These words galvanize Gerda. She heads for the door, almost fleeing the room before Kai blocks her exit.

"You can't run into a fire."

Thyra appears at his elbow. "Is Anders there?"

"Anders definitely, and probably Erik," I say, joining the group at the door.

Thyra stands near Kai—so close, yet their bodies do not touch. "Our concerns can wait. These two young men are friends of Gerda and Varna. They're also brave soldiers we must help." Thyra spreads wide her hands. "If there is anything we can do … "

"Very well." Kai focuses on Gerda's stricken face. "We will go."

"Now." Gerda pushes past Kai and heads for the stairs.

It is all Kai can do to close and lock the door behind us before Gerda reaches the street.

CHAPTER THIRTEEN: UP IN FLAMES

I TUCK THE TOP OF MY skirt over my waistband, freeing my ankles from the heavy folds of the material, and run. Thyra simply pulls up her lighter-weight skirt and grips it with both hands, exposing her riding breeches. She receives stares and comments from people on the street, but pays them no heed.

"Cover your mouth and nose!" Kai lunges in front of us, pulling the lapels of his coat over the lower portion of his face.

I recognize the sense in his command as we draw close to the Opera House. Black smoke billows from its upper stories and rolls in waves over the growing crowd. Several of the onlookers fall back, rubbing at their eyes and coughing. I pull the edge of my cloak over my face, leaving only my eyes exposed.

The entire opera house pulses with heat. Flames shoot through the roof and race along the sides of the building, feeding on the dark beams and melting whitewashed plaster from the wooden framework. My eyes water from the smoke. All I can make out are indistinct shapes—swirling shadows that fill the balcony at the top of the staircase and occasionally coalesce into a single body that pierces the curtains of smoke and tumbles down the marble stairs.

I spy a tall figure with hair the color of the flames. "Erik!"

Sweat drips from his nose and chin, streaking the soot coating his skin.

Kai throws out a hand to stop Gerda. "The whole structure could collapse," he yells over the din. He pulls Gerda and me close, pressing us against his ribs.

Thyra walks past us to stand beside Erik, who scans the crowd. He seeks Anders, of course.

What if he never made it outside? I still my shaking hands before turning to Gerda. *I'm sure he is safe,* I mouth at her.

With one arm pressed against her mouth and nose, Gerda nods, but I read terror in her eyes.

"There!" Thyra grabs Erik's arm and shakes it. "Against that street lamp."

Gerda slips free of Kai's grip and trails Erik and Thyra as they force their way through the jostling crowd. As Kai and I follow, a scream pierces the rumble of voices. I look up to see a young man fling his body through one of the upper windows. The man has blond hair and wears a white tunic over dark tights. Is it Christiane's friend, who was flirting and laughing not long ago? I force myself to focus on Kai's slender back.

When we reach the lamppost, Erik squats down in front of Anders and grips the other man's forearms. Gerda kneels at his side as Thyra bends over them, her pale hair spilling from her hood.

I push past Kai. Falling to my knees, I lean in and examine Anders carefully, despite his protests.

Anders's hazel eyes are glazed. "I'd just stepped outside." He lifts a trembling hand to wipe his damp brow. "I was waiting for you, Erik. Christiane had to go to rehearsal and I thought ... I wanted to wait outside the building, to make sure you could find me."

"Glad you did," Erik says grimly.

"He seems all right." I use the edge of my cloak to wipe the soot from Anders's face. "In shock, but no additional injuries."

Erik picks up the wolf-head cane lying across Anders's legs. "What happened? Do you remember?"

"Yes, I ... " Anders clutches one of my hands. "It was sudden, like a lightning strike. I was leaning against this lamppost when I heard a crackle and a snap like a whip, then flames appeared, inside the building and across the roof." He stares over Erik's shoulder and his eyes widen. "It was you! I was not sure before. Now, in this light ... It was you."

I follow the trajectory of his gaze and realize he's staring at Thyra.

Her pale face glows against a backdrop of dark smoke and the flames roaring behind us tip her white curls with red. Her light gray eyes are clear as ice.

Or bright as a blade.

I gasp and tighten my grip on Anders's fingers.

"What are you talking about?" Erik's gaze slides from me to Anders, finally coming to rest on Thyra's expressionless face.

"She was my angel. The one who saved me from the battlefield. Only it wasn't an angel, it was her."

Thyra straightens. Behind her, Kai's face expresses all the emotions her icy visage does not.

"What are you saying?" Kai stares at Anders. "Thyra rescued you?"

Anders nods. "Yes. There was a wolf by her side. It was odd, but I wasn't thinking clearly at that point. I didn't seem impossible. I don't know much about angels."

Thyra lifts her chin. "I was on my way to the village to check on Gerda. I hid in the woods when I ran across the battle, hoping to escape notice until it was over."

"You could've been captured." Gerda gazes up at Thyra, her blue eyes very wide.

Thyra shrugs. "I was careful. No one could see through all that smoke, and I was hidden in the trees. I planned to ride on, when the soldiers marched away, until I heard something."

"Me." Anders leans against Gerda's shoulder.

"Yes. And I thought … Well, I didn't want to leave you behind, alone in that place." Thyra pulls up the hood of her cloak, shadowing her face. "It was a bit selfish, really. I worried how I would feel later. Anyway, it seemed logical to try to save you. I did not want … I didn't think leaving you was my best choice."

Erik rises to his feet. "Whatever the reason, thank you."

Kai steps up beside Thyra and clutches her hand. She does not meet his intense gaze but also doesn't pull her hand away.

"Christiane … " Anders grips the lamppost and pulls his body to a standing position. "She could still be inside. We must look for her."

Erik grabs Anders's arm, steadying him while holding him back. "No one can get close to that building, much less go inside."

Gerda stands, wobbling a bit. "Perhaps they escaped out the back door?"

"I have to do something." Anders takes the cane from Erik and grips it tightly, his eyes focused on the Opera House. "I can't live with myself if I do not try."

Through the smoke I spy a slender figure leaning over the balcony railing. It's a woman with dark hair and a pale face, wearing a sweater that blends into the gray of the smoke.

Anders has seen her too. "Christiane!" He stumbles forward, leaning heavily on his cane.

Erik throws out an arm to halt his progress, but he's chosen the wrong person to protect. It's Gerda who takes advantage of a parting of the crowd to rush the marble stairs.

When I scream and jump to my feet to race after her, Kai and Thyra grab my arms and pull me back.

Quickly exhausting my knowledge of curse words, I struggle in their grip. Erik pushes past the gaping onlookers to chase Gerda until a muscular man takes offense and knocks him roughly to the ground.

I yell Gerda's name but even if she hears me, I know she will not listen. *She never listens. Not when she is doing what she thinks is right. She would walk into hell to save someone, even a stranger.*

Tears drench my cheeks. Kai tells me to be still. I am not about to listen either.

That is my sister, and I love her. Nothing else matters. I will run into hell too, if that's what it takes to save her.

Thyra slaps me, hard across my cheek. "Stop it. Hysterics will not help. Kai," she commands, "hold her. I'll go after Gerda."

Kai's brown eyes flash. "The hell you will. I forbid it."

"You are not my master, Kai Thorsen. I will do what I must." Thyra pushes me into Kai's arms and runs toward the building. The milling crowd blocks her, forcing her to one side. She joins Erik, who sits up, holding his head.

We are so caught up in this drama we miss it—Anders limping forward, some inner strength lending him the power to reach the bottom step. He drops the cane, which rolls off the sidewalk into the gutter, and crawls up the stairs. He reaches the halfway mark before any of us realize what he's doing.

As Thyra helps Erik to his feet, Kai marches me to where they are standing. "We can't reach them now." He gestures toward the building.

Flames have sprung up between the sidewalk and the steps, like a curtain pulled across the base of the stairs, blocking any approach.

It is something designed to keep us from aiding Gerda or Anders. Something unnatural.

I turn my head. There, at the edge of the crowd, stands a tall, dark-haired figure, wrapped in a black greatcoat. Beside him is a slighter figure, hidden in the folds of a hooded cloak. His servant, perhaps.

Sten Rask. I meet his sardonic gaze. He nods and raises his walking stick, as if in greeting.

There's a crystal orb topping the cane. It catches the light of the flames, making it appear the orb contains actual fire.

Because it does. Look closer, Varna. That is no ordinary walking stick. That is a scepter, like in the paintings of kings and queens.

Rask flicks his wrist and flames shoot from the scepter, arcing over the crowd and setting another section of the building alight.

There are too many people separating us. I focus on those beautiful dark eyes.

I will kill you. If Gerda is harmed in any way, I will hunt you down and I will destroy you.

Rask's smile broadens. He lowers the scepter. *Varna, my dear, you will come to me one day. But not to kill me. You will come because you choose to do so. To embrace your true nature. To accept what only I can give you.*

I cry out and slam my fist into Kai's ribs. He releases me and I elbow my way through the crowd, but the tall figure in black has disappeared, along with his mysterious companion. Turning my gaze back to the Opera House, I spy Gerda on the balcony, holding the hand of the dark-haired girl.

It *is* Christiane. Gerda guides her toward the stairs just as Anders reaches the top step and pulls his body onto the balcony floor, rolling to Gerda's feet.

A thunderous roar drowns out every other sound. The stairs, their wooden underpinning scorched by the fire, give way and collapse in a thundercloud of smoke and ash. Only the landing and its balcony still stand, hoisted on a rickety framework of wooden poles and beams, forlorn as a ship in dry dock.

"Come away," shouts a voice in my ear and I turn to see Erik staring directly into my eyes. Behind him stand Kai and Thyra, covering their faces with the edge of their cloaks.

Erik tugs at my sleeve. "We need to fall back. Now."

"We can't leave them there!" I push at Erik's hand. He grabs my flailing fingers and pulls me into a tight embrace.

"We cannot help them, Varna. Only God can help them now."

Erik drags me across the street, away from the worst of the rolling smoke and ash. "Wait here." He presses my back against a rough brick wall.

I stare at the Opera House. Gerda's golden hair is still visible amid the drifting clouds of smoke. On one side of her stands Christiane, dark head held high. On the other side is Anders, leaning against her shoulder.

I silently pray for God to save them. Or if not God, then I beg the same of the man who obviously caused this conflagration.

Whatever you wish of me, I will give you. Whatever you ask, I will do, if you will just save them. Or Gerda, at least. All of them, if you can. If not, save Gerda.

It is madness to think Rask can hear me, or will heed my plea. But everything is madness now.

If there is anything you can do ...

A shadow falls over the street. A black cloud glides overhead, blocking any sliver of sky.

No, it is not a cloud. It is wings—dark wings, as wide as the street. It is a great bird, sailing straight for the burning Opera House.

The screams and shouts of the crowd intensify. The huge creature pulls its wings against its body and dives toward the balcony.

Slender, ridged legs extend, displaying black talons curved like sickles. The bird—or whatever it is, for it looks like no bird I've ever seen—reaches with clawed feet and plucks Gerda from the balcony.

She is imprisoned in its talons as if in a cage. Clutching my arms across my chest, I rock on my heels and pray she's unharmed.

Just as the great bird lifts off, Anders grabs hold of a leather strap dangling from its other leg. So this is no wild bird, acting by instinct. This creature was sent by someone.

You have saved her from the fire. Now return her to me.

Words wind through my mind, sensuous as a snake. *Come to me, Varna. If you want your sister back, you must come to me.*

Erik shouts his friend's name, but Anders is swept away, clutching the great bird's fetters, his legs fluttering like pennants beneath him.

The creature sails into a cloud of smoke and vanishes.

I stumble into the street. Kai dashes forward and grabs me before I collapse onto the cobblestones.

As quickly as they sprang up, the flames recede, leaving only embers and coils of black smoke. A stiff wind rattles the framework under the balcony, and it lists to one side. The bodies of those overcome by smoke or flame slide into the balustrade like so much cordwood.

Seated on the railing on the opposite side of the balcony, Christiane dangles her legs over the edge.

She is going to jump.

The four of us run toward the burnt-out building.

I notice the alley near the stage door, not far from where Christiane perches on the balustrade above. "Over here!"

I guess her plan—a hedge of bridal veil bushes lines the wall just below this side of the balcony. Their slender branches are already covered in delicate green leaves and soft clusters of white flowers. It's a smart choice, if one must jump.

It is still a tremendous leap. I gaze up into Christiane's dark eyes. They're as lifeless as cold coals.

Another blast of wind tips the balcony farther. Christiane only stays in place by gripping the railing with both hands.

She has no choice, if she doesn't want to be sucked down into a whirlpool of rubble when the balcony collapses.

The others join me at the edge of the singed bushes. We link arms and press our bodies into the arching branches of the shrubs, ready to keep Christiane from tumbling onto the stony surface of the alley.

"Now!" Erik shouts.

The bridal veil bushes shudder under the impact of the dancer's body. Curled in a tight ball, she rolls from the swaying branches into Erik's arms.

Erik gathers her still form to his chest and strides across the street to an alcove under the stairs of a narrow brick townhouse.

The rest of us follow, Kai pausing to snatch up Anders's cane, still lying in the gutter in front of the smoking building.

As Erik gently lowers Christiane to the ground, I notice one of her legs is twisted the wrong way. I still my chattering teeth. I cannot go to pieces over Gerda's abduction right now. There is work to be done.

Christiane's eyes are closed. "Do not wake her." I cast about for anything I can use as a splint. "I need to brace her injury."

Kai catches my eye and holds out Anders's cane.

I whip off my cloak and squat down beside the prone form of the dancer. "We need to stabilize her knee." I take the cane and place it next to the dancer's leg.

"You must help." I look up at Erik and Kai.

The two young men follow my instructions as Thyra slides around to hold Christiane down by her shoulders. As we yank the leg back into place, the dancer's eyelids fly open and she utters a heart-rending wail.

"Again," I say, closing my ears to the sound.

While we work on her leg the ballerina whimpers and moans. Thyra strokes her forehead and murmurs soothing words with a gentleness I'd never have expected.

We manipulate the limb into some semblance of a normal position before I use my cloak to tightly bind the cane to Christiane's leg. After I finish this process, Kai and Erik stand and help me to my feet.

I wipe my sweaty face with my sleeve. Even though the fire has died down, residual heat and smoke blanket the air. "We need to get away from here, but cannot move her far."

"We must." Thyra turns to look at me, her eyes bright as steel. "This was no ordinary fire, nor was that bird anything natural. Is it the work of Sten Rask?"

I clench my jaw and nod.

"He has Gerda and Anders then?" Erik's fingers clutch something inside the pocket of his coat. The pistol, no doubt.

"Probably." Thyra shares a significant look with Kai. "We should carry Christiane to Sephia's cottage. She will receive the best care there."

Erik pulls his hand from his pocket and rakes his fingers through his hair. "We need to go after Rask to find Gerda and Anders. We can't backtrack now."

Thyra takes Kai's proffered hand and rises to her feet. "If this is the doing of a master sorcerer, we need Sephia's assistance just as much as Christiane does. We cannot face Rask on our own."

Erik bangs his fist against the brick wall of the foundation. "So we let Rask take our friends to God knows where? How will we ever find them if we don't track them now?"

"Perhaps Erik is right." Kai strokes his chin with two fingers. "No, seriously, Thyra, spare me that look. Listen—Erik and I can try to track

Rask. We will not confront him, but we can determine where that bird carried Gerda and Anders. You and Varna take Christiane to Sephia and we'll meet you there when we locate the others."

Thyra looks like she wants to argue, but sighs instead. "I concede. But take Bae with you. He's just outside the city walls, waiting in the woods. Luki and Freya are with him—they can come with us. We'll need Freya to transport Christiane, at any rate."

"And Luki for protection." Kai smiles. "A logical plan."

"Always." Thyra's lips twitch upward.

A great roar and crash split the smoky air. It is the balcony, finally giving way. I focus on the small group of people near me, refusing to look at the Opera House.

More bodies, more blood on Sten Rask's hands, and for what? To find the mirror? Or to draw me to him?

Or both, Varna. Probably both.

Erik bends down to pick up Christiane. "Enough talk, let's get her to the woods. The sooner you carry her to Sephia, the better."

Thyra lifts her pale eyebrows. "Very well, Master Stahl. Lead on."

"After you accomplish that, Erik, meet me at my rooms. I need to throw together a travel pack or two." Kai rattles off the address. Erik nods as if he knows the street well.

"I would like to go with Erik and Kai," I say. "Gerda is my sister. I must find her."

Thyra shakes her head. "No. It is not the impropriety," she adds, after a quick glance at my face. "I don't care about such nonsense. It's simply that I believe you are connected to Rask as more than just a casual acquaintance. I'm afraid he will sense your presence if you are anywhere near him, and that could betray the others."

I bow my head. She is right. "I just want to be there when he is defeated."

Thyra takes my arm as we follow Erik and Kai down the street. "I'm afraid you must be there, Varna, and I'm not sure you will really want that, in the end."

CHAPTER FOURTEEN:
THE POWER OF A MIRROR

ISHIFT THE STRAP OF MY bag from one shoulder to the other. Both shoulder blades are equally sore and I'm glad I decided to abandon Gerda's bag when I retrieved my rucksack from the lean-to. Although I did pull the blue gown from her bag and stuff it into mine.

Because she will wear it again. I know she will.

Our travel back to Sephia's cottage is uneventful, even though Christiane's obvious pain makes each mile seem longer. Fortunately, Erik gave me the remaining bottles of Sephia's special potion. I feed Christiane a few drops when she's conscious. It's the only thing that allows us to move forward without constant cries of pain.

My feet swell inside my boots, but with Christiane slumped against the horse's neck, her face pale as milk, I decide not to complain. Instead, I remark on Freya's gentle gait—she takes great care in placing her hooves so she doesn't jostle her semi-conscious rider.

"She is well trained." Thyra guides the mare around a fallen tree limb. Luki trots ahead of us, occasionally glancing over his shoulder to make sure we follow.

"I was afraid she might pull away, or break into a trot or something."

"She will not."

"Yes, but if she's startled; if something spooks her … "

"She fears me more," Thyra says, without looking in my direction.

"Fears you? Not loves you?"

Thyra shoves her curls behind her shoulders. "She remembers me as the Snow Queen. Despite any fondness developed since those days, she retains a shadow of fear." Thyra quickens her pace. "We need to make it to Sephia's by evening. I don't want to spend another night on the road."

"What about Luki?"

"What about him?"

"Does he fear you as well?"

As if he knows we're discussing him, Luki turns his head and looks back, his tongue lolling from his half-open mouth. Those teeth. I still can't get used to keeping company with a wolf, no matter how friendly.

Thyra's smile softens her angular face. "No. Luki loves me. He never feared me, even when he should have. Even when I was wielding my power and other creatures shrank back in terror."

I lengthen my stride to walk beside Thyra. "You gave it up. Your magic. Do you ever miss it?"

Thyra side-eyes me. "No. I relinquished it willingly, as I'm sure Gerda told you. It was a burden, not a blessing."

"But the power." I stare at my hands. What could I accomplish with such power? Healing beyond my dreams.

Healing, Varna? Be honest. You also want to be admired or adored. You want to wield authority over others. To know they can never laugh at you, or pity you, again.

I kick a pebble from the path into the woods. "I sometimes long for power. I don't have any, you see."

"Is that right?"

I turn my head to meet Thyra's scrutiny. "No. I am not rich, or beautiful, or talented at socially acceptable pursuits. I'm just a girl from an ordinary family living in a small village, learning to make a few ointments and potions."

"I'm not sure I would say your family is ordinary. There's Gerda, after all. And I think"—Thyra casts me a little smile—"there is more to you than meets the eye, Varna."

"Well, I certainly hope so. I am not much to look at." I toss my head as I say this, to show it doesn't matter. *Even though it does. It always does.*

"I think it depends on who is looking." Thyra slaps the reins against her palm. "Do you think Kai loves me for how I look?"

"Maybe. I mean, you are beautiful, so I'm sure that comes into it."

Thyra laughs. "No, not at all. I suspect he would prefer someone who looks like Gerda. No doubt, given a viable option, he'd choose someone who does not annoy him with intimidating stares, or constantly remind him of a world of ice and snow. Someone warmer and sweeter." She shrugs. "He likes how I look because he loves me, not the other way around."

Easy for a beautiful woman to say. I swallow my sharp reply and fall back a few steps.

"Finally," Thyra says, as we step into the clearing where Sephia's cottage sits, squat and comforting as a rocking chair.

Sephia opens her door before we even reach the stoop.

"What is this?" She hurries to Freya and helps Thyra lift Christiane from the mare's back.

"Her leg is badly broken." I follow them inside the cottage. "I did what I could, but I doubt it's enough."

Sephia carries Christiane to the bed, with Thyra shoving back the alcove curtains so the enchantress can lay the injured dancer down in one swift motion.

She examines my makeshift splint. "Not bad, given the circumstances, which must have been dire. What happened?"

As Thyra launches into an explanation, Sephia motions for me to take her place beside Christiane. "You sit with her, Varna. I'll boil water and gather some other things we may need." She glances up at Thyra. "Sorry, please continue."

Thyra steps back. "It's actually Varna's story. She's the one who saw Rask at the fire. She believes he sent the bird that took Gerda and Anders."

I duck my head. "I'd rather not talk about that now. Let's focus on Christiane."

Sephia nods before rising and crossing to her iron cook stove. As she rattles utensils and fills the kettle, I help Thyra undress Christiane, who looks up once to ask where she is, then lapses back into a stupor.

"Do you have a nightgown?" I ask.

Sephia points to her magical cupboard. "Check there. I'm sure you will find something."

Thyra crosses to the wardrobe and opens its painted doors. She picks up the first item her fingers land on and looks at it for a moment before tossing it to me.

It is a nightgown, white as milk and soft as rabbit fur. I slip it over Christiane's head and tug it down over her limp body.

I shoot Thyra a sharp glance. "I could use some help."

She stares into a mirror lining one door of the wardrobe. I catch my reflection there and look away.

"That's what he wants, Sephia." Thyra closes the door and turns around, leaning back against the cupboard. "The mirror. I should have destroyed it again. Smashed it to pieces."

"No, you did the right thing, sending it to Holger." Sephia crosses the room, carrying a basin of water and a crocheted bag filled with bandages and other supplies. "Varna, would you please get the ointment I left on the counter?"

As I rise to fetch the jar of ointment, I look from Sephia's verdant green eyes to Thyra's icy gray ones. "Holger? Gerda mentioned the name, but claimed she never met him. He's some old man who lives in a cave in the mountains, right?"

"A wise old man," Sephia says, with a gentle smile. "And a friend."

I hand her the ointment. "You said something before, about Gerda and the mirror. Something about a tear? What was that all about?" I sit beside Sephia on the edge of the bed and take a vial of amber liquid from her outstretched hand.

"A few drops on her lips will be sufficient." Sephia glances at Thyra. "Ah yes, the tear. I think Thyra should tell that tale."

Thyra twists her hands in the folds of her gray gown. "I'm not sure I should say anything without Gerda's permission."

"I don't believe Gerda would mind." Sephia bends her auburn head over Christiane's prone form, her attention seemingly focused on her patient.

"It was magic," Thyra says, after a long stretch of silence. "Not the kind I knew. Not anything, my master, Mael Voss, could have conjured. Or Sten Rask. Or even Sephia."

The older woman continues working on Christiane, but I catch the crescent moon curve of her smile.

"The mirror was complete except for one piece. It was a fragment Voss took with him to his icy grave." Thyra lifts her chin and meets my inquisitive stare with a steely gaze. "I sent him to his death, knowing he might possess that piece. Hoping he did not, and knowing he might." She grips her hands together so tightly her knuckles turn white. "He did. I thought it was over—that he'd won. One missing piece and I was doomed. When the clock struck midnight, when I turned eighteen, I would disintegrate into a wraith. A horrible, never-ending existence, without a body, or any real thought. With no hope for death to release me." She closes her eyes. "I prepared myself for this fate, but then something happened. It was magic none of us expected." She opens her eyes and I'm taken aback. A fire burns there, brilliant as diamonds. "It was a miracle."

"What does Gerda have to do with it?"

"Everything." Thyra lifts her hands. "She wept, and one of her tears fell and hit the mirror and somehow made it whole. It saved me. Perhaps it was God who intervened, or the mirror itself. I do not know. I only know why. It was because Gerda cried. She wept for the girl who treated her rudely and stole the boy she loved. She cried for someone she had every right to hate. But Gerda didn't think like that, did not feel that way. She wept because her heart held more love than the deepest well. She cried for me."

Sephia sits back, pulling a light woolen blanket over Christiane. "I have done all I can. She sleeps peacefully, and I think she will heal quickly, although I doubt she'll ever dance again."

"Like Anders." I stroke the ballerina's soft cheek.

"Like Anders." Sephia rises to her feet and crosses to Thyra, who stares at the enchantress as if she's never seen her before. She stiffens for a moment when Sephia pulls her into a close embrace. Then her shoulders sag and she presses her head against Sephia's shoulder.

"I have waited to hear you say it, Thyra. To accept a power mightier than any you ever wielded, or knew. To admit love was the magic that saved you." Sephia pushes Thyra back, still holding onto her arms. She brushes the tears from the former Snow Queen's very human face. "I know love compelled you to sacrifice your chance at freedom when you called down the avalanche that killed Voss. You were willing to throw away your life to save Kai, Gerda, Bae, and Luki. So remember, it was not only Gerda's love that saved you, Thyra Winther. It was also your own."

I leap to my feet. "Can such magic save Gerda? She holds so much love in her heart. Will it protect her from Rask?"

Sephia releases Thyra and turns to me. "I hope so, Varna. That is my prayer. I know if anything can keep her safe, that will."

"We must find her, and Anders, and stop Rask. He wants the mirror."

Sephia smooths down the front of her sea green gown. "I know. And he cannot have it. In his hands it could be used for great evil. I would be better to smash it to pieces than allow him, or his mentor, to wield such power."

Thyra's face displays a mixture of determination and fear. It solidifies a thought chasing around my mind like a will-o-the-wisp. "The restoration of the mirror is what saved Thyra. What will happen to her if it is broken again?"

I can tell by Sephia's expression that, for once, someone has considered an idea that has eluded her.

Thyra has considered it. She has probably wrestled with this thought for some time. I stiffen my spine and look Sephia in the eye. "What will happen to Thyra if we destroy the mirror?"

Thyra steps around Sephia and touches her arm before speaking. "No one knows. How could they? No one truly understands the magic of the mirror, do they?"

"No." Sephia's voice is muted and her lashes lowered, veiling her green eyes.

"You could still become a wraith?" I bite the inside of my cheek.

"No, I don't think so. That was a spell Voss created—he drew on the mirror to do so, but I don't believe that is part of its intrinsic powers."

"You might die?" I turn to Sephia. "Will destroying the mirror kill Thyra?"

"As she says, no one knows."

I look from one beautiful face to the other. "Does Kai know?"

"No, although I'm sure it will occur to him, in time. Especially if it appears we must destroy the mirror to stop Rask." Thyra tosses her head. Her curls catch the light and seem to spark, like lightning flashing across a night sky. "It doesn't matter. We must find Gerda and Anders, and make sure Sten Rask does not gain access to the mirror, no matter what it takes."

Sephia grips Thyra's hand.

"No matter what," I echo.

If that means you must make the sacrifice, Varna, then so be it. Rather than Thyra, rather than anyone else, let it be you.

Thyra pulls her hand free and forces a smile. "Now I must go and tend to Freya and Luki. They've been waiting patiently for some time. I will leave you to take care of Christiane."

After Thyra leaves, I catch Sephia's eye. "I'll sit with Christiane, if you wish."

The enchantress slides two fingers down her long, slender neck. "Thank you. I think I shall try to send a message to Holger. Someone must warn him about Rask."

"How can you do that? Isn't he in a cave somewhere, far from any roads or trails?"

Sephia's smile lights up the room. "I have some special messengers." She turns and walks to the door to her garden, but pauses with her hand on the latch. "You have the makings of a great healer, Varna Lund. I just want you to know that."

I hug myself when she leaves the room, and contemplate a future spent here, learning from Sephia. I could become more than a simple village healer. I could grow into someone who mirrors cannot define. I could become something more.

Someone who matters.

I smile and lay the back of my hand on Christiane's brow to check for fever.

CHAPTER FIFTEEN:
BEFORE THE STORM

E RIK AND KAI RETURN A week later.

Bae lumbers into the clearing as I drape damp sheets over a blanket covering a low tree limb. Erik and Kai straggle behind him, their clothes caked with dust and dried mud. They look like they've been traveling for months.

I raise my hand in greeting. "Welcome back. You bring good news, I hope."

"News, yes, but … "

"But what? If you didn't you find Gerda and Anders, why have you returned?"

"We have news. I'm just not certain how good it is. Give me a moment, would you?" Erik strides to the pump and works the lever until water gushes out. He sticks his head under the spout.

"We've been on quite a journey." Kai looks abashed as Erik swears and shouts, "Cold as ice!"

Erik straightens, slams down the lever, and steps away from the pump. His red hair is plastered against his skull and the dripping water leaves pale trails in the grime coating his face.

I toss him a towel. "It's a bit damp, but since you're soaked, it should do."

He grunts and wipes his face clean before rubbing at his hair.

The door to the cottage flies open. Luki dashes out and heads for Kai, yipping and running in circles. Thyra crosses the clearing in several long strides before pulling up short before Kai.

Sephia waits in the doorway, her arm around Christiane's slender shoulders.

Luki butts his head against Kai's leg and howls once before loping into the woods, where Bae has already disappeared. Looking for food, no doubt.

"So you are back." Thyra reaches out and plucks a twig from Kai's dark hair. "Did you fall into a bog?"

Kai's hand shoots up and his fingers encircle her wrist. "A bog, a stream, and two forest pools. We also tumbled down a steep ravine and climbed the side of a mountain. But we're just fine, thank you very much." He pulls her toward him, until they are standing toe to toe.

"That's good." Thyra uses her free hand to trace a line from Kai's temple to his chin. She taps one finger against his rigid jaw. "I did worry a bit."

"Did you?" Kai reaches up to trap her moving fingers with his. "I mostly did a lot of thinking. I considered all the elements of a certain equation."

Thyra stands absolutely still. "Oh? And what answer was revealed when you completed this inquiry?"

"This one," Kai says, and leans in to kiss her.

I turn my head to focus on Erik's wide grin. "Now—what did you find out? Where are Gerda and Anders?"

He runs the towel roughly over his face. When he pulls it away, his expression is somber. "At Rask's fortress. He owns a great stone pile of a house up in the mountains, hidden in the forest. We were able to walk the perimeter, but there was only one gate, and we couldn't get past it. Fortunately, Bae was able to wander in when Rask rode back from wherever. Bae managed to catch a glimpse of Gerda and Anders through some barred windows before he was chased from the enclosure by that great bird we saw at the fire. It didn't raise any alarms, so I guess Rask doesn't take much notice of a wild reindeer roaming his property."

"Which tells us he is not as perceptive as he may think," Sephia says. "We can save the details for later. You need to clean up and rest."

"Yes, you both require a change of clothes." Thyra's voice is merrier than I've ever heard it. She presses close to Kai's side, leans into his shoulder, and sniffs. "Definitely."

Kai laughs and tightens the arm he's draped over her shoulders. "I can strip right here if you wish. I certainly don't want to taint Sephia's cottage."

Thyra widens her gray eyes. "Kai Thorsen!" She pops him in the side with her fist. "Behave yourself. There are actual ladies present."

Christiane giggles, but the bright sound devolves into a hacking cough. Poor Christiane. Although her leg is healing, I'm afraid the smoke she inhaled from the fire has permanently singed her lungs.

Sephia pats Christiane on the back. "Enough nonsense. Come inside, Thyra and Varna. I will provide these young gentlemen with some robes, so they can stroll to the river to bathe and tote back their dirty garments. Wearing the robes," she adds, wagging her finger at Kai.

He grins and gives her a little bow.

I pick up the willow laundry basket and carry it inside as Kai and Thyra share another passionate kiss.

"It's romantic," Christiane says, as Sephia helps her to the armchair. "I just hope when Anders and Gerda return ... " Her rosebud lips tremble. "They *will* return, right, Sephia?"

"Of course." Sephia arranges a blanket over Christiane's legs. As she turns to head for the wardrobe I catch her troubled expression.

"We'll go fetch them, now that we know where they are." I perch on the edge of one of the hard kitchen chairs. "I mean, with Sephia's help, and all of us working together ... "

"We shall see." Sephia shoots me a sharp look before crossing to the front door.

I tighten my lips. *See? Nonsense We'll go and rescue Gerda and Anders and that is that.*

Sephia steps outside to hand the robes to Erik and Kai, and pull Thyra, who lingers on the stoop, into the cottage. "Come inside," she tells the younger woman. "He has waited for you long enough. You can wait a few minutes."

Thyra wanders into the center of the room, looking as if she's not entirely sure where she is. When she lifts her head I notice a rosy hue tinting the skin over her sharp cheekbones. Her eyes are soft as spring rain.

She is more beautiful than ever. *This is what love can do.*

Yes, Varna, but you must possess some sort of beauty before anyone will love you. I slap my arm with my opposite hand. *Stop this now. Do not think about yourself—think about Gerda and Anders and how to rescue them.*

Christiane's dark eyes fasten on me with curiosity.

"Fly." I lightly swat my arm again. "Got it that time."

Sephia lifts her eyebrows as she heads for the stove. "Tea is what we need."

"They need food." Thyra follows her. "I'm sure they're starving." She pokes around the shelves of the larder. "Is there any of that honey left? And the lovely bread?"

No matter how many times I have seen Thyra help around the cottage over the past week, watching her perform domestic tasks always feels odd. She should be sitting in some parlor, discussing the finer points of a complex theory with a circle of scholars, not slicing bread.

Slicing bread is what girls like I do. We wash clothes, polish woodwork, and take care of all the little, mundane tasks fine ladies need not consider.

You are mistaken, Varna. She is not a fine lady. She's a girl from your village, even if she was once the Snow Queen.

Sephia leans in to whisper something in Thyra's ear.

Two women who are not fine ladies, yet demand more respect than most that are. Because they are confident in themselves, happy with who they are, and don't care what anyone else thinks.

No, because they have power, Varna, or had it once and still act as if they do. Because they know what power is, and how to wield it. I press my hands over my ears. It's Sten Rask's voice I hear, even though I know these thoughts are mine.

"Are you all right, Varna?" Lines pucker Christiane's forehead. "I know you must be worried, like me. I'm so lucky to be here, with everyone taking care of me. All snug and safe, while Gerda and Anders ... "

I stand, brushing off the pine needles clinging to my woolen skirt. "Don't worry, we'll bring them home as soon as we can. We'll leave tomorrow, once the men have rested."

Kai and Erik clatter into the cottage, wearing the odd robes Sephia provided. Their faces shine with scrubbing and their hair clings damply to their scalps. Although Erik tops Kai by a few inches and is bigger-boned, they are equally handsome. I walk to the fireplace and lean against the cool stones. Yes, and nice enough, yet they'll never consider me as anything more than Gerda's sister.

Sephia orders them to sit at the table and brings tea and a platter of fruit and cheese, while Thyra passes around the sliced bread and a ceramic jar filled with honey. The young men eat greedily, wolfing down two helpings of everything.

I wait until they finish eating before I cross to the table. Standing at one end, I tap my finger against the oaken surface. "So, when do we leave to rescue Gerda and Anders? Tomorrow? I know you're tired, so I can pack for all of us, if you wish."

Sephia and Thyra share a glance. "The truth is, we cannot make that journey yet." Sephia turns back to the stove and fiddles with the lid of the kettle. "Thyra and Kai must warn Holger first."

"No!" I shove the table. Erik's cup bounces off and smashes against the plank floorboards.

Sephia's face hardens like carved stone. "Yes, they must. I've sent several of my messengers and received no reply. They have returned with my messages unopened, unread. Perhaps my old friend sleeps, or rests in a state that prevents him from answering my missives. It is possible, given his age and the perfection of his spirit. Still, I must be sure. Holger is the guardian of the mirror and he should be warned. Thyra and Kai will take Bae and Luki and travel back to the lands Voss once held—the former kingdom of the Snow Queen. Only they know they way, and only they should travel it. The less who know the path to Holger's cave, the better."

I press my palm against my heaving chest. "We should rescue Gerda and Anders first."

"Sit down, Varna," Erik says.

I turn on him. "This is none of your business."

"It is." He pushes back his chair and stands to face me. "Anders is like a brother to me. I want to rescue him as much as you want to save Gerda."

"It's not the same." I fight the urge to stomp my foot.

Erik moves closer and looms over me. "You're acting irrationally. You need to take a walk or something. Cool your head."

I stare up into his green eyes. That expression—so dismissive. "You are not my master, Erik Stahl. Or my brother or father or anything to me. You have no right to tell me what to do."

Kai whistles. "Erik, my friend, I suggest you sit down."

Erik leans in and grips my shoulders. "I have the right of someone who knows what's best. Sephia, who has always been helpful and kind, says we must wait, that Thyra and Kai must warn this Holger person before we travel back to Rask's fortress. I don't like it either, but I will not throw a childish fit over something Sephia calls necessary."

The eyes of everyone in the room focus on me. I lift my chin and meet Erik's angry gaze with a fierce glare. "Childish? You are no older than me, and I've seen how you behave when something thwarts you. You're just saying this to impress Sephia, even though she will never bend so low as to love you. You're an ordinary man and she, as you have admitted, is far above anyone ordinary. You must find your perfect beauty elsewhere."

Erik thrusts me aside. "Bah! Talking to you is like spitting in the wind." He stalks to the middle of the room before wheeling around. "You talk about beauty as if it doesn't matter, yet you're more obsessed with appearances than anyone else." He jabs his finger at me. "Well, let me tell you, Varna Lund, it would not make any difference if you were as lovely outside as Sephia. Because all that petty, childish anger inside would still make you ugly."

I suck in a breath. Not *make* you. *Still* make you.

I won't cry. Not in front of this boy. Never. I swallow and tuck a loose strand of my hair behind my ear.

"That is enough, Erik." Sephia steps between us. "Perhaps it is you who had better take a walk."

"Perhaps." He slams the door as he leaves the cottage.

"He's upset about Anders," Kai says.

I shoot him a sharp look just as Thyra elbows him.

"So no one is going to rescue Anders and Gerda?" asks Christiane.

Sephia sighs. "Yes, someone will. Soon. But tomorrow Thyra and Kai must travel to Holger's cave." She pats my rigid arm before turning to face the others. "I still have your furs, Thyra. You will need them for this journey."

Kai frowns. "As well as boots and hats and mittens. And here I thought we'd left winter behind, at least for a little while."

Thyra glances at Sephia. "I know Bae can still fly, but we have no sleigh."

"I will provide one. You'll find it in a little shed, at the point where you cross into the lands of eternal winter. You may leave Freya there and travel on with only Bae." Sephia holds up one hand as Thyra protests. "Freya will be well cared for, I promise. She'll be waiting on your return."

Kai slumps in his chair. "I suppose there's nothing for it. I don't relish going back there, but if must, I must."

Thyra places her arm over his shoulders. "We will go together. With Bae and Luki, just as we did before."

"Well, not exactly." Kai covers her hand with his. "Then you possessed the powers of a Snow Queen. Now we are both mortal, with no power at all."

"Nonsense." Thyra leans in to kiss him on the cheek. "We have each other. There is power there."

Christiane claps her hands. "The power of love!"

Observing her bright face, I swallow my harsh retort.

Thyra and Kai rise from the table and follow Sephia to her wardrobe, where she uncovers winter clothes I don't recall seeing stored in there before. Thyra and Kai stand side by side, their bodies almost touching, as Sephia fills their arms with hats and gloves and other garments they need for their journey.

They are traveling to a land that can kill with one blast of wind. Without any magic, except possibly the sorcery Thyra spoke of when telling the story of Gerda's tear.

I don't know if I believe in magic arising from love, but I believe if anyone could use such power, it would be Thyra and Kai.

And Gerda, of course.

I smile grimly. *Really, Varna? Some sorcery of love? Surely you do not believe such a ridiculous notion.*

Because even after hearing the tale of the tear, I doubt such magic exists.

Kai pulls one of the thick woolen hats over Thyra's head, causing her curls to spring out from under the cap and halo her face. He says something about a daisy and they both laugh.

I hope it does, though. I desperately hope it does.

CHAPTER SIXTEEN: SHADOWS IN THE FOREST

EPHIA'S GARDEN IS ALIVE WITH color and the mingled scents of flowers. An indigo butterfly, its wings filtering light like stained glass, flutters about my head. I lean against the stone wall of the cottage and study the riot of vegetation, trying to name all the plants. It's impossible now, but I will learn them, in time.

Christiane sits on a blanket spread across a small lozenge of lawn, her injured leg stretched out straight before her. She reaches up to touch a waving frond of chamomile and laughs when it curls about her finger.

"She has a gift." Sephia steps through her back door. She examines Christiane for a moment. "It is not something everyone possesses, that connection to growing things."

I shoot her a suspicious look. "Christiane seems sweet, but she's very young."

"She's only two years younger than you, Varna."

"I'm not talking about age, exactly."

Sephia turns her brilliant gaze on me. "Her childlike nature may be what's needed for someone who draws magic from the earth."

I can't stifle a snort. "Like you?"

Sephia's expression grows wistful. "I was once like Christiane, long ago. Before I learned too much about the evil in this world. Before …

" She shakes her head. "You needn't hear the tale of my folly. Come inside. I must speak with you."

As she turns I catch a glimpse of her somber face. "You haven't received a message from Thyra and Kai, have you?"

"No. But they only left a few days ago. Their journey is much longer than yours will be."

"Journey?" I follow her into the cottage. "What journey?"

"Rescuing Gerda and Anders, of course." Sephia sweeps into the center of the room. "Erik, enough rummaging about in the larder. Come and hear what I have to say."

He emerges with an armful of tins and small cloth bags. "You mentioned a journey, so I thought I'd gather some food."

"Very wise, but you needn't pack it all yourself. I will help, as will Varna. Pile those things on the table." Sephia motions me toward the rocking chair as she settles in the armchair. "Then come sit with us."

Erik drags over one of the wooden chairs and straddles it, the chair turned so the wooden slats face us. "So, is this a scouting mission? I know we must wait for the others before we attempt a rescue."

"Ah, there you are wrong." Sephia leans back against the soft upholstery of her chair. "To defeat a sorcerer like Sten Rask does not require arms or armies. No, the only hope for success is through cunning and the element of surprise." She glances from Erik's puzzled face to mine. "That is why I sent Thyra and Kai on ahead, to complete their own mission. It's also why I am sending the two of you, and no one else, on this rescue."

"The two of us?" Erik shoots me a sharp glance. "Surely not. I'm happy to go alone, if you think that best, but I'm certainly not taking Varna with me."

Sephia taps the arm of her chair with one finger. "It is the only way."

"It is improper!" Erik blurts out, as color rises in his cheeks. "I mean, the two of us, traveling together, with no chaperone?"

Sephia rises gracefully. "I did not take you for such a narrow-minded person, Erik. I think I know your true nature, and have no fear of you taking advantage of any young woman under your protection. As for Varna, I'm convinced she will not throw herself at you." She crosses to stand behind my chair. "You are not that irresistible, Master Stahl."

I cover my mouth with my hand. A guffaw right now is probably not the best way to convince Erik to travel with me.

Erik's cheeks shine almost as red as his hair. "That's not what I meant."

"At any rate, Varna must go. Rask wishes her to come to him, I believe?"

"Yes," I reply, all humor gone.

"And so she shall." Sephia strolls over to a small cabinet hanging on the wall. Opening it, she pulls a vial of golden liquid from a row of brightly colored glass bottles. "This tincture," she raises the vial, "will make one invisible. Only for a short time," she adds, holding up her hand as Erik leaps to his feet. "There is only one dose. So it must be used wisely."

"You want me to present myself at Sten Rask's fortress, as if I am accepting his offer, then Erik will sneak in when Rask allows me entry?" I look to Sephia and receive a dazzling smile in return.

"Just so. The spell will last for an hour, perhaps a little less, but that should allow Erik time to locate Gerda and Anders and free them."

"While I keep Rask occupied?" I rise and cross to stand before Sephia. "How shall I do that?"

Sephia gives me a pitying look. "However you can."

Erik's gaze slides from Sephia's solemn face to mine. "I don't understand. What does Rask want with Varna?"

Sephia tilts her head and studies me for a moment. "I'm not quite sure. He has seen something in her that interests him. That is all I know. Yet it's enough of a weapon to use against him, if Varna agrees." The glint in her eyes softens. "I think this is the best chance to free Gerda and Anders. I will not command you, Varna Lund. Go with Erik, understanding the risk, and approach Rask only if you choose to do so."

I clench my fingers into fists. "I'll do it. I will do anything, if it will save Gerda." I glance at Erik. "And Anders."

Sephia moves toward the kitchen table. "Now I'll help you pack."

"You can't come along?" asks Erik. "Your magic might prove useful."

Sephia places both hands on the table and leans forward, her hair shadowing her face. "No. Now that he has encountered my power, Rask would sense my presence. I'd be a hindrance to our plan, not a help." She straightens, tossing back her flaming hair. "I shall be with you, in spirit. Call on me in any extremity." She turns to us, and I glimpse the fearsome enchantress beneath the human mask. "But only then. There are limits to all powers, and a cost to all magic. It is not to be used lightly."

"That applies to Rask as well, I hope," Erik says.

"Oh yes." Sephia's smile brings the color back into Erik's face. "Yes, indeed. And it is my dearest hope he does not realize this yet."

Erik and I ride in silence for most of the day. The dappled gray gelding and dun mare Sephia whistled from the woods, the tack she produced from a shed behind her walled garden, the pearl gray cloak she pulled from the wardrobe and fastened about me with a silver pin shaped like a lily—these feel real as anything I've ever touched. Yet they're all undoubtedly touched by some enchantment. As we move closer to Sten Rask's fortress, my thoughts dwell on the magic enveloping my life.

I did not believe, or disbelieve, in magic when I was a child. I simply never considered it. Only when Gerda returned from her sojourn in the Snow Queen's kingdom—telling tales of sorcerers and talking reindeer and an enchanted mirror—did I spare magic any thought.

Now it spins about me, seeping into my skin like a fog. I shiver and pull Sephia's cloak tighter.

Erik glances over at me. "Need to stop and rest?"

I shake my head. "No. I'm simply thinking over everything—trying to make sure I consider all the possibilities, so I'm not taken by surprise. I don't want to be the reason we fail in our quest."

"I'm certain you won't be." Erik's voice is gruff, but he offers me an encouraging smile. "You're pretty brave and resourceful, from what I've seen."

"Thanks." I lower my head, not sure how to respond to such compliments.

"And I'm sorry," he continues, keeping his gaze fixed on the road ahead of us, "for being rude to you the other evening. I was upset over the situation with Anders, and when you said ... To be honest, I confess your arrow struck its mark, when you spoke of my adoration of Sephia, of wanting to please her. Because of course I do. I admire her great beauty."

"Inside as well as outside." I fight, and fail, to keep bitterness from tainting my tone.

"Yes. But your words struck me to the bone for another reason." He turns his head and I'm shocked by the naked emotion playing across his face. "The bit about me being beneath her. Well, of course I am. But I've heard those words so often, they cut me to the quick."

"What do you mean?" I tighten the grip of my thighs on my mare's sleek sides. Following Thyra's lead, I'm wearing breeches under my rolled up skirt, a choice that earned raised eyebrows, then a shrug, from Erik.

"Oh, it's just my history. You see, my family's always thought my love of beauty was ostentation. I was getting above my station, being dismissive of my own class, that sort of thing." The lines bracketing his mouth deepen. "They're wrong. I don't care about being a gentleman—I would prefer to manage a business, or work with my hands. But when they see me rhapsodizing over a painting or some perfectly worked piece of silver they call me a wastrel." He offers me an ironic smile. "They don't understand. I love beautiful things for themselves, not because I wish to own them. Not even because I want to be rich, or to dismiss my family as if they're beneath my notice. Not at all. I'm not in love with beauty because I want to use it to better myself, but because I want to experience it wherever and however I find it. And add to it somehow, if I can."

"With your carvings? They are stunning."

Erik slaps the ends of his reins against the palm of his free hand. "Yes. I love creating beauty, even if I'm just a craftsman, not an artist."

Twilight dapples the road with dancing shadows. "Is there a great difference between the two?"

He meets my inquisitive gaze with a genuine smile. "Perhaps not."

We drop back into silence, though more companionable than before. "Are we far from Rask's fortress?" I ask at last.

"No. We should reach it by tomorrow morning. It makes a difference, having the horses."

"Yes. I wonder where Sephia found them." My mare delicately side-steps a fallen tree limb. She's a better horse than I am a rider. I've ridden a bit before, but never known the luxury of owning my own mount. Thankfully, Sephia's horses are so well trained I can stay in the saddle without much effort.

Erik raises his eyebrows. "Found them? Or called them from the mist?"

I pat the mare's neck, which is soft as chamois. "She feels solid enough."

"I didn't say they were phantoms. I simply believe she's enchanted them." Erik pulls up his gelding. "We should stop and make camp for the night. The dark is coming on fast."

We dismount and walk into the woods that border the narrow road. Erik leads the way, beating back the underbrush until the thin branches break.

"This will do," he says, when we reach a tiny clearing, only wide enough for a few people to lie down beside each other. It's scarcely an ideal spot, but I soon realize why Erik chose it. A spring bubbles up at the edge of the clearing, offering fresh water for us and the horses.

I sneak into the woods to relieve myself. When I return Erik has removed the saddles and bridles from our mounts. He checks to make sure they are cooled down properly, then gives each a swat on the haunches to chase them into the trees before he hangs the saddles over a low-hanging limb. "Sephia told me they'd find their own food, and always return when we whistle," he says, when I protest this action. "Let's see about our own supper. Even though we can't make a fire."

"It might draw too much attention?" I rummage through our saddlebags.

"Yes. No use inviting guests. I have this"—he pats the pocket of his greatcoat, where the outline of his pistol is visible—"but would prefer not to use it."

I hand him an apple, a slice of bread, and chunk of cheese. "Should we take turns staying awake?"

"Sounds good. I'll take the first watch, then wake you for the second." Erik finishes off his food in a few bites. "Hand me your water flask, would you? I can fill yours as well as mine."

I fish the leather-covered flask from my bag and toss it to him before I sit down on a fallen log to eat my own supper.

Erik returns from the spring and moves in close, the tips of his books touching mine. He thrusts the full flask toward me "Here you go. Fresh and cold."

"Thanks." I drop the remainder of my bread into my lap and grab the flask, not looking up. "Please have a seat. There's room for both us on this elegant settee." I wave my hand over the log.

Erik doesn't move. "Varna, I want you to know I don't believe you are ugly—inside or out."

I finally look up to meet his intense gaze. "All right."

"*All right*? What does that mean?"

"It means I'm glad you said it, but I know I am not beautiful, so you needn't pretend."

Erik snorts and steps back. "Don't worry, I never said you were beautiful."

I lift my chin. "As long as we understand each other. I hate when people try to make me feel better by lying to me."

"I'll never lie to you. I have many bad habits but that is not one of them." Erik takes a long swallow from his flask before speaking again. "You know," he says, studying me dispassionately, "beauty's not everything. You act like you'll never have a chance at marriage, but there are plenty of men seeking more than looks in a wife."

I yank a blanket from my rucksack and toss it across the ground. "Oh, I know. There are widowers with several children, hoping for a nursemaid, and farmers seeking someone to help milk the cows or work the fields. Not to mention old merchants mourning beloved wives, just wanting someone to cook and clean. Yes, there are many men who'd consider marrying me. The problem is, that is not what I want." I slump down onto the blanket, keeping the log at my back.

Erik sits down beside me. "Looking for love, are you?"

I lower my head and toy with the silver brooch on my cloak. "What if I am?"

"That's always a dangerous pursuit, regardless of one's appearance. Pull out the other blanket, would you? We need to cover up. The night air is cold."

"You don't want to fall in love?" I peer up at him from under my lashes.

"I am not sure." He pulls me to his side and tucks the blanket so we're cocooned together. "Body warmth," he says, when I make a noise. "It's the best way to keep from getting too chilled. Nothing to twist your lips over—I used to pile up with the other soldiers in camp, especially in winter. As to your question, yes, I would like to fall in love. It just has never happened, and despite some rather romantic notions about beauty, I am a practical person. Besides, I 've not seen love last, or experienced much of anything that makes me believe it can."

I turn my head to examine his profile. His last statement, along with his comments about his family, make me wonder if he's had a tougher life than I ever imagined.

"So you don't believe in lasting love?"

Erik drapes his arm over my shoulders and pulls me close, until my head rests on his broad chest. "Think about it. Your own sister took off on a journey, all alone, with no money or companions, to track down her great love. Now she claims she and Kai are like brother and sister, and she's delighted he and Thyra are together. What happened to *that* eternal love?"

Erik's heart beats steadily beneath my ear. It's a comforting sound. I allow my body to relax in his arms. "That's not a good example. Gerda was only fifteen at the time, and had adored Kai for years. Once she saw the truth—how his love for her was nothing like his love for Thyra—Gerda came to her senses."

"But that's my point."

I tap my forefinger against his shoulder. "You must admit Thyra and Kai seem truly devoted. I believe their love will last. They've been apart for four years, with only letters to keep their romance alive, and haven't lost their feelings for one another."

Erik huffs. "Those two. They are like peas in a pod. I think they love each other for their minds as much as anything else."

"What's wrong with that?"

"Nothing, I suppose. Kai did surprise me. I thought a scholar would be weak, but he had no problem keeping up."

I nudge Erik's thigh with my knee. "Perhaps you aren't as superior as you think. Anyway, Kai grew up in my village, and worked hard at our family mill long before he went to the University. We villagers are tougher than you city folk."

"Oh, fearsome, are you?" Erik's fingers dig into my shoulder blade. "Hold still."

I roll my shoulders to loosen his grip. "What are you doing?"

"Keeping you alive. Stay still, and quiet too, if that's possible. I'm going to reach into my coat pocket and pull out my pistol."

"What ..." I follow the trajectory of Erik's fixed gaze.

He shushes me and levels the pistol with his right hand.

Then I spy it—a shaggy creature hidden in the shadows. A bear. It lifts its snout and sniffs the air

It probably smells the food stuffed in our saddlebags.

Or you, Varna. Another kind of food. I press closer to Erik's side.

"Dammit, don't throw off my aim."

Before I can reply, Erik fires the pistol. Smoke clouds my vision and the acrid scent of gunpowder fills my nostrils. "Did you hit him?" I rub my eyes.

"No, but I did not mean to." Erik lowers his weapon. "I wanted to scare it off, not kill it."

"What if it comes back?"

"It won't. And anyway, I will keep watch." He whistles for the horses, who trot into the clearing, still chewing the grass they found somewhere.

Erik frowns. "No sleep for me, it seems. I need to stay awake, pistol at hand. You should get some rest, though."

"I'm not sure I can."

"Nonsense." Erik presses my head back down on his chest. "Stop talking and close your eyes."

"Are you always so bossy?"

Erik makes a harrumphing noise. "Are you always so argumentative?"

"Yes," I say.

I'm rewarded with a chuckle.

Erik's body is warm and I am tired. I bury my face in the folds of his wool coat. He smells of horse and leather and a trace of gunpowder. It is not an unpleasant mixture. Not at all.

Stop it, Varna. Yes, it's nice to be held by a man, but this is Erik, and he's simply being practical. Stop acting like a dithering idiot and get some sleep.

My eyelids droop and close. "That bear could have charged us. Why not shoot to kill?"

Erik rests one hand on my head, his fingers loosely entangled in my hair. "There's no need to shoot a wild creature when you can scare if off. And anyway," Erik's voice fades as sleep takes me. "I've seen enough of killing."

CHAPTER SEVENTEEN:
THE PULL OF MAGIC

I N THE MORNING, WE EAT a hasty breakfast of bread smeared with honey. As Erik saddles the horses, I stuff the blankets back into the saddlebags and refill our flasks with spring water.

I examine Erik's red-rimmed eyes. "Did you get any sleep?"

"No. Perhaps I dozed off once or twice. It's no problem—I'm trained to stay alert even when drowsy. That's a necessity in the army, when the enemy's all around." He elbows the dappled gray in the ribs, causing the gelding to exhale a gust of air. "We should move as quickly as possible," he adds, tightening the girth to his saddle. "I don't want to enter Rask's fortress after nightfall."

"Me either." I roll up my skirt, tying it in an untidy knot at my waist. One foot in the stirrup and a hand at the pommel, I swing my body up into the saddle before Erik comes to my aid.

His eyes narrow as he studies my face. "I would have helped."

"Did not need it," I reply, adjusting my grip on the reins. I tend to hold them too tight, or so Erik claimed yesterday.

I flush as I recall what else he said when he first observed my riding skills. *"Reins are for guiding the horse, not hanging on. Hold them together in one hand and lay them against the horse's neck to direct it right or left. Don't yank the bit back and forth like a saw."*

"See?" I lift my arm, displaying both reins held loosely in my right hand. "I'm a quick study."

"I will give you that." He swings up onto his own horse. "And quite tenacious."

"That can be good." I kick my mare and follow Erik as he guides his gelding toward the road.

"I never said it wasn't." He urges his horse into a trot.

At this pace, there's no opportunity for further conversation until almost noon, when we reach a narrow track leading off the main road.

Erik pulls up his horse. "This is where we must start the climb to Rask's fortress. We can't make good time now—which is the reason I was hurrying us along earlier."

I rise up in my stirrups and rub the small of my back. "I won't complain about slowing down."

Erik grins. "Backside a little sore, is it?"

I huff. "That's not a proper question to pose to a lady."

He glances around. "Are there ladies present?"

"I can't throw anything at you right now, but just wait."

He kicks the gelding into a walk and directs it onto the path. "There you go, proving my point."

Although the path's barely wide enough to ride abreast, I urge my horse forward, until I'm close enough to bump thighs. "So, I know you're skeptical about lasting love, but do you have a sweetheart, Erik Stahl?"

"Not at the moment."

"I am not surprised." I slow my mare and fall in behind the gray gelding.

Erik quickly silences his laughter, which rings too brightly through the thick forest flanking the path.

We ride on, the chirp of birds and rustle of unseen small creatures the only sounds breaking the silence. Hardwood trees give way to pines with branches drooping over the narrow track, their green needles darkening to black as I peer deeper into the forest. I rub my right arm with my left hand, smoothing down the raised hairs.

Erik stops short in front of me. "We must ditch the horses. The path grows rocky and I don't want to risk broken legs. They can wait here for our return." He dismounts, pulling his reins over the gelding's lowered head. "Drop your reins on the ground. They appear to be trained to stay, as if tied to a post."

"Useful." As I swing my body out of the saddle, Erik moves beside my horse and helps lift me to the ground.

He keeps his hands on the small of my back for a moment, so I stand in the circle of his arms. "I'm afraid you must climb the final portion of the path alone. We can't allow Rask to sense my presence. I hope he will be so focused on you he'll not notice me sneaking through the forest."

I look up into his face. His jaw is clenched. "I will do my best."

"I know." Erik releases me and steps back. His gaze remains fixed on my face. "Think about Gerda and Anders, and how we can get them out of there. Focus on the task and don't allow Rask to get inside your head."

I'm not sure this is possible, but don't want to admit my fears to Erik. Our relationship has changed, and I'm reluctant to do anything that might make him think less of me.

My fingers clutch the skirt fabric I retie about my waist.

Friends. You are friends, Varna. Nothing more.

Still, "friends" is good. I've never had a male friend before. I like it.

The track ahead of me is steep and riddled with rocks. "Keep following this path?"

"Yes. Kai noticed it before, although we approached the fortress through the woods."

"Which is what you plan to do now."

"Yes." Erik's pistol weighs down one of his coat pockets.

"I see you have your gun. Do you also have the vial Sephia gave you?"

He pats his other pocket. "Right here."

"And you recall its effect only lasts for an hour or so?"

"Yes, Mistress Lund, I do." He grins. "I may not be as smart as Kai, but I can remember basic instructions."

I fight back an answering smile. "I don't want you to get caught."

He leans in to kiss me on the forehead. "Stay safe."

Before I can reply, he turns and walks into the shadowy trees.

I take a deep breath. It's time for me to take the path that leads to Gerda and Anders.

And Sten Rask. I hitch up my bundled skirts and step forward.

The path grows steadily rougher, forcing me to bend forward and grab rock outcroppings to aid in my climb. By the time I reach a plateau where the narrow track widens into something resembling a road, my fingers are cross-hatched with scratches and my hair has tumbled out of its hastily fastened bun.

I stand on a dirt road, rutted from the wheels of some carriage. How a carriage traversed the path to reach this point eludes me, until I recall Gerda's tales of flying horses and reindeer. Rask probably employs the same enchantment.

I straighten and push my lank hair behind my ears. On either side of the road, majestic oaks rise like wooden sentinels. Or perhaps they are giants—their bodies buried beneath a shell of wood. Anything is possible, with so much magic at work.

I draw my gray cloak tighter about my shoulders. Strange, despite its lightness, it blocked the heat of the sun when I was on the main road, yet also warms me in this dank forest.

Silly, it is magic. Like the power crackling through these woods. You feel it, swirling around you, like a swarm of bees.

It does not matter. Whatever happens, I must persevere. I straighten my back and walk, focusing my thoughts on Gerda.

When I round a corner, I see the house. It's just as Erik and Kai described—a great, stone pile that rises from the forest as if it's grown from the earth.

And who says it was constructed by human hands? I shiver, lapping the edges of my cloak one over the other.

A tall stone wall surrounds the main building—an impenetrable expanse punctured at the front by a set of massive iron gates. On the other sides, scraggly pines cluster close to the walls like vagrants seeking shelter. The road ends at the gates, in a circle only wide enough to turn one carriage.

I move closer and stand before the gates, peering into an empty, packed-dirt courtyard.

The manor house is a three-story central building, with one-story wings stretching forward from each side. No embellishments decorate the façade of the main structure—its windows are small and blank as the eyes of beetles.

There are bars on the windows on the third floor.

I curl my fingers around a section of iron filigree—a strangely fanciful design of entwined vines and flowers, with the silhouette of a peacock emblazoned in the center of each gate.

Pressing my forehead against the cold metal, I send a mental message to Sten Rask. *I am here. As you wished. Will you let me in?*

Nothing happens. I open my eyes as a rustle disturbs the woods to my right.

Erik creeps from the trees, hugging the wall as he makes his way to me.

"You haven't taken the potion?" I whisper when he's close enough to hear me.

"I'm saving it. Might need it later." Erik presses his back against the wall. "No sign of Rask?"

"No. What do you mean, saving it? Thought you planned to sneak in behind me, if Rask ever opens these gates."

Erik flashes a devilish grin. "I didn't spend hours wandering the city, escaping chores, without picking up a few skills. I can get in without magic, and no one will notice, trust me. We'll save the potion for a more difficult maneuver."

"What? You can climb these walls?"

"No, but I can climb trees, and there are plenty overhanging the courtyard. You stay here and catch Rask's notice, and I'll shimmy up a pine and be inside the walls before you."

I frown. "What if Rask's minions catch you? He must have servants or something."

"Do you see any? No, me either. I think he conjures them when he needs them. Don't worry. I know what I'm doing." Erik raises his hand in a mock salute. "Now, go forth with honor, and spare no thought for me. Sorry, old company saying. First time it's really felt appropriate."

"Be careful," I say, as he slides away from me. He disappears into the trees with only a slight rustle of the undergrowth.

I step away from the gate and stare at the upper level of the facade. Somewhere, behind those barred windows, Gerda and Anders await rescue.

As I scan the windows for any flash of movement, the iron gates before me creak. I take two steps back. The long metal bars latching the gates slide and clang against the frame. The gates swing inward, sweeping dust and piles of dried pine needles into the courtyard.

I spin around at the sound of hooves. Barreling down the road, an ebony coach pulled by two black horses approaches the open gates. No one sits in the high seat—the horses appear to be driving themselves.

I scramble to the edge of the circle. The coach, its dark shades drawn, slows as it enters the circle. It makes one complete turn before stopping close to me.

One shade rolls up. Leaning out the open window, Sten Rask meets my open-mouthed stare with a smile.

"Welcome, Varna." He unlatches the coach door and steps out.

Despite my fear, I marvel at the beauty of his appearance. The collar of his black greatcoat is turned up to frame his elegant jawline. Dark hair spills over his broad forehead, hiding his fine brows, and fawn-colored trousers are tucked into his gleaming black leather boots. A white cravat froths over the neckline of his coat.

He's tucked the scepter under his left arm. It could be mistaken for a walking stick, and probably is, by most observers. I spy the fire flickering in its crystal finial and narrow my eyes.

All those people at the Opera House, dead or damaged, because Sten Rask wanted to capture Gerda. To use her to track down the mirror.

And to draw you here, Varna.

All that suffering, to satisfy one man's whims. My fingernails dig into the palms of my clenched fists.

Rask sweeps one hand through the air and the black horses jangle their harnesses before pulling the coach through the open gates and into the courtyard.

Pulling off a leather glove, he holds out one hand. "Come, my dear. It is time you visited one of my real homes. It's rather more elegant than Madame Margaret's cottage."

"I love the cottage." So stupid, so pathetic, but it's all I can think to say.

"I know. But it's time to expand your horizons, Varna Lund."

Rask crooks his fingers, and I walk forward, as if pulled by some invisible thread.

When I reach him, he takes hold of my right hand and tucks it inside the bend of his elbow. He leads me through the gates, which close behind us with a clang that vibrates the still air.

The horses stand quietly beside one of the low wings of the house, where an arched colonnade separates the barren courtyard from the stables. Rask snaps his fingers and the silver buckles of the harness spring open. The horses step free of the wooden shafts and leather straps and make their way into two stalls whose open half-doors slam shut behind them.

"You don't have servants?"

Sten Rask tightens his grip without slowing our march to his front doors. "Magic is my servant."

I gaze up at the blank, cold, face of his home. "So you live here alone?"

"For now. Although, as you know, I am entertaining a few guests at the moment."

"Yes, that." I plant my feet, the toes of my boots pressed into the final riser as the wooden doors open before us. I see nothing inside except a stretch of stone flooring and shadows. "I will enter on one condition. You must release Gerda and Anders immediately."

Rask's laugh rips through the quiet like the roar of some great beast. "Oh, Varna," he says at last, yanking me through the doors and into the front hall, "what fun we shall have, you and I, once I transform you into everything you should be."

CHAPTER EIGHTEEN: CHOICES

S THE DOORS SLAM BEHIND us, Rask releases my arm. He steps away to lay his coat and the scepter on an ornately carved wooden chair—the only object pressed against the stone block walls.

The hall extends the entire width of the house, ending in a row of tall, arched windows set into the back wall. Although pieced and leaded like stained glass, the windows are devoid of color.

Except for the windows and the one chair, the only object of interest in the room is a curving mahogany staircase. It's a marvel—spiraling upward to landings on the second and third floors without any obvious central support. I stare at it, trying to imagine how anyone could build such a structure, and how it could hang there without crashing to the stone floor below.

"Craftsmanship, not magic," Rask says, as if reading my thoughts. "It is amazing what can be accomplished by someone who possesses enough skill and determination."

He crosses back to me and takes my chin in his hand, forcing me to look into his eyes. "It's what I see in you, Varna. Something magic cannot supply."

I can't allow his gaze to enchant me. "You just said 'transform'. What do you mean?"

"Why, give you beauty to match your spirit, of course." He turns my face to one side and studies my profile. "Personally, I see no need, but

I know how this world judges appearance. So many people cling to a narrow definition of beauty."

I force myself to remain still. Gerda is here somewhere. I must do whatever I can to engage Rask and focus his attention on me. I need to give Erik and the others time to escape. "You mean you'll create an illusion of beauty."

"Not at all." Rask releases my chin and steps back, his gaze sweeping from my head to my toes. "The magic I work will change your appearance, not simply gift you with glamour to fool others' eyes."

"Why?" This is the question I need answered, regardless of Gerda's fate or anything else. The one thing I cannot understand. I reach out and grasp one of Rask's fine-boned hands. "Why me? There are many beautiful women in the world. No need to use magic to create another."

Sten Rask stares at my fingers, curled about his own. His dark eyes widen, as if he's thrown off-guard by my action. "Because, my dear"— he pulls me closer, using our clasped hands—"it does not require a great deal of magic to change outward appearance. Oh, it's not an easy process, I grant you. There is some pain involved. Still, it is child's play compared to altering someone's basic nature." He uses his free hand to tip up my chin before he leans in, his lips only inches from mine. "I can give you beauty and power. I cannot give a beautiful woman your intelligence or your innate passion. No magic can do that."

I hate myself—my desire to kiss those lips, to press against that body, to allow Sten Rask's seductive voice to enchant me. Beauty and power. It is my dream.

But ... The screams of those trapped by smoke and fire, a young man flinging himself to his death, my sister and Anders carried off by a frightful, unnatural creature ... I turn my head. "I need to see Gerda. To know she's all right. I want your promise to free her and Anders Nygaard if I agree to stay here with you."

Rask takes hold of my shoulders. "And I need the location of the mirror. So if you can convince your sister to tell me that, we can broker a deal." He pulls me close and brushes his lips against my skin, tracing a line from my temple to one ear. "A deal that will benefit you, my dear, more than anyone. The beauty you desire. The power you crave."

I sigh and sink into his embrace, allowing his mouth to slide to my lips. Heat surges through my body as he kisses me. I feel as if I'm suspended in some light-drenched pool, weightless and warm, my skin tingling. Light blossoming into fire.

A crash resonates through the hall. I trace the source of the sound to the third floor, and all pleasure evaporates from my body.

Rask's grip tightens until pain shoots through my shoulders. He lifts his head. "There is someone else here. What have you done? Brought along a bodyguard?"

Erik. I try to still my mind, to block all thought of him, but I'm too late. Rask drags me along the main hall and thrusts me into one of the rooms, slamming the door behind him.

I don't move. Nothing will improve this situation.

You have failed, Varna. You couldn't keep his attention, could not protect Erik, or Gerda or Anders.

I swallow a sob. I might be beaten, but I will not give Sten Rask the satisfaction of seeing me cry.

As I await the inevitable, a glimmer of gold catches my eye. I glance around the darkened room. Shadows fill the space—a jumble of objects piled like boxes in a storeroom. As if drawn by a magical cord, I walk to the window and throw back the heavy damask drapes.

The room bursts into life, a riot of shapes and color. I circle the furniture in a daze. It's like a dragon's hoard—beautiful objects are stacked on antique tables and chairs, while paintings line the walls. Everything is of the finest workmanship, from the silver tea set balanced on top of a hand-painted cupboard, to the perfectly detailed carving of feathers on a sculpted marble owl.

My gaze lingers on a portrait of a woman. Although she is clothed in garments from long ago, there's nothing antiquated about her face. It is vibrant and alive, her wide dark eyes fringed with impossibly thick lashes, and her full lips barely parted as if she's about to speak. Her hair, dark and glossy as a raven's wing, falls like a shimmering veil behind her pale shoulders.

I wonder who she is, or was. The painted arches framing her lovely face and figure resemble ancient buildings, and her clothing matches the sculpted images of saints. But, unlike those chaste depictions, this woman's robes outline her figure in a sensuous fashion. My eye is drawn to her hand, where tapered fingers curl about the handle of an exotic feather fan.

Peacock feathers. I recall the emblem on Rask's front gates and squint as I examine the portrait's mesmerizing eyes. "I wonder if she was truly that beautiful," I say aloud, "or if the painter flattered her."

"She is that beautiful," says Sten Rask from the doorway.

He stares at the painting. His face is as cold as a stone carving, although a blue flame dances in his dark eyes.

It's someone he knows. But who? I can't spare further thought for this puzzle, because Gerda and Anders are standing on either side of the sorcerer, his hands gripping their shoulders. He shoves them into the room and turns sideways to allow Erik to walk past him. From his shuffling feet and blank expression, I suspect Erik is trapped by some spell.

Of course he is. Otherwise he would fight back, no matter how futile the effort.

I run to the door as Rask releases his hold on Gerda. She stumbles forward and falls into my waiting arms.

"Are you all right?" I ask repeatedly as Gerda buries her head in my shoulder and sobs.

Rask marches Anders to a gilt chair and forces him to sit. "She is fine. They all are, for now." He turns to Erik and snaps his fingers.

Erik's clouded eyes clear. He lunges at the sorcerer, fists raised.

I push Gerda aside, ready to step in if necessary. *Stop, Erik. No matter how strong you are, you cannot fight this man.*

"You truly thought you could sneak into my home?" Rask grabs Erik's arms and shakes him. "Foolish boy. I remember you from the fire, huddling with Varna and the others. You were utterly useless then as well." He lifts Erik by his arms and tosses him across the room.

Erik's head slams into a brass-bound wooden trunk with a sickening thud. I run to him, but before I can reach his side, Rask stands before me.

I did not see him move. I press my palms against his velvet waistcoat. "He may need my help."

"He is fine." Rask grips my hands. "Unfortunately, he won't stay that way, unless you do as I say."

I look up into his expressionless face. "Please release them. I will stay if you will free them."

"It's too late. You have aided in this deception. I see that now. Your pleading means nothing to me."

Gazing into his haunted eyes, I can tell this is a lie, but can't pursue that mystery now. I lower my head. "If you seek the mirror, we can't help, since none of us know where it is hidden."

"That's not precisely true." Rask releases my hands. "I've sensed something buried in Gerda's mind, but have not been able to extract the information." He meets my furious expression calmly. "I could use stronger magic, but unless it is willingly accepted, it might damage her mind. I prefer to avoid that possibility. I'm not inclined to torture innocents."

Erik jumps to his feet, green eyes blazing. "You had no trouble killing them in that fire."

"Christiane?" Anders glances from Erik to me. The skin under his eyes looks bruised.

"She is safe," I reply. "She was injured but is recovering."

"No thanks to you." Erik strides forward to face Sten Rask. He lowers the hand he's holding to the back of his head.

I spy blood on his palm. Anders also sees it, and pushes his body out of the chair. "Steady, Erik. Perhaps we should negotiate." He limps to stand at Erik's side.

Gerda runs to them, brandishing a handkerchief Erik plucks from her fingers and presses against his head.

Gerda stands between the two young men, her face flushed with anger. "You hurt him. Is that all you can do, hurt people?"

Rask strolls over to confront my defiant sister. "I do not enjoy harming others, little sparrow. However, I must do whatever it takes to recover the mirror. There are forces that compel me, in addition to my own desires. And I still believe you can help me, if you will."

Examining Gerda, I realize she's perfectly clean and wearing different garments than when she was captured. As is Anders. I look to Rask, whose lips curl into a smile.

I want to slap that smile off his face.

And kiss those lips.

No, Varna, that is not real. That is some enchantment. It must be.

I clutch the fabric of my skirt with both hands. "You don't have anything to tell, Gerda. I keep repeating the truth, and this man keeps ignoring me."

"I never ignore you, Varna. I simply know there's something buried in Gerda's mind that might prove beneficial to my quest."

"You have no rights to the mirror." Anders's voice rings out, perfectly steady, although he leans heavily on Erik's arm to remain on his feet.

Rask looks him up and down. "No one has *rights* to the mirror, Master Nygaard. But I will find it, with or without your friends. The question is, will Gerda aid me, and gain their freedom, or fight me, and condemn them to imprisonment. You see, if she helps, I promise to free Master Stahl, and even Gerda, eventually. As well as you, of course."

The muscles in Erik's neck bulge. "And Varna?"

Sten Rask's gaze sweeps over me. "I have other plans for Varna."

Erik lunges toward him, but Rask lifts his hand and Erik stops as if he's hit a wall. Gerda seizes the opportunity to fly at the sorcerer with her fingers outstretched like claws.

Rask grasps both of Gerda's wrists and lifts her off the ground "Calm down, little sparrow. I have no intention of harming Varna. Quite the opposite. I wish to help her." He sets Gerda back on her feet.

Anders releases Erik's arm and grabs a silver-tipped walking stick from a table at his elbow. He balances his weight with the cane and straightens, his head held high. "You? What could you do for her? Surely nothing good. None of us will allow you to lay a finger on Varna."

Rask looks him over, amusement sparking in his dark eyes. "I doubt you could stop me."

Erik steps up next to Anders. "You'd have to go through both of us."

Rask brushes a piece of lint off his waistcoat. "Not really a problem. At any rate, the question of Varna's future is not relevant to this discussion. It's also not your decision." He shoots me a piercing look. "What *is* important to me at this moment is the location of the mirror. If Gerda can provide me with information, everyone can have what they want." His gaze remains fixed on my face. "What they truly want."

Beauty and power, Varna. Is that not worth a little sacrifice?

I cover my ears with my hands, even though I know these words are ringing in my head, not falling from Rask's lips.

Gerda's shoulders slump. "Please stand back, Erik and Anders. I don't want more harm to come to you through this man." She stares up at Rask, her face set. "If I know anything, if you can discover it, I will allow you to try—but only if you agree to release Varna along with the rest of us."

Rask grabs her and pulls her to his chest. "Open your mind then, Gerda Lund." He presses his fingers against her temples. "Stop fighting and allow me to search your memory."

Gerda stills her body and closes her eyes, while Erik holds Anders back.

"Take your hands off her!" Anders struggles in Erik's grip. "He can't have the mirror, Erik. Imagine what evil such a devil could do!"

"We will deal with it later." Erik glances over at me. "Right now any action we take could harm Gerda. You don't want that."

I unclench my fingers, releasing their hold on the crumpled material of my skirt.

"A cave." Gerda's eyes close. Her voice is hollow as a shell. "Bae told me once. He pointed it out when we were traveling through the kingdom of the Snow Queen. He said if we were ever separated, I should try to reach the old man who lived there."

"Holger," I say under my breath.

"I didn't think much of it at the time," Gerda continues, in that ghostly tone. "My mind was focused on other things. I remember now— it was in the mountains that ring the Snow Queen's castle. Just above the cave there was a strange formation in the rocks, like a great bird with its wings outstretched. A giant bird … " She gasps and collapses in a heap on the wooden plank floor.

I run to kneel at her side, glaring at Rask. "No more. Keep your word and let us go. You have what you want."

"Not entirely." His eyes remain fixed on my face. "And I never promised anything. To be honest, I believe I should take Gerda with me to find this mysterious cave. Her memory may aid me, and I need a hostage to prevent you from doing anything foolish, such as alerting your friend Sephia to my plan. At least until it is too late."

"You are not going anywhere with Gerda!" Anders lifts the cane as if to swing it against the sorcerer's head. He's knocked back with one wave of Rask's hand and falls into the chair, breathing heavily.

Erik runs to his friend and kneels beside him.

I must draw the sorcerer's attention. "Take me, not Gerda," I say, as my sister yanks at my sleeve.

"No, no, I will go. I will go."

Rask stares down at the two of us, huddled on the floor. "Ah, the Lund sisters. So very brave. Perhaps I should keep both of you." He holds out his hand. "No, Gerda will do for now. But only because I know Varna will honor her vow later."

Out of the corner of my eye I see Erik pass something from his pocket into Anders's hand. Of course, the invisibility potion. Erik wants Anders to have it, in case …

In case Erik dies, trying to protect us. In case Anders must use it instead.

"I will. I always keep my promises," I say, locking onto Rask's gaze.

"What promise?" Gerda allows Rask to pull her up, as I struggle to my feet without aid. "What promise, Varna?"

Rask takes her by the arm and ushers her into the hall. "Master Stahl, please escort Varna," he calls over his shoulder.

Erik stands and shuffles over to me like a reanimated corpse. He clutches my arm and follows Rask and Gerda.

"Spell," he spits between clenched teeth. "Or I would shoot him."

"I know." I lay my fingers over his.

Gerda must jog to keep up with Rask's longer strides. "What of Anders?"

"I think we can leave Master Nygaard where he is. He cannot move quickly enough to do anything to stop us, so there's no need to waste magic on him." Rask waves his hand and the front doors swing open. "Don't worry, Gerda. I said I would free him and the others, and I will. Now—in the room across the hall you will find a fur cloak and some boots and mittens. Go and collect them. You'll need protection on our travels."

Gerda nods. As she disappears into the shadows of the other room, my mind spins wild scenarios of rescue.

What can you do, Varna? If Rask can control Erik so easily, he can surely circumvent any action you take.

I sigh, causing Rask to turn back to me and Erik.

"Kill you," Erik says, although the words seem to choke him.

"I've no doubt you would like to, but I'm not ready to die quite yet." Rask reaches into Erik's pocket and pulls out the gun. "Such a primitive weapon." He tosses the pistol to the foot of the spiral staircase.

Erik only manages a strangled cough in response. I don't look at him. I stare at Rask. "You must free Gerda as soon as you find the mirror."

"Well, perhaps not immediately." The sorcerer moves closer and takes my chin in his hand. Beside me, Erik's fingers tighten on my arm like a vise. "We'll be in an icy wilderness, after all. Still, in time I will deliver her back to you, Varna. I promise to transport her to

Sephia's doorstep, safe and sound." He leans in and kisses me, full on the lips, before stepping back. "And you will then honor your vow and come with me."

Erik's body, pressed to my side, vibrates with suppressed rage.

I lay my free hand over Erik's rigid fingers. "I'll keep my promise."

"Of course you will." Rask turns aside as Gerda reappears, her arms laden with furs and other winter garments. "Come." He strides to the front doors, pausing only long enough to snatch up his greatcoat and the scepter.

Forced by sorcery, Erik and I follow.

We step outside. The coach waits, the black horses harnessed by unseen hands.

I shudder. Rask glances back at me. "There is nothing to fear. Gerda will be perfectly safe. Although I must warn you, I travel in a most unusual way."

"Through the air?" Gerda's clear voice rings out. "That's not so unusual. I've done that before."

She walks past us, clutching the winter garments to her breast. Boots, hanging from their leather shoestrings, dangle from her fingers. With the furs bundled in her arms, she looks like a guinea hen, small and plump and entirely harmless. It's the fire in her eyes that betrays her. She pauses at the coach, waiting for Rask to open the door.

The black horses paw at the ground, their harnesses jangling. There is no driver. Apparently magic controls them.

Rask gestures grandly with one hand. "The rest of you will be free as soon as we depart."

He flings open the coach door. "We must hurry, Gerda. I've already given the command and even I cannot hold these horses back much longer." As he steps onto the footrest, an unseen force grabs him and pulls him inside. The door slams behind him.

The coach jerks forward.

Rask's roar of anger drowns out Erik's shouts and Gerda's cries.

"Anders!" Erik leaps at the coach, but it's rolled beyond his reach. The horses, as if chased by devils, make a circuit of the courtyard.

The tincture. Anders took it from Erik as if he meant to keep it safe, but all along, he planned to do something, anything, to help us.

He must have swallowed the potion, and once invisible, made his way outside without our knowledge. He walked past a sorcerer without a weapon, without even a cane or any other support. Dragging his damaged leg behind him. Driven by sheer will.

I glance at Gerda's stricken face. No—driven by love.

As the coach passes the steps again, Anders's disembodied voice sails out. "Gerda's not coming. I will be your hostage, Sten Rask. Either take me, or kill me."

"You promised to free him!" I shout, praying Rask will honor that vow.

The horses pull the coach through the open gates, their trot rolling into a gallop.

Gerda dashes after them. She only makes it to the gates before the horses soar into the sky, the coach sailing behind them like a dark flag.

I stare upwards until clouds obscure the magical sight. Erik says something about getting back to Sephia's cottage as soon as possible, but all I hear is Rask's voice echoing inside my head.

I will keep my promise, Varna. But in exchange you must fulfill your own vow. One day, and soon, you must come to me. Or no one you love will ever be safe again.

CHAPTER NINETEEN: OUT OF THE GARDEN

W E FLEE THE MANOR HOUSE and head for the horses, who wait down the trail. Erik attempts to navigate the steep hill at the end of the road on his feet, but Gerda and I just sit down and scoot. I figure we will end up on our backsides anyway. Erik proves my theory when he falls and rolls to the bottom of the hill.

After much swearing and dusting off, Erik places Gerda in front of him on the gray gelding, leaving me the dun mare. We ride without stopping, ignoring the change of day to night and back again. We push past hunger and weakness, sheer willpower driving us forward.

"The sooner we can inform Sephia, the better," Erik says, when Gerda stirs in his arms.

Gerda nods, her lips quivering. "I'm fine. Keep going."

I say nothing, despite Erik's piercing looks. I obsess over Rask's final demand, turning it over and over in my mind.

When we reach the cottage, Erik dismounts and locks his trembling legs before Gerda gives into exhaustion and tumbles into his arms.

Erik waits until Sephia rushes outside to take charge of Gerda before turning to me. "I'll help you down if you wish." He raises his shaking arms.

"Thanks, I can manage." I slide off the mare's back. As my boots hit the ground, my legs give way and I crumple.

"Such foolish pride." Erik kneels and hugs me to his chest for a moment before helping me to my feet.

I lean against him as we make our way into the cottage. "I'm sorry about Anders."

"I know." Erik pats my shoulder. "It wasn't your fault. It was his choice."

I straighten as we cross the threshold. "He made that sacrifice for Gerda."

"For all of us, I think."

Christiane runs in from the garden, her arms laden with lilies. She looks from Erik to me to Gerda. "Where is Anders?"

Erik tightens his grip on my arm. "With Rask. He sacrificed his freedom to save us."

Christiane blinks rapidly. "No, that cannot be." The glossy white flowers spill to the floor.

I hold out one hand. "Rask has promised to bring him back, after he locates the mirror."

"And you believe him?" Christiane slumps against the kitchen table. "The word of an evil sorcerer?"

"I believe it, but only because it's also the word of a man." I pull away from Erik and meet Christiane's stricken gaze. "He's kept his word before."

Sephia shoots me a sharp glance. "We can only hope. Christiane, please collect those flowers and place them on the table. I need your assistance arranging some sleeping quarters for our travelers. Pull some comforters from the wardrobe, please."

Erik shifts from one foot to the other. "Any word from Thyra and Kai?"

The enchantress shakes her head. "No, although I expect them back any day. Now, as for you three—time for some rest. No, do not argue. You look like you might fall asleep on your feet."

"I need to go after Rask, to rescue Anders." Erik slurs his words like a drunkard.

"Of course you do, and you will. But only after some sleep." Sephia guides Erik to the bed in the curtained alcove. "Take off those dusty clothes and boots and lay down," she commands, pulling the curtain behind him.

Sephia crosses to Gerda and me. "You two can share the quilts Christiane's arranging in the corner. Strip down—you can wash up later." She leads us to far side of the room, where the pile of comforters waits, soft and inviting.

I touch the back of Christiane's hand. "He'll come back. Rask will keep his promise."

She limps toward the kitchen without a word. Of course she doesn't believe it. Why should she?

Why do you, Varna?

"And if not, we'll go after him." Gerda slumps into the down-filled quilts. "I will, anyway. It was my fault. I shouldn't have allowed Anders take my place. I should have stopped him, somehow."

I remove my outer garments, mechanical as an automaton. Clothed only in a chemise and pantaloons, I fall into the mountain of comforters. "No, it was my fault." I yank a soft blanket up to my chin. "I should've gone with him. It's me he wants. Rask wants me."

"Does he?" Sephia kneels beside the makeshift bed. "What does he want with you, Varna?"

"I don't know." Exhaustion deprives me of the ability to make sense of anything.

Sephia presses the back of her hand against my cheek. "Be careful, my dear. Whatever it is, it could prove dangerous for you."

"Do not know," I mutter, before drifting into the blessed darkness.

When I wake, the light filtering through the curtains is tinged pink. It must be morning. I sit up and stretch my arms above my head.

"Welcome back," Sephia says.

I blink and look up into her lovely face. Her auburn hair falls forward as she bends over me. "Is it morning?"

"Yes, but it's the morning after the day you slept through." Sephia smiles and holds up her hand. "Hush, no need to feel ashamed. The others are still asleep. Except for Christiane, of course. She's gone for a walk in the woods. The trees seem to call to her these days."

I slip out of the pile of comforters, careful not to disturb Gerda. "I slept an entire day?"

"You needed the rest." Sephia helps me to my feet and hands me a silken robe the color of spring violets.

I slip on the robe and tighten the sash. "How is Christiane? I'm sure it was hard on her, expecting to see Anders and then discovering he's still in danger."

"She is fine. She's stronger than she appears." Sephia looks me over. "Walk with me in the garden, Varna. I believe we should talk."

I follow her out the back door. As we step into the luscious jumble of scents and colors, I stop and breathe deeply. "I will never get enough of this."

Sephia lays her slender fingers on my arm. "I know. I see how much you love it—how you desire to step away from the world and stay here, enclosed within these garden walls." She presses her nails into my skin, forcing me to look at her. "This is not your destiny, Varna Lund. I wish it could be, but I know in my heart you must walk a different path."

"Why?" I try, and fail, to silence the whine in my voice.

"I do not know. I only see it, or glimpse the shadow of it. I cannot see the future with perfect clarity. No one can. Each decision we make shifts the images."

I shake off her hand and walk deeper into the garden. Pausing in front of the herb bed, I touch one finger to the star-shaped flowers of a borage plant. "So you see me doing what? At least working as a healer, I hope."

Sephia appears at my elbow. "Your future is hidden in a mist. It's one reason I wanted to speak with you alone."

I turn on her. "To tell me to forget about being your apprentice, because you've already chosen Christiane?"

"I have not chosen Christiane. She's been sent to me by a greater power. But I do hope she'll elect to stay and become my pupil. She has a connection to growing things I have rarely seen. I do not believe she ever suspected this, living in the city. She started dance training at such a young age, and has been buried in rehearsal rooms and the artificial world of the ballet all her life."

"But she loves Anders. If he ... *when* he returns she will abandon you for him."

Sephia's red-gold eyebrows arch higher over her green eyes. "Will she? Christiane and I have spoken on this subject at some length, and she's admitted her love for Anders was as ephemeral as dew. Oh, she still cares for him—she just knows her feelings were tied up in pretty words and dancing and other baubles. It was nothing substantial. Now she seeks something real and true. Which is for the best, since I believe Christiane will realize, soon enough, who Anders loves."

"Gerda." I twist off one indigo flower from the borage and roll it between my thumb and forefinger. "But he's very loyal. He will not abandon Christiane, especially not now."

Sephia smiles. "Love has its ways. I cannot envision any future where Anders chooses another girl over Gerda. And Christiane will break their pledge before forcing him to give up his true love." Her smile fades. "We must bring him home safely first."

I stroll beneath an arbor blanketed in wisteria. "Can you see that?"

"Unfortunately, no. Perhaps because his fate is in the hands of another sorcerer."

I lean against the wooden frame of the arbor, allowing the heavy scent of the blossoms to fill my nostrils. "I hope Thyra and Kai won't encounter Rask. I don't want any harm to come to them. Or to Luki and Bae."

"They will be fine. Thyra Winther is a resourceful young woman, and Kai Thorsen is her equal in all ways." Sephia moves close to me and takes hold of my wrists. All the softness melts away, revealing a visage as terrifying as it is beautiful. "Varna, what has Sten Rask promised you?"

I stare into her eyes, now hard and glittering as gems. "He says he can give me beauty and power." I lift my chin. "I am not a fool, Sephia. I don't expect he means me any good. Nor do I necessarily believe him."

"I never said you were a fool." Sephia lays her hand on my rigid arm. "I simply know the lure of magic. It's difficult to resist, even for the wise."

I pluck a cluster of the wisteria blossoms dangling over my head. They look plump and solid as grapes, but the blossoms crush easily between my fingers. "It's not his offer of some mysterious transformation that will send me to him, Sephia. It is my own promise. When Gerda and Anders were caught in the fire, with no way to escape, I vowed I'd do anything he asked, if he would save them." I toss the crumpled flowers to the ground. "Somehow he heard me, and he did save them, even if it was by a kidnapping."

"He also probably started the fire."

"Yes, but … I made a vow. Perhaps it was foolish, but I was desperate."

"Of course." Sephia touches my cheek. "You did what you had to do, to save your sister and friend. No one can fault you."

I grab her hand as it falls away from my face. "So, must I fulfill this vow?"

The enchantress studies me for a moment. "Wait and see what your heart tells you. Besides, if Rask breaks his promise and harms Anders, you have no reason to comply. Varna"— Sephia squeezes my fingers— "I see something in your eyes. A deeper concern. What troubles you?"

I focus on the light filtering through the wisteria leaves. "It's nothing. Just—I don't understand why Sten Rask desires my return. Frankly, I can't imagine why he wants anything to do with me. I'm not beautiful or rich, and I hold no power. I'm sure there is a reason for his actions, but I cannot fathom it."

Sephia takes hold of my chin and turns my head until we are face to face. There's a sadness in her eyes I've never noticed before. "Varna, one thing you must understand—those gifted with magical power experience life differently than others do. I see something in you—a fire burning within your heart. It is likely Sten Rask has seen this as well. Why it interests him, I cannot say, but you must consider every possibility, no matter how illogical. Rask's reasons for desiring your company may have nothing to do with his quest for the mirror. Sorcerers possess powers that remove them from normal life, yet at their core they are still human. Never forget that."

I toy with the sash of my robe, wrapping it around my hand. "I'll try not to."

"Good. Because you must never assume we're above human frailty." Sephia's face softens, until she looks like a lovely woman again. "Someday I must tell you the story of a young enchantress and the boy she loved far too much. For now, trust your instincts, Varna. Do not allow magic, or desire, or even love, to blind you to the truth." She places her arm around my shoulders. "Come, let us join the others."

She pulls me from the shade of the arbor. I blink and allow my gaze to wander as we walk to the back door. The morning sun outlines every stem and leaf with light.

I *do* want to stay here. There is nothing I want more, not even the possibility of beauty and power Rask dangles before me. But I know, as we cross the threshold and enter the cottage, I can only visit, never live here.

It's a paradise, but not mine. And I don't even know what sin I've committed to be cast from this garden.

Two days pass quietly. I help Sephia and Christiane in the garden, while Gerda spends most of her time in the kitchen, whipping up batches of bread and other items to stock Sephia's pantry.

Dissuaded from chasing Rask by Sephia's warnings—and, I suspect, a touch of her magic—Erik swims in the river or hikes the forest trails. He returns one day with another pistol. "I traded the rose brooch for it," he tells me. "Some fellow wanted a trinket for his sweetheart more than his gun." Frown lines crease his forehead as he examines the flintlock. "I can't say that's a bad trade."

In the evening, bathed in flickering candlelight, the five of us talk about many things, although never about Anders, even though I suspect he's at the forefront of our minds.

On the third afternoon, Christiane's shrieks of joy draw us to the clearing. She'd volunteered to hang some damp clothes, but when I reach the front steps and trip over the laundry basket I know something else has captured her attention.

Stumbling forward, I fall to my knees, scattering a pile of dried pine needles. A cool nose bumps my arm and I look up into the golden eyes of a wolf.

"Luki!" I drop back, sitting on the ground, and gaze at the cluster of animals and people before me. Luki nuzzles my arm once before bounding back to join the others.

Freya side-steps gracefully in reaction to my shout. On her back sit Thyra and Kai, fur coats draped over their laps.

Sephia steps out from the garden's back gate, wiping her earth-stained hands on her white apron.

Beside Freya, Bae's liquid brown eyes are shadowed under lowered eyelids. Christiane stands by his drooping head, looking up.

There is someone on his back.

"Anders!" Gerda dashes past as Erik helps me to my feet.

"He is alive, he's back." I pat Erik's wrist repeatedly.

He curls his hand back and grabs my fingers. "Yes. Thank God. Yes." He squeezes my fingers, then releases his grip and jogs forward. "Stand back," he tells Gerda and Christiane, before reaching up to help Anders down. Erik keeps his arm about the slighter man, holding him steady, while the two girls flit about him.

Thyra and Kai dismount. Kai stays at Freya's head, holding onto her bridle, as Thyra crosses the clearing to stand before Sephia.

"We failed." Her gray eyes are clouded with regret. "I'm so sorry, Sephia, but we were too late. Holger is dead and Sten Rask has the mirror."

CHAPTER TWENTY: VOWS

S EPHIA USHERS US INTO THE cottage—all except Kai, who volunteers to look after Freya and Bae. Luki stays glued to Thyra's side, lying next to her when she takes a seat on the rag rug, her back to the flower-filled fireplace.

Sephia instructs Erik to seat Anders in the armchair. "Now, tell me what happened," she commands, as she pulls up a stool by the hearth.

Leaving Christiane and Gerda to fuss over Anders, Erik crosses to the settee and sits beside me. "Yes, I'm confused. You had such a head start. How did Rask beat you to the mirror?"

"I can answer that." Anders sits up straighter. "You know about flying reindeer and such. Well, Rask's horses appear charged with the same magic. As you saw, they require no driver, and we didn't just sail through the air at a normal gallop, we moved so fast, everything outside the coach was a blur. I couldn't tell where we were, but I did spy wings and knew Rask's horrible creature—the enormous bird that snatched Gerda and me—was keeping pace with us."

Sephia and Thyra share a worried glance.

"Rask left you there?"

Erik side-eyes me. The cheery tone of my voice must confuse him, but I don't care. With Anders safe, the fact that Sten Rask reneged on his vow may free me from mine.

"Not exactly," Anders says, making the knot under my ribcage twist again. Christiane places one hand on his shoulder. He sits forward, breaking contact with her.

Thyra shifts to allow Luki to lay his head across her knees. "When we arrived, Anders was insensible. He lay behind Holger, who was still sitting up, although his eyes were closed and no breath stirred his ribcage." She absently strokes Luki's head, her eyes focused on Sephia. "I'm sorry. I know he was your friend."

"He was a great man. A mighty sorcerer, although he rarely used his gifts." Sephia rises to her feet and leans against the stone fireplace, one hand gripping the plain wooden mantle.

Anders lowers his head. "He sacrificed himself to protect me. As soon as we arrived at the cave, Rask demanded the mirror. Holger just laughed and said something about being careful what you wish for. Rask pointed his scepter at Holger. I guessed what that could mean. I tried to jump in front of the old man, but he pushed back and took the blast from the scepter without flinching. He was not burned." Anders looks up, meeting Sephia's stoic gaze. "It was as if the fire could not touch him. But it must have drained him somehow, fighting Rask's power. He held out as long as he could, then slumped forward."

"He was very old." Sephia's voice is as brittle as dead leaves.

Luki, dreaming in his sleep, whimpers. Thyra leans in and speaks some unintelligible words into his twitching ear.

"After Holger collapsed, Rask used his scepter to levitate the mirror out of the cave. I imagine he had that great bird of his carry it off."

"Sten Rask was supposed to return you here." I curse the tremor in my voice. "Why did he leave you?"

Anders sinks back into the chair. "He couldn't get to me. The protective wall Holger created held. Rask could not shatter it, although he tried. He was very angry, and kept muttering something about a promise. He had to leave me, in the end."

"Oh, you must have been terrified! Thinking you were going to die, all alone." Christiane's bright face loses some of its luster, and I remember she also recently faced death.

"No, I was resigned at that point. I've received a couple of reprieves from death recently." Anders's gaze sweeps over Thyra, Erik, and me before coming to rest on Gerda's face. "I felt the extra time I was given was perhaps enough—just enough for me."

It's all unfolding as Sephia predicted. Gerda and Anders will soon declare their love and Christiane will stay here and I ... I must go to Rask.

I feel a tiny thrill of anticipation, like a moth fluttering its wings, deep within my heart. There's something in me that wants to go. And that is the most terrifying feeling of all.

I sniff back a sob. Erik turns to look at me, his eyebrows knitted together.

Before he can question me, Kai enters the cottage, pausing by the door to yank off his boots. "Freya and Bae are cooled down, fed and watered."

"Thanks, my love." Thyra pats the rug. "Come sit with me and rest."

As Kai settles beside Thyra, Luki stretches out a paw to touch Kai's leg.

"Comfortable?" Kai pats Luki's head, and the wolf opens one golden eye and looks at him expectantly. "I know, I know—ear skritch."

Erik stares at Thyra. "So how did you break through the protective wall around Anders? I thought you gave up your magic."

Thyra meets Erik's gaze with an icy glare. "I did. No magic was required. We found Anders lying on the floor of the cave, with nothing surrounding him."

"It had faded by then," Kai says.

Erik crosses his arms over his chest. "Just seems convenient."

Anders shoots a warning glance at Erik. "Please don't doubt Thyra. She took good care of me on our return trip. She kept me warm, but only with furs and blankets. No magic was involved."

"I'll take your word for it."

Erik jerks as I jab him in the ribs. "What was that for?" he asks, rubbing his side.

"Being a total ass."

"I'm just sick of all this magic stuff."

"We are all sick of it." Anders glances over at Sephia. "I mean, the evil kind. Not the good kind."

Sephia smiles. "I think Erik is tired of it all, good and bad alike. It does tend to complicate things."

"Thank you." Erik stretches out his long legs. "I'm glad someone actually understands."

Thigh muscles ripple under the tight cling of Erik's breeches. I purse my lips and look away.

You are the ass, Varna. Those thoughts in your head—no lady thinks like that. Especially about a friend. I shift my position on the settee until no part of my body touches Erik.

Focusing straight ahead, I catch Kai leaning in to kiss Thyra's cheek. I close my eyes.

Kisses … I now know how kisses feel. Fire on my lips. An image of Sten Rask's handsome face flashes through my mind.

My eyes fly open and I leap to my feet. "Does anyone want tea?"

Six pairs of eyes focus on me, while Luki sits up, ears pitched forward, poised to confront danger.

"Tea would be nice." Sephia casts me an inquisitive look as she heads for the kitchen.

Kai stands and helps Thyra to her feet. He keeps his arm about her as they walk to the center of the room. "Champagne would be better."

Sephia turns slowly to face them, her hands on her hips. "So what's this then? Do you have something you wish to say, Kai Thorsen?"

Thyra lifts her sharp chin, her haughty expression at odds with the smile tugging the corners of her mouth. "Well, in light of the possibility our world might end, courtesy of Rask and the mirror, Kai and I decided we should, perhaps, get married."

Gerda's squeals are almost drowned out by the babble of congratulations. Almost. Brimming with excitement, she rushes to hug Kai and Thyra, then dashes to Anders, who has risen to his feet.

Gerda throws her arms around Anders and hugs him tight. "It's the most wonderful thing, don't you think? Love is the best magic of all!"

Christiane catches Sephia's eye and smiles wistfully. It's true, then. She has already given him up.

"Very nice." Anders stares into Gerda's joyous face for a second before kissing her full on the lips.

"Very nice indeed." Erik stands and moves to my side. He tips his head toward Gerda and Anders, who remain locked in a close embrace.

Thyra places her arm around Kai's waist and presses closer to him. Her eyes sparkle like crystal. "Perhaps we should plan a double wedding?"

I glance at Christiane, who has backed away to stand behind the kitchen table. She knows. Nothing will stop her from accepting Sephia's offer now.

If Gerda's happy, isn't that enough? I turn my gaze back to the kissing couple.

"I've heard of stealing thunder, but this is ridiculous." Kai's eyes are filled with merriment.

"Stop staring, Kai." Thyra uses her forefinger to tip down his chin until he looks at her. "Anyway, Sephia, we would like to be married here, and soon."

"Tomorrow, if possible." Kai taps Thyra on the nose. "We dare not make Thyra wait any longer. You can see how desperate she is."

"Hah!" Thyra leans back but Kai places his hand behind her head and pulls her in for a kiss.

Erik shuffles his feet. "This is all very well, but we must also come up with a plan to stop Rask."

"We will. After the wedding." Sephia hugs Christiane before crossing to Kai and Thyra. "I know a priest who owes me a favor, so I think I can arrange things for tomorrow. If you're sure." She taps Kai on the shoulder.

He waves her aside and continues kissing Thyra.

"Good lord," Erik says. "Does no one need to breathe?"

I can't help it—I laugh.

Erik looks down at me. "Speaking of which, why did Sten Rask kiss you in that passionate fashion?"

I instantly sober up. "He was trying to manipulate me, nothing more."

Erik's eyebrows lift. "Kissing can do that? Perhaps you shouldn't share such information too widely, Varna."

"Not a problem," I say, before I stalk off.

Gerda and Anders finally come to their senses and walk, arm in arm, to join Thyra and Kai in a discussion about the wedding. Christiane slips by me as I fill the kettle with water from the pitcher. "Going to the garden," she murmurs, and I nod. I can't really blame her. She may have gained a vocation, but she has lost her dance career and first love.

What have you lost, Varna? Without gaining anything, it seems.

I bang the kettle onto the top of the cook stove.

Erik appears at my elbow. "I am happy for Gerda and Anders, but we can't forget our mission. We must either take back the mirror, or destroy it."

I glance over at the cluster of happy faces. "Of course. But first, as Sephia says, there should be a wedding." I look up into his eyes. "What's the point of saving the world if there's no joy left in it?"

The shadow of a smile crosses Erik's face. "I will say one thing—you have a talent for making me see things differently. How do you do that, Varna Lund?"

I concentrate on packing herbs into the silver acorn tea ball. "I speak the truth, Erik Stahl."

He presses his palm against my shoulder blade. "Well, keep doing it. I need more friends who do that."

Friends. It's not just my imagination. He said it.

"Oh, you can count on that." I toss my head as if this means nothing, allowing the steam rising from the kettle to mist my face and hide my single tear of joy.

The next day flies by in a flurry of preparations. With Bae pulling a cart Sephia produces seemingly from midair, Erik and Anders are sent to fetch the priest. Christiane and I help Gerda make food. "For a feast!" Sephia says, although there're only a handful of us.

The priest, poor man, spends most of the day sitting in the front clearing, watched over by Bae and Freya. He's an odd choice for an officiant—wizened as a dried apple and wearing robes frayed at the hem. His surplice, although elegantly embroidered, is faded and fuzzy with loose threads. I'm certain he does not understand why he's been transported to a cottage in the woods to perform a ceremony for people he's never met before.

"Where is the deceased?" he asks, when Erik settles him into one of the wooden chairs pulled from the kitchen.

"It is a wedding," Gerda shouts in his ear.

He nods and flips through his prayer book, changing the location of his tarnished silver bookmark.

"Are you certain this is legal?" Kai asks Sephia, who just laughs and pats his shoulder.

"I have the certificate." Erik holds up a thick piece of paper, embossed on one side with the seal of the neighboring town. "That's all you really need, plus the blessing of the minister, of course."

"We'll have to file it somewhere, I guess." Thyra stares at the priest. "He does know we aren't part of his congregation, or even his denomination, I hope?"

"Oh, he no longer has a church. It's been many years since he did anything but putter around the monastery gardens. Don't fret—he will marry you as well as anyone, and without asking too many questions." Sephia levels her brilliant gaze on Thyra. "We do not want too many questions, now do we?"

Thyra shrugs. "I guess not."

"What did you do for him anyway, that he owes you a favor?" Erik asks.

Sephia smiles. "Together we saved a child condemned to death as a witch, although it was I who provided the miracle. He is a good man. One of the few truly good men I've ever known. He tried desperately to save the child, and failed, until I made the dead staff in his hand burst into bloom. He told the authorities it was a message from God, but he always knew who granted that blessing." Sephia gazes at the old man with affection. "Not to say God didn't have a hand in sending him to me."

Erik examines the old priest, who mumbles some prayer. "What happened to the girl you rescued?"

"She became a healer." Sephia glances at me. "Margaret—that was her name. I believe she lived for many years and saved countless lives."

I snap my mouth shut and nod.

By mid-afternoon, Sephia insists we bathe and prepare ourselves for the ceremony. She sends the young men to the river, with instructions to dress in the clothes she gives them, then wait in the clearing with the priest until she calls. The girls take turns washing up in an elegant porcelain tub set behind a screen of lilacs, before Sephia shoos us into the cottage.

She disappears into the garden. "Don't come out until I give the word."

Gerda and I dress in the hyacinth blue and sunflower yellow gowns Sephia gave us before, aired out now from their travels. Christiane uncovers a similar gown, pink as a summer sunrise, in the magical wardrobe.

Sephia's provided a special bundle of clothing for Thyra. Gerda lifts the gown from the soft folds of its lace petticoat. It's the silver-tinged white of moonflowers. The elegant but simple cut fits Thyra perfectly, clinging to her slender figure and cascading in soft folds to the floor. Long, tapered sleeves open at the wrists in a waterfall of fabric beaded with tiny seed pearls. The bodice is also covered in opalescent pearls. I recognize the pattern as Sephia's emblematic vines and flowers, now rendered in shades of white, like snow drifted over a blooming garden.

There are satin slippers, and a crown of white roses. Gerda and I help Thyra arrange her pale hair—pulling it up with pearl-encrusted hairpins while allowing a few curls to spring free and frame her face. When we place the crown of roses on her head, Christiane claps her hands.

"You look like a queen!"

Thyra's smile transforms her angular face into a beauty so bright I blink.

Sephia appears at the back door to usher us into the garden. "Come," she says. "I have worked a little magic to match this day."

When I step into the garden I gasp. Each petal and leaf is touched with drops of water—tiny liquid pearls that sparkle like diamonds. The entire garden glows and reflects the light, as if everything has been turned to crystal.

Christiane, her cheeks blushed pink as her dress, follows Sephia, who somehow has changed into a pale green gown with a bodice embroidered in emerald green vines and vivid violet blossoms. Gerda and I follow Christiane, our slippers making no sound on the soft paths. When we reach the wisteria arbor, Sephia opens the back gate and calls for the men.

The priest wanders in, still looking befuddled. Sephia slips her arm into the crook of his elbow and leads him to one side.

Anders and Erik stride in, both dressed in fawn-colored breeches and crisp white shirts, their tall leather boots gleaming like mirrors. Anders sports an embroidered waistcoat worked in the colors of autumn leaves, while Erik's vest is as green as a summer forest.

Kai appears behind them, walking slowly, but with great deliberation. Like the others, he wears pale fawn breeches, a white shirt, and dark brown boots, but his waistcoat sets him apart. It features an intricate pattern of swirls and geometric forms, picked out in colors as vivid and varied as Sephia's garden.

Luki trots at Kai's heels, his head held high.

The priest stares at the wolf and blinks. "I usually do not include dogs at such ceremonies."

Luki moves closer and licks his hand. The priest pats Luki's head, clears his throat, and opens to the place marked in his prayer book.

I take Gerda's hand, but she pays no attention to me. She gazes at Anders like a lost soul might look upon the gates to paradise.

He stares back, and it's clear he's also glimpsed his heaven.

Sephia guides the priest to the center of the arbor and motions for Kai to join them.

"It is beautiful," whispers Christiane. "If only we had some music."

At that moment, a light wind wafts through the garden. The lilies-of-the-valley swing back and forth, setting off a sound like chimes. It's as if all the blossoms dancing in the breeze are ringing.

A voice lifts, bright as a silver bell. Sephia sings a song as beautiful and pure as the clearest rippling brook, as sparkling as the first star at twilight, as rare as a double rainbow. It's a song whose words I do not understand, in a language I cannot fathom. But I know it's a song about love.

No, it *is* the song of love.

Thyra appears in the doorway and walks toward us, her head held high and her face lit from within.

Luki yips with excitement. Kai lays a hand on his back to calm him.

I stare at Kai and tighten my grip on Gerda's hand.

This is what love looks like, Varna. This is what it is. Not perfection. Not without flaws or problems. A commitment that can accept everything and rise above it. Wide as the sea and deep as the heart of a rose. Fragile as a snowflake, strong as the mountains.

I want this. No matter how impossible, this is what I want.

Gerda leans into me and I wrap my arm around her shoulders. "You are next," I whisper, and she blushes.

Sephia's glorious voice falls silent as Thyra takes Kai's hand. The priest, his rheumy eyes suddenly sparkling with life, reads the service. After they share vows, Erik produces two simple, but beautifully carved, wooden rings from his pocket.

So that's what he was doing late last night, when he disappeared from our company.

He hands the rings to Kai and Thyra. "For now."

"Forever." Thyra clasps Erik's hand and kisses his fingers.

After the exchange of rings, the priest raises his hand to bless them as husband and wife.

A swirl of white blossoms fills the air, drifting over their heads like snow, as Kai takes Thyra in his arms and kisses her.

When they break off their kiss, Erik sends up a "huzzah!" and Anders joins in. Gerda, Christiane, and I clap and stamp our feet. Luki circles Thyra and Kai, yipping and banging his nose into Kai's legs. Sephia leans in and kisses the priest on the cheek.

Kai and Thyra laugh and run down the garden path.

We gather in the cottage to eat the cakes and other treats laid out on the kitchen table. From some mysterious back shelf in the larder, Sephia produces bottles of champagne, already chilled, and we drink toasts until the words no longer make sense.

The priest snores in the armchair as Erik swings Christiane around the floor, lifting her up so her injured leg is no impediment. Sephia raises a crystal glass and taps it with a silver spoon.

"Now we send the happy couple off, to spend the evening in each other's arms." Her smile renders this announcement as pure as the pearls on Thyra's gown. "I have another cottage prepared for you, just down the forest path. Quite tiny, but big enough for two."

Kai's grin illuminates his face. "I thank you, my lady." He bows to her before turning to Thyra. "What do you think, my love? Are you ready to leave this company and spend the night with me?"

Thyra reaches up to stroke the side of his face. "I want nothing more."

He lifts her up in his arms and carries her out into the dark.

Luki attempts to follow, but Gerda lays a hand on his back, burying her fingers into the thick fur of his ruff. "Not tonight, my friend. Tonight they must be left alone. Tonight you stay with us."

The wolf whimpers and sits back on his haunches, gazing trustfully into Gerda's face.

"There is more champagne." Erik waves a bottle over his head. "It would be a shame to waste it."

"Nothing will be wasted tonight." Sephia sweeps into the kitchen and holds out her glass. "Tomorrow we must return to the fight, but tonight … Tonight is for joy."

CHAPTER TWENTY-ONE: INTO THE FIRE

W E MUST DO SOMETHING." ERIK paces the floor of the cottage, running his hands through his hair until it stands up in spikes. I sigh and settle back in the rocking chair. We've engaged in the same argument for three days.

"What can you do?" Christiane glances over her shoulder. She stands at the kitchen table, stripping leaves from a bundle of herbs. "Rask is a powerful sorcerer. None of us can fight against him."

"I would not say that, exactly." Sephia leans over Christiane's shoulder, pointing out something. Instructing her in the finer points of herbal concoctions, no doubt.

I sigh again. I've resigned myself to Christiane taking my place as Sephia's apprentice, but now … What am I to do? What am I to be?

"If we can track Rask to his current location, perhaps we can figure out something from there." Anders leans on the new cane Erik carved for him. This one boasts a simpler design—a finial of smooth wood, etched with a sunburst—but is still a fine piece of craftsmanship.

"I agree." Gerda places her hand under Anders's elbow, providing extra support.

Also touching him. Which she seems obsessed with lately. Not that he minds.

I study Christiane's narrow back, bent over the table, and marvel at the grace she displays over Anders's defection. I'd have pegged her as a brainless flirt, but she's actually nothing of the kind. Childlike, yes. Yet while she enjoys attention, she does not demand it, nor act sullen when it is withheld.

I read her wrong when I met her. I expected the worst, and kept trying to find it. *Something to remember, Varna. You may discover strength in the most unexpected places. You might even uncover a kernel of goodness in the darkest heart.*

"What if we were to track Rask and discover his whereabouts, but take no action?" I stand and cross to the center of the room. "Then we can alert Sephia, and see if she's able to confront him unawares." I step in front of Erik, forcing him to stop pacing. "Sephia said the only way to defeat such a sorcerer was by guile and surprise. If we can find him, tell her where he has hidden the mirror, perhaps she could do something?"

"That might work." Erik looks me up and down. "But only Anders and Kai and I need to go. You girls should stay here with Sephia."

I place my hands on my hips. "Excuse me?"

"There's no need to put you in danger." Erik takes a step forward, until we are close enough to touch, but he keeps his hands clasped behind his back.

"Nonsense," Gerda says.

Erik casts her a glare over his shoulder. "Now look, I'm not about to argue with both the Lund sisters. I simply state the obvious. There is no point to the women coming with us."

"Oh really?"

Thyra stands in the open doorway.

"Yes." Erik faces her, his mouth set in a tight line.

"So, you see no use for us, is that right, Erik Stahl?" Thyra stalks into the room, stopping a few feet from where Erik and I stand.

Kai follows her. He widens his eyes as he shakes his head at Erik.

Who pays no attention. "I see no point in putting you in danger. If this is a simple reconnaissance mission, we don't need everyone."

"You mean you do not want the women." Thyra moves closer and I step back to allow her to face-off with Erik.

"I want to protect you."

Thyra pokes a finger into his chest. "What if we don't desire your protection, Erik Stahl? What if you need our help for things like—oh,

I don't know—my ability to speak a few foreign languages, or Varna's healing skills?"

"You speak other languages?" asks Gerda.

Thyra tosses her head. "Yes. I learned more than mathematics on my travels. Now, Erik, I appreciate your concern, but I think it's misplaced. This mission could require all our talents, not just your brawn."

Erik throws up his hands. "I am not just …"

"My friend, give it up." Kai takes Thyra's arm. "We travel together, or not at all."

"Very well. But I must register my disapproval."

Sephia turns around. "So noted, Master Stahl. However, I approve Varna's plan. The six of you must work together to track down Sten Rask. Once you know his location, send me a message, and wait. I will remain here with Christiane until I receive word from you. That should prevent Rask from being alerted ahead of time."

Erik bends his head. "I bow to your command, my lady."

Sephia laughs. "I am not so high-born as all that. Still, I think this is the best plan. Something tells me you will all be needed to complete this task."

"How can we send you a message?" Anders asks.

"Thyra knows how to reach me." Sephia crosses to a cabinet and pulls out a small, glittering, object before walking over to Thyra and Kai. "Take this." She presses a silver whistle in Thyra's palm. "It will summon one of my messengers. You should recall them—falcons, trained to carry information in cylinders attached to their legs."

Thyra clenches her fingers about the whistle. "I will send you a message as soon as we determine Rask's location."

"But do nothing." Sephia closes her fingers over Thyra's fist. "Please allow me to confront him first."

Thyra nods. "Understood."

Kai pulls Thyra closer to his side. "Sephia, if you choose to destroy the mirror … "

Sephia lays her other hand on his shoulder. "I understand your concern, Kai. No one knows how the destruction of the mirror could affect Thyra. I think she is resolved, in any case."

"Yes," Thyra says, as Gerda rushes forward and jostles Sephia aside to face her.

"What do you mean?" Gerda focuses on the former Snow Queen.

Thyra smiles. "Only that the mirror, made whole, saved me. Made whole by you, my friend." She strokes the side of Gerda's face. "No one knows what smashing the mirror again may mean to me, but that doesn't matter now. What must be done, must be done. And I have known such joy since"—she lays her head on Kai's shoulder—"I think I can accept whatever fate has in store."

Kai kisses her temple. "Not me. I'm going to fight to save you, whatever it takes."

Thyra nestles closer to him. "I know you will. Still, we must never allow fear to rule our actions."

"Just remember the mirror is neither good nor evil," Sephia says. "Any harm it causes is due to the evil in the hearts of those who wield it."

Anders frowns. "I have seen the face of the man who hopes to wield it, and I'm afraid it could prove evil indeed."

Christiane turns and brandishes her paring knife like a sword. "If it's the sorcerer who started that fire, he is wicked beyond all hope."

"No one is beyond hope. I have seen … " Sephia's gaze rests on me, sharp as a sword and unearthly as mist, before she transforms her expression and smiles brightly at Thyra and Kai "I have seen many changed in ways no one would expect."

"So, we pack and prepare?" Erik asks.

Sephia taps his arm. "Yes. All of you."

He nods and heads for the front door. "I need to check on the horses."

Thyra and Kai join Anders and Gerda, who are collecting food from the pantry.

After the front door slams, Sephia tilts her head, and glances at me. "This is your charge. Anders and Gerda have one another, as do Thyra and Kai. Erik needs you to watch over him."

"But who watches over me?" I ask, my tone more plaintive than I intended.

Sephia's smile is as mysterious as the moon. "We all will, Varna. And, perhaps, you will discover your own strength is sufficient, in the end."

We depart at daybreak. Thyra rides Freya, while Erik and I ride the gray gelding and dun mare Sephia provided for us. Somehow, she is also able to whistle up additional horses for Kai and Anders. Gerda insists on riding Bae, who refuses to allow her to travel without him. Luki lopes along, ducking into the woods to follow us unseen whenever we encounter anyone else on the road.

We don't see many other travelers at first, but as we draw closer to the city a trickle of riders and carts turns into a steady stream of travelers. People of all ages appear, burdened under rucksacks and other bundles—walking as well as riding.

"Headed in the wrong direction," says one old woman, perched on the seat of brightly painted caravan. Her ancient horse, who looks more suited to pulling a plow, paws at the dirt as she tightens her hold on the reins. "Turn back now, if you have any sense."

Erik leans over his gelding's neck to talk to her. "What do you mean? Is there trouble ahead? Did something happen in the city?"

"Not the city." The old woman fiddles with the whip laid across her lap. Her clothing, an odd mix of colorful patterns, layered gold necklaces, and chunky leather boots, identifies her as someone who wanders from fair to festival, providing entertainment or selling trinkets. "City's fine, but out in the country, along the old River Road, there has been a mighty fierce fire, or so they tell me."

Erik straightens and casts a look back at the rest of us. "Fire?"

"In one of the villages. Everything burnt to a cinder. That is why this lot's taken to the road. I was already traveling—it's what I do—but this bunch, they look like refugees to me."

A small hand reaches out of the window of the caravan. "Are we stopping?" asks a childish voice steeped in an accent I cannot place.

"No. Get yourself back inside, missy, and close that curtain."

The hand disappears.

"Sorry, nothing worse than an ungrateful child, eh?" The old woman looks us over. "So where are the likes of you headed? All these young folks, without a chaperone." She makes a guttural noise of disapproval.

Gerda flashes one of her sweetest smiles. "Our chaperones are behind us. They're a bit slow."

The old woman cackles. "Or you have ridden fast to lose them. Yes, I can see the besotted looks on your faces. Having a little lovers' adventure, are you?"

Erik clears his throat. "Not exactly. Now, we must move on. Thank you for your information."

"You still headed that way?" The woman waves her whip in the direction of the city.

"Yes. Good day to you." Erik kicks his horse into a brisk trot, forcing the rest of us to keep pace.

"Good luck to you!" yells the old woman. "Never say Madame Skarkazy did not warn you!"

As we ride past the caravan, I peer at the window to see if I can spy the child inside, but I can't see past the dusty black curtains.

Pausing on the outskirts of the city, Anders suggests we take the River Road. "Just to check things out."

Erik's grim expression betrays his hesitation. "I suppose we must." He turns his horse onto the wider road.

I ride up beside Thyra. "Did we lose Luki?"

"No. He just likes to keep out of sight when we are close to civilization." Thyra casts me a quick smile. "Don't worry. He can track me anywhere."

We ride on, navigating through the river of travelers rolling in the opposite direction. Erik questions anyone who will talk to him, but we learn little more than the old woman told us.

"Fires, just like the Opera House," Anders says at one point.

I glance at his taut face. "It could be something natural. Fires occur all the time."

"Right after Rask steals the mirror? That's not likely." Anders sighs and lapses into silence.

He does not want to see another fire. Neither does Gerda, I suspect. I don't want to face this possibility either, but if they ride on, so must I.

A young man gripping a staff of rough wood stops us, waving us to side of the road. He's covered head to foot in a fine gray powder, like the ashes left in a fireplace grate. "You should take care. There's a village aflame just up the road. I barely escaped with my life. Thank God I was simply traveling through, and didn't lose my home like those other poor souls."

"Does anyone know what started this fire?" Thyra urges Freya closer. He looks up and down and away from her, as if to avoid the question.

"You do, apparently. Tell me." Thyra's tone could command a regiment.

"It sounds crazy," the young man replies, finally looking at her.

"We've seen many strange things," Gerda says. "We will not judge you."

Focusing on Gerda's gentle face, the young man clutches his walking stick to his chest. "The Usurper. One of his battalions has apparently been camped on the outskirts of this town for some time. Until now, our army has always been able to fight them back. It's been a standstill, with neither side gaining any ground. People in the villages around here, they took precautions, but the battles never touched them. Not 'til today." He swallows hard.

Gerda guides Bae to stand near the young man. "It's all right. We know how hard it is. We've seen horrors too."

The man shakes his head. "I'm not usually like this. I have worked my family's farm all my life, dealt with lots of trouble, seen some things … Nothing like this." His fingers tighten on the staff. "It was just a day like any other, you see. Someone spotted the enemy troops on the hill overlooking the town. These folks, they've seen that before. Soon our men would appear to drive them back. Only, this time, they didn't."

"The enemy has a new weapon?" Kai rides up beside Freya, his leg bumping Thyra's thigh. Out of the corner of my eye I see Thyra clasp his outstretched fingers.

"Yes, it must have been. I didn't see it, but that's the only explanation. I was inside, talking to a man about a price for my corn crop, when a great light blazed through the windows. Then there was fire, flames everywhere, and smoke so thick I had to use my hands to feel my way to the back door. I got outside, I saw …" He rubs at his eyes with the back of one sooty hand. "I saw terrible things. So I ran. I just ran, until I made my way to this road. Now I am walking home. I need to get home. Need to see it."

"Of course." Thyra's voice is now as gentle as Gerda's. "We will not keep you. Thank you for your time."

"Do not go there." The young man reaches up and grabs Bae's halter, staring into the reindeer's eyes as if he's guessed Bae's secret. "Listen to me. Do not take them there."

Bae just butts the young man's shoulder with his muzzle, pushing him away.

Gerda turns to look at us. "We must."

"Yes." Anders kicks his horse into a trot.

We leave the young man behind, swallowed up by the crowd of refugees, and follow Anders.

The flow of travelers slows as we ride on. Kai shades his eyes with one hand and surveys the road ahead of us. "I suppose everyone who needed to get out has already done so."

Gerda wrinkles her nose. "The fire. I can smell it."

An acrid scent permeates the air, as ashes drift and settle on our hair and clothing like dark flakes of snow. We round a corner and spy the remains of a small village.

The smell is worse. It's the terrible odor of burnt flesh.

"Ride on," Erik says. "We'll ask our questions in the next village. No one here can tell us anything."

We stay on the main road, but as we pass the village I can't escape the sight of houses and shops fallen to pieces. Their stone foundations rise up like broken teeth amid drifts of bone-white ash.

Overhead, the vultures circle, frustrated.

There is nothing left here, not even for them.

CHAPTER TWENTY-TWO:
ASHES TO ASHES

E RIK CONVINCES US TO CAMP for the night in the woods outside the neighboring village. "I can't imagine they would welcome a group of strangers, especially at night, with the way things are. We're better off staying out of sight and sending in one or two of us in the morning."

After a rather heated argument over who will take watch, and when—made more contentious when Erik again suggests only the men need to do so—we finally settle in next to a fire.

"It won't attract the enemy?" Anders gazes at the rising smoke with concern.

"I doubt it. Every report places them on the other side of the village, and our troops stand between us and them."

Anders massages his injured leg. "It did not stop them from leveling a town."

"That was some special weapon, though." Kai absently strokes Luki's back. He and Thyra sit as close as possible, given that the wolf has wiggled his body in between them.

Thyra rests her hand on Luki's head. "The mirror."

"Perhaps." Kai leans back and stares at the stars, just visible through a break in the trees. "Do you think Rask has already handed it over to the emperor? If so, it is protected by his elite guard as well as the regular troops."

I snap a twig between my fingers. "No, he has not."

"You sound certain." Erik kicks a fallen branch into the fire before settling next to me on the blanket I've spread over the hard ground.

I sit forward, hugging my knees to my chest. "I just do not believe … I don't think he would do that."

"Because you know him so well?" Erik glances down at me, his face unreadable in the flickering light from the fire.

"No. Still, it seems out of character, even for the little we do know. I doubt he would ever give up something so valuable so easily."

"He said he supports the emperor," Anders points out.

"I know. But even that does not ring true. Why would a sorcerer hand over an object of such power to someone else?"

Erik shoots me a quizzical look as he stretches out his legs. "Sephia said you had some mysterious connection to Rask."

He remembers that? I pull the blanket up to my chin. "It was all part of his plan—manipulating me to get to Gerda. Since he now has the mirror, I'm sure he's forgotten I exist."

Varna, what a liar you are. Why not tell these friends about your promise? Surely they, like Sephia, will understand.

I know why. It's because they, unlike Sephia, will do everything in their power to prevent me from fulfilling it. I can't sacrifice that final option—not if it turns out to be the only way to protect them.

"I'm going to sleep." I sink down and roll until I am pressed up against Gerda.

She leans over to whisper in my ear. "I might take a walk."

I snort. "Walk? All right, but please avoid dragging Anders too far afield. He can't run back if something happens."

Gerda slaps my arm, but the thump is buffered by the blanket I've pulled around me.

After some time drifting in and out of awareness, I sense someone leaning over me.

"I told you, I want to sleep."

"Wake up, Varna."

I roll over. Erik looms over me, his arms holding him up, inches above my body. I mutter one of those words he claims I use too often.

"Shhhh …" Erik drops back on his heels. "Do not wake the others."

I fight my way free of the blanket and sit up.

"What is it?"

"I was keeping watch and saw something I think we need to check out."

I look around. I don't know if Gerda and Anders actually took a walk, but it must have been a quick stroll, because they're now snuggled next to one another on his blanket, fast asleep. Kai is stretched out on another blanket, his arms around Thyra, with Luki pressed up against his back.

As I lace my boots, Luki lifts his head and examines me with interest. Erik makes a low whistling sound, and Luki leaps up and pads over to us.

"Watch over them."

Luki sits on his haunches, his golden eyes gleaming. I could swear he understands this command.

"Come on," Erik says. "At the very least, he will alert them to any danger."

He won't allow anyone to harm Thyra, that's certain. Which should wake the others in time. I stand and pull on my cloak. "Where are we going?"

"To the village. I saw lights moving on the road, right outside the gates."

"Wait." I lean over and grab my rucksack. "My healing supplies," I say, when Erik raises his eyebrows.

Erik shrugs. "All right, but keep up with me. I need someone at my back. I don't want to put you in the middle of anything, but I need you to keep a lookout."

"I'm thinking of the fire at the Opera House. The supplies would have been useful."

Erik does not respond. He moves so quickly, I must run to keep up with him.

We reach the edge of the woods and pause behind the tree line. The open ground rolls away in a gentle hill that leads to the road.

There's no activity outside the village gates, but soldiers march farther up the road. A few carry torches—enough to provide some light, but not enough to draw attention. I press my fingers into Erik's wrist and realize, by the pull on his hand, he holds his pistol.

"Ours?" I remove my hand. He might need to use the gun.

He shakes his head. "No. See the coach in the middle? It looks familiar."

I squint at the dark mass of figures as they veer onto a path that winds up a hill as barren as a plowed field. A larger form rolls in their midst. It is Rask's coach.

Will he sense my presence? I slide behind the trunk of one of the larger trees.

Erik shuffles his boots in the piles of old leaves. "What are you doing? I need you to watch my back."

"You are not going after them."

"I must. I need to see what they are up to."

I peek around the tree. Directly before us, the town is a jumble of buildings, huddled and quiet as some sleeping animal. Like half-open eyes, a few windows flicker with the light of lanterns or candles. The brightest building is probably the tavern. I imagine lingering drinkers clutching tankards, avoiding some trouble at home.

"The village." I tug at Erik's coat. "Forget following those soldiers. We must warn the village first."

His face is bone-pale in the dim light. "You're right. I wasn't thinking straight."

"I want to go after Rask too," I say, although this is not exactly true. "But the two of us—even the six of us if we wake the others—cannot possibly stop those soldiers. We *can* warn the village."

Erik nods. "We'll wait until the troops round the hill. Then I'll go and warn the townsfolk while you keep watch here."

I hoist my rucksack higher on my shoulder. "I am coming with you."

"No, you are not."

"Yes, I am."

Erik stares into my eyes. I don't know what he sees there, but he sighs and leans in to kiss me on the forehead. "So stubborn, you Lund girls. I pity Anders, I really do."

I pat his shoulder. "That is a lie. Now, we should go. They have moved behind the hill."

Erik runs toward the village with me at his heels. We approach the wooden gates just as the enemy's troops reach the top of the nearby hill. High on the rocky promontory, they appear like a gathering of birds. It's as if Rask's great winged creature has spawned an army of raptors.

I hike up my skirts, thankful I still wear my riding breeches, and climb the low fence enclosing the town. Erik pockets his gun, steps up, and vaults over the top, landing on the other side in time to help me down.

"Look." He points toward the high hill. "That's Rask, I think."

I do not need to look, as I feel the pull of the sorcerer's will from here, but I allow my gaze to follow Erik's outstretched arm.

Sten Rask stands at the edge of a cliff. Beside him is another man, wearing a uniform decorated with so many jewels and medals his body sparkles in the torchlight. On Rask's other side stands a slighter figure, wrapped in a dark cloak. A boy, perhaps. Maybe it is that same hooded figure I saw at the Opera House. A servant, staying close to his master.

Rask raises one arm above his head. Moonlight touches the object he holds, illuminating its crystal crown until it burns like a falling star.

The scepter.

"Get down!" Erik grabs my arm and throws me to the ground, curving his body over mine. My rucksack is under me, clutched to my chest, and my thoughts focus on that—on foolish, trivial things. *Did the bottles break? Not sure they were packed well enough. And the ointments, in their little ceramic jars, are they smashed? Do not let them be smashed.*

Because to think on what is happening is too terrible.

The warmth of Erik's body is nothing compared to the heat exploding around us. Even though my eyes are closed, the flash of light is so bright I see red behind my eyelids.

There's a roar like an onrushing wave, or the wind before a storm. Erik tightens his grip, holding me so close I feel as if our bodies could merge.

Skin to skin. Bone to bone. Ashes to ashes.

Erik slides off and pulls me to my feet. "Run!"

I drop one of his hands and throw the strap of my rucksack over my shoulder. Around us flames feed on the air and leap from roof to roof. They eat through the thatch like devouring birds.

Erik pulls me toward the gates, now shoved open, as a mass of people make for the road. Some are pale as ghosts, a film of ash covering their bodies. One man, his hair aflame, dashes past us, and Erik trips him. When the man falls to the ground Erik kicks him.

"What?" I scream, then realize Erik's rolling the man in the dirt, extinguishing the fire in his hair.

He must be in pain. Such great pain. I drop Erik's hand and fall to my knees beside the injured man.

"Move!" Erik circles behind me and grabs for my arm. I swat him aside.

"Varna!" Erik yells, but I concentrate on the man in front of me. I roll him closer to the wall, away from the flying feet of those escaping the fire. Erik's forced to keep moving to avoid being trampled.

My patient groans, his fingers flailing at his burnt scalp. I push his hands down to his sides. "Hush, stay still. I have something that will help." I dig into my rucksack for an ointment for burns.

The wails and screams of the injured and terrified float around me. I focus on gently rubbing ointment into the scalp of the man lying before me. He whimpers and clutches his knees, drawing his body into a ball.

After a moment, he falls silent. I press my fingers to his neck to ensure blood still throbs there. He grabs my wrist and pulls me down, inches from his reddened face.

"Thank you." His voice cracks like shattered glass. "Bless you."

"You need to get out of here." I stroke his shoulder. "Can you rise to your feet?"

He grimaces as he holds out one arm. I grab it and stand, pulling him up with me.

He shakes like a leaf about to fall, but thanks me again before staggering away to join the others fleeing the burning village. I catch no sign of Erik. Hopefully he escaped, forced along by the inexorable movement of the mob.

I cannot leave. I know that now. I have a job to do, a mission of my own. It must be why I felt compelled to carry my rucksack. Why I am here at all.

The flames are dying down more quickly than they should, but I understand. The first blast was so hot, so devastating, there is little left to burn, and, like the Opera House, this was no natural fire.

Everything is gone, leaving a wasteland of gray powder, collapsed walls, and half-charred timbers. The odor of burnt flesh—animal and human—sickens the air.

I hoist my rucksack higher on my shoulder. Suffering people are lost in this wreckage. I can provide healing, or if no healing, comfort.

No fear, no hesitation. Only the call of the injured and dying.

Everyone else runs away, as they should. Anyone with sense will flee this hell.

But I am a healer. I must walk in.

CHAPTER TWENTY-THREE:
DUST TO DUST

I DON'T NEED TO GO FAR to find people who require aid. There are so many, I fear my meagre supply of medicines and ointments will be used up before I can help half of them.

I focus on one patient at a time. I can't think of the total number, just as I cannot allow my mind to dwell on their injuries—the bones shattered by fallen timbers, the eyes scratched by cinders, the gashes from glass blown from windows, the burns ... Oh, my God, the burns.

No, Varna. It is not about your horror or repulsion. It's not about the nausea rolling up your throat, or the smoke burning your eyes and clogging your nose. It is not about the sharp bits of debris that tear at your clothes and etch your arms with scratches. It's about the people who live here, who are buried in the rubble, who slump like discarded bags of grain against the walls of what used to be their homes.

It is not about you. Only what you can do.

I do whatever I can. Sometimes that's providing a potion for pain, or splinting a limb, or cleaning and bandaging a wound. Sometimes it is simply holding the hand of someone so close to death their breath is the merest wisp of air.

When I find a covered well, I cry tears of joy. I unseal jugs I dug from the rubble of the tavern and pour the contents out of most of them so I can refill them with water, saving a few jugs of liquor to clean wounds or dim the pain of the wounded.

I have no idea how long I've been here. Time is suspended like the embers still dancing through the air. Smoke turns day to night—it could be noon, or twilight. It does not matter. This is not a normal day, marked by clocks or the sun. This is an endless day in hell, searching for the damned, offering them aid.

Many cannot be helped. They are already gone—killed in the first blast of flame. I step over bodies, closing my mind to any thought of who they were. Soon they will be mourned. For now, I must think only of the living.

Sounds dim and voices fade away. I curse, knowing I can't work fast enough to help them all. After more time passes, the only noise is the crash of falling timbers and clatter of collapsing stone. Then I hear it—one more voice. Hoarse as a crow, but insistent. Fighting to survive.

It comes from a building whose walls still stand, although the roof has given away. Crawling over half-burnt timbers and wooden chairs that disintegrate at my touch, I batt at charred paper swirling around my head like moths. So much paper— this must have been a library. It does not matter. I can't stop to examine anything. I must follow the anguished cries of someone trapped in this wreck of a room.

My boot catches in a pile of fallen beams. I tug, yanking my foot free. No matter. I will come back for the boot later.

Heat sears the sole of my foot as I step onto a metal grate that holds the memory of flames. Pain shoots up my leg, but I move forward. The cries grow louder. I am close.

I stumble over a broken ceiling beam, now lying on the floor.

Lying across the legs of a woman.

I kneel beside her and take her hand. My heart's squeezed as if someone has grabbed it in their fist. I cannot move that beam. I can't free her.

The woman's face is covered in ash, lending her the appearance of a wraith. Shining through the ghostly mask, her light brown eyes burn with pain.

She manages a weak smile. "Are you my angel?"

"No, but I'm here to help you, any way I can."

A blistered burn encircles her neck, and I realize her necklace must have melted into her flesh. I bite the inside of my cheek.

"I prayed for an angel." Her voice is as ghostly as her face. "For an angel to come and carry me to heaven."

"Well, I'm no angel, and I'm not here to escort you to the afterlife. I am here to save you." I dig through my rucksack for burn ointment and the last bottle of Sten Rask's mysterious potion.

The woman halts my rummaging by laying her hand over mine.

"Do not waste your time, or your supplies. There's no use, you see." She pulls my hand closer and presses it into the folds of material rumpled about her waist. "Everything is broken. Everything inside is broken."

Warmth seeps through my splayed fingers as blood oozes all around my hand. I pull it back to my side, my eyes still focused on the liquid pooling in the folds of material. Where her lower ribs should be there's only a strange indentation, filled with a mangle of fabric, blood, and bone.

"It really is an angel I need now," the woman says. "Unless you are a sorcerer, or have such powers, you cannot help me, try as you might."

I close my eyes for a moment and take a deep breath.

"If you will sit with me … "

"Yes," I say. "Yes."

I slide next to her, careful not the jostle her shattered body, and pull a piece of bandage and my water flask from my rucksack. Finding the special potion bottle, I give her drops of the liquid, alternating with sips of water. When she ceases trembling, I dampen the bandage and wipe the ash from her face.

"Feels good." She drops her head upon my shoulder.

We sit like that for some time. I tell her stories—funny tales I remember from childhood, then Gerda's story of a sojourn in the snow, complete with sorcerers, an enchanted mirror, and a talking reindeer.

The woman mutters something.

I lean in close to hear her.

"A tear. She saved the Snow Queen with a tear?"

"Yes," I say, wishing my own tears held such power. But all they do is blur my vision.

Which is why I don't see him at first, standing at the door to this roofless room.

Erik steps forward with great deliberation. "Come out now, Varna."

I shake my head. "I must stay. She asked me to sit with her. I can't do anything else, you see, except sit with her."

Erik moves a little closer. "You have done enough. More than enough. For her, for all of them. Your friend is already gone. Now you need to come with me."

I glance down at the woman by my side. She is dead. I have seen enough death to know.

"I just want to sit here a little while longer."

"No, Varna. This building is not sound. It could collapse any minute. Stand up, grab your bag, and walk toward me." Erik holds out his hand.

I lean over and kiss the woman's forehead and close her eyes. Sliding away from her limp body, I crawl to a spot where one post still stands, broken at waist-height. It's just tall enough for me to pull myself to my feet.

As soon as my burnt foot hits the ground, I cry out and stumble, falling forward on my hands and knees.

Fingers reach under my armpits, and strong hands lift me, then swing me up to cradle me in well-muscled arms. Erik has come to find me. To rescue me. I bury my face in his shirt, which smells of smoke and sweat.

"What have you done, Varna?" He clutches me tighter as he picks his way through the rubble. "Your foot is burnt so badly. Where is your boot?"

"Lost," I mumble into the folds of his shirt. A breeze stirs my tangled hair "Where are you taking me?"

He doesn't break his stride. "Somewhere safe."

"There might be more people. I need to help them." My voice sounds odd, like sandpaper rasping over wood.

"You have helped already. More than enough. More than anyone should ever be asked to help." Erik adjusts his arms so I can rest my head on his shoulder.

"Never enough. It is never enough."

"It will have to do," he replies. "Now, just so you know, we are not going back to the camp. I've already sent the others away. I told them I would come back for you. Your sister and Thyra argued with me, of course."

Safe in his arms, I allow myself a little chuckle.

"Yes, you can laugh, although it was not funny at the time."

Erik carries me for some time. I drift in and out of consciousness, until a thought flashes through my mind. He said he told the others. "Where are they? The others?"

"They are safe. We'll meet up with them tomorrow. I told them to wait for us."

"You were so sure you would find me?"

"Not sure, simply determined to take the village apart, stone by crumbled stone, if necessary. Fortunately," he adds, "there were people who told me you were alive. Told me all about you, as a matter of fact—what you did, what they thought of you."

"Hope it wasn't too bad." We pause before the doorway to what looks like a shepherd's hut. My injured foot, swinging, brushes the door frame and a squeak escapes my parched lips.

"Sorry." Erik ducks his head to enter. "No, it was not bad. It was … illuminating."

The hut is a round structure, like a squat stone tower. There are no windows, but one section of the thatched roof has been left unfinished, creating an opening. Erik must have carried me some distance from the village, because there's no smoke blurring the dark sky. It's night again, which means an entire day passed amid that devastation.

Erik deposits me on a pile of quilts covering a narrow cot, careful to prop up my foot with an extra blanket. "Do you have anything in your supplies we can use?" He removes my remaining boot.

"Yes, bring me the bag. There's some ointment I can rub into the burn."

"That *I* can, you mean." Erik hands me my rucksack and waits while I locate the ointment.

I struggle to sit up. "I can manage."

Erik pushes me back. "Lie still. I may not be a healer, but I can handle this. First, a little wash up wouldn't hurt." He pulls his water flask and a clean handkerchief from his coat pocket. Soaking the cloth, he kneels at the bottom of the bed and wipes the dirt from my foot.

"*Does* hurt," I say, between gritted teeth.

"Do you need something to bite down on?" He rubs the burn ointment into my damaged flesh.

"Your hand?"

Erik's laugh is only a low rumble, but I hear it, all the same.

"Done." He sits back on his heels. "Now, what about the pain? Do you have something for that in your bag?"

"There's nothing left."

"Pity." Eris stands and dusts off his breeches. He digs around in my bag, finds another clean bit of bandage, and pours some water over it.

"What's that for?" I push myself up on my elbows.

"I thought you might feel better with some of that grime removed." He sits on the edge of the cot and pushes me down again. "Relax."

I frown, but close my eyes and allow him to scrub the ash and sweat from my face. It does feel better.

As he wipes my neck, I open my eyes and look up into his face.

Odd. He studies you with such intensity, Varna. Like he's trying to figure something out—uncover some secret that eludes him.

"I must look rough. It feels like every inch of my skin is covered in scratches."

He smooths my hair away from my face, tucking several tangled strands behind my ears.

"I need a comb. Do you have one of those stashed in that bottomless sack as well?"

"I do, but draw the line at you combing my hair."

"Why?" Erik sits back, balling up the dirty cloth and tossing it onto the dirt floor.

"It seems a little outside your experience."

"Nonsense. I have two younger sisters. I've combed and brushed their hair plenty of times." He turns so I can't read his face. "My mother, you see, was always busy with the store."

"It's in the side pocket."

Erik brandishes the pewter comb. "Here, let me help you sit up for a minute." He settles onto the bed behind my back, allowing me to lean against his right side. Using his left hand, he carefully pulls the comb through my hair, working out the tangles.

"Bravo. Not a single hard tug," I say, when he finishes and drops the comb back into my rucksack.

"I have hidden talents."

"Apparently." I run my fingers through my smooth hair.

He hands his water flask to me. "You need something to clear the smoke from your throat."

I take a long swallow before speaking again. "So it was Rask, no question about it. But he does not have the mirror, just his scepter."

"No, he has both, or so I hear." Erik pockets the flask, then slides to the edge of the cot to allow me to lie down again. "I met a barkeep who's had dealings with the Usurper's troops. He occasionally sold them some brandy."

"Anything for some coin." I stare up at the opening in the roof. The moon is almost full. Only a sliver of darkness shadows one edge of the pale disc.

"Money is money and people have to survive. Anyway, he said the emperor does not have the mirror yet. Apparently Rask has hidden it at some old castle not far from here. It's located somewhere on the other side of the hills, closer to the sea."

"So just the scepter caused these latest fires?" I shiver. If Sten Rask can use the scepter to create such devastation, what can he do with the mirror?

"Not exactly. The soldiers bragged to the barkeep, claiming the emperor's sorcerer used the mirror to infuse more power into some magical staff. I assume they meant the scepter. They said everyone would soon see how useless it was to fight against their forces."

"What do you think?"

"About what?" Erik stares down at me.

"Do you believe our country can stand against the Usurper, especially now? With Rask in control of the mirror, and this demonstration of its terrible power … "

"I don't know if we can, but we must try." Erik presses his hand against my cheek. "You should get some sleep. You have pushed your body beyond all limits today."

He stares at me in the strangest way.

"You as well. Look how your fingers shake."

Erik jerks back his hand as if he's touched fire. He jumps to his feet and crosses to a stool on the other side of the room. "I will keep watch." He pulls his coat tight and buttons it.

"No, you were awake most of last night. You can't continue to do this, Erik. You will ruin your health."

"Says the girl who crawled around a burnt-out village to save a few lost souls."

I glance over at him. He is perched on the stool like a bear balancing on a rock far too small for its bulk. "So, what do we do now?"

"If we can locate the mirror, and destroy it somehow, we have a chance. We need to track down Rask at this castle of his and send a message to Sephia, as we discussed. We must stick to the plan and hope for the best."

I can't see his face clearly in the dim light, but his voice sounds oddly hoarse. "You look so uncomfortable. Lie down with me if you want. I mean, we are friends, and you can't sit on that stool all night."

Erik mutters some obscenity, then clears his throat. "No, I think I am better off here."

"Suit yourself. I just wanted to offer." I look away.

My foot throbs. I focus on other things to dull the pain, but it's the dying woman's words that haunt my thoughts. *Unless you are a sorcerer, or have such powers.*

It was power Rask promised me. Not just beauty, but power. The kind of power capable of confronting, perhaps even defeating, the evil I have seen today.

I glance at Erik again. His head has dropped to his chest. He must be exhausted after keeping watch last night, enduring the trauma of the fire, and searching for me amid the rubble.

Searching for me, and finding me, and carrying me to safety.

I stare at that red-gold head, now turned to gray by dust and the shadows.

He is a difficult young man, always trying to take control. Obstinate. Always arguing.

Brave. Loyal. Willing to sacrifice his life for others.

Stubborn, brash, and quick to anger. Someone who speaks the truth, even when it is not kind.

A boy who stares into pieces of wood and gives life to the amazing objects he sees there. Who loves beauty more than anything. Who combs his little sisters' hair.

I turn my head and stare up at the cold, uncaring moon.

A rush of emotion swamps my heart. It is love, I admit, although not the kind I've always expected. Love for the person he is, for a dear friend.

But not a love that includes desire. I sink back against the hard mattress, wondering why I do not feel more for Erik than friendship. Is my heart so shriveled I cannot feel romantic love, not even for a young man so worthy?

Yet I am grateful, in a way, that I do not. Because I know Erik worships beauty, and I am not beautiful. I cannot be what *he* desires, either.

I *can* protect him, though, as well as my sister and our other friends. I can prevent them from walking into danger.

They don't have to go after a treacherous sorcerer, Varna. You know who can find Rask. Only send a thought. Call to him with your mind, tell him you are coming, and he will guide you to his castle.

More people need not die. Perhaps if you fulfill your promise, you can reason with Rask and convince him to stop using the mirror as a weapon. And if that doesn't work, you can still do good. You know he keeps it near him. Go to him and find it there. You can destroy the mirror, even if it requires sacrificing one more life.

Only one more. Only yours.

CHAPTER TWENTY-FOUR:
IN GOOD COMPANY

AS ERIK LEADS OUR HORSES from the woods, Luki bounds forward to greet me. Erik remarks that Thyra left Luki behind to watch over the horses.

I pat Luki's head, no longer afraid. He may be a wolf, he may need to kill to survive, but no evil shines from his golden eyes.

"I'm not quite sure what town they headed for, but Thyra said to instruct Luki to find her and follow him."

"That sounds reasonable." I wait for Erik to help me up onto my horse. My foot is too sore to put any weight on it.

Erik swings up into his saddle. He gives the command to Luki and waits for me to ride beside him before setting off. "It appears I must make you a cane too."

"We don't have time. I'll just find a sturdy stick when we dismount." I lower my head and fiddle with my reins. I don't want him to guess my new plan.

Because I've decided to go to Rask once Erik joins the others. It will be better if they are together when I disappear. Perhaps cooler heads, like Kai and Thyra, can prevent Erik—or Anders and Gerda—from attempting to find me.

They will send for Sephia, of course, but I don't fear for her as I do the others. She has formidable magic on her side.

Luki trots before us, occasionally looking back to ensure we follow him. Seeking a way to pass the time, I question Erik about his sisters, a subject that brings a welcome smile to his tired face. Promising me a laugh, Erik launches into a tale about the time Anders snuck Erik and his sisters backstage at the ballet. One of the girls tugged on a cord and brought down a piece of scenery in the midst of some sylphs flitting about a painted forest glade.

"It looked like a large stone, but was only papier-mâché. Still, it made the audience think those ballerinas had some hard heads when it burst into pieces around them."

I do laugh. "What did you do?"

"Grabbed up the girls and made a swift exit out the stage door. You should've seen us run!" His merry expression sobers. "Anders was always so light on his feet."

I face forward and fix my gaze on Luki's swinging tail. "What will you do about the army? You can't spend the rest of your life worrying you might be arrested as deserters."

"I'm not sure yet. Still trying to work that one out. I'll think of something."

"I'm sure you will."

"You're being awfully agreeable today. Did you bump your head as well as burn your foot?"

"No, but when I do find that stick, I can think of another good use for it."

"Ah, there we are. The Varna I know."

"Peevish and sharp-tongued?"

There's a stretch of silence before Erik speaks again. "No, honest. Not afraid to put me in my place. God knows someone needs to."

Luki's yips break off this conversation. The wolf pauses for a moment, glancing back at us, before loping down a side path.

We follow him to a gatekeeper's cottage—a tumbled-down building attached to the remnants of a stone wall. Saplings rise up in place of the missing gates.

Erik lifts me off my mare and keeps one arm around me as I limp toward the entrance to the cottage.

"This estate is in bad shape."

Kai steps out of the open doorway. "Exactly why we chose it."

He's elbowed away by Gerda, who dashes to me and throws her arms around my neck, knocking away Erik's hands. "We were terrified you might be dead. Oh, thank you, thank you, Erik, for finding her." She releases me to stand on tip-toe and kiss him on the cheek.

With my support removed, I wobble. Kai runs and grabs me before I pitch forward.

Gerda turns to me with a stricken face. "What happened? Are you hurt?"

"She badly burned her foot." Erik watches as Kai offers me his arm. "After giving aid to heaven knows how many of those poor souls."

"I was only doing what I'm trained to do. I had my supplies, and I am a healer, so I had to help." I brush aside Gerda's hands. "It's not that bad."

Taking a couple of steps with Kai's help, I forget to lift my injured foot and bang it into a rock on the path. I make a noise that sounds like something being slaughtered.

Kai moves to provide more support, but before he can do so, Erik swoops in behind us and lifts me up into his arms.

"Enough of this nonsense. Gerda, please push the door open. Kai, can you see to the horses?"

"Of course," Kai says, moving out of the way.

Thyra walks around the corner with Luki at her heels. "What is this?"

Gerda pauses with one hand on the door. "Erik found Varna, but she's hurt, and he is taking her inside."

"I see." Thyra sets down a pail of water. She examines Erik before sharing a glance with Kai. "It is all perfectly clear, actually."

Kai grabs the bridles of our horses. "Absolutely." He grins at his wife.

"The door, Gerda," snaps Erik, and carries me inside.

Anders, resting on an old bed pushed up against one wall, rises to his feet as soon as he spies us.

"Varna is alive!" Gerda hands him his cane. "She's a little hurt, but not too much." She leans in to kiss him on the cheek. "Now we are all together again."

Erik crosses the room and lowers me onto the bed. "I hope that is one of ours." He frowns, staring at the dusty coverlet beneath the wool blanket.

"The blanket? Yes," Anders replies. "I was not about to sit on the bed without it."

Erik places me on the blanket and I scoot until I can press my back against the iron bedstead. I want to sit up, not lie down like some invalid.

Gerda perches on the edge of the bed and clasps one of my hands. "All this misery might soon be worth something. Thyra has a lead. We hope to receive news tomorrow."

"Oh?" I look up and meet Thyra's speculative gaze. "What have you found?"

"I contacted someone I knew from my travels." She sets the pail on a rickety table near the door. "It's a person we can trust," she adds, with a sharp look at Erik.

"You are sure?" he asks.

"Absolutely. This is someone I met at my mentor's home. It's the person who warned me about the emperor's interest in the mirror."

"A spy?" Anders raises his wispy eyebrows.

"I suppose you could say so. At any rate, someone who's just as anxious to see the mirror destroyed as we are." She does not turn around when Kai enters the cottage, but I can tell by her sudden stillness she's aware of his presence. "Because it must be destroyed. I see that now. There is no way to hide it again, not when Rask has demonstrated what a touch of its power can do."

Erik leans against the stone wall of the cottage, his head brushing the low beams. "Now we just have to find it."

"That is where Thyra's contact comes in." Kai crosses to his wife and puts his arm around her waist. "They're connected to someone in the emperor's retinue. It seems the Usurper is as anxious to locate the mirror as we are, and Rask has not revealed its location yet."

"A dangerous game," Erik says. "Is Rask turning against his master?"

"I don't think the Usurper *is* his master."

The words leave my mouth before I consider what the others might think. I lower my eyes and fiddle with the lacing on my bodice. "I mean, Rask is a sorcerer. Surely he does not fear a mere man, no matter how many troops the emperor commands."

Thyra examines me with her icy gaze. "Not even a sorcerer can stand against battalions. At least, none I have known. However, I've learned one other important fact—Rask is not the Usurper's only sorcerer."

"He has more than one?" Anders taps his cane against the rough wood floor. "We are doomed, then."

"Not necessarily." Kai pulls Thyra closer to his side. "This is Rask's mentor, the woman who trained him. Apparently, she's thrown her lot in with the emperor, and pledged the support of her apprentice as well. However, from what we hear, Rask left her estate some time ago. Supposedly to search for the mirror, although there are rumors he's broken with her, or wishes to. Which could benefit us."

Erik straightens, bumping his head on a rafter. "We could set them against one another?"

"That's the hope," Thyra says. "But we can't take any action immediately, I'm afraid. We need to stay here, out of sight, and wait for news."

I sit back and study the faces of the five people in the room as they discuss these developments and make plans.

They are brave, all of them, and determined. I know each one would willingly risk their life to save any of the others.

I must ensure they never need do so. But how will I make it Rask's castle if I can barely walk? Even if he provides me with directions, even riding my mare, it will be impossible.

Varna, you idiot, he is a sorcerer. Explain the difficulty and see what he can do.

I need to get outside. Sometime tonight, when the rest are asleep. I must do this without waking Luki, or allowing any of my friends to catch me. That's all I have to do.

I clap my hand over my mouth to stifle a bubble of hysterical laughter. Five pairs of eyes turn on me.

"Shock. All that horror ..."

Gerda, Anders and Kai look sympathetic. Thyra narrows her eyes and thins her lips.

Erik crosses his arms over his chest and stares at me, an unreadable expression on his face.

"I'll be fine after some rest."

This comment compels Gerda to pull things out of rucksacks and fuss over me—bundling blankets behind my head so I can sit up comfortably, taking off my remaining boot and loosening my clothes. Thyra joins her to help unwrap, clean, and dress my foot. Kai brings me fresh water, and Anders offers up the last soft roll from his rations.

Erik strolls over after all these activities have subsided.

"My turn." He holds up the pewter comb.

It's a blessing the light has faded in the cottage, so that shadows hide my face.

Erik sits on the edge of the bed and combs out my hair. If he is bothered by the obvious astonishment of the others, he does not let it show.

As darkness falls, and the others settle in for the night, I silently recite recipes for potions and ointments to force myself to stay awake.

When I feel certain everyone is asleep, I swing my feet over the edge of the bed. The problem of getting from the bed to the door remains, but fortunately Anders's cane still leans against the bottom of the bed frame. As I grab the walking stick I consider pulling on my boots, but reject this idea. Either Rask will provide a way for me to reach him that does not require much walking, or I cannot go. I pull Gerda's rucksack onto the bed and find the slippers she wore at the wedding. Trust Gerda to carry those on this trip.

Fastening my cloak with Sephia's silver lily pin, I gingerly slide my feet into the slippers and stand, leaning heavily on the cane. Thank goodness Thyra decided Luki should sleep outside tonight, to keep watch over Bae and the horses. I limp across the floor, resisting the urge to rush.

I reach the door without anyone waking, although Erik rolls over and mutters, "Never saw it. Why didn't I see it?" rather loudly. I pause, frozen in place until I realize he's simply talking in his sleep.

Slipping outside, I lean the cane against the outside wall and force myself to place my injured foot on the rough ground. I shuffle forward, knowing I must reach a spot in front of the cottage where the trees open up onto the clear night sky.

Stars wink like candles blown by the wind. I close my eyes.

I will come to you, as I promised, if you can show me the way. But I cannot walk, or even ride. I need your help, one more time.

The breeze ruffles my hair, still hanging loose about shoulders. Still as smooth as when Erik's fingers drew the comb through it.

No, I can't think about that. I must put such things out of my mind.

I am ready to honor my vow, but I'm injured, and can only come if you will send your coach, or some other aid. Still, I will come, if you will have me.

Crickets chirp and leaves rustle. Somewhere in the distance, a wolf bays at the moon.

Varna.

The word rises on the air, so much a part of the wind I'm not sure I've actually heard it. It repeats, over and over, like waves rolling into shore.

If you still want me, I am here.

The rustling of the leaves grows into a sound like the rush of wings. I open my eyes.

Luki crouches on the ground, his ears flattened to his head. Next to him, Bae stands in front of the frightened horses, protecting them with his bulky body. I meet the reindeer's soulful gaze. He lifts his head, motioning toward something in the trees.

A dense shadow fills the latticework of dark branches. It moves, and I catch the sweep of wings.

Of course. I fight back a giggle. Of course. I lift up my arms.

Luki growls. Bae shambles forward.

"Do not do this, Miss Varna. This is a great mistake."

"No, Bae. This is a great sacrifice. If you tell them anything, tell them that." I take two painful steps forward.

Rask's great bird sweeps down from the trees, dark as a thundercloud, and imprisons me in the grip of its claws. I clutch my arms over my breast and lay back against the bone-hard cage of its talons. I know it won't drop me, or hurt me. Its master wants me, alive and unharmed.

The creature soars into the air. I can see little in the darkness. Only the cooling of the wind tells me we are rising higher and higher.

I experience a moment of panic. I'm flying, trapped in the clutches of an unnatural beast. I am being carried away, to some unknown fate, to some unexpected destiny.

As if he senses my fear, Rask's voice is in my head, drowning out the wind. *Varna. Do not fear. You are safe. Nothing will harm you. Close your eyes. Soon you will stand before me. Then your life can truly begin.*

CHAPTER TWENTY-FIVE: EMBRACING DESTINY

THE BIRD DESCENDS. THROUGH THE bars of its talons, I spy the tops of trees swaying like a dark and restless sea.

The true sea is soon below us. Salt spices the air, interlaced with the pungent scent of seaweed and beached ocean creatures. I lean forward and catch a glimpse of sand, pale as an ivory ribbon, bordering charcoal-gray cliffs.

The great wings lift and close. We glide toward a fortress set high on one of the cliffs. The castle. It glimmers in the moonlight, as if its gray stones are studded with diamonds. *Not diamonds, quartz.*

I can't remember where I acquired such knowledge. Honestly, I can't remember much of anything. I recall standing before a tumbled-down cottage, and a huge bird descending and grabbing me, then flying and flying. Before that, what was there? A wolf, a reindeer with liquid brown eyes, faces of young people gathered around me, a rough hand gently combing my hair …

No, I must not forget. *Do not let me forget*, I cry, and instantly it all comes flooding back—my sister and Anders, Erik, and Thyra and Kai, Sephia, and our quest.

My friends. My family.

I will not lose my memories. No matter how much pain it causes me, I do not wish to forget.

The bird glides to the terrace of the fortress—a wide expanse of flagstone, bordered on one side by glass doors leading into the castle, and on the other by a crumbling, curving balustrade overlooking the sea. The creature lifts the clawed foot that imprisons me and doesn't set it down again until we safely land.

The talons open and I tumble out. Stones lie cold and slick under my hands. I push my body to a sitting position. I long to rise to my feet, but I know I cannot. The rough surface of the terrace, with its chipped stones and film of dew, is too treacherous.

Wings flap over my head, blowing my hair across my face as the bird flies away. I watch it sail into the sunrise.

The doors to the castle open and Sten Rask strides out, his leather boots slapping the damp stones. He reaches me, leans over, and swiftly lifts me to my feet.

"My poor Varna, so cold and mussed." He brushes my hair away from my face. "We must get you inside and warm you."

"I can barely walk," I say, between chattering teeth. "I burned my foot in that fire."

The fire he set. I recall the faces of the people I aided and slap his hands. "Your fault. It is all your fault."

"Yes." Rask lifts me, ignoring my protests.

Once again, I am in a man's arms, being carried into some building. But this time I refuse to relax, or press my head against his chest.

"Do not struggle. You'll feel much better once we get you into some dry clothes and sit you before a fire."

We enter the castle, the glass doors swinging closed behind us. I hear the click of a lock.

"No need for that, I can't escape. I can't throw myself over the railing, or even walk," I mutter as I look around me.

In contrast to its dilapidated exterior, the interior of the castle is beautiful. More of Rask's treasures line the walls and fill all available spaces. But instead of a storehouse, this is an elegantly appointed drawing room.

Rask lowers me onto a couch covered in gold brocade. I slide away from his hands and recline on a pile of velvet pillows. As Rask steps back, I see it, off to one side, leaning against one damask-papered wall.

The mirror.

Rask follows my gaze. "Ah yes, a plain thing, is it not? Just glass in a simple wooden frame. Yet it is worth more than everything else in this room." He turns back, studying me. "Well, almost everything."

I squirm under his scrutiny, acutely aware of my disheveled clothes and hair.

"Now, let's see to that foot." He kneels beside the couch and slides off my slipper. "You received this in the village fire?"

"Yes, my boot came off, and I couldn't stop to retrieve it. I was trying to save lives, you see." I meet his concerned gaze with a glare.

"Hmmm ... Well, I think we can take care of this easily enough." He closes his fingers about my foot, sending a shaft of pain shooting up my leg. "Sit still, my dear. This may hurt a little."

"You think?" I grit my teeth, press my back into the pillows, and grip the carved wooden arm of the couch.

I catch Rask's smile as he bends his head over my foot. He strokes the sole with two fingers.

It does hurt, at first. Then the skin tingles and relief spreads. The heat in the burn evaporates under Rask's touch, which is cool as a gentle fall of snow.

"There." Rask lays my foot back on the couch and rises to his feet. "It should be fine now."

I wiggle my toes. There's no tug of blistered skin. Sitting up, I pull the foot into my lap and stare at its unblemished sole. "How did you do that? Can you teach me how to do that?"

"Yes, that and many other things. I told you I could give you power. This would be part of it."

I recall the people I attempted to help in the burnt-out village. It might be worth accepting his offer, if I could learn to heal such terrible injuries.

I look up at Rask. "Why?"

He settles into a wing-backed upholstered chair. "Why what?"

"Why me?"

"I have already told you why." Rask snaps his fingers and flames to leap up in the marble framed fireplace.

I sink back into the cushions, stretching out my legs on the couch. The warmth from the fire soothes me. Without the constant throbbing of my foot, I could easily fall asleep.

No, I want something to eat first. I count back and realize I've not had a decent meal in days.

"I'm hungry. Do you have any food?"

Sten Rask looks me over for a moment before he rises to his feet, the flickering flames reflected in his polished black boots. He brushes a bit of lint from his pale gray breeches. "I will bring you something. Wait here."

He leaves the room. I turn and stare at the mirror. I could smash it now, while he is gone. Of course, he would probably kill me, but isn't that what I expected when I agreed to come here?

I stand and cross the room, reveling in my ability to move easily again. When I reach the mirror, Rask reappears, carrying a silver tray.

"Come. You can eat in your room."

I take a deep breath and back away from the mirror. "My room? I have a room?"

"Yes, everything has been arranged. It's just down the hall. I have laid out some clean clothes, and there's a pitcher and basin waiting, so you can wash up."

"Were you expecting me?" I follow him into the hallway.

Rask marches to a door standing ajar. He balances the tray on one palm and pushes the door open with his other hand. "I have been expecting you for quite some time."

The room is lovely—a perfect retreat in shades of gold and green. A marble fireplace, decorated with carvings of flowers, blazes with a welcoming fire. Pressed against one wall is a tall, narrow table, covered in bottles and ceramic jars. It's a workbench for creating healing potions and ointments.

Yes, everything has indeed been arranged. I sneak a look at Rask, who sets the silver tray on a small table placed before a mullioned window.

"You should eat and rest. We will talk more later." He exits the room without looking at me and closes the door. The lock clicks into place.

So, a prison. An elegant, comfortable, prison.

I slump onto one of the gilt embossed chairs at the table. On the platter are small plates, each covered with a silver dome.

Lifting one, I'm assaulted by steam, along with the delicious scent of potatoes boiled with butter and rosemary. I poke at the food with my fork.

It could be poisoned, or drugged, but I am so hungry, I don't care. I dig in.

Anyway, it's unlikely Rask wants me dead. He needs me for something, probably something related to the mirror. Perhaps, if I play along, I will have a chance to smash it, sooner rather than later.

I stuff a forkful of potatoes into my mouth, eating like it's my last meal.

Rask knocks on my door an hour later. The lock clicks open and he pushes the door slightly ajar before asking me to join him in the drawing room.

I wash up and change into the clothes I find draped over the tall, curtained bed—a simple shift of white linen, satin slippers, and a gold robe embroidered with rust-red chrysanthemums. I know it's nightwear, but it covers my body as well as any gown. I twist my hair up into a bun without looking in a mirror and fasten it with silver pins I find on the dressing table.

I rehearse various speeches as I walk the short distance to the drawing room. Since I do not know what is wanted of me, I must consider all options.

Sten Rask stands by the fireplace, one hand on the marble mantle. As I enter the room, he turns and looks me up and down.

"Ah, Varna, come in. And may I say, you should always dress in exotic robes. They suit you better than those stuffy garments you usually wear."

I cross to the center of the room. "I wear what's practical and acceptable for a girl of my station. I certainly couldn't wear something like this in my village."

"I know. More's the pity." Rask strolls over to me. "So, are you ready to begin your transformation?"

I swallow. "That depends. What does such a process entail?"

"A little pain, but nothing you can't bear." He strokes my jawline with one finger. "It's one of the many reasons I chose you. Some girls cannot endure the transformation process. Some go mad. Some die. But"— he presses his finger to my lips—"you will do neither, Varna Lund. I know you're strong enough to withstand almost anything. You can certainly tolerate a little magic."

"What do you intend to do—turn me into someone I cannot recognize?"

"No." Rask pulls the pins from my hair. "You only need slight alterations. You are not far from ideal, just as you are."

I snort. "I'm plain as a post. I've heard that enough times to know it must be true."

"As I have told you before, you shouldn't listen to the nonsense most people spew." He takes hold of my chin and turns my head from side to side. "No, not so very far. In fact, I wouldn't change you at all, had I not promised to do so, and if it were not necessary to advance my plans."

I pull back, breaking his hold. "So, do it. Whatever it is. But there is one thing I want first."

Rask's eyebrows disappear under the fall of his dark hair. "I am gracing you with beauty and power and you want one more thing?"

"Yes. I want you to promise to never use the mirror's power the way you did in those villages. Swear to never again use it to harm innocents."

"It was not my choice to do so, but that is another story. Still, I think I can promise I will never use it to harm innocents. Although, in my experience, those are few and far between."

"Swear."

He lifts his hand. "I swear I will not use the mirror to harm innocents. Now, my dear, place yourself in my hands."

I stare into his dark eyes, which burn with some mysterious passion. "Why?"

That's still the question, the one thing I do not comprehend.

"Because it is what I want." He draws me into his arms.

At first I feel nothing, except Rask's embrace. His body, lean but strong, presses against mine. Under my ear, his heart pounds like a hammer against a forge.

Then the pain hits—just flashes at first, like needle stings in a limb held in one position too long. But it grows and spreads, until I feel my blood is on fire. I gasp and try to pull away, but Rask clasps me tighter.

His lips brush my ear. "Hush, stay strong. It will all be over soon."

Heat, so much heat. It's as if molten gold pours down my throat and oozes through every pore. My fingers claw at Rask's chest, ripping off buttons and tearing through the soft fabric of his shirt. My bones crumple like paper. I bury my face in the folds of Rask's shirt and scream and scream.

The pain subsides, rolling out like a tide. Hollow as a reed, I shudder and slide to the floor at Rask's boots, my hands and feet twitching.

Rask bends over and sweeps me up into his arms. Striding down the hall, he kicks open the door to my room. He drops me onto the downy mattress of the bed and pulls off my slippers and robe, although I'm shaking so hard he must avoid being kicked or slapped by my flailing limbs. When I'm clad only in my linen shift, he tucks me under the sheets and pulls the coverlet up to my chin.

"Now you must sleep." He strokes the side of my face. "Rest."

I sink into the mattress like a drowning soul sliding to the depths of the ocean. All my limbs are limp, my hair floats like seaweed, and my heartbeat slows. Everything above me is lost in a blue-green haze.

Rask leans over me, his face as strange and inhuman as some sea creature. A merman, dragging me down to join him in the depths. His lips are close enough to kiss mine, but he does not, yet I feel he is drawing all the air from my lungs.

"Dying." My voice is barely a whisper. "I am dying."

Rask strokes my cheek again before he sits back. "No, my beautiful girl, you have only just begun to live."

The blue water turns black, and I give myself up to the uncaring sea.

CHAPTER TWENTY-SIX:
BEAUTY REVEALED

A SHAFT OF SUNLIGHT SPILLS ACROSS my face. I sit up, throw off the covers, and swing my legs over the edge of the bed. Strangely, after the trauma I endured earlier, I experience no stiffness or pain.

I glance at the window. The sun hangs low over the sea. I slept most of the day, or maybe it was more than one day. There is no way to tell.

I stand and walk toward the tall worktable, but stop dead when I catch my reflection in a full-length mirror.

Who is this girl? I creep closer, staring into the eyes of the young woman walking toward me.

She is beautiful. Reaching the mirror, I touch my lips, now full and shaped like a perfect bow. My nose is shorter and its distinctive hump has been ironed straight. My jawline is softer, my cheekbones higher. My eyes, still hazel, are wider, and fringed with long dark lashes.

I run my hands over my body, which remains slender, but now includes sensuous curves in all the right places.

Strangely, I still see Varna Lund smiling back at me. Sten Rask kept his word. He only changed my appearance in subtle ways, yet how much difference those slight changes make! I spin, attempting to catch a vision of every angle. It's amazing. Rask did not turn me into someone else, or some artificial doll. It's still me, but me without flaws.

I laugh and run my fingers through my hair, which is no longer dull brown and broomstick straight. Now it's thick and wavy and the color of polished walnut.

Examining my new face and body, I lose all track of time. As I stare into the mirror, something tugs at my thoughts. A memory—something I need to do about another mirror, something about destroying a terrible weapon.

Smash the mirror, Varna. You must smash the mirror.

Not yet. I want to enjoy the experience of being desirable. I wish to revel in a beauty even Erik Stahl would admire.

A wardrobe fills a corner of the room. One of its doors stands ajar and I spy a flash of gold silk. I skip over and throw open the carved wooden doors. There are so many beautiful robes and gowns and cloaks and shawls stuffed into the wardrobe, I can't decide what to choose first.

In the past I never gave much thought to clothes. I just concentrated on keeping my appearance clean and neat. Now I want to try on every one of these gorgeous garments. As I pull out an armful and carry them to the bed, I notice all the colors flatter my newly heightened coloring.

Remembering Rask's comments, I choose a forest green silk gown cut in a simple style, almost like a robe, but cinched tight at the waist. Its only trim is an intricate, twisting pattern embroidered around the square neckline—exotic birds on branches, picked out in tones of gold, green, and brown.

I slide my feet into a pair of suede slippers and run to the door, which is thankfully unlocked. I step into the hall and make my way to the drawing room.

Rask sits in the wing-backed chair, reading a book. He looks up as I enter the room, then leaps to his feet, allowing the leather-bound volume to fall, unheeded, to the floor.

"So you are awake at last. Come and let me look at you properly."

I run to him. "I had no idea it would be like this. It's perfect. Perfect in every way." I complete a spin, holding out my full skirt with both hands.

"It is indeed." Rask looks me up and down. "My sorcery has definitely not failed me."

"Can I do magic too?" I dash to the fireplace, where the fire has died down to embers, and snap my fingers.

"Not like that." Rask steps up behind me. Placing his arms around me, he grips my wrists. "You still need instruction. Relax and concentrate on the power within you. You will feel it. The tiniest tug at first, like the pull of a thread, then it will rise and rush through your body like a river."

I close my eyes and allow Rask to lift my right arm as if I am his puppet. He slides his fingers from my wrist to lightly cup my hand.

"Concentrate," he whispers in my ear. "On warmth, on fire and flame."

It feels as if his fingers are shooting sparks into my skin. My upraised hand trembles.

Warmth. Fire. Flame.

"And there it is." Rask drops my hand and steps back.

Flames leap up amid the ashy logs, reigniting a roaring fire.

I wheel around to face him. "I did that?"

"Yes, but that is very simple magic. There's much you still need to learn. Much I must teach you."

"I can work magic." I hold out my hands, examining them with wonder. "I have such power."

Rask smiles. "You do. Of course, you always possessed the potential. I would not have attempted to transform you otherwise. It wouldn't have worked. It might have killed you instead."

I turn my hands over, examining my palms. Totally unmarked, yet somehow I called forth fire. "Gerda said that's what happened to some of the girls she encountered as wraiths. Mael Voss attempted to convert them into the Snow Queen, but they went mad, or died."

"Not died, as you recall. It was a more horrible fate—living forever with no mind and no will of their own."

Rask speaks these words with such violence I look up from my hands to study his face.

"That's what Thyra Winther feared above all things."

"As do I." Sten Rask turns his head so I can no longer see his eyes. "Anyway, now that you have the beauty you've always craved, I think we should allow you to have a little fun with it." He crosses to a small table with legs carved like a falcon's talons.

"What do you mean?"

He picks up a thick ivory card and waves it at me. "We should take you to a ball."

"These people support the emperor. So it's best if you do not refer to him as the 'Usurper.'" Rask leans over me to adjust the fall of my brown velvet cloak. "Also, you're my ward, don't forget that."

"I remember." I brush his hand away. "Stop. I know how to dress myself."

"It appears not." He slaps his leather gloves against his bare palm. "Based on the way you've pinned that cloak."

I huff and stare out the window of the coach. We're not flying this time and somehow Rask has produced a man outfitted in ebony and gold livery to drive the black horses. At least I assume it's a man. Perhaps it is a transformed rat.

"Something amuses you?"

I shove my black net gloves against my lips to stifle my giggles.

"You're supposed to wear those, not eat them."

"I never wear gloves."

"Which explains the condition of your hands when we first met. Never mind, just slip them on when we arrive." Sten Rask looks me over. "You are quite lovely. I'm sure the young men will forgive a few peccadillos in someone so beautiful."

"You do not?"

"My dear, I know your true nature, don't I? And still, I enjoy your company, for reasons that escape me right now."

"So, what am I to do about the dancing? All I know are country dances. Reels and such."

"That's another benefit of your new powers. Simply observe the other dancers for a few minutes and allow the knowledge to seep into you, right to the bone, and you will be able to waltz like a grand duchess."

I stare at the manicured forest rising up on either side of the gravel road. We've entered the grounds of some great estate, owned by a family who support the Usurper.

No, Varna, these people would never call him that. You must say "emperor." Remember, you are walking into the halls of the enemy. Be aware, be wary. Perhaps you can even learn something of value to share with the others ...

The others. I chew on the finger of one of my gloves. I wish Gerda could be here to celebrate me looking as beautiful as any lady in the land. I would love for her to see these fine traveling clothes, and admire the gorgeous gown resting in my trunk. I want her standing beside me when I make my entrance into the ballroom.

I press my forehead against the frame of the coach window. It's likely I'll never see my sister, or any of my friends, again.

"Varna, we're almost there." Sten Rask turns me to him, taking my face in his hands. "Do not lose sight of our mission. I have come to conduct some business—you are here to enjoy yourself and revel in the power of your new-found beauty. You may dance, flirt and collect admirers. Lead men on and break their hearts for all I care. But remember, it's all a game." He leans in until our foreheads are touching. "You can amuse yourself and learn how to make good use of your beauty, but do not fall in love. Never do that."

I stay very still, clearing my head of the thoughts crowding my mind.

Rask lifts his head and stares deep into my eyes. "Be very careful. While I must associate with these people, they are not my friends. Enjoy yourself, but don't expose our secrets. You are my ward, given into my care when your parents died unexpectedly. Stick to that story, smile, and find me if anything worries you." His face displays a concern that looks oddly real.

God forgive me, I want him to kiss me. *No, Varna, this is magic. He has spun some enchantment.*

I twist the soft fabric of my cloak around my hands.

Rask releases me and sits back, calmly pulling on his gloves. He taps me on the wrist to remind me to put on mine. "We've arrived. Tidy your hair and straighten that cloak. It is time to dazzle them, my dear."

CHAPTER TWENTY-SEVEN:
THEN AND NOW

I T IS AN HOUR BEFORE the ball is set to begin. A livered footman ushers us through the front doors of the manor house, into a two-story hall with polished floors laid out in a black-and-white chessboard pattern. A white marble staircase sweeps up to the second floor.

A maid, who looks no older than fourteen, leads us upstairs, while two additional footmen follow with our trunks. We are shown into rooms next door to one another, although I can tell by a swift glance that Rask's is decorated in a masculine style, while my room is a feminine boudoir, complete with rosebud wallpaper and white lace curtains.

The young woman offers to help me dress, since I have no lady's maid of my own.

"I've never had a maid," I tell her, as she bustles about, pulling garments from my trunk and shaking them out.

"This is lovely." She holds up the gown I am to wear tonight.

Made from velvet the color of a rust-red October leaf, it has puffy cap sleeves and a square neckline. Elaborate gold embroidery decorates the sleeves, bodice, and lower portion of the full skirt.

The maid lays the gown across the bed before turning to help me out of my traveling clothes. "It suits you so. Must've been designed with you in mind."

It's true—the gown's a perfect match for my new figure as well as my lustrous brown hair and light brown eyes. Strangely, I found it hanging in the wardrobe at Rask's castle, so if anyone had it designed for me, it must have been him.

The thought sends color rushing into my face.

"You will be quite the queen of the ball." The maid slips the gown over my head and loops the numerous tiny buttons that fasten the back of the bodice. "We just need to do something with your hair."

She asks me to sit at the dressing table and expertly pins up my hair with golden hairpins we find in my luggage.

"Need to leave it a little loose, a few strands here and there." She tugs curls free to fall around my temples and down the back of my neck. "You have such lovely hair, miss. It doesn't need any decoration. Not like all those other ladies, with their jewels and such."

"You are quite right." Sten Rask walks into the room and appraises me in the mirror. "She needs nothing more. We will allow those who don't shine so brightly to wear the jewels."

The little maid bobs a curtsey and disappears, but not before eyeing Rask up and down.

As I rise to my feet and study him in the mirror I can understand why. He's wearing his usual impeccably tailored fawn breeches and knee-high leather boots, with dark brown cutaway coat and a white shirt with a wide, flyaway collar. His waistcoat is beige velvet, embroidered with a flame pattern in rust and gold.

"We are wearing the same colors." I speak without thinking, then press my hands to my face to hide my blush.

"So we are. A well-matched pair," Rask holds out his arm. "Now, come. Allow me introduce you to these thieves and vultures."

We saunter down the stairs and into the main hall arm-in-arm, occasionally pausing for Rask to introduce me to a bevy of well-dressed ladies and gentlemen. The eyes of the young men light up when Rask mentions I am his ward.

"They think they stand a chance. The fools," Rask whispers in my ear before he straightens and offers the men a dazzling smile.

When we reach the ballroom, Rask kisses my hand before releasing me. "Go fill your dance card, my dear. I must take care of the business I mentioned earlier." He strides off in the direction of the main hall.

I stand next to one of the marble pillars supporting a painted dome that soars above the dance floor. Within moments, a crowd of men appears. Many of them carry glasses of punch, while some offer to escort me through the gardens.

"I am here to dance." I hold up the gold-bordered card pressed into my hands when I entered the room.

The young men elbow one another to get close to me; to have their names penciled onto the card.

This is what it's like to be beautiful. To be desired. The same boys who'd sneer at you, who would call you names, jostling one another for the chance to spend a few minutes with you.

I toss my head and laugh and allow them to fight for the honor of a dance.

As the evening draws to a close, my card is full, and men still press around me at the end of each dance, begging me to strike out a signature and pencil in their name.

I simply laugh and spin off with my next partner, executing the steps with thoughtless grace while the man chatters about his wealth, title, or military achievements. I listen without hearing, knowing their words mean nothing. Sometimes one of the dancers clutches me a little too close, or slides his hand too far down my back, and I casually adjust our positioning to discourage such attentions.

I could take any one of them for my lover. All I have to do is ask.

Smiling and spinning, moving across the polished floor on slippered feet, I'm a fine lady, a princess, an enchantress.

A desirable object.

I pause, my hand still held above my head, forming an arch my partner—a short, pudgy young man who claims to be the heir to a great fortune—ducks under. "Forgive me." I drop his hand and flee the promenade of dancers.

I head for the open French doors that lead to the balcony. Crossing the flagstone-floored balcony, I reach the marble railing and lean against it, my hands gripping the balustrade.

Voices waft up from the dark foliage of the formal garden. One in particular captures my attention. I haven't seen him since he left me in the ballroom, but it is definitely Sten Rask. I lean over the rail, but only see two shadowy figures facing one another. One is tall and broad-shouldered, the other short and willowy.

"You have the mirror, my pet," says a woman's voice that's low and sweet and utterly seductive. "So when may we expect it to be delivered, as promised?"

"In due time." Rask's tone is strangely sharp.

"And when may I expect you to return home?"

"What home might that be?" Rask turns away, and the torches positioned on the edge of the terrace illuminate his face.

His eyes burn in his sculpted face—fathomless and dark as the sockets in a skull.

I gasp. He looks up and catches my eye, warning me to silence with a shake of his head.

The woman steps into the light. She's ethereal as some fairy creature. Yet earthy too—her tiny figure boasts sensuous curves, and her wide, dark eyes glow with passion. Everything about her is smooth and polished, from her porcelain skin to the silken dark hair pulled into a simple bun with loops of hair framing her face.

That face. Somehow it looks familiar, although I could not possibly have encountered her before. I'd never have forgotten such a creature.

"Sten, you cannot stay away from me forever. You are bound to me by more than simple affection."

"Affection?" Rask practically spits the word. "You know I hold no affection for you."

The woman's laugh echoes her appearance—delicate as fine china, yet infused with fire. "Desire then. Call it what you will. You cannot deny its power."

"I do not deny your hold over me, since it was forged in magic and forced upon me as an enchantment. But I now possess the means to break that bond, and I will, as easily as you might shatter a mirror."

The flickering light of the torches transforms the woman's face into a ghastly, yet gorgeous, mask. "You are a fool. Try as you might, you cannot best me. I made you. I can unmake you again." She points her fan at Rask.

A peacock fan. A dark-haired, dark-eyed beauty. A face I recognize from a portrait painted centuries ago.

I cross my arms over my breast and step away from the railing.

The woman alters her expression until she once again appears as sweet and innocent as a child. "You are playing a dangerous game, my pet. One you may not survive."

"I think I will. And prosper." Rask bows deeply, sweeping his hand through the air. "Now I must bid you farewell, my lady. Other matters demand my attention."

The woman slaps her fan against her palm. "That girl? Really, Sten, do you think I care about such things? But go if you must. I know we shall meet again soon, when you deliver the mirror to the emperor."

"Perhaps." Rask sketches another, less elegant, bow before crossing to the terrace doors. "And perhaps," he calls over his shoulder, "by then the emperor will have tired of your so-called affections, as I have."

I turn and walk back into the ballroom, desperately seeking the next partner on my card.

The rest of the evening I dance as if possessed, only pausing to catch my breath or take a swallow of punch.

My last partner—a burly nobleman from a southern country, according to the words I can decipher from his heavily accented speech— leads me out for the final waltz. He guides me once around the dance floor, then releases me when another man taps his shoulder. I spin right into the arms of Sten Rask.

"You dance?" I ask, although it's clear he does, and well.

"Of course. I possess all the skills of a gentleman." His hand presses into the small of my back, drawing me close to his body. "Although without, perhaps, some of the finer qualities."

"I saw you, earlier."

"I know. We will speak of it later. For now—dance with me, Varna."

We sway and spin about the floor, the three-two-one beat relentless as waves crashing to shore. Caught up in his arms, I lose all sense of time and place. We could be waltzing through the heavens, the stars our candles, our orchestra the music of the spheres.

When the music dies away, Rask leads me from the dance floor to the central hall. He leans in to whisper in my ear. "Go back to your room and get some rest. You'll soon have more opportunities to test the limits of your powers."

I look up at him. "I was not using any magic this evening."

He smiles. "Truly? Not all magic is sorcery. Go upstairs. I have business to conduct with some fine, if rather stupid, gentlemen." He kisses my temple before striding toward the smoke-filled billiard room.

I climb the stairs to the second floor, my head filled with images of light and music and a woman wielding a peacock fan.

In my room, I contemplate my reflection in the oval standing mirror.

I touch my cheek. Not much has changed. I still look like Varna Lund, only perfected. I spin, holding out my full skirts. Such little changes, yet such a great difference in how men see me.

They desire you now, all of them. You could crook your little finger and invite any one of them to your bed. And they would say yes.

But it is only because I look a certain way. I have not changed, otherwise.

I frown at the mirror and press my palms into my sides. The soft velvet fabric swings once, then falls into elegant folds.

I must consider how to disrobe. I could call for the lady's maid who dressed me earlier, but despite a lacy white nightgown and robe laid across the tall bed, there's no evidence of her in my room. She's probably helping other ladies at the moment. I reach behind my back, stretching my arms to see if I can unfasten the gown by myself. My fingers brush the tiny bone buttons, but I can't reach around far enough to work them loose.

"No need for that."

I look up at the mirror. Sten Rask stands behind me.

"Where did you come from? I locked the door."

"I am a sorcerer. More to the point, we have adjoining rooms. With a hidden door." He points toward a tapestry, now pushed back to reveal a narrow door. "Which was not locked."

I take a deep breath. "I see. I thought you had business with some gentlemen?"

"I'm afraid they were entirely too stupid." Rask moves in close behind me.

In the reflection we are a beautiful couple. Both dark-haired and handsome, with fine figures and elegant features.

"You did well tonight. Every man here was smitten." Rask's fingers slide across my bare shoulders before he applies them to unfastening my gown. "You see now, the power you possess, even without using magic?"

I concentrate on my breathing as his fingers work each of the tiny buttons loose. "Yes, but I also see how foolish most of these men are. They wouldn't spare a thought for me if I were still plain Varna Lund. Which is ironic, as I am the same person as I ever was, inside. Yet they would spurn me if I looked as I did before, while now my outward beauty instantly convinces them I am worthy of their attentions."

"Ah yes. You *do* understand." Rask kisses my shoulder. "There, you are unbuttoned. Can you manage the corset?"

"Yes, it fastens in the front." *Thank goodness.* I pull the sleeves of the gown up and hold them in place so it does not fall to the floor. "I need to change."

"Over there." Rask points to a tall, painted folding screen in one corner of the room. "You duck behind it and I'll hand over your night things."

"That's not really necessary." I scuttle toward the screen, still holding up the gown with both hands.

"Nonsense. It's rather amusing, playing the lady's maid."

After I duck behind the screen, Rask tosses the nightgown and robe over the top.

"You see, Varna—" Rask's boots tap against the wooden floor as he steps away—"when one learns all the ways, and kinds, of power, nothing is impossible."

I tug loose the corset ties before venturing to speak again. "That woman I saw you with, is she your mentor?" I step out of my corset and pull off my chemise and stockings, until I am standing in only my pantaloons. "She seemed to know you well."

"She *was* my mentor. No longer."

I slip the nightgown over my head. It falls to my feet in perfect folds of white lawn. "I heard her name once, from Sephia. The Lady Dulcia, is that right?"

"Yes."

I pull on the matching robe and realize this ensemble actually covers more skin than my ball gown. No need to hide, then.

"Sephia claims she is powerful sorceress." I step out from behind the screen.

"She is indeed." Rask, who has his back to me, turns around. "Well." He clears his throat. "An enchanting ensemble."

I walk toward him. "Is she your lover?"

Rask covers his mouth and coughs—or is it a laugh?—before replying. "She was, once."

I stop a few feet in front of him. "She is in league with the emperor too."

"Not *too*, as I have broken with him, although he does not know it yet. However, she is indeed in league with him. You see, he's her lover now."

"I see." And at last, I think I am beginning to catch a glimmer of the truth.

Rask sweeps his gaze from my head to my toes. "I'm not sure you do. Not entirely. Please, take a seat, my dear, and indulge my strange whim to enlighten you." He motions toward a winged-back chair.

I sit, crossing my ankles primly and clasping my hands in my lap. "Proceed."

He grabs a simple wooden stool and places it beside my upholstered chair. Sitting, he stretches out his long legs. "You see, I was raised in a great house, a lavish home befitting a wealthy and titled family. But they were not *my* family."

I turn my head to meet his searching gaze. "You were a servant?"

His ironic smile disappears as quickly as it appears. "I was the son of servants. My mother was a cook. My father was a valet. I was a nothing."

He turns his head so I can only view his aristocratic profile. "A very handsome nothing, but still … Then, one day, we entertained special guests. One of them was a lady. She was so beautiful, so gracious." His voice falters for a moment. "She saw potential in me, or so she told my parents. I was to be trained to be something very fine—a lord's valet, or even a butler.

Of course, what she actually noticed was my innate magical ability. I used to play little tricks, you see. I didn't think of them as sorcery—it was just something I could do. Throw my voice, move objects across a table, snuff candles without touching them, that sort of thing."

"So she took you as her apprentice?"

"Yes. My parents were thrilled. They thought they were sending me to a great house, to be trained in an honorable occupation." He leans forward, gripping his knees with both hands. "And, in a way, they were correct. Unfortunately, there was a price to pay."

I study his face for a moment, noting the sharp lines bracketing his mouth. "How old were you?"

"Younger than you are now. Only fifteen. Anyway, the Lady did teach me many things. She revealed my innate powers, and granted me more. She showed me the secrets of wielding magic of all kinds, and taught me other skills, such as healing." He casts me a rueful glance. "Things that have come in handy over the years."

I think of the beautiful woman in a portrait painted hundreds of years ago. "And she became your lover."

He shakes his head. "Not exactly. She took me as *her* lover. A rather different thing."

"You did not love her?"

"I did, or at least thought I did, once upon a time. Quite desperately. Of course, I was so young and green, I knew nothing of what love could be, or should be. I thought desire was all that mattered. But I eventually realized that Dulcia wasn't interested in returning my foolish affection. Oh, she enjoys my body. She craves my companionship for my appearance alone, just as those men tonight desire you."

My fingernails dig into my palms. I unclasp my hands and slide them across the soft fabric of my robe before resting them on my thighs. "Just how old are you now?"

"Twenty-seven. It's my actual chronological age. I have not taken any measures to halt my aging, or extend my years unnaturally. It has not seemed necessary yet."

"But you will."

"Probably. I like this age, actually. Perhaps I shall choose to stay as I am."

"Forever?"

"There is no forever, Varna. Not even for those of our kind. We can still die, by various means. And eventually we grow too old to care anymore and simply … fade away."

I think of the beautiful young woman I spied earlier this evening.

"The Lady Dulcia has not reached that point yet, despite the many years she has lived?"

Rask's laugh holds no humor. "No. She wishes to live forever. Perhaps she shall. She's very powerful, as Sephia said, and as egotistical as she is beautiful."

"Do you still love her?" I can't believe I've asked this question, but once the words are out, I am glad.

Rask rises from his chair to pace the floor. "I still feel desire," he says at last. "But trust me, that is not love, merely an obsession that torments. The truth is, I don't know how much I ever felt for her was sorcery and how much was reality." He turns to face me, raking his hands through his hair. "I desire her and hate her at the same time. I am drawn to her, but want to destroy her. She made me a great sorcerer, yet never her equal. She didn't want that. She still does not. She wants me to worship her—to fall at her feet, not stand by her side. She does not want a partner, she wants a vassal, an acolyte ... "

"A servant," I say quietly.

"Yes. Which I will not tolerate." Rask crosses to my chair and holds out his hands. "I will be no one's servant, no woman's mindless plaything. I left her. She thought I was merely traveling, searching for the mirror, but now she knows I never had any intention of returning. And I do not."

I allow him to pull me to my feet. "You plan to keep the mirror for yourself."

"Yes." He raises one of my hands and kisses the palm. "But not just for me. It could be for us. You and I, as true partners. Together we could stand against anyone, even the Lady Dulcia."

His eyes are alight with passion, but his words shake me from the warmth of this enchantment.

"That's why you wanted me." I yank my hands away and clasp them behind my back. "You needed to be her equal in all things. You wanted to prove your sorcery matched hers. So you decided to choose someone and create your own apprentice, your own acolyte. Or perhaps"—I straighten my back and lift my chin—"you sought to best her, because she chose a beautiful boy, and you began your transformation with someone so plain and ordinary."

Rask grabs me about the waist and pulls me into an embrace. "You are not ordinary. I saw something special in you, just as she did in me."

"And like her, you thought only of yourself. Of what you wanted." I stare into those dark eyes—clouded now, unreadable. "I was never really a person to you, was I? Just an ingredient in your vindictive potion. A weapon for your revenge. Is that right?"

He leans his forehead against mine. "Perhaps. In the very beginning."

"And now?"

He releases me, takes two steps back, and studies my face as if it holds some magic he must master. "And now"—closing his eyes for a moment, his hands clenched into fists, Sten Rask sighs deeply—"go to bed, Varna."

He strides to the connecting door and passes through it without looking back.

I run to the door and lock it, just as I hear the tumbler click on his side.

CHAPTER TWENTY-EIGHT:
FIRE WITH FIRE

AT BREAKFAST I AM SURROUNDED by a cluster of admirers whose chatter and constant attempts to gain my attention make it impossible to eat. From across the room Sten Rask catches my eye. I raise my fork and cast him a desperate look.

He strolls over to my table. "Give us a moment." He shoos away the men, who squawk like roosters squabbling over the last kernel of corn.

Rask sits beside me. "The price of beauty."

"One of them proposed over a plate of salted fish," I reply, before stuffing some eggs into my mouth.

"Only one?"

I narrow my eyes and finish chewing before I reply. "There was another one last night, during a waltz. And one earlier this morning, before I even had my coffee, which was a mistake on his part. Although he did almost convince me, with his talk of two estates and a townhouse."

Rask's laugh makes heads turn in our direction. "You know you should hold out for four estates and a title, at the very least."

I make a disparaging noise and turn my attention back to my plate.

Rask leans close enough to speak into my ear. "Although, you must tell them all 'no'. You do understand that, I hope, my dear?"

I turn my head to stare into his eyes. "I have no plans to marry anyone, if that's what worries you."

"I am not worried." He sits back, tipping up the front legs of his chair. "I believe you know where you belong."

"Do I?" I continue to hold his gaze as I wipe my mouth on my napkin. I touch the fabric to my lips, shielding them from his eyes.

He pulls the napkin from my fingers and tosses it on the table. "If not, I must show you."

His lips are only inches from mine. I press my hand over my heart, as if to prevent it from leaping from my breast.

"At last, we can be properly introduced," says a seductive voice. "This must be Varna."

I sit back and look away from Rask, gazing straight into the face of Dulcia. She stands before us, waving the peacock fan.

"Yes, and you are the Lady Dulcia. I have heard much about you."

Her laugh is bright and twinkling and entirely artificial. "You should not believe everything you hear, little one." She snaps the fan shut.

"I didn't say it was bad."

"No need, my pet. I know who has been telling you tales." She looks past me. "Ah, Sten, do not get up."

Which she says in jest, because he has made no effort to do so.

Lady Dulcia moves close to me and taps my arm with the fan. "I am delighted to finally make your acquaintance. It seems your benefactor could not take the time to introduce us last night. Of course, he is such a busy man. Those elegant fingers seem to be stuck in so many pies."

Rask finally rises to his feet. "Varna, this is the Lady Dulcia, as you have already guessed. Lady Dulcia, may I introduce Varna Lund, my ward."

I realize he's not spinning this tale for the ears of Dulcia, who knows better. He's keeping up the charade for the edification of the guests milling about the room.

"Ward? How extraordinary? How did this come about?" Lady Dulcia no longer spares a glance for me. She stares at Rask.

With the hungry look of a barnyard cat.

Rask places a hand on my shoulder. "Her parents were my friends. They died. I agreed to take in Varna and provide for her."

"Friends? I did not think you had any friends, Sten."

"It seems you don't know me quite as well as you think, my lady."

Lady Dulcia lifts her elegant brows. "Apparently not. For instance, I heard the strangest story last night. Someone reported a rumor that you do not plan to honor your agreement concerning a certain looking glass. Of course, I told the speaker such a thing was impossible. Sten Rask is not a stupid man. He would never try to keep such a valuable item for himself. Not when he knows how much the emperor desires it." She slaps the fan against her palm. "Not when he knows I have promised to deliver it, and how I never renege on my promises."

Rask shrugs. "Because you never make any, my lady. You suggest everything, yet promise nothing."

"I promise this"—she lowers her voice until only Rask and I can hear her—"give up the mirror or I will destroy you."

Rask's grip on my shoulder tightens. "I have no idea what you are talking about. You must have misheard something. Perhaps the punch went to your head?"

Lady Dulcia's dark eyes flash and she looks, for one moment, like the terrifying sorceress I glimpsed last night. "And you"—she points the fan at me—"do not think because he has taken you into his bed he will remain true to you. He will use you and discard you like that napkin he tossed earlier."

Only Rask's pressure on my shoulder prevents me from leaping to my feet. "How dare you suggest ..." I take a deep breath. "For your information, Lady Dulcia— although it is not your affair—Sten and I are not lovers."

"Really? How extraordinary." She looks Rask up and down.

Not a cat, but a bird of prey. A raptor, half-starved, sighting its next meal.

Rask grabs my arm and pulls me to my feet. "I'm sorry to break off this delightful chat, but we are leaving this morning, and must pack. Come, Varna." There is no bow offered. He simply nods at Lady Dulcia and drags me from the room.

Taking the stairs two at a time, he forces me to run to keep up with him. Outside our rooms he makes a fist and slams it against the wall. "Forgive me," he says, when I stare at him in surprise. "I did not plan for the two of you to meet."

"She looks at you like she would like to kill you—or kiss you. I can't tell which."

"Both, I think." Rask brushes down his suede waistcoat. "Now, please pack. We must leave."

"I thought we were staying for a few days."

"Circumstances have changed. Go— I will call for a footman to pick up your trunk." He turns on his heel and disappears into his room.

As I pack, I recall Lady Dulcia's face when I said Rask and I were not lovers. Her expression was so strange. It wasn't amusement or disdain. It was something I never expected.

Fear.

We arrive at the road to the castle by late afternoon. Rask either sleeps, or feigns it, during most of the ride. It is clear he does not wish to talk to me or answer my questions.

I spend my time staring out the coach window, striving to recall the faces of family and friends, and growing terrified when I cannot. Gripping the window frame I force my mind to reconstruct images—Thyra's pale curls and Kai's dark hair, Sephia's green eyes, Erik's strong jaw—but although I can remember descriptions, I can't see anything. It's as if they exist in some tale told to me long ago. Even Gerda. I can't remember Gerda's face.

I swallow a shriek and Rask stirs beside me.

"What is it?" He sits up, tugging down the sleeves of his coat.

"I can't see them anymore. My family. My friends. I try to recall their faces and I cannot."

"No, you may not be able to." Rask turns to me, his expression solemn. "I should have told you before, but I did not wish to frighten you. Also, I wasn't sure it would work the same way for everyone." He takes hold of my hand. "The transformation—it's rather like rebirth. You enter a new life, and everything in the past fades. Oh, you remember, but it means nothing. As time goes on, it all seems like a something that happened to someone else."

"I don't want to forget."

Rask pulls my hand upon his knee and caresses my fingers. The action sends a wave of calm throughout my body.

Magic, Varna, magic.

"You have not lost your ability to feel, if that's what worries you. It's just that you have a new life now."

I look up at him from under my dark lashes. "And this new life, does it include the possibility of love? Or is that something else I must relinquish?"

Rask drops my hand back onto the seat. "There is always that possibility."

I will not let this go. If I've lost my friends and family, I must know there's hope for some type of human companionship in my future.

"The Lady Dulcia seems surprised I'm not already your mistress. If I think about it, I suppose I am too."

Rask is seized by a sudden fit of coughing. "Oh God," he says at last, "what am I to do with you, Varna?"

I straighten my back and stare at him. "Yes, what is your plan?"

He tips his head, gazing up at the ceiling of the coach. "You are very young. Yes, I know girls younger than you are married off in your village. I'm not talking about chronological age. I mean you are very young in the understanding of your new powers."

"And that matters?"

"It does." When he turns his gaze on me, I'm shocked by the pain haunting his eyes. "I was so young when the Lady Dulcia took me in— and lured me into her bed. Too young, in all ways. My lack of control over my own magic was the worst thing. I could not separate myself from her power, from her being. It's what still ties me to her, still torments me." He sighs and strokes the side of my face before pressing two fingers over my lips. "It is why I will not touch you, Varna, not in that way, not now. I won't do to you what she did to me. I do not want someone tied to me by shackles they cannot break. I want a partner, not a servant." He lifts his fingers. "I will wait until you are in full control of your powers."

I realize I am holding my breath and release it. "How will you know?"

"I won't." He leans in and brushes my lips with his. "Not until you tell me."

The coach shudders to a halt.

"Who is that?" Rask throws open the coach door and leaps out, striding to the wide stairs that lead to the front doors of the castle.

Sephia stands on the steps.

I climb out, but stay huddled by the coach.

Rask places one booted foot on the bottom step and glares up at her. "You have no business here, Lady of the Roses."

"I do. You have taken one of my friends captive. I am here to free her."

"I took nothing." Rask holds out his hand to me. "Come, Varna, and explain to this woman what really happened. How you called to me. How you came to me of your own accord."

I don't want to move closer, but the pull of Rask's will is too strong. Walking with carefully measured steps, I cross to him and take his hand.

Sephia examines me, her face darkening. "I see you could not resist changing her. Why choose this girl, Sten Rask, if you had to alter her appearance to suit your tastes?"

"It was what Varna wanted, not me." Rask pulls me to his side. "She has always desired beauty and power. To please her, I have given her both."

"I see." Sephia takes a step down.

"After all, why not choose my offer, when you refused to give her anything?"

I dig the fingers of my free hand into the folds of my velvet cloak. I know Rask is trying to make Sephia believe I acted out of anger because she wouldn't take me as her apprentice. "I never said anything about you, or about the garden, or … about anything."

Sephia does not look at me. Her gaze is fixed on Rask's sardonic face. "I know, Varna. I won't be swayed by this man's lies."

"Neither will I be convinced by yours." Rask releases me with a little shove to the side. "I know why you are here, my lady. And it has nothing to do with Varna."

Sephia takes another step down. "Of course it does."

"No. You seek the mirror. To destroy it, I assume? Or to keep it for yourself? Do you hold hope it might resurrect your lost love? Yes, I know the story of your liaison with Mael Voss."

I take two steps back, stumbling over the cobblestones in the courtyard, and stare at Sephia, my mouth agape. What had she said, that day in the garden? *Someday I must tell you the story of a young enchantress and the boy she loved far too much.*

Sephia's face appears sculpted from ice. "I would never attempt such a thing. Obviously, you know nothing about me, Sten Rask. I do know much about you. I know how you vowed to deliver the mirror to your mistress, so she could in turn hand it over to her lover, who seeks to conquer these lands. It's a rather sordid scenario, all in all."

Rask covers the steps separating them in two leaps and faces off with Sephia. He is taller than she, but somehow I don't feel that gives him the advantage.

"I have broken with them. The mirror is mine."

I realize Rask does not have his scepter. He left it behind on this trip, claiming it was unnecessary. Sliding sideways, I reach the edge of the steps and climb to the landing flanking the front doors, while Rask and Sephia face off on the lower steps.

"No one may own the mirror." Sephia swings her arm in a wide arc.

A mist rises around the two figures. The swirl of vapor twists until it looks like a rope. Wrapping Rask's hands and feet, it topples him and sends him rolling down the stairs.

He roars and jumps to his feet, thrusting out one arm, forefinger pointed at Sephia. A flash of light crackles through the air and Sephia crumples.

In a moment, she is on her feet again, conjuring a wind that sweeps Rask across the courtyard.

He holds up his hands and a wall of fire springs up, surrounding him.

They will destroy one another. I cannot allow that.

I push one door open and dash inside the castle, my mind focused on the scepter. If I can find it, can wield it, perhaps I can stop this battle. I can make Sephia and Rask stand down before they kill each another.

I run to the drawing room fireplace and there it is, just as I remembered, sitting beside a wrought iron poker.

I grab the scepter and turn to run back outside, but … The mirror.

You could smash it, Varna. End it now. Rask is consumed by his fight with Sephia. He cannot stop you.

Smash the mirror, Varna.

I stand before it, breathing heavily. My reflection stares back.

I am beautiful and powerful. No longer a creature who must accept scraps and make do with whatever life hands her. Not a girl who feels inferior, but a woman who can have anything, be anything, she desires.

I turn from the mirror and run back to the front hall, the scepter clutched to my breast. When I reach the front door, I trip over a vine snaking its way across the threshold. The courtyard is a tangle of brambles and vines which spring from the cobblestones as if they require no roots.

As fast as they appear, the plants burst into flames and shrivel to husks.

Sephia stands to one side, her hands moving as if working a loom, weaving foliage from thin air. In the middle of the courtyard, Rask wheels about, his fingers flinging fire at every new sprig of green.

Vines climb the courtyard walls, dislodging stones. Brambles spring up, forming a cage. Rask is able to leap away from such traps, or set them alight, but it's clear Sephia currently has the advantage. His rage causes him to make mistakes, while she remains perfectly calm.

"Cease this foolish battle, you cannot defeat the power of the earth with fire," Sephia calls out.

Rask sends a blast of flame in her direction. It sweeps through a barrier of briars, but cannot reach the enchantress, who throws up a wall of mist that diffuses the fire.

Exhaustion marks both their faces. Soon, one will make a fatal error. Holding up the scepter, I raise my voice. "Stop, both of you!"

Rask spins around. His face blanches to the color of parchment. "Varna, please put that down."

"I will use it if I must."

"You cannot yet wield such a thing. It will kill you." Rask moves closer, kicking aside burnt brambles.

"Then I will break it in half." I wave the scepter over the iron railing flanking the stairs. "Smash it to pieces."

As Sephia walks toward me, all the vines she's conjured wither and crumble to the ground. "Varna, I do not know what magic the scepter may contain. I only know it is an object of great power. Lay it down and step away."

"Not until you promise to cease this fight." I swing the scepter back and forth.

Rask runs up the stairs. "You have stopped it. Now, give that to me." He holds out his hand.

I press the scepter to my breast. "No. First swear Sephia will be able to walk away. Unharmed."

He looms over me, his dark eyes burning like the flames he conjures. "Do you wish for death? Because you are holding it to your heart."

"Swear."

"I swear," he says, between clenched teeth.

I glance at Sephia. "You must go. Without the mirror, and without me. Go back to Gerda and everyone else. Tell them I'm fine. Tell them I'll make sure there are no more tragedies like those villages. Tell them goodbye."

Rask takes hold of my waist with one hand. "Give me the scepter, my dear." His voice has regained its seductive tone. I loosen my grip, allowing the scepter to slide into his other hand. As his fingers tighten about it he closes his eyes for a moment and takes a deep breath.

Sephia crosses to the base of the steps and gazes up at me.

"Come with me, Varna. You do not belong here. You've been bewitched by this man, enchanted by an unnecessary transformation. Come home to those who truly love you."

Rask tucks the scepter under one arm. "Varna is where she is meant to be. She has asked me to allow you to go in peace. So—go."

Sephia doesn't move. "You think he will love you, but he will not. He may desire you, respect you, and even adore you. Yet he will never truly love you. Because love demands sacrifice, and he will never make such a choice. Not even for you."

I lay my head against Rask's chest.

He takes me into his arms. "Leave us," he commands Sephia, then draws me close and kisses me, driving all other thoughts from my mind.

When he pulls away, he puts his arm about me and guides me back into the castle. I cast a final glance over my shoulder. The courtyard is empty. We walk inside and the doors swing closed behind us with a clang of wood against metal.

I can't remember the past as anything other than a rather dull story, but it does not matter. I have a new life now.

"Teach me," I tell Sten Rask as we stroll toward the drawing room, "everything you know about magic."

He tightens his arm about me. "I will teach you, Varna Lund, everything about everything."

CHAPTER TWENTY-NINE: THE DIVIDING LINE

O NE DAY A MONTH OR so later, a steady rain prevents me from taking my usual stroll outdoors. I explore the castle instead, wandering through its numerous corridors and empty rooms. Sten has not wasted time or resources decorating spaces we don't use, although he spares no expense otherwise.

There's one door I cannot open. It leads to a tower that overlooks the sea. I always hoped to climb those stairs and take in the view, but the door remains locked.

Sten is away, dealing with business he will not discuss. Even when he's gone I practice the magic he's already taught me, although I admit I don't spend the time on it I should. Despite the exhilaration of power, the actual working of sorcery is exhausting. I can see why Sephia and Sten avoid using it when it is not required.

I wander into the drawing room to stare into the mirror, something I do far too frequently. Sten has warned me not to touch the glass. Which, naturally, tempts me to do so.

It is such an ordinary looking thing, with its frame of plain dark wood, wide as the span of a man's hand. Except for its size, it could be a mirror in any village home.

I move closer and slide my fingers down the frame. One touch of the glass could not hurt. I have learned so much recently about harnessing my new powers, surely I can manage this.

Allowing my fingers to drift to the glass, I steel myself for a violent reaction.

Nothing happens. The mirror, cool and slick as ice, simply reflects my face and figure. I pause for a second to admire my transformation.

If only those boys from the village could see me now. *No, Varna, that is all in the past.*

I press my palm against the glass.

The mirror shimmers and clouds over and my hand grows warm. I pull it from the glass and step back. The surface of the mirror swirls like a whirlpool. Colors spin, coalescing into images.

It is the village, after the fire.

The scent of burnt timber and flesh permeates the drawing room. I fall back against a chair, clutching at the brocade upholstery with flailing fingers.

In the mirror are the faces of those caught in the fire, some blistered with burns and others covered in ash. All are terrified and in pain. There are also images of the dead—their bodies mangled and broken, or burnt beyond recognition. In an instant, all the horror of that day floods back.

Sinking into the chair, I stare at the mirror until the glass clears. Until it no longer reminds, only reflects.

My face gazes back at me, wide-eyed and open-mouthed. I had forgotten. How could I forget?

Sten Rask caused those fires. He cast flames from the scepter and set two villages ablaze. He destroyed homes and livelihoods, killed countless people, and injured many more.

The man I allow to kiss me. The man I contemplate allowing much more, and soon. He did these terrible things. How can I love a man like that?

I sink deeper into the chair. *Do you love him, Varna, or is it just desire?*

So much desire. Just thinking about him makes my entire body flush. Yet when I recall what the mirror showed me—those images of terror and destruction—I go cold.

I rise to my feet and cross to the fireplace. Flicking my wrist, I set the half-burnt logs ablaze. I grip the marble mantle with one hand and lean forward, staring into the flames.

I do love him, and yet ... It is not the love I ever expected, or imagined. I always thought I might, through some miracle, find a gentle, warm, and comfortable love. Not this fierce attachment I do not understand.

Not this fiery passion. I cannot deny my feelings, but all my logic fights against succumbing to something so challenging and conflicted.

I think of the simple, happy, times I have spent in my village, allowing myself to imagine my life with some ordinary young man. Someone like Erik. We would join our families for holiday meals, and have picnics by the river, and share a quiet, simple life …

After a few minutes, I straighten and step away from the fireplace. It's best to erase those images from my mind. I need to forget any laughter shared with friends. Bury all memories of Gerda, or our mother, or anything from the past.

Forget it all. Forget.

A warning tugs at my mind. Intruders. Sten cast an enchantment around the castle before he left, so I doubt anything can breech the outer walls. Yet something lingers out there, near the gates.

I run to the front doors, grabbing my hooded cloak and tossing it about my shoulders before I dash outside. With my new ability to cast fire and other magical skills, I'm not concerned about my safety. I'm more worried about someone finding this hidden castle and the mirror. Even though I no longer plan to destroy it, I don't want it to fall into the hands of the emperor.

I splash through the puddles that riddle the courtyard. I don't know why I feel such urgency, but something draws me forward.

I clap my hands and the gates swing open.

Drenched to the bone, their clothes plastered to their bodies and their boots sunk into the mud, Erik and Gerda stand before me.

I wait for a surge of joy, for love for them to flood my heart.

I feel nothing.

Their horses wait patiently behind them. I narrow my eyes. There are too many hoof prints stamped into the soggy soil of the path. "Where are the others?"

"Gone," Erik says. "Off to carry news of this castle to those who need such information."

"Varna?" Gerda stares at me, her blue eyes widening. "Is that really you?"

I throw back my hood, heedless of the rain. "Yes, it is."

"No, it can't be." Erik steps forward, his gaze fastened on my face. "You are so changed."

"Why not?" I toss my head. "Sten Rask released my full potential. I am not the girl you knew before."

"I can see that." Erik's expression does not hold the admiration I expected.

He loves beauty, and I am gorgeous now. Yet he appears unmoved.

I turn on my heel and stalk toward the castle doors. "We should not talk out here. You'd better come with me."

Glancing over my shoulder, I make sure Gerda and Erik are safely inside the courtyard before I sweep my arm, closing and locking the gates.

"You can work magic now?" Gerda runs to catch up. She circles in front of me, forcing me to pause.

"Yes. I possess powers, and grow stronger every day."

Gerda holds out her arms. "Still, no hug for me? Is that another change—not caring about your family or friends anymore?"

I look her over, taking in her bedraggled condition—her clothes splotched with mud, her braids springing free of pins and flopping against her shoulders, and her face damp with rain.

Or tears. I straighten and brush past her. "Come inside. There's a fire blazing in the drawing room."

Their boots clomp against the floor of the hall. Closing the front doors with a wave of my hand, I march into the drawing room.

"Just drop those wet things in the hall. We can deal with them later." I walk to the fireplace and push a couple of chairs closer to the blaze. "Now, come and sit. We'll talk when you are more comfortable."

I snap my fingers to draw up another chair. It's not really necessary to use my powers for such a trivial task, but I can't resist demonstrating my magical ability.

Erik crosses to one the chairs. He sits down and examines me with a critical gaze. "You seem to have settled in here quite cozily."

"Of course. It is my home now." I take the chair facing him.

"No, it isn't." Gerda stops in front of my chair and glares at me. "Your home is in our village, with me and Mother and the twins. This is some sorcerer's lair. It cannot possibly be your home."

"I am a sorceress now, so … Please sit down, Gerda. I'm sure you're tired after your journey." I place my hands in my lap. "How did you find me? Did Sephia tell you where I was?"

Gerda sinks into the other chair. "No. She said we should leave you alone, that you had to make your own choices. But I had Bae follow her without her knowledge. He was able to lead us back here."

Erik, who's been looking around the room, stares at the mirror. "The damned mirror. I could smash it and be done with it."

He attempts to stand but I hold up my hand and force him back into his seat. "You will never get close enough to do that."

"Varna." His freckles blaze against his pale cheeks as he studies me with that odd expression. So strange—it almost looks like disappointment. Or despair.

He has not acknowledged your beauty, Varna. Not once. He seems blind to it, even though it drives other men to distraction.

I tap my foot against the hardwood floor. "I assume Thyra and Kai and Anders were in on this little mission as well?"

Erik stretches out his legs and leans back in the chair. "Yes, and Luki and Bae. They journeyed with us to the castle gates, but decided to travel on ahead to make sure we weren't all captured. I planned to come alone, until Gerda insisted on accompanying me. She believed her presence would convince you to return with us. I thought it was a bad idea, but you know how Gerda is when she sets her mind on something." He offers me a grin, but it fades as soon as I do not respond.

"It was a foolish gesture."

Gerda slides to the front edge of her chair. "You've forgotten everything? Even those who love you? Even what day this is?"

"Day? Is today something special?"

"It's your birthday. You're nineteen now."

I look away from her bright face. I had forgotten. All my days bleed together, and such ordinary events don't seem significant.

"Still the same age as me," Erik says. "I turned nineteen last week, although there was no time for celebration. We've been too busy trying to avert a catastrophe."

I glance at him. "What catastrophe?"

"The Usurper obtaining the mirror, of course."

I rise to my feet. "He will not."

"Because Rask will not turn it over to him? Sorry, that is not good enough." Erik jumps up and closes the short distance between us. He looms over me, his green eyes blazing. "The emperor has already amassed his battalions to storm this castle. Yes, he knows where it is. Apparently his sorceress is a bit cleverer than Rask. That's why the others traveled ahead to alert our generals through Thyra's contacts. Our army will arrive soon, and they will clash here, in a battle to determine the course of the war. You'll be sitting in the middle of it. Is that what you want?" He kneels before me and clasps one of my hands. "If not for Gerda, or your other family, or your friends, come away for yourself. Please, Varna, save yourself."

He bends his head over my hand. I long to smooth the flyaway strands of his red hair, almost as much as I want to pull him to his feet and force him to look at me, really look at me, and finally see me.

"You fools!"

I jerk up my head and glance toward the open doorway. Sten stares at our little tableau, his eyes bright and hard as ebony.

He storms into the room and yanks Erik to his feet. "Do you know what you have done? Condemned us all to death, you idiots."

Erik shakes off Sten's hand and faces him, feet planted apart, head high.

I must intervene. "Erik and Gerda have done nothing. They simply came to convince me to return home. I told them I *was* home, so that is that."

Sten turns on me. "Varna, please stay out of this. I heard your friend talking about the emperor's battalions and your country's troops. Do you have any idea what that means?"

He softens his voice to speak to me, but anger still darkens his face. I tug on his sleeve. "Please, they have seen me and know I am fine. They cannot harm us. So let them go."

"Sadly, I am not sure that is possible."

"Because you are a vindictive bastard?" Erik asks, his tone quite pleasant.

"Perhaps, but more to the point, because you have information I do not wish to share. I'm afraid you are stuck here with us, as rather unwelcome guests."

Erik crosses his arms over his chest. "Guests? I think you mean prisoners."

Sten looks him over. "I suppose I do."

Gerda jumps up. "You cannot hold us here!"

"I am afraid I can, little sparrow. It is not what I want, but I truly see no other option."

"You can let them go, and you will."

Sten gazes down at me, his face registering surprise at the command in my voice. "My dear, they will join those allied against us. We can't allow that, since they know more than the castle's location. They also know exactly where I keep the mirror."

"Then move it." Out of the corner of my eye, I spy Erik's face. It expresses, finally, his approval.

Sten strokes my jawline with one finger. "I do not want to."

I tilt up my chin. "It is my birthday."

"Is it? Congratulations, my dear. However, I don't follow your line of reasoning. How are these things connected?"

"This is what *I* want. As my gift from you. Let them go."

Sten pulls me into an embrace. "I would rather give you the world." He turns his head toward Gerda and Erik. "I don't know what you think of me, other than I am a bastard, but let me assure you I have no intention of handing over the mirror to any army, yours or the emperor's. In fact, I soon plan to leave this country and disappear, taking the mirror with me."

Gerda eyes us with distaste. "And Varna?"

"And Varna, if she agrees." Sten gives me a look that raises the color in my cheeks.

Erik opens his mouth and snaps it shut before saying anything.

Sten examines Erik's face. "Ah, now I see how things stand. I am sorry, Erik Stahl, but Varna is not for you."

I look up at Sten's averted face in amazement. Surely he doesn't think Erik has feelings for me. Not romantic feelings, anyway. No, that's ridiculous.

Erik's face turns the color of his hair. "Varna is my friend. I want what's best for her. I doubt that is you."

"Wouldn't it be preferable to allow Varna to decide?" Sten slides his fingers down my neck and across my shoulders before releasing me.

Erik shakes his head. "Normally I would agree, but not now, because Varna is not herself. It is my turn to speak truth. You have enchanted her mind as well as her body. You've turned her into your plaything. Now she is just your doll, or some mindless puppet. You don't know her, so how can you truly care anything about her?"

Sten stares at Erik, his dark eyes glittering. "You are mistaken. I know her, far better than you. You did not spend months working beside her in a tiny cottage, making healing potions. You never traveled out together on midnight calls to save the sick. You didn't struggle side-by-side to aid the injured. Yes, I know her—the girl who toiled tirelessly, with little thought for her own comfort, and the woman whose intelligence and passion shine like the stars, although most cannot see it. I know her true self, below the surface, beyond this transformation. It is you, Master Stahl, who have never seen her as she really is." Sten steps away and raises his arm.

Erik sails backward. He hits the floor with a thump, banging his shoulder into the stones of the hearth.

I rush forward and kneel beside him. "You did not have to do that." I gaze at Sten, my lips trembling.

Admit it, Varna, you more shocked by his words than this action. Amazed that he might be jealous of Erik, or that he would claim to care for you, the real you ... No, it is another manipulation. It must be.

He crosses to me. "Please get up, my dear. You should never grovel."

Gerda kneels down beside me. "Leave her alone. You've done enough damage."

I check over Erik, who pushes my hands away. I sit back. "You seem to be fine."

He grips of one of my hands. "What about you? Are you all right? What has that bastard done to you?"

I pull my hand from his grasp. "I am fine."

"No, you are not." Erik struggles to a sitting position and looks me in the eye. "This is not you. I know it isn't."

"You know no such thing."

Erik gazes at me as he did that night in the shepherd's hut, and I finally realize what it means. I recognize the cause of the shaking hands, the searching looks, and the determination to save me, whatever the cost.

Foolish, foolish, Varna. You couldn't see it before because your lack of confidence, your stupid self-hatred, blinded you. Do you see it now?

Yes, I do. Now, when it is too late, I know the truth. Erik Stahl loves me.

He loves me in a way I cannot love him. No matter how incredible such a thing seems, Erik desires me, while I only care for him as a friend.

But I do love him, and Gerda too. And that love is just as important as any fantasies of romance.

I rise to my feet. "Let them go," I tell Sten.

Gerda stands beside me as I extend my hand to help Erik to his feet.

Flanked by Erik and Gerda, I meet Sten's furious gaze. "I will stay here with you, as I promised. In exchange you must allow them to leave."

"No, Varna," Gerda says, as Erik keeps my hand clasped in his.

"That is not how this works, my dear. You choose my side or you choose theirs. There is no middle ground." Sten's eyes appear glazed. So odd—if I didn't know better, I would say he was in pain.

"I will stay. So you must let them go."

"Or?"

Erik tightens his grip on my hand as I stiffen my spine. "Or I will fight you."

Sten laughs. "You cannot win, dear one."

"No, but I can force you to battle me. Which may allow my sister and Erik time to escape." I squeeze Erik's fingers. "I don't think you can concentrate on them when you're engaged in such a fight, can you?"

"Varna." My name rends the air like a desperate cry. "Do not do this. I need to keep them prisoner, but I promise not to harm them. That must be enough."

"It is not. You said yourself we will be caught between two warring armies. Perhaps you and I can escape, but if they remain here, imprisoned, what will happen to them? No. I will not allow it. Let them go."

Erik releases my hand and steps away, placing his arm around Gerda. He knows what's happening, what I am about to do.

And you know what to do, Erik. Whatever happens, escape with Gerda. If you love me, do this one last thing for me.

I curl my fingers into a fist. Heat blazes in my palm—a fire that does not burn me. I swing my arm and cast a ball of flame at Sten Rask.

He blocks the flames with invisible shield formed by the palm of his hand, then wheels about and throws a stream of fire at my feet.

I leap aside and spin the fire into a ribbon of flame I cast into the fireplace. "Go!" I shout at Erik. "Get out!"

Sten casts a wall of flame around me. I push the fire down with my hands and break free, running toward the mirror.

"No!" he roars, chasing me down. He grabs me about the waist.

Out of the corner of my eye I spy Erik dragging Gerda from the room.

That is all that matters. Nothing else. I turn in Sten's hands and stare up at him. "I will smash the mirror. If not now, later. I will do it. Unless you kill me."

Sten's chest heaves. "I cannot kill you. You know that."

"Why?"

His dark eyes bore into me until I feel the flesh is being flayed from my bones. "You have betrayed me, but I know it was only a momentary lapse. Those two reminded you of the past. You forgot who you are."

"No." I caress the side of his face with the back of my hand. "I remembered."

He pulls me close and kisses me. A long, slow kiss that melts all my bones. It's as devastating as my transformation, but with pleasure replacing the pain.

"I will cast you into the tower," he whispers in my ear. "I will place a spell so you cannot use any of your new-found magic. I will imprison you, if you don't bring them back. They have only made it as far as the gates. Call them back, my love."

"No." I snap my fingers. "I have opened the gates. They are gone."

Sten thrusts me from him. "You have chosen. You go to the tower."

I hold out my hands, crossed wrist over wrist. "Do it then."

He swears, grabs my arm, and drags me out of the room, down the hall, up the stairs, and straight to the locked door leading to the tower.

"Varna"—he turns to me as he throws open the door—"say the word and I will release you. Give your allegiance to me. Vow you will never smash the mirror."

I look him in the eye. "No."

He takes me then, up the stairs and into a small, round room with one window. He tosses me to the stone floor and leaves me there, and locks the door behind him.

CHAPTER THIRTY:
THE VIEW FROM THE TOWER

S TEN PROVIDES ME WITH FOOD, water, and all the necessities. Clean clothes, water to wash up, even a brush for my hair. And a mirror.

It is not a magical object, of course, simply a full-length looking glass set in an oval oak frame. I assume it is a reminder—a way for me to admire my transformed face and body.

He visits me, bringing little gifts—flowers from the garden, a book of poems, a delicate puff pastry, filled with raspberry cream.

I know what he is doing. I know what he wants.

What I want is not so clear.

"Varna, this is foolishness." Sten stands behind me as I stare out the tower window.

I do not turn around. "No, it is not."

He moves closer, until he can wrap his arms around me. "It makes no sense for you to remain here, so far from me, over a little misunderstanding."

Although I long to melt into his arms, I stiffen my spine at his touch. "You wanted to imprison my sister and my friend. You have murdered innocents in the most horrible way possible, and not blinked an eye. You would destroy anyone who stood in the way of your ambitions, even me."

"Not true." He kisses the back of my neck. "I would never harm you."

"Just everyone around me."

"Does that matter so much?" He turns me around in his arms, until I am forced to face him. "We could leave now. Take the mirror and disappear. Create a new life, just you and me."

"No." I lean away from him. "I suppose you could force me to go with you, if you wished. Why not do so?"

He looks over my shoulder and stares at the scene displayed in the window.

I know what he sees. Troops are massing on the beach and the cliffs. In the forest, blue banners indicate the emperor's camp, while ships sail along the horizon, one fleet preparing to face the other. Not yet engaged in battle, but soon.

"It would mean nothing if I forced you to go. If you insist on opposing me, we will stay here, whatever comes."

"And die together?"

"If necessary."

I sigh. "You need not do this. Take the mirror and go. I will stay. Perhaps my friends will secure my safety before it is too late."

Sten takes my face in his hands. "You know I can't do that. I chose you. Transformed you as a weapon in my war against Dulcia. Used you for my own purposes. Then learned your true worth. Now ... "

I tilt my head and study his face. "Now?"

He shakes his head. "It is too late. I suspect you no longer care for me, not as you once might have, but I cannot abandon you."

"You could burn down two villages and an Opera House, but abandoning me is beyond the pale?"

"Those were not things I wanted to do. I was forced by circumstances ... "

"Nonsense." I place my fingers against his lips. "We choose. I forgot that for a time, among other things. Now I've come back to my right mind, and I know we can always choose. Oh, it might mean bad things will happen to us—disapproval, disgrace, even death—but we have that power, Sten. To do what we know is right and best. No matter the consequences."

He pulls me close and buries his face in my hair. "Please do not do this. We could have everything. Not just wealth and power, but all the things I've never known—companionship, joy, and even love."

"Love?" I push him back, my palms pressed against his chest. "Are you saying you love me? Do you even know what that is?"

"I know how I feel."

"That is desire, not love. If you loved me, you would allow me to leave this tower."

Anger flashes in Sten's eyes. "To run back to your village? To Erik Stahl?"

"If that is what made me happy, yes."

He shakes his head. "It would not. I do not believe you know yourself as well as you think, Varna Lund."

"You are in no position to determine that. What do you love, Sten Rask? This face and figure? The power you gave me? A woman you formed from a foolish girl? Because I think this transformation is what you love, if anything. Not me. Not the real Varna Lund, who's merely a villager who wants to help others. A plain girl who dreams of alleviating suffering, not gowns and dances. An ordinary woman who only wants to live a life that matters."

"I know you. I told Erik Stahl that, and I meant it."

"You know a lie. This is not me. This is your creation. That is what you love."

"No, it is you who are mistaken, my dear. You have allowed your self-doubt to cloud your mind." Sten releases me and strides away. At the door, he turns, casting me one last look. "I do love you, the real you. What will it take for you to believe me, Varna?"

"A sacrifice," I say, turning my head so I cannot see him leave.

As the days pass, nothing changes except the movement of troops outside my window. I don't know what they are waiting for—what signal will cause the battle to erupt. I have no idea how long it will be before they swarm the castle, before one side or the other breaks through Sten's protective spells.

I hope it will be our soldiers, but it will probably be the emperor's troops, aided by his lover, the Lady Dulcia. I have prepared myself for that eventuality. The window in the tower is not wide enough for me to crawl through, but I study the stones and ancient mortar and know, if necessary, I can break it open. My wooden chair will do the trick.

Of course, once that's accomplished, the only thing I can do is jump to my death.

Still, it is a better option than placing my life in Lady Dulcia's hands. I know this without a doubt.

Sten has not returned to the tower since our last conversation. I suppose he has given up on me. Perhaps he has already fled, leaving me to my fate. *No, Varna, you know he's still here. Waiting. You can sense it, despite the spell he's cast to dampen your magic.*

I lean against the stones surrounding the window and dangle one hand outside. It comforts me to feel the sun warm my hand and the air caress my fingers.

Dropping my hand, I encounter a bump. I look down. A green vine climbs over the sill and burrows its tendrils into the cracks between the stones.

I lean against the window and look down. A web of vines covers the tower, reaching from the foundation to my window. The vines interlace to form a living ladder.

There is only one person who could create such a thing. I scan the bottom of the tower, where it connects with the terrace, for any sign of Sephia.

I do spy a red head, but it is not the enchantress.

"Erik!" I press my face against the narrow opening.

He gazes up at me and raises a hand as he climbs the vines.

Oh, Erik, why are you here? Placing yourself in danger, once again, for me? I know why. It breaks my heart, yet warms it at the same time.

I grab the chair and slam it against the window. Mortar flies in all directions. I hit the wall repeatedly, until I can pry a stone loose. I toss it to the floor and use my fingernails to dig out one stone, then another, and another.

My fingers bleed and it doesn't matter. Not at all. Erik reaches the window, now open wide. I throw my arms around him and help him crawl into the tower.

We tumble onto the floor, still wrapped in each other's arms.

"Well, hello, Varna." He kisses me.

I allow the kiss, hoping it will ignite my own passion. But although it is enjoyable, it does not.

What is wrong with you, Varna? Erik is a handsome and intelligent young man, with an undeniable core of goodness. You've looked at him with desire before. What is different now?

I know, but will not admit it, not even to myself.

Erik pulls away from me. Lifting his body to a sitting position, he stares at me, his cheeks almost as bright as his hair. "Sorry, I'm just glad you are still alive, and safe, and … Well, not still attached to that sorcerer, to tell you the truth."

I sit up and face him. "No need to apologize. I'm actually quite flattered. But, happy reunions aside, don't you think we'd better get out of here? I can't vouch for our safety otherwise."

Erik stands and helps me to my feet. "We must climb down. Do you still have on breeches under your skirt?"

"I doubt that's important at this point." I tuck up my skirts and my petticoat, exposing a bit of leg between my stockings and my pantaloons. "Are you going to be able to control yourself if you glimpse some skin?"

Erik's eyes have gone very wide. "I think I can manage."

"Good. Now, who descends first?"

"I do. So I can provide some support if you slip."

"Or I can send both of us crashing onto the flagstones." I take a deep breath. "All right, let's make the attempt. Whatever happens, it is better than staying here."

Erik nods and kisses my cheek before he climbs out the window.

Clinging to the vines, he makes his descent. I follow him, not looking down. Concentrating, I move hand over hand, my slippered feet feeling for the next sturdy rung of the vine ladder.

Erik reaches the terrace and drops down. "You must jump the last little bit." He holds up his arms. "But I am right here."

I release my grip, allowing my body to tumble into his arms. I know he won't let me fall.

"About time." Kai and Thyra walk out of the shadows.

Sephia steps up beside them. "We must act quickly. According to Erik, the mirror is just inside those doors. We need to gain entrance and destroy it, then leave before Rask is aware of our presence."

I wobble slightly as Erik places me on my feet. He puts an arm around me and I lean against him. "Where are the others? And how did you get up here?" I look out over the terrace. "There's no way up or down, unless one can fly."

Sephia smiles. "Bae carried us, two at a time. He is waiting, hidden in the woods outside the front gates. As for Gerda and Anders, they are safe with some allies in a nearby village."

"Luki watches over them," Thyra says. "So they are well protected."

"Good." I glance up at Erik. "Sten is still here, somewhere. I can sense it."

"All the more reason to move swiftly," Sephia says, with a sharp look at me. "We cannot allow the mirror to fall into the hands of the emperor, or his concubine."

The glass doors to the drawing room swing open. "I must correct you." The Lady Dulcia strolls onto the terrace, holding her peacock fan against her breast. "I may be the emperor's lover, but I am certainly no concubine." She flicks open her fan and languidly waves it before her face.

In the drawing room, Sten thrusts the scepter at the mirror, and instead of breaking, the glass gives way, like water. Sten yanks the scepter free and crosses the terrace to stand behind Lady Dulcia. From the set of his jaw and the look in his eyes, I can tell he isn't moving under his own volition.

"You should leave." Sephia straightens to her full height.

"Or what? You will drown me in roses? No, I do not think you can stand against me. Against Sten, perhaps, but not me."

Sten clutches the scepter. I wonder why he needs it, especially infused with the mirror's magic. Perhaps he intends to burn us all to cinders, if his mentor demands it. I stare into his tortured eyes.

Fight her, Sten. Not just to save me and my friends, but also to save yourself. Break her hold on you, now and forever.

"My apprentice thought he could keep the mirror from me, but of course he was mistaken. Such a naughty boy, although he has his uses." Dulcia slaps Sten on the arm with her fan. "Go, take out some of this country's troops, would you, my pet?"

He shuffles to the edge of the terrace, his face a mask of agony.

"This is not necessary." Thyra step forward to confront the sorceress. "Take the mirror and go. Do not kill innocent men to prove a point."

"Innocent?" Lady Dulcia's delicately arched eyebrows lift. "They are the enemy."

Thyra stares her down. "They are my countrymen."

"Which means you are my enemy as well. Be very careful, little girl, who you choose to confront. Besides, I know your story, Thyra Winther. I suppose you *would* wish me to carry off the mirror. Smashing it, as some of your friends are inclined to do, might kill you, yes?"

From the play of emotions on Thyra's face, I can tell she wishes she still possessed all the powers of the Snow Queen. "That is of no consequence. I will shatter it with my own hands if necessary. I simply wish to prevent more needless deaths."

"How noble of you, but"—Dulcia taps Thyra's rigid arm with the fan—"I scarcely think you have any right to the moral high ground. I have it on good authority that, as the Snow Queen, you allowed at least one innocent to die."

"That scarcely places us in the same circle of hell. Besides, I deeply regret my actions, while you seem to have no compunction about murdering any number of people. I suspect you forced Sten Rask to destroy the Opera House and those villages, just as you are controlling him now."

"Why, yes. Because he is my creature. He must do as I say." Dulcia tilts her head, studying Thyra for a moment. "You will not be killed by the mirror's destruction, by the way. That much I know. So you need not fear. Yet, seeing such courage and resolve, perhaps I have overlooked a possible ally. I could use another apprentice, since Sten has failed me so miserably. Yes, perhaps you possess a will strong enough to help me wield the mirror. What do you say, Thyra Winther? You have tasted power before. Will you join me? Together we could achieve more than you ever dreamt of."

Thyra's eyes glitter like diamonds. "I would kill myself first."

"If that is your answer, you must allow me that privilege." Dulcia flings up her right arm, throwing Thyra and Kai to the ground.

Sephia rushes forward to kneel beside them. "You are insane." Her eyes shoot daggers at the sorceress. "I will not battle you now, for fear of the harm that might befall my friends, but I promise I will find you one day, and make you pay for this."

Lady Dulcia laughs. "I am terrified. Truly." She swishes her fan and strolls over to Sten. "Now, my pet, you see those little figures in the green uniforms? The ones with the gold and emerald banners? Take out that regiment for me, would you?"

Sten raises the scepter above his head. Lowering his arm, he points it in the direction Dulcia indicates with her fan.

"No!" shouts Erik. I grab his arm and hold him back.

In the moment Sten flicks his wrist, I glimpse his slight correction. It's a movement that buckles his knees and drops him onto the flagstones.

An arc of blue flame pierces the sky, soaring high before descending like a falling star. A terrible explosion rattles the woods, and fire and smoke obliterate one section of the gathered battalions.

"What have you done?" shrieks Dulcia. She grips the balustrade, staring out over the chaotic landscape. "You missed. I said the green and gold banners, not the blue. You hit the emperor's camp, and have undoubtedly killed him, along with his elite guard."

Sten struggles to his feet. Leaning against the railing, he allows the scepter to dangle from his fingers. He offers his mentor his most dazzling smile.

"On the contrary, my lady. I did not miss. I hit my target."

CHAPTER THIRTY-ONE: SACRIFICE

I HOLD MY BREATH, AWAITING LADY Dulcia's next move. It's doubtful I can stop her, but I am determined to try. I move closer to Sephia. She stands beside Thyra and Kai, who've risen to their feet with their arms wrapped around one another.

"Can we do anything?" I ask her, keeping my voice low.

Sephia lays a finger to her lips and shakes her head as her voice fills my mind. *She is too powerful, Varna. We would simply enflame her anger, and place our friends in more danger. We must wait for the right moment and use cunning, not magic.*

I nod my understanding, even though my thoughts won't stop racing. *She will kill him.*

Sephia looks at me, lifting her eyebrows.

I know what she's thinking, although she sends no more mental messages. She wonders why I care what happens to Sten Rask.

No, she knows, Varna. That pitying expression—yes, she understands only too well.

Erik slides sideways to join our group as Lady Dulcia focuses on Sten.

"You ungrateful cur." Her once sweet voice is curdled as sour milk. "Do you know what you have done?"

"Yes." He brushes his dark hair away from his forehead with one hand. "If all went well, I have killed your lover and sent his troops scurrying like ants fleeing a smashed anthill."

"You have also shattered my plans for our future."

"Our future? Did we have one?" Sten's voice slips into a familiar bantering tone.

Dulcia steps closer to her former apprentice. She's tiny compared to him, but her size is deceptive. Power radiates off her in shimmering waves.

"You and I and the mirror. Nothing could stand against us. Why do you think I seduced the emperor? For love?" Dulcia's laughter rings like silver bells. "That stupid, egotistical, fool? Nonsense. I was using him. I promised to help him conquer all the lands he could hold with his armies, while I waited for his sickly wife to die. Of course, I had plans to hurry that process along." She slides her delicate fingers through the shining fall of her hair. "Then, once he married me and made me his empress, the emperor would meet with a tragic accident. It would not be anything too obvious. Perhaps a tumble from his horse."

Sten's lips curl in distaste. "Orchestrated by your magic, of course."

Dulcia shrugs. "Or yours. The end result would be the same."

"Not the blame, however."

"And that matters? Really, you have become pathetic. I scarcely recognize you."

Sten bows from the waist. "I take that as a compliment, my lady."

"You think because you hold the mirror you can defy me?" The mask slips from Lady Dulcia's face. Her skin pulls tight, hard and pale as a skull, and her eyes blaze like heated coals.

"It is in my possession, and thus must answer to my magic, not yours." Sten's voice is as cold as his mentor's face. "You can try to take it from me, but I will burn us both to cinders before I allow you to succeed."

"You will relinquish all the power you have sought for so long? You were meant to rule beside me, you fool."

A bark of laughter escapes Sten's lips. "Please stop this pretense. You can't dupe me any longer. I know how it would be. You—the empress. Me"—he bows again, this time making it a grand, sweeping gesture—"your humble servant."

"Which is what you are. What you always were. Did you think I would raise you to my level, you foolish boy? Did you imagine I would ever truly love you?"

"Once, perhaps. But not for some time. And I am finally, thankfully, quite happy about that." Sten turns from Dulcia and strolls to the center of the terrace.

He stops and surveys our huddled group. "Now, these rather bothersome creatures—why not let them go? They are not likely to survive, at any rate, since they must make their way through the chaos of the troops battling below. Honestly, they're an impediment, if we truly wish to come to terms over the mirror."

He catches my eye and I know, in that instant, he's trying to save us.

Erik grabs my hand. "I'm happy to leave, if you guarantee my friends will not be harmed."

"Not by me." Sten meets Erik's stoic gaze with a sad smile. "Just take care of her," he whispers.

The Lady Dulcia crosses to stand at Sten's side. "I agree. I have no use for these children. They should be gone. I will even help. However, since you are so attached to the mirror, perhaps you should sit with it, my pet." She flings Sten backward with one sweep of her hand. A gale-force wind catches and carries him into the drawing room. In an instant the glass doors close and lock and a thick plate of additional glass materializes over the entrance, trapping Sten inside.

Dulcia raises her arm again, as if brushing away an annoying insect.

Erik's fingers are torn from my grasp. I shriek and reach for him, but he's flung into the air to dangle like a poorly controlled marionette.

"Stop it!" I shout, as Dulcia flicks her wrist and sends Thyra and Kai sailing upward.

The sorceress does not acknowledge me. She turns on Sephia. "Now, Lady of the Roses, save your friends, if you can."

Dulcia purses her lovely lips and blows a tiny puff of air. The puff grows into a gust that blows my three friends off the edge of the balustrade. They hang, helpless, above the long, deadly drop to the beach.

Sephia wheels about, spinning a web of vines with her hands. The vines encircle Erik, Thyra, and Kai, wrapping them together. Just as Lady Dulcia flicks her wrist once more, and my friends fall from the sky, Sephia whips the living net tight about them and casts it higher.

I scream, certain they will be dashed to death on the rocks, but Sephia whistles and leaps up, grabbing the end of the vine that ties off her green web. She spins in the air like a ballerina turning pirouettes, keeping the net, and our friends, aloft. Just when I think she must fall, dragging the net with her, a bulky form appears, pulling a sleigh.

Bae, the reindeer enchanted by Sephia's former lover, Mael Voss. I stifle an exclamation, as my thoughts acknowledge the irony that the sorcery wielded by a mage who fell to the darkness may be what saves her, and the others.

Thank heavens, the others too. I fall to my knees. If they are all safe, I can endure anything.

The flying reindeer sweeps up under Sephia, allowing her to drop onto his back. She grips the web of vines and swings it into the sleigh. Bae sails away, pulling the sleigh carrying Thyra, Kai, and Erik behind him.

They *are* safe, at least for now. I bend my head over my hands and weep with relief.

"I see the enchantress of flowers has some uses. Now, child"—Dulcia pokes at me with her slippered foot—"what shall we do with you?"

I leap up to face her. "You should know I also possess magical abilities. I'm not powerless."

Lady Dulcia makes a tutting noise. "Silly girl, if Sten Rask cannot stand against me, what do you think you can do?"

"Whatever I can, even if it kills me." Cracks form in the glass imprisoning Sten. If I can hold out long enough …

"That can be arranged." Dulcia examines me, her eyes narrowed. "He did well, though. He made you into a pretty thing, a lovely toy."

"I am no one's plaything," I say, as a large section of the glass shears off and falls from the castle doors.

Sten strides out, pointing the scepter at Lady Dulcia. She grabs my arm and faces him, a little smile playing about her lips.

The crystal finial glows blue, spitting sparks of fire. Sten raises the scepter as if to cast its power, but halts his motion when Dulcia holds me before her like a shield.

"Go ahead. Destroy me. Just know you will be incinerating your little ladylove as well."

I create fire balls that fizzle in my hands as I struggle in her grip. "Do it," I tell Sten. "Free yourself, and our world, from this evil."

He lowers the scepter. "I cannot."

"This is the sacrifice!" I shout at him.

Sten shakes his head "No, it is not. There is one I must make, but it is not this." He rubs his hand over the crystal until its blazing light dims and fades. "There. It is a dead thing now. A simple walking stick." He lays the scepter on the ground at his feet. As he lifts his head to face us, the anguish in his dark eyes makes me gasp. "Lady Dulcia, I will give you the mirror. I will even accompany you when you travel to whatever country you wish to torture next. I will do this, will promise to return to your service, if you allow me to call my winged messenger to carry Varna safely from this place."

"Such a pretty scene." The sorceress's taunting voice fills my ears, almost blocking out the roar of the cannon fire from the battles below. "Really, Sten, do you think I would allow this creature to retain your transformation? Why—so if you escape again you can run back to her? I think not."

Dulcia thrusts me away, tossing me to the flagstones. "Yes, she is quite lovely now. Also, I am sure, clever enough to grow into a powerful sorceress. But without those things, what is she? Simply a plain village girl with nothing to offer. That is all she really is. Everything else is your creation."

I hear Sten's shout right before a blast of power engulfs me. I scream and roll into a ball, clutching my knees. My entire body is wrapped in a blanket of fire—it burns as if the skin is being ripped away. My bones melt and twist like silver hammered on a forge.

Pain blinds me until all I see is white light, as if I have stared straight into the sun.

I am dying. Here on this terrace, at this castle, without friends or family beside me. This is where I die.

No. My fingers encounter damp moss. I slide my hands over flagstones and push up, raising my body from the ground. Lifting my head, I realize I am still on the terrace. The sounds of battle rage below the castle. Still alive.

"There," says the Lady Dulcia. "There is your precious apprentice, reduced to her true form. Just as you found her."

I sit up, banging my knee into something. The scepter. My fingers tighten around the object. It must have rolled in my direction when Dulcia blasted me.

"I will allow her to leave, unharmed, if you swear you will honor your earlier vow."

"I swear," Sten says.

His face is an unreadable mask. He crosses to me and whistles. Calling his great bird to take me away, while he remains, chained to his mentor by his vow.

Even worse, the mirror will fall into the hands of one who will use its tremendous power for evil.

I attempt to stand, but my legs are too weak. Sten bends down and places his hands under my arms and lifts me to my feet, my fingers still clutched about the scepter. He slides his hands to my waist, steadying me.

Dulcia laughs and points at me. "She is not such a prize now, is she? Come, my pet. She no longer matters. Instruct your bird to carry her off and drop her wherever you wish. We will flee this place with the mirror. I may have lost these lands, but there are many more we can conquer. You and I, so well matched. We belong together. I am sure you see that now."

Sten turns me with his hands until my face is pressed against his chest. "I see nothing of the kind. I will honor my vow. Yet know this, my lady"— his tone turns this title into an insult—"I choose Varna over you, even now. You think your beauty and power make you more desirable? You are much mistaken." He tips up my chin with one finger, leans in, and kisses me.

Still steeped in passion, but a sweeter kiss than all the others. A kiss goodbye.

As he lifts his head, he whispers in my ear. "Take the scepter. Break the mirror. I will buy you time."

I stare into his eyes. *She will destroy you*, I mouth, afraid to speak aloud.

"She will try." He brushes my lips with a final kiss. "Smash the mirror, Varna."

"Enough of this." Anger vibrates Dulcia's voice.

Sten pushes me away and steps forward to face his former mentor. "I will keep my vow to travel with you, but I will never again touch you. Not willingly."

Her lovely face twists. She hisses like a cat. "You will crawl on your knees, begging for one kiss."

"Never," Sten says, and casts a river of fire around her.

She shrieks and draws the flames into a ball she throws back at him.

He holds up one palm and the orb of fire dissolves into smoke. He blows it in Dulcia's direction. Before it reaches her, it coalesces into the shape of a snake, its mouth open to display fangs dripping with poison.

Lady Dulcia laughs and grabs the creature behind its glittering head. She throws it about her neck, transforming it into a scarf that mimics the colors of a peacock's tail. In an instant it shimmers and dissipates.

Sten sends another blast of fire in her direction, which she swiftly deflects.

He cannot win this contest, but that is not his goal.

I run to the shattered doors that open into the drawing room. Dulcia, focused on her battle, her anger overwhelming all sense, does not notice me.

Once inside the drawing room I race to the mirror. Before I lift the scepter, I pause and consider my reflection. My beauty is gone, as my power must be too. But that does not matter, not now. I lift my head and stare at the two embattled sorcerers.

Smoke and flame fill the terrace. Sten has been forced to kneel before Lady Dulcia. She laughs. She thinks she has won.

Sten turns his head and my gaze locks with his. Using both hands, I raise the scepter over my head.

Dulcia stops laughing. She has seen me, but even for her, it is too late. The scepter swings through the air in an unavoidable arc of destruction. In an instant, it smashes into the mirror.

I close my eyes. An avalanche of sound fills my ears as glass flies in all directions. Miraculously, none hits me. Opening my eyes, I drop the scepter and turn toward the terrace.

Sten Rask laughs now. Even though Dulcia still holds him on his knees. Even though in her fury, she has drawn all the glass shards from the drawing room and raised a whirlwind of jagged fragments around him. They cut his hands and other exposed skin, but not his face.

Of course not. The sorceress doesn't wish to disfigure him. Her revenge will be subtler. She will force him to honor his vow. She will make him her prisoner.

Her servant. Her slave.

I step onto the terrace. Before I can run to him, Sten lifts a hand and I'm engulfed in a rush of feathers. Talons close carefully about me and I'm lifted above the terrace, beyond the swirling glass, far from the battles raging around the castle. The last thing I see is a dark-haired man bowing at the feet of a small, raven-haired woman.

There is no final goodbye, only this image, burned into my mind.

CHAPTER THIRTY-TWO: MANY PATHS

CRADLED IN THE BIRD'S CURVED talons, I am carried from the castle and the battlefield. We fly into the clouds, the mist obliterating any view of the ground. I curl inward, hugging my knees to my chest, and rock back and forth.

I'm right where I started—plain Varna Lund, who holds no magic.

No, that's not true. I am not the same person at all. I press my fingers to my lips, where I still feel Sten's final kiss.

He made the sacrifice I demanded, yet I can do nothing for him. I know he understands; that it's all part of the choice he made. But someday, somehow, I will help him. Even if we can never be together, even if I must live the rest of my life alone, I won't allow him to suffer forever.

I am a healer. I must find a way.

We descend, brushing the tops of trees. The bird lands in a clearing and opens its talons, tumbling me onto the pine needles blanketing the ground.

I roll over and stare up into a circle of dark sky. The bird's wings blot out the stars for a moment before the creature disappears from view.

A cool, wet nose bumps my arm. Luki. I sit up and stare into the wolf's golden eyes. "Can you lead me to the others?"

He yips once and waits until I am on my feet before heading into the woods. I follow him to another clearing, where a group of people cluster around a blazing fire.

Luki bounds over to Thyra and Kai, who sit beside each another on a fallen log. Gerda and Anders are nestled together on a blanket spread over the ground, while Erik leans against a pine tree.

Gerda's the first to reach me. "Varna!" She hugs me tight. "I was so worried, especially when the others returned without you. Yet here you are, safe and sound." She releases me and looks me over. "He changed you back?"

"No, the Lady Dulcia did." I turn to the others, spreading my arms wide. "She let me go, at Sten Rask's request. After he sacrificed his freedom for mine." I take a deep breath. "And after she stripped me of any power or beauty."

"No." Erik walks forward "She did not take anything from you, Varna. Nothing that matters, anyway." He pulls me close and kisses me.

Amid the claps and whistles, I clearly hear Anders say, "It's about time."

I sit next to Erik and listen to tales of espionage and escape from the others, including the good news that Thyra's contact has secured pardons for Erik and Anders.

"They have aided our country, even out of uniform," Thyra says, "so it wasn't difficult."

I look up into Erik's smiling face. "So you can go home."

He tightens the arm he's draped over my shoulders. "Sooner or later, anyway. Anders is more excited than me, since he has a partnership with his old master waiting for him. My older brother's set to inherit the shop, so I have less to look forward to."

"You would own the shoemaking business?" I ask Anders.

"Yes. Co-owner for now, but my mentor has no children. Before I enlisted he told me he would eventually bequeath the shop to me, if I returned after the war." Anders pulls Gerda a little closer. "So I will have a decent livelihood, for myself and a family."

"Ah-hah." I look at Gerda, who has lowered her lashes so I can't read her eyes. "Are you thinking of starting this family with my sister, Anders Nygaard?"

Anders's face flushes to match the fire. "Not until I marry her, of course."

"That's a good plan." I wink at Gerda. "I'm sure Mother will approve, although she'll be distressed to lose her mill manager."

"Well, about that ... " Erik scratches the back of his neck with his free hand. "I wonder if I might be considered for that position."

"You want to manage the mill?"

"I would like to give it a try. I thought perhaps you could put in a good word?"

"I will, but you'd better ask Kai as well."

Kai waves his hand. "I've already said yes. It would be a relief, really. Thyra and I plan to return to the University, although we need a new place to stay. I don't believe my landlady will allow a married couple to rent her garret."

"It would difficult to explain a wolf, as well." Thyra pats Luki's head.

Kai grins at her. "Yes, and there is that."

I tap Erik's knee. "I don't see why we shouldn't give you a chance. At least on a trial basis," I add, wrinkling my nose at him. "Allow you time to prove yourself."

He grunts. "See, nothing has changed. Same practical Varna."

Everyone laughs and I join in, although my mind is elsewhere.

Things *have* changed. I have changed. I glance up at Erik's merry face and wish this was not true, but I must be honest, if only with myself.

You love him, but feel no burning desire. And when he kisses you, memories of other kisses cloud your mind. What will you do about this, Varna? What does your heart truly desire?

"If you will excuse me," I slip out from under Erik's arm and rise to my feet, "I must disappear for a moment or two."

"Stay close," he says. "There are still troops milling about, even if the Usurper's armies have withdrawn."

I nod and smile and walk into one stand of trees surrounding the clearing. I don't actually need to relieve myself. I just need a moment to think.

A rustle in the undergrowth—I pause and prepare to run. Then I see who it is.

"Hello, Varna," Sephia says. "I hoped to find you alone, sooner or later. I thought you might need to talk"

"I do. How did you know?"

She smiles. "Oh, I can sense these things."

We walk in silence for a minute before I can muster the courage to ask the question on my mind. "You know how I feel?"

"I do." She takes hold of my hand. "You care deeply for Erik."

"Yes, although more like a dear friend. But really, that should be enough. It's more than many girls can expect. He's good man, and kind, and will make a great mill manager, and if we were to marry, everyone, even my mother, would be thrilled. And he is even handsome, and I like being around him, but ..."

"But you love someone else."

I stop walking. "Yes."

"And you are not certain what you want to do about that."

I lower my head. "I understand what I should do, what is probably best. I know what makes sense, and yet I feel ... conflicted."

Sephia squeezes my fingers. "You are allowed to be confused. You've lived through a transformation, and I do not mean just what Sten Rask did to you. You have experienced something most people can never understand. Do not torture yourself over how you feel right now. You need to give yourself time." She turns her head and stares at me, her green eyes mesmerizing me into silence. "Time. That is what you must demand of yourself, and others. Don't make rash decisions, Varna Lund. Don't make choices based on what everyone else wants for you—or anything except what your heart says. It will tell you the answer, if you will listen, although it may not speak clearly for a while. So wait. This is the best thing you can do now—allow yourself time to decide."

I nod, swallowing a lump in my throat.

Sephia releases my hand and strokes the side of my face with her fingers. "I have faith in you. You will know what to do when the time is right. Just remember to trust your own heart. It is a mighty heart," she adds, with a little smile. "Now, let's join the others. We can be happy for them, and with them, and perhaps, find some happiness ourselves. What do you say?"

"I say you are very wise, and I'm glad you are my friend."

"Now that," Sephia says, as we walk back, arm in arm, "makes me very happy."

When we reach the outskirts of the village, I'm thrilled to see the enemy's troops have abandoned their camp.

"They don't have the stomach for a prolonged occupation," Erik observes. "Not with their leader gone. It seems he was the driving force behind the invasion."

Encouraged by a wicked sorceress. I shift in my saddle and offer Erik a smile, but don't voice this thought aloud.

"I'm just glad they are gone. It's time we were home. I can't wait to tell Mother and the twins everything." Gerda casts me a sly smile. "The twins will be *so* outdone to have missed all the excitement." She kicks Bae into a lope.

We urge our horses faster to follow her. Luki slips into the woods.

"He won't go into the village," Thyra says. "He knows better. Don't worry, he will be waiting when Kai and I leave town."

By the time we ride into the town square, the noise of our arrival has drawn most of the villagers out of their shops and houses.

Expressions of amazement fill the air. The villagers cluster around us as we dismount.

"We thought you were dead," Nels Leth says.

Anders takes Gerda's hand. "Nearly, but not quite."

Nels, who'd raced forward with his arms extended, as if to take Gerda into an embrace, drops his hands to his sides and stops in his tracks. He can see the love shining in Gerda's eyes when she looks at Anders. Anyone can see it.

My mother pushes her way through the crowd. She hugs Gerda, then me, complaining the entire time about our irresponsible behavior. "Who is this then?" She steps back and glances from Anders to Erik and back again.

Gerda lifts her chin and looks Mother in the eye. "These are the soldiers you wanted to turn over to the authorities. These are the men who saved our lives, several times."

Franka and Nanette jostle their way to Mother's side. Erik meets their astonished stares with a grin.

"Anders Nygaard, Madame Lund." Anders leans over his cane to give her a little bow.

Erik follows suit. "Erik Stahl."

Mother huffs and slides her hand over her head, pushing the cap off her hair. "Well, I never."

"Anders and I are getting married," Gerda says.

The twins shriek in unison.

"If you will allow it." Anders bows his head again.

"And even if you don't," Gerda says, while a blush creeps over Anders's face.

Mother sighs. "Well, we should not talk about this in the street. Come along, all of you, and we'll discuss this at our home. Yes, you too, Kai Thorsen. Your mother is there—she's visiting us today. I'm sure she'll be delighted to see you again." Mother examines Thyra. "As well as whomever this is."

Kai drapes his arm over Thyra's shoulders. "My wife, Thyra Winther Thorsen."

Mother's blue eyes widen. She shakes her head. "Very well. I suppose we can sort all this out, one way or the other."

She continues to mutter and shake her head as we make our way through the crowd and head for home.

The twins, as if stricken dumb, keep shooting glances at Anders and Erik.

Nels Leth is the only one who speaks again, and that is to offer Gerda and Anders sincere, if stammered, congratulations.

Later, after enduring a barrage of questions, too much tea, and demands to detail our adventures one more time, Erik and I slip out into the back yard.

"Are you sure you want to work for us?" I ask, as he takes my arm.

Erik laughs. "Yes, as long as I can avoid too many meetings with your mother."

I lead him to a bench placed beneath a wisteria vine. "Look." I tug on one of the leaf clusters. "It reminds me of Sephia's cottage."

"Only, no longer blooming." Erik slides my arm through the crook of his elbow and rests his hand on my knee. "Finally, a moment alone."

"Yes." I study my fingers.

"We haven't really had a moment to talk since ... "

"Since you kissed me?" I glance up at him from under my lowered eyelashes.

"Yes, since then." Erik tips his head and stares up into the tangle of wisteria vines.

"You must realize you've given Gerda ideas."

"I think she already had them." Erik looks back at me with a smile. "I mean, it does sound perfect, you must admit—me, managing the mill for your family, and being Anders's best friend, and you, being Gerda's sister. It would be a fairytale ending, wouldn't it, if we were to marry?"

"Yes, but we can't allow others to decide such things for us."

"No, I agree." Erik's expression turns pensive. "I'm very happy for Anders and Gerda, of course. And I do want to marry, and you and I ... well, we have the makings of a great relationship. But I think it would be good if we didn't rush into things."

"I agree. Now Master Stahl, you needn't look so surprised. I have goals to accomplish before I'll even consider marriage. For one thing, I'd like to take over Dame Margaret's cottage and establish myself as the local healer. Also, you need time to prove yourself at the mill."

"Prove myself—yes, I suppose I do." He gazes down at me, a smile tugging the corners of his mouth. "To you too, I think."

"No, I didn't mean ... "

"It's all right. The truth is, I would like to court you. Take my time, and do it properly."

I tap his knee with my fingers. "Picnics by the river? Village dances? The annual parish festival?"

He grins. "Exactly. Perhaps those things aren't as exciting as what we've already experienced together, but I think that's best. It gives us time to see how we feel about each other in the midst of our ordinary lives."

"I like that idea." I lay my head on his shoulder.

"Although, I admit it's a gamble for me. Over time, given my charming personality, you may decide you prefer someone else."

Erik's off-hand tone alleviates my anxiety, but I'm still glad he can't see my face. "Just as you may decide you actually prefer a beauty,"

"Now, about that." He straightens, forcing me to sit up and look directly at him. "There is one thing I want you to understand. Honestly, it's important you know this, whether we end up married or not." He clears his throat. "I need to tell you a story. Will you humor me?"

I nod.

His expression turns solemn. "All right, here it is. Listen very closely, Varna Lund." He places his left hand over both of my hands. "When I was searching for you in that burnt-out village, I stumbled over people you'd helped and asked if they knew where you had gone. I attempted to describe you, but they stopped me and said they knew who I was talking about. 'The lovely lady,' they said. 'The girl with the eyes of a saint.' Their faces lit up when they mentioned you, the same light I've seen in the eyes of people admiring a work of art— awed and adoring.

Then I found you, sitting with that poor dying woman. You held her hand and gave her comfort. Shared her pain. Once, near the end, she gazed up at you and I glimpsed a look in her eyes that took my breath away. It was as if she saw an angel, or the loveliest person she'd ever known. The most beautiful girl in the world.

And then I looked again.

And I saw it too."

With my hands captured, I cannot brush away the tears rolling down my cheeks. He leans forward and gently uses his right thumb to wipe them away, one by one.

"Who knows what the future holds, Varna?" He releases my hands and pulls me into a close embrace. "I just want you to know, regardless of what we decide to do with our lives, and whether we marry or simply remain dear friends, I will always love you."

"And I you." I lift my head to look into his eyes. "That much we know. Time must decide the rest."

Erik smiles and sits back. As he tilts his head to look upward, he drapes his arm around my shoulders and pulls me to his side. I lean into him and follow his gaze, until we're both watching wisps of cloud sail like small boats on a clear blue sea.

Yes, time will tell. And whether I ultimately walk alone, or with someone by my side, I know my best future will be revealed if I'm brave enough to open my mind and heart to all possibilities. Sephia's recent words resonate within me. Even if it requires years, I must not make my final decision until I find my own path—the one my heart knows, without a doubt, is right and true.

The one I choose.

ACKNOWLEDGEMENTS

I wish to thank the following people for their contributions to this book and their support of my writing career:

My agent, Frances Black of Literary Counsel – thanks for always answering my questions, providing guidance, and boosting my confidence throughout this process.

My critique partners, Lindsey Duga and Richard Pearson – thanks for your advice and support.

My cover design and formatting team at Deranged Doctor Design – thanks for the beautiful work on this series.

My author colleagues at Silver Wings Publishing – thanks for your support.

My family, especially my Mom and my late Father – thanks for your love and guidance throughout my life.

My husband, Kevin G. Weavil – thank you for being my best beta reader and fan. I truly appreciate your unwavering belief in my writing.

Finally, I must acknowledge the genius storyteller without whom SCEPTER OF FIRE could not exist. Thank you, Mr. Hans Christian Andersen.

AVAILABLE NOW

CROWN OF ICE

Book One in *THE MIRROR OF IMMORTALITY* Series

Snow Queen Thyra Winther is immortal, but if she can't reassemble a shattered enchanted mirror by her eighteenth birthday she's doomed to spend eternity as a wraith.

Armed with magic granted by a ruthless wizard, Thyra schemes to survive with her mind and body intact. She kidnaps local boy Kai Thorsen, whose mathematical skills rival her own. Two logical minds, Thyra calculates, are better than one. With time melting away she needs all the help she can steal.

A cruel lie ensnares Kai in her plan, but three missing mirror shards and Kai's childhood friend, Gerda, present more formidable obstacles.

Thyra's willing to do anything — venture into uncharted lands, outwit sorcerers, or battle enchanted beasts — to reconstruct the mirror, yet her most dangerous adversary lies within. Touched by the warmth of a wolf pup's devotion and the fire of a young man's love, the thawing of Thyra's frozen heart could prove her ultimate undoing

ABOUT THE AUTHOR

Victoria Gilbert turned an early obsession with reading into a dual career as an author and librarian. An avid reader who appreciates good writing in all genres, Victoria has been known to read seven books in as many days. When not writing or reading, she likes to spend her time watching films, listening to music, gardening, or traveling. She lives in North Carolina with her husband, son, and some very spoiled cats.

Through Snowy Wings Publishing, Victoria is the author of The Mirror of Immortality series (Crown of Ice, 2017; Scepter of Fire, 2017), a YA fantasy series adapting Hans Christian Andersen's classic fairy tales. Her short story, The Cat and the Conjurers, is part of the 2019 Snowy Wings anthology, A Touch of Magic.

Victoria also writes mysteries. Her Blue Ridge Library Mystery series -- which includes A Murder for the Books (2017), Shelved Under Murder (2018), Past Due for Murder (2019), Bound for Murder (Jan. 2020), and a fifth book in 2021 – is published by Crooked Lane Books. She is also writing a new series for Crooked Lane, the first book of which, BOOKED FOR DEATH, will be published in June 2020.

Social Media Links:

Website/blog: http://victoriagilbertmysteries.com/

Facebook author page: https://www.facebook.com/

VictoriaGilbertMysteryAuthor/

Twitter: https://twitter.com/VGilbertauthor

Instagram: https://www.instagram.com/victoriagilbertauthor

Made in the USA
Middletown, DE
24 April 2022